# DIAMONDS AND PEARLS

## MAGGIE DAVIS

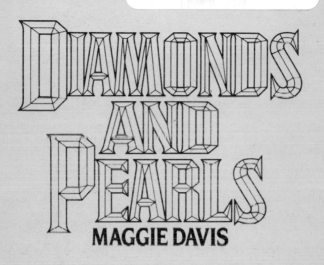

*12468*

Ⓑ

BERKLEY BOOKS, NEW YORK

DIAMONDS AND PEARLS

A Berkley Book/published by arrangement with
the author

PRINTING HISTORY
Berkley edition/May 1985

ISBN: 0-425-07705-5

## DATE LOANED

| MAY 2 2 1985 | | |
|---|---|---|
| AUG 6 1985 | | |
| SEP 1 7 1985 | | |
| OCT 2 5 1985 | | |
| DEC 1 9 1985 | | |
| FEB 4 1986 | | |
| MAR 4 1986 | | |
| APR 1 1 1986 | | |
| Sept 24, 1990 | | |
| DEC 1 4 '90 | | |
| DEC 2 8 '90 | | |
| | | |
| | | |
| | | |
| | | |
| | | |

PRINTED IN U.S.

# PROLOGUE

AT FIVE minutes to five on a particularly busy day in the second week of June the hum of the history department of Northeastern University came to a stop. The footsteps and voices of student traffic on the stairways ceased, and the click of typewriters and the ringing of telephone bells in the department's administrative offices gave way to a satisfying early evening quiet.

In the office of the director of graduate studies, Francesca Lucchese sank back in her desk chair to wait. Everyone else was going home. But for Francesca the biggest part of the work day was about to begin, thanks to the personal habits of Professor Wesley Montburn, the director.

She gathered together the tall stacks of processed applications of college students wanting to come to Northeastern to do graduate work in history and glanced at the clock. June was the month when graduate-student applications descended on colleges like a landslide. From the looks of the pile of paperwork from those hoping to take their master's or doctoral degrees at Northeastern, she knew she was going to be lucky if she got out of the office by nine that evening.

The secretary to the chairman of Northeastern's history department, Marjorie Anderson, stuck her head in the door of the graduate studies office and said, "Don't work too late, Frannie," in a warning tone. It was what she always said. This was like any other day.

Francesca looked up and smiled.

"I mean it." Marjorie's voice rose a decibel. "Don't just sit there and smile, turkey! Not past seven-thirty this time, remember?" She made an aggressive gesture with both hands, thumbs up. "Frannie, tell him you're not getting paid for all this!"

At five-thirty, never earlier and sometimes later, the red-faced and sometimes irascible person of Professor Montburn would arrive in the graduate studies office for an evening's work. When he arrived, he expected Francesca to have all the work of graduate studies laid out for him, and her entire evening free.

"If old Wes Heartburn wasn't what he is," the chairman's secretary said from the doorway, "anybody'd think you two had something going on in here at night."

Francesca stuck out her tongue at her friend. Of all the things that might be suspected of her, this wasn't one of them, and with good reason.

Marjorie shrugged. "Frannie, you can't waste your life like this! Honest to God—don't you want to go out, see movies, have dinner, go dancing? Don't you want to meet men? There are half a dozen guys in the department, including the gorgeous hunk we just got as an exchange instructor from Oxford, who are *dying* to have you say something to them besides 'I gotta work.' What does Joe say when he calls? Doesn't he raise hell about your working until eight or nine o'clock every evening with Montburn?"

Francesca opened her desk drawer and took out her coffee

cup. Joe Iaccone was a more-or-less steady boyfriend who worked for her uncles in their east Boston concrete and construction company. And Joe knew better than to raise hell with Francesca about anything. All the Italian and Sicilian men her own age walked very softly around Carmine and Anthony Lucchese's niece. It was one of Francesca's very real problems. It was only non-Italians, like Steve Livermore, who raised hell with Francesca about everything. Problem number two, Francesca told herself.

Francesca walked with Marjorie out to the corridor water fountain to fill her coffee cup. "Who wants to go out?" she murmured. "Do I have to go on dates with just *anybody?*"

Marjorie leaned against the wall while Francesca directed a steady stream of icy drinking water into the coffee cup. "Frannie, how can you say a thing like that, when you're so beautiful men's eyes hang out on their faces when they see you? Listen, you've got to get out and look for men! Meet men—before you find out whether they're interesting or not! What's the matter with you, anyway?" she cried. "Here you are hiding out at Northeastern, wearing college bags for camouflage—" She pointed to Francesca's chambray work shirt and long denim skirt and wooden-soled clogs. "Hiding how gorgeous you are, hiding from *everything,* actually—and letting an old wimp like Heartburn treat you like a coal miner! An Italian princess like you, Francesca, who's had all those uncles pampering her and standing guard! Somebody hasn't gone and broken your heart, has he? I mean, you're not going to use the history department of Northeastern as a permanent psychological bomb shelter, are you?"

Marjorie followed Francesca back into the graduate studies office as she talked. Francesca took down the asparagus fern from the top of the bookcase and watered it, and then went on to the two pots of philodendra on each side of her desk.

"It all depends on what you're willing to settle for," Francesca said softly. "Nobody's broken my heart. It's just that I've had such a hard time getting my family to let me move out on my own after all these years, that I've had to find this ultra-respectable job to reassure them. My family is very impressed with colleges. Working for Montburn is only one step down from working for the Diocese of Boston, or being the Cardinal's file clerk, or something like that as far as they're concerned." Francesca turned to look at her friend, a troubled expression in her eyes. "Marge, I was *twenty-five* when I left home! I hadn't been anyplace—not even to summer camp as a kid. And I almost didn't make it when my uncle Carmine started reading newspaper stories on how many rapes take place on Boston campuses."

"Francesca—" Marjorie began.

She handed her friend a battered arrow plant to hold while she watered it. "Marge, it's really hard to explain how old-fashioned Sicilian families are to people who don't know them, or anything about their traditions. Both of my uncles are from Sicily; they were born over there. Then my father died in an accident when their company was just getting started and left me in their care. Which is a sort of sacred trust my uncles can never forget. They didn't let my aunts forget, either. I really had a strict upbringing, even stricter than their daughters'!"

Her friend's eyes narrowed. "Is that what you're hiding from, Frannie—a strict upbringing?"

"Am I hiding?" Francesca asked, putting the arrow plant back up on the shelf beside the asparagus fern. She looked thoughtful. "If I am—hiding, you know—it doesn't make me unhappy. It won't make me unhappy if I never get married, honestly. I'm twenty-eight-years old and, frankly, I don't think I can find anybody my family will think is good enough. And all the Italian guys are scared half to death of me. And you know something? I don't think I'll ever find anybody *I'll* want to marry, either!" Francesca put the coffee cup back in her desk drawer. "Being an Italian princess has a lot of drawbacks, you know." Her lips quirked up in a half smile. "One of them is that you get so spoiled and overprotected you can't make up your mind."

"You're not serious," Majorie protested.

"Oh, no?" Francesca opened her mouth to confide in her friend and then thought better of it. The chairman's secretary stood observing her skeptically, her hands on her hips.

"You could always get a better job, Frannie," she declared. "You know you can. After three years of taking Montburn's nonsense you've certainly got enough to build up a good resumé. And you've got a master's degree in business administration that you're certainly never going to get a chance to use here!"

The telephone rang and Francesca said, before picking it up, "Marge, that master's degree doesn't open any doors for women. In fact, you know it opens fewer doors than being able to type."

As Marjorie Anderson mouthed a silent "good-bye" and left, Francesca heard a man's voice say, heavy with sarcasm, "Don't tell me you're still at the office!" It was Steve Livermore on the line.

Francesca sighed and sat down at her desk, holding the telephone receiver slightly away from her ear. Steve was a lawyer, one of the types Marjorie had been so eager for her to meet. And Steve, unlike the Italian-American men who dated her or who wanted to date her, was supremely self-confident, even overbearing. With Steve, Francesca knew, her ego stayed mostly at ground zero while, in his arrogant voice, he questioned the importance of her job, her relationship with Professor Montburn, her clothes, that part of Boston where she lived, and why she wasn't more physically responsive when he tried to make love to her.

Steve Livermore was very tall, very blond and very Beacon Hill Boston. Francesca knew these were the things that had attracted her to him in the first place. She didn't really need to speculate on what had attracted Steve to *her*, because she already knew. Steve was on record as saying she was the most gorgeous, sexy, desirable creature he had ever met. And that his one goal in life was to possess her and awaken her fully to love and womanhood. The young Italian men her uncles watched over so carefully talked of love and marriage. Steve Livermore was interested in having an affair.

The clock said six-thirty-five.

"I can't talk, Steve," Francesca said into the telephone. "Professor Montburn is due right now, and we have a pile of work because of graduate student applications this month."

"Francesca, *listen to me!*" This was Stephen Hill Livermore, the Third, the Beacon Hill lawyer speaking. "You told me you'd get out of this mess of working at night, especially since you're not getting paid for it. Woman—is it impossible for you to stand up to this slobbering academic, just once? I honestly don't know what the hell's the matter with you, Francesca! I'm sitting here with reservations at the Copley for dinner and a show afterward, hoping that for once when I called—"

Francesca looked up to see a man standing in the doorway of the graduate studies office. He was a rather distinguished-looking middle-aged man in a light gray summerweight suit, small in stature, silver-haired, and he carried an old-style but very expensive-looking calfskin briefcase. He smiled.

He said, "I'm so glad you're still in your office, Miss Lucchese. I was afraid I'd missed you. Finding one's way around a college campus is not the easiest thing in the world. I've been lost for about an hour."

The voice of Steve Livermore was saying, "I've come to the conclusion it must be some neurotic need on your part, Francesca, to let this graduate studies flunky subject you to this sort of idiotic treatment. And I'm not fully convinced he doesn't understand the implications of his demanding, night after night, that you stay until all hours while he catches up with work he's paid to do during the daytime! I swear, I feel there are strong overtones of sadism in all this—"

"You're looking for me?" Francesca said, surprised.

"Oh my, yes." The small distinguished-looking gentleman stepped into the office and looked around. "Do you suppose I could have a word with you right here? Since I'm running late, and you seem to be closed for the day, it would seem to suit, very nicely."

". . . about nine-thirty, do you think you could make it this time?" the voice on the telephone said. "Look, Francesca, I realize I pushed things too fast last Saturday night, but you've got to realize I'm not made of stone. We've been seeing each other for—"

"Steve," Francesca interrupted. The small man with the briefcase was watching her, and the office was so small he couldn't help but overhear. "I'll have to talk to you some other time. Do you mind?"

"Is he there?" Steve demanded. "Is that what's the matter? He just walked in and you've got to drop everything? Francesca, are you listening to me?"

Francesca's lips tightened. People tended to underestimate her, and it was her own fault. She always waited until the last minute to make up her mind. She thought of what she had said to Marjorie about not ever getting married. It sounded better and better all the time.

What she really wanted to tell Steve Livermore was that she didn't think she would ever want to go to bed with him. She knew how devastating that news would be. So she wouldn't be able to make it tonight at nine-thirty, and probably never would be able to make it.

Instead she said, "I'm sorry, Steve, I'll have to call you back. Are you at home? I'll call you later," and hung up.

She could see the man with the briefcase was not only listening, he was regarding her keenly. She knew her face was slightly pink.

Francesca said, frowning, "I'm sorry, but I have to tell you I'm not really through with work. Professor Montburn will be in shortly. In fact, I'm expecting him now. We plan to work on graduate-student applications, which take a long time. So if you—"

"Of course," he said promptly. "I'll make it quick, and

to the point. I'm Harry Stillman of Stillman, Newman and
Vance, attorneys, of Miami. We specialize in estate work."
He presented Francesca with a business card. "At this time
I'm acting for the estate of the late Carla Bloodworth Berg-
strom. Your father, Giovanni Lucchese, is named in Mrs.
Bergstrom's will as sole inheritor of her very substantial
fortune." He put his briefcase on the edge of Francesca's
desk and drew up a chair and sat down in it. "I understand
you lost your father some time ago, Miss Lucchese, and
I'm very sorry to hear that, but now let me get to the point.
Under the terms of Mrs. Bergstrom's will, you are the sole
inheritrix of the estate."

"Oh," Francesca said. The words really had little impact,
perhaps because she was still thinking of Steve Livermore.
She gathered someone had left her some money. Francesca
could only stare, remembering that Professor Montburn was
due to arrive at any moment. Personal business was not
supposed to be transacted during working hours.

On the other hand, didn't business hours end at five
o'clock?

"Is it good news?" she said, rather inanely.

The twinkle had returned to the lawyer's eyes.

"You could say that, my dear. Yes, you could. Mrs.
Bergstrom's estate entails, among other things, the Bloodworth Palm Beach house, *Ca' ad Carlo,* a condominium in
New York City, a cattle ranch in Wyoming, a house on the
island of Maui in Hawaii, a collection of jewels that belonged to Mrs. Bergstrom and her grandmother, Mrs. Charles
D. Bloodworth, Senior, fifty percent of the shares of common stock in Bloodworth's, Incorporated and the Bloodworth Foundation, and assets generally estimated in the
neighborhood of between forty and sixty million dollars."

Francesca was silent for a long moment. The blood began
to pound in her head, making it hard to think. What she
was hearing was unbelievable. She knew she didn't believe
it.

Finally she said, "Is that Bloodworth's, the dime store
company?"

* * *

"FORTUNATELY for you," the lawyer said some few minutes later, "Mrs. Bergstrom died without other heirs—that is, she had no children of her own, so your position is assumed to be virtually unassailable under the terms of the will. It's all very exciting, I suppose."

"I don't understand it," Francesca insisted stubbornly. "It says, 'To Giovannni Lucchese, my former chauffeur and being the only man I have ever truly loved, I bequeath all my worldly goods and chattels, to wit . . .' and et cetera. But I know my father didn't have an affair with this woman! He wasn't that sort of person."

The lawyer looked sympathetic. "I think," he said gently, "that we will have to conclude that whatever the true meaning and circumstances of this document some thirty years ago, we will never really know the facts, and let it go at that. After all, it is for the living, not the dead, to explain themselves."

"It's too much money," Francesca said dazedly. It was impossible to try to conceive of sixty million dollars.

"It's all rather unusual, I realize," the lawyer said, "but people do inherit money rather unexpectedly. It's not all that unique. The question is, my dear young lady, how do we get you introduced to a set of very new and different circumstances and responsibilities with a minimum of difficulty? The answer is, we hope, that you will let us propose a simple plan." His smile grew broader. "It's my wife's contribution, actually, but a very good one. She remarked that if she were a young woman about to inherit the Bloodworth millions, she would want to proceed very slowly and cautiously. That prompted our thinking—that we would like to try not to throw everything at you at once." He opened his briefcase again.

In spite of all that was happening to her and the state of shock that was beginning to settle over her mind, Francesca could detect in Harry Stillman's kindly manner a very smooth and sophisticated professional at work. One who was proceeding with the utmost tact.

He handed her a sheaf of papers. "Here are some photographs of *Ca'ad Carlo*, the Palm Beach estate. It's very
quiet down there in the summer, as you probably know.
We like to think it would be a very good place for you to
start picking up the reins of your new position. The house
also has the advantage of being ready for occupancy—
something the Hawaii estate and the New York place do
not. But most of all—" The smile faded and was replaced
with a serious expression. "Most of all a move like this will
not only provide a transition period, but it will also help to
protect you, a young and very beautiful young woman, from
premature publicity which could make your life very difficult. One needs time to cope with a very public life. In
the past very rich young women like Doris Duke and Barbara
Hutton and more recently Mrs. Jacqueline Kennedy Onassis
became what the business calls 'media queens,' in that their
every move was chronicled in the press and television, and
they lived their lives in the public eye. We'd like to spare
you that, at least for the first few months, by suggesting
that you live quietly in Palm Beach at *Ca'ad Carlo*, enjoying
yourself, and that you learn as much as you'd like about
the details of your inheritance and go about making some
friends unencumbered by the spotlight. Palm Beach is a
very good place to start. People there will be very much
like yourself, with substantial incomes and a good bit of
property, and so you won't be excluded from a relatively
normal sort of life. As it is lived at this level, of course."

After a few moments Francesca said slowly, "Live in
Palm Beach?"

"Oh, I think you'll find *Ca'ad Carlo* quite comfortable.
You have an excellent staff there to maintain a main house
of twenty-eight rooms, five guest cottages on the grounds,
two swimming pools, a nine-hole golf course that is, regrettably, not in usable condition at the moment, six tennis
courts, a yacht basin and—at your disposal—at least one
Rolls-Royce which is, I believe, a very well-kept Silver
Ghost. It was Mrs. Bergstrom's favorite car."

Francesca turned wide eyes on him. Her brain was not really absorbing all this. The lawyer leaned forward, his hands clasped between his knees.

"Please allow us to do it this way, my dear. We have a charter Lear jet out of Boston's Logan International Airport which can be made ready for you any time you decide to leave, and which will deliver you in comfort and the utmost privacy to the West Palm Beach airport, where you will rendezvous with me and members of my staff and be taken out to the island. We'd like to ask, in order to insure that everything goes smoothly, that you try to tell as few people as possible about your inheritance at this time. If you can confine the news to your immediate family, that would help. Within a few weeks, when you've settled in, you can then write or telephone your friends and tell them and, of course, invite them down to *Ca'ad Carlo* if you wish."

Over the lawyer's shoulder Francesca saw the figure of Professor Wesley Montburn looming in the doorway. Professor Montburn did not look pleased.

"Hello, what's going on here?" he boomed. "Francesca, are you ready to work now, or what?"

Francesca still held the copy of Carla Bloodworth Bergstrom's will in her hand. Her first impulse was to hide it, to open her desk drawer and slip it inside. Then she thought, *What am I doing?* Francesca looked at the face of Harry Stillman, ready to be of immediate service, and then to the thundercloud visage of Professor Wesley Montburn, director of graduate studies of the Department of History of Northeastern University. A dizzy, frantic sense of excitement rose in her suddenly. It was real! She was incredibly, unbelievably rich! She was *free!*

For the barest of seconds Francesca saw the stack of graduate-student applications and had a wild impulse to jump up, grab them up in handfuls and throw them up in the air while Professor Montburn watched. She gave a sob of choked laughter, aware that she could hardly breathe. The air seemed to be growing very dim.

She saw Professor Montburn glaring at her.

"I think I'm going to faint," she whispered.

"Nonsense," the Miami lawyer said firmly. "You're too rich now to faint."

# 1

# ThE HousE of ChARlEs

# CHAPTER ONE

FRANCESCA LUCCHESE looked up into the late afternoon shadows of the great hall of the Bloodworth mansion to the arched ceiling almost three stories above, its white clouds and nearly nude gods and goddesses encircled by a plaster frieze of fruits and vegetables in the della Robbia style, and wondered, with a pang, what it was going to be like to live in such a place. And how long it was going to take to become accustomed to calling a house as huge as this "home."

The vast room was filled, at four o'clock in the afternoon, with the sweltering stillness of a south Florida July. Somewhere in the recesses of the big house could be heard the faint roar of an air conditioner and the muted sounds of servants' voices, but where Francesca stood, flanked by the Miami lawyers and their accountant, the temperature hung in the nineties.

While the junior law partner droned on with his account

of how the former owner built his dime store empire, Francesca lifted her hand and scooped up a handful of damp black curls and held them away from the back of her neck, glad for a moment's relative coolness. And as she did so she was aware that the young accountant's eyes followed the sudden bulge of the front of her linen suit jacket, which opened to reveal a tantalizing view of her bared breasts in the gaping V. She lowered her arm quickly, and the accountant looked away.

The once crisply tailored linen pants suit she wore had grown tired and limp in the steamy heat; Francesca knew she no longer looked as she had when she left Boston a little over five hours ago—sleekly turned out in the white suit and French high-heeled sandals that showed her long-legged figure to advantage. But, she told herself resignedly, there was nothing she could do about it. She simply hadn't expected Florida to be so hot. Summertime weather, yes. Humidity, yes. But nothing so stunningly, paralyzingly *tropical*. She hooked her finger through the top buttonhole of the jacket, where she had opened it to get a fraction cooler, and buttoned it up again, hoping, as she did so, that she looked more dignified and confident than she felt.

The junior lawyer, Maurice Newman, was explaining the lifestyles which had built Palm Beach. "They lived like kings here then, or in a style, actually, that few kings could afford. All the names—they're like a roll call of American finance and industry in the first part of the twentieth century—J. P. Morgan, Horace Dodge, William Vanderbilt, Henry Flagler, John Jacob Astor, Jay Gould, and of course old Charles D. Bloodworth himself." The small middle-aged man couldn't keep a slightly awestruck note from his voice. "They really ruled a good part of the world, and they knew it. The story goes that one night Charlie Bloodworth, Senior, was in a poker game with some other millionaires in a private railroad car parked on the fourteenth green of the Breakers Hotel golf course, and the New York banker Morty Schiff joined the group and asked what they were playing. Charlie Bloodworth said the table stakes were ten thousand dollars. 'Count me in,' said Schiff, and they threw him *one* chip!"

The three men laughed, shaking their heads. Francesca smiled politely. Anecdotes about Palm Beach millionaires were a dime a dozen, she was finding; she felt as though she had heard at least that many since the estate lawyers had met her Boston plane that morning. What really concerned her at the moment was the vast house. A squadron of butterflies romped alarmingly in her stomach at the thought; the Bloodworth mansion had been staggering enough from photographs and inventory lists sent to her and now, as she stood looking around the enormous hall that authentically replicated the audience chamber of a Venetian doge's palace, the reality was overwhelming. She was having trouble just thinking about it.

For the past two years Francesca had been living in a one-room efficiency apartment, saving her money from her job at Northeastern College toward the goal of getting a better place to live in a better neighborhood, perhaps over the river in Cambridge. Where she could have a full kitchen, not just fixtures hidden behind a folding screen, and a glorious bedroom with a full-sized bed instead of a studio couch. Now, she understood from the Bloodworth estate lawyers, she owned nine bedrooms, all with their own private dressing room and bath, and she had only to choose which one she wanted to use for her own.

"I'm sorry about the heat in here, Miss Lucchese," the accountant murmured, moving closer. He held his clipboard clamped to his side under his elbow, and his expression was definitely admiring. His look rested a moment, almost unwillingly, on Francesca's rather delicately boned oval face, the gray eyes that were almost a silvery color rimmed with dense black lashes, and her soft, lusciously full mouth, before he dragged it away. "Ah, some of these window air conditioners date back to World War Two, when the second Mr. Bloodworth was a War Department consultant for the

Miami district. When you take a look at them, you'll see what I mean."

The lawyers had passed on to the far side of the great hall to examine the large pipe organ there. Francesca and the accountant followed them slowly.

Beyond the stained glass windows of the east wall the sun beat down on the brilliant aquamarine waters of the Gulf Stream, reflecting back in patterns of red, yellow and blue light against the checkerboard of black and white marble floor tiles. The vast hall was alive with garish color. Great ruby glass lamps hung suspended on gilt chains from the mural ceiling, and fantastically twisted purple- and red-striped columns supported a second-story Renaissance gallery with a railing that was set at intervals with gilt wood panels of heraldic devices of Adriatic dukedoms.

The accountant continued, "Mrs. Bergstrom wanted everything kept as it was in her father's and grandfather's day, so nothing's been changed. The maintenance guys on the estate, the groundskeepers, take turns fixing the air conditioners when they break down."

When they joined the lawyers the senior partner was saying, "The reason you have this arrangement, the open hall surrounded by the other rooms—which is damned expensive to heat in the wintertime, by the way—is that Bloodworth senior fell in love with Venice, totally, and nothing would do except an exact replica of some place he'd seen off St. Mark's Square. When he got back to the United States the only thing he wanted was to build a Venetian palazzo on his new property in Palm Beach just like that one. He was dissuaded from taking the original apart piece by piece and shipping it over here, as the experts told him it would never survive the trip. So he started a new one. *Ca'ad Carlo* was completed in a little over thirteen months, which was quite a feat considering the interiors had to be bought up by Bloodworth agents in Italy, dismantled, shipped across the Atlantic and then reassembled here by crews of workmen brought down especially for the job from New York and Philadelphia."

The accountant said to Francesca in a low voice, "Miss Lucchese, there's a booklet on *Ca'ad Carlo* if you're interested. We've got one in our files in the Miami office. Mrs. Bergstrom's second husband, DeLacy, got it together when she was thinking of turning *Ca'ad Carlo* over to the State of Florida for a museum. It has an inventory in the back that describes some of the better Italian pieces and where they came from. You might want to use it if you're going to live here."

Live there? Francesca stared at him, knowing he saw the doubt and confusion in her eyes. Even the last owner, Carla Bloodworth Bergstrom, hadn't done much living there. The granddaughter of the founder of the worldwide chain of Bloodworth's variety stores had spent her last years in an upstairs room as a bedridden recluse.

"Well, how do you like it, young lady?" the senior lawyer said, turning to her with a smile. His gesture included the dazzlingly ornate room around them; his voice was, if anything, a little too cheerful. "This is *Ca'ad Carlo,* which, as you probably know by now, means 'House of Charles' in the Venetian dialect, after the first Charles Bloodworth. And I assure you, it's much more comfortable than it looks." He took Francesca's arm reassuringly and strolled a few feet with her toward the pipe organ. "You've got a good staff here, even though it's been cut back some in recent years. The cook's been here for the last fourteen, and Delia Mary knows everything there is to know about the place. Carla's personal maid, Mrs. Schoener, is staying to look after you. She's a fine employee, reliable and discreet. Then there are the grounds and maintenance people, nice young guys, very efficient."

"And Kurt Bergstrom," Francesca murmured.

The lawyer stopped, but did not turn to look at her. His face was bland. "Oh yes. Kurt Bergstrom, too."

The other lawyer was already at the gigantic pipe organ which dominated the south wall of the room. He climbed up onto the velvet seat quickly and faced the banks of curved ivory keyboard. "This looks in good shape," he observed.

"Mrs. Bergstrom—Carla—was very attached to her grand-father's pipe organ. These things are an interesting feature in the big Palm Beach houses—there isn't a mansion of note that doesn't have one. They must have been some status symbol of the era. Mrs. Horáce Dodge had a big yacht, the *Delphine,* that had a pipe organ on it that would disappear into a panel." He said suddenly, "You don't play, do you, Miss Lucchese?"

They all turned to look at her.

Under their gaze Francesca turned rather pink. She wasn't a very accomplished person by their standards, she was sure, she didn't come from that sort of background. She had never taken a music lesson—any sort of music lesson—in her life. In fact, she came from a working-class Italian family that had not been very enthusiastic even about her want-ing to go to college; they had thought good secretarial courses, maybe, at night school would be enough. And Francesca knew this would not be the first time her lack of cultivation would make her feel ridiculously uneasy before other people.

The other lawyer said quickly, "Well, no one's played the organ here for at least a couple of decades. But Mrs. Bergstrom always kept it well maintained—it's quite a large item on our books. The organ people come down from Healey's in Jacksonville every—" Eyes raised inquiringly, he turned to the young accountant.

"Six months," the accountant said, consulting his clip-board. "With mileage."

"Well, if you can play the piano," Newman declared, "they tell me you can play the pipe organ. Here's the switch, apparently." As he pressed a lever a low, humming sound filled the shadows of the great hall. "All you need is a little practice." He placed his fingers tentatively on the ivory tabs.

Immediately a high soprano chord like a musical shriek sprang into the air. It vibrated over their heads in the wooden beams and panels of the gallery and far up into the dim reaches of the painted ceiling.

They all jumped violently. "Turn that damned thing off!" Stillman, the senior partner, barked.

Hastily the other lawyer turned the switch to off.

But the musical scream seemed to hang in the air. The lawyers had looked shocked. The accountant had paled visibly. Francesca, startled and confused, thought the pipe organ had sounded uncannily like a woman's desperate wail.

The accountant said in a low voice, "Maybe it shouldn't be played until somebody's checked out that ceiling."

They became aware there was a faint haze in the air like drifting plaster dust.

"Nonsense, *Ca'ad Carlo*'s sound," Harry Stillman said loudly. "It was just checked for termites and that sort of thing a few months ago."

THE walls of the downstairs music room were paneled in fine Louis Quatorze beveled mirrors. The reflecting light from the sea which filled all of *Ca'ad Carlo*'s rooms caught them in a rather eerie brightness and repeated the group of three men and the young woman in the mirrors several times: the tall attractive girl with her dark mop of curling gypsy hair, the two middle-aged lawyers perspiring in their summerweight suits, and the shirt-sleeved accountant carrying his clipboard of lists. They all blinked.

Beyond a rococo white and gold pianoforte was a life-sized portrait of a woman in a filmy ball gown of the twenties, her hair arranged in stiff blonde waves to frame a pale, flowerlike face. The eyes held a rather vague expression.

"Edna Bloodworth," the senior lawyer murmured. "I didn't know this was still here. She was a famous beauty of her time—San Francisco China trade and Texas oil. Styles in beauty change, don't they?" He cocked his head to one side, critically. "Two years after *Ca'ad Carlo* was built she finally gave way to what was described in those days as a 'nervous condition' and was in a sanatorium for the rest of her life. But Charlie Bloodworth continued to come back to *Ca'ad Carlo,* though, every winter—to play the pipe organ and keep up his golf game."

A broad, strong-looking woman with graying blonde hair and wearing a pink maid's uniform had appeared silently in the doorway.

"Here's Gerda Schoener," Harry Stillman said. "She's going to show us the upstairs rooms."

The gallery and second floor of the house was, if anything, hotter than the downstairs had been. The heavyset blonde woman went ahead of them, opening doors and windows to start the stagnant air circulating.

"There's actually very good cross ventilation," the junior law partner said. "It helps when the air conditioners go out."

The ponderous old-fashioned bedroom for the master of the house had a mahogany bed the size and shape of a medium-small sailboat. Charles D. Bloodworth's dressing room, complete with professional barber chair where the dime store tycoon was shaved by his valet every morning, adjoined it. A portrait of the founder of Bloodworth's, Inc., hung against a wall covered in rich red silk moiré. The painting showed a stocky, florid middle-aged man in a dark blue business suit. The eyes were an arresting, surly steel gray.

The bedroom suite for the mistress of *Ca'ad Carlo* was next door. The room where Carla Bloodworth Bergstrom had been secluded for so long and which had originally been designed for her grandmother Edna, was, by contrast, almost suffocatingly feminine. Layers of heavy yellowed lace were everywhere, especially at the windows. A thronelike bed with tester was covered in yellowed Brussels rose point and piled high with pink satin pillows edged in the same lace. The adjoining bathroom was decorated in age-darkened white and gold, and the sunken tub was white marble. Only a television set and a French telephone on the bedside table struck a modern note.

Harry Stillman seemed to breathe a small sigh of relief. He muttered, "It was wall-to-wall pill boxes and medicine bottles in here. You've done a good job, Mrs. Schoener."

The maid's broad, lined face was impassive. "I just put it back the way it was, that's all. What you see is how it was when Mrs. Edna, Mrs. Bergstrom's grandmother, was alive. That was always the way Mrs. Bergstrom wanted it."

When he turned to Francesca with a question in his eyes she said quickly, "Oh, I'm not going to change the room. I'm going to use another bedroom for the time being."

Francesca supposed the room had been pretty once, a half century ago, but its elaborate fussiness was oppressive. The one redeeming feature was the brilliant sea light which seemed to fill most of *Ca'ad Carlo*. It seemed impossible to forget that Palm Beach was an island, surrounded by the sea, hammered by the blazing Florida summer sun.

Francesca moved to the French doors which opened on a small balcony looking out on the circular front drive of the house and acres of green lawn, and a part of a crumbling concrete boat basin beyond which was the blue-green Atlantic mixed with the more brilliant waters of the Gulf Stream. In the far distance across the greensward was the larger swimming pool like a sapphire in the hot sun, and a complex of red-tile-roofed guest houses.

"Which one is Mr. Bergstrom's house?" Francesca wanted to know.

The maid had come to stand beside her. "It's the largest, Miss Lucchese. Not there by the swimming pool, no—those are the others. You have to go down the lane of daturas." She indicated a darker green among royal palms and banyan trees. "Down there."

Maurice Newman said quickly, "Oh, I talked to Kurt before we left Miami this morning, and he wanted you to know he'll be around all day in case you need him to show you anything. Since Carla's death, incidentally, he's been moving his things out of the main house. The boat, the *Freya*, is his. So's the Porsche and some other things." He paused, then said, "He wants you to know how much he appreciates your letting him use the guest house for the time being."

Both lawyers looked carefully noncommittal and the accountant was busy with his clipboard lists, but it was an awkward moment. Kurt Bergstrom should have, by all rights, inherited his wife's money and estates. The last will, found in Carla's safe deposit box a few days after her funeral, specified that all the Bloodworth property was to go to Giovanni Lucchese and, in the event of his demise, to his heirs. There was only one, his daughter, a twenty-eight-year-old woman working as assistant director of graduate studies in the history department of one of Boston's larger colleges.

"I certainly want Mr. Bergstrom to stay for as long as he wants." Francesca caught her lower lip between her teeth with an expression of great seriousness. "He's lived here for several years—"

"Five," the accountant said, not looking up from his lists. "Five years."

"And I don't want him to feel that there's any hurry about getting out. He's just lost his wife—" Francesca looked around the group with a small frown perched between slim black brows. "And he has to have some time to get over that."

"Oh, Kurt can help you," the senior lawyer said quickly. "Of course. He ran things around here for the last few years and really held the place together while Carla was sick. Yes, he can help."

As they filed out of the bedroom Francesca paused, then stopped to look at the lace-covered dressing table and its display of silver-backed brushes, and the collection of price-less cut glass perfume bottles. There were several photographs in solid gold frames, one a carefully posed studio portrait of a lovely young woman in the close-cropped hair-style of the 1950s. The blonde hair, small pointed flower face and pale eyes struck a disturbingly familiar note. The photograph was that of Carla Bergstrom, but it was also curiously the face of Edna Bloodworth, the woman in the portrait in the music room.

Beside Carla Bloodworth's photograph was an enlargement of a snapshot showing a handsome young man, curly black hair under a gray uniform cap, his mouth curved in an engaging grin. The upper part of his body, all that was visible in the photo, wore a gray jacket with round collar and two rows of brass buttons descending his chest—a chauffeur's uniform.

With a cry of recognition, Francesca picked up the photograph in its heavy gold frame.

"I've never seen this before!" she exclaimed.

The others turned around in the doorway.

The maid said quickly, "Oh, Mrs. Bergstrom kept that picture right there on the dressing table. All I knew was never to touch it." Her lips tightened. "Nobody knew who he was until she died."

Francesca replaced the photograph very carefully.

"I don't remember him this young," she murmured. "I guess this was taken before I was born. But he was always so handsome. I'd recognize my father anywhere."


THERE were two dining rooms. The larger, formal one, featured a twelve-foot-long marble dining-room table, made to order in the Medici marble works of Florence, Italy, to Charles Bloodworth's specifications. The smaller dining room was painted in green and pale yellow and the inevitable gilt, but the table and chairs were human-sized and agreeably designed. French doors opened out from the little dining room to the great balustraded terrace and the sea.

"This was one of Edna Bloodworth's rooms," Maurice Newman explained. "She designed her bedroom, the music room and the little dining room the way she wanted. Bloodworth and the architects did all the rest."

Beyond the informal dining room was a passageway with a butler's pantry that opened into a vast kitchen filled with the outsized restaurant ranges of another era. Huge copper hoods hung over the stoves, and the room was full of giant refrigerators, sinks, and wooden chopping blocks.

"You want to hang on to Delia Mary," the lawyer said, eyeing the cast-iron ranges. "Nobody else can cook on those monsters."

A large and dignified black woman in a starched white cook's jacket appeared at the doorway to what was obviously a storeroom. She gazed at them for a moment, eyes finally coming to rest on Francesca.

She said, "We got microwave ovens now. We don't use the big stoves for much."

Through the open doorway they could see a man on a stepladder, shirtless and in old khaki shorts, reaching up with both hands to complete the splicing of two electric cables.

"This is Delia Mary," Harry Stillman said, introducing the black woman. "Delia Mary knows about everything there is to know about *Ca' ad Carlo*'s kitchen. I had to take inventory with her, and believe me, she knows every spoon!"

The man on the ladder bent down to look at them.

Francesca had shaken hands with the cook. Now she extended her hand to a man who was the most beautifully bronzed and muscular giant she had ever seen. His face was covered with a blond beard, trimmed short, and his bright blue eyes spoke of the sea. In Boston, Francesca had been sent a list of *Ca' ad Carlo* employees, including some names that had been scratched out because they had left the estate since Carla's death. The grounds and maintenance men, both of them, had decided to stay on. This was either John Turtle or Peter Peavey. She put out her hand and smiled.

"I'm Francesca Lucchese," she said. "I guess you could say I'm your new employer."

The bronzed giant's sea-blue eyes regarded her smilingly. "I'm delighted to meet you." He took her hand and did not release it. "I'm Kurt Bergstrom. I guess you could say I'm the *old* employer."

They all laughed. Francesca pulled back her hand quickly, her face burning.

"I'm sorry," she said in a small voice.

They were still laughing.

"Not at all." The big man continued to look her over with his strange eyes. "This cable is a 220-volt line that feeds the kitchen equipment, and Delia Mary needs it. If you'll excuse me, I'll be with you in a minute."

"Yes, it's time for a drink," Harry Stillman announced. "I believe we could all use one."

# Chapter Two

Harry Stillman's idea had been to have happy hour on the terrace overlooking the Atlantic, but they found the half acre or so of red tile at that side of *Ca'ad Carlo* to be a blistering gridiron under the Florida sun. They settled for drinks served by the maid on the small porch off the informal dining room that had been used as a breakfast nook. Even so, it was hot.

The lawyers suggested a bottle of Moët from the wine cellars, the accountant wanted vodka and tonic, and Francesca asked for a Coca-Cola, although she would have preferred something stronger. The idea of having wine cellars, and being able to order champagne from it on a moment's notice, made her rather subdued.

In about a quarter of an hour Kurt Bergstrom joined them, dressed in a navy blue shirt and white slacks. Watching him out of the corner of her eye, Francesca had come to the conclusion that Carla Bergstrom's widower was the hand-somest man she had ever seen. She tried not to look at him any more than was necessary. The bronzed man lounged in a small wrought-iron chair, almost overwhelming it with his size, and joined in the conversation in a desultory way. He made no effort to hide his interest in Francesca; she felt herself grow very awkward and uneasy under his steady appraisal, and very aware of her rumpled pants suit and heat-flushed face. She tried to keep her eyes on the water and a handful of sailboats in the distance, and look uncon-cerned. But Carla Bloodworth's third husband puzzled and intrigued her.

If there was bitterness in him over the loss of the Blood-worth money, Francesca couldn't detect it. His tone of voice, the way he looked as he studied her, was perfectly relaxed and good-humored. The biggest surprise was that she found him so much younger than his dead wife. According to the papers Harry Stillman had turned over to her before she left Boston, the Bloodworth heiress would have been fifty-five in December. Francesca had visualized a much older man when she had given permission for Kurt Bergstrom to stay on at *Ca'ad Carlo* in one of the guest cottages. Now she estimated this tanned giant with the Viking look was—what?

It was hard to tell, she thought, studying the burning horizon and deliberately keeping her face turned away from him. *Thirty-seven? Forty? As much as forty-five?* If she had to guess, she would say at least ten years younger than his late wife. He didn't really fit any mental picture she had of a man with a rich, much older wife—an adventurer who would deliberately seek out and marry a woman of fifty or so. Which was, apparently, Carla's age when they married.

Carla Bergstrom's photograph in the upstairs bedroom showed her to be a woman in her late twenties or early thirties who had been very beautiful in a blonde and fragile way. Perhaps, Francesca told herself, the Bloodworth heir-ess had been still beautiful at the time of their marriage, but she doubted it. That was five years ago when Carla had been fifty. And fifty was *fifty*, after all.

As she listened to his conversation with the lawyers, Francesca couldn't help but wonder what Kurt Bergstrom's reactions had been when he had heard of the new will; what he had felt when he had read a copy of it, provided by these same lawyers who sat drinking champagne with him now, which said that his wife had left *Ca'ad Carlo,* the Wyoming cattle ranch, the estate in Hawaii and all the Bloodworth millions to her former chauffeur, the handsome young Italian who had worked for her during her second marriage almost thirty years ago. And whom the will described, in Carla's words, as "the only man she had ever truly loved."

Or, she thought, what Kurt Bergstrom had felt when he found that the will applied not to Giovanni Lucchese, now more than a dozen years dead, but his twenty-eight-year-old daughter and only child, Francesca? It had taken the law firm of Stillman, Newman and Vance four months to locate her. In all that time, she wondered, had Kurt Bergstrom hoped that Giovanni Lucchese's heir would never be found? Or, if found, that she be conveniently dead, like her father?

Slowly, she turned her head. Kurt Bergstrom wasn't watching her now, but she saw the assured movement of his blond head, thrown back to laugh, his teeth showing very white against his tanned face. His hands were huge but, as with most big men, his gestures were controlled and gentle. She thought, finding it suddenly difficult to breathe, it was his eyes that caught and held you. That clear green-blue look was like the unending reaches of a cold, calm sea. They seemed to look right through you. In response, something deep within her body quivered in a purely sensual reaction.

He looked, she thought nervously, as though nothing ever really disturbed him. But how had he felt, she wondered, when he had to move his belongings out of the main house, where he was no longer master, and into the guest cottage? The use of which, as the new owner, she had so graciously granted him?

Suddenly Kurt Bergstrom turned his head and met her eyes as though he had known she was watching him. That blue look was full of electricity as it raked her.

The young accountant was saying, "Well, what do you think of it?"

With a great effort Francesca dragged her eyes away from Kurt Bergstrom's face. "Think about what?" she murmured.

"About this. *Ca'ad Carlo*. And Palm Beach."

The accountant was about her own age, maybe a year or two older, she judged. Francesca tried not to look at him as though she couldn't remember who he was. But she wasn't listening; she really had no idea what he was talking about. The impact of Kurt Bergstrom's look still vibrated in her senses.

She said, in a low voice, "Is he really a count?"

He studied her for a moment, an odd expression on his face. "Yes, Miss Lucchese, he's a count. That much is for real."

With a voice that was not quite steady Francesca said, "Do you know how old he is?"

The accountant hesitated. The look of hungry admiration in his eyes faded as he said, "Older than you." He shifted in his chair. "Miss Lucchese, do you mind if I give you some advice?"

At that moment Harry Stillman said, "Ah, here's the remainder of the staff. I see they've finally found us."

Two youngish men in blue jeans and T-shirts were approaching the veranda. One was tall and lean and walked with a noticeably effortless, catlike grace. His thick black hair, worn somewhat long and shaggy, and his black eyes reminded Francesca of her cousins, but his skin was coppery rather than olive. Not Italian, she decided; perhaps Cuban or South American, but she could not be sure. The tight T-shirt showed well-developed shoulders and arms and a broad chest tapering to a flat belly and slim hips. He looked interesting, in spite of a flat, almost hostile stare. Much more so than the wiry young man beside him with the tow hair and freckles of a native Floridian.

Harry Stillman got up to open the screen door and let in the maintenance men. "Miss Lucchese," he said formally, "this is John Turtle and Peter Peavey, grounds and maintenance staff for *Ca'ad Curlo*. John doubles as chauffeur and general security guard. Peter maintains the swimming pools, both of them, in addition to other duties. Incidentally, John can make arrangements for you to rent a car in West Palm Beach if you want something other than the Rolls-Royce to run around in. Just let him know."

Francesca longed to get over the terrible uncertainty which she felt on meeting *Ca'ad Carlo*'s employees, and which welled up in her again at that moment. She might be the heiress to the Bloodworth fortune, but she couldn't forget that she had been a wage earner herself so recently. *I'm going to have to practice this,* she told herself as she got up to shake hands.

She felt the flicker of John Turtle's black eyes on her and they made her wonder, ever so briefly, what he was doing at *Ca'ad Carlo* mowing grass. Then his look turned veiled, and remote.

"Turtle," Francesca said, as he released her hand. "That's an unusual name."

It was only something pleasant to say. But again there was the challenge of those dark eyes.

"In some places, perhaps," he said tersely.

Francesca felt her already flushed face redden. Her grounds and maintenance supervisor was obviously not burdened down with charm. His eyes had seemed to assess her, to take in the once-fresh pants suit, her shiny face and damp mass of black hair with an air of being greatly unimpressed. Francesca felt she'd been given an unqualified "F" in her grades.

"I'll get back to you about the car," she said, knowing that her voice showed her dislike.

When the grounds crew had left, Harry Stillman said, "Don't let John Turtle put you off, my dear. He's an independent cuss like all the Brighton reservation people, but you can depend on him. His father—was it his father?" he said, turning to the other lawyer, who shrugged. "Or his grandfather worked here shortly after *Ca'ad Carlo* was built. There were still Seminoles on the Palm Beach estates in the old days. They had something of a monopoly as gardeners."

"Seminoles?" Francesca said. "You don't mean he's an *Indian,* do you?"

At her expression they all laughed.

"It's not the Wild West, Miss Lucchese," Newman, the lawyer, assured her, "only Florida."

Unexpectedly, Kurt Bergstrom said, "Brighton Indian Reservation is on the other side of Lake Okeechobee, and there are Indians here, yes. But 'independent' is too nice a word, I think, to describe that one. The Indians are good gardeners, maybe. The trouble is, they do not think of themselves as gardeners. My wife liked this one, so she let him stay. You know how Carla was, to keep everything always the same. It was his grandfather, Sebastian, who worked here first." His calm face was slightly disdainful. "But this one, John, is not purebred."

The senior partner put in quickly, "The whole Palm Beach area knows the Turtle family. And the Hominees, and the Oraras. The mother was an Orlando girl, wasn't she, Kurt?"

"The mother was a white woman, yes." He smiled, revealing beautifully even white teeth. "That is what the word Seminole means, does it not? *Mixed?* This is one Turtle who is even more so."

Harry Stillman said to Francesca, "John Turtle is a good man. You'd do well to keep him around for a while. Good grounds and maintenance people are hard to get anywhere, and the Turtle family knows *Ca'ad Carlo* like the back of their hands."

Francesca pushed away the half-emptied glass of Coca-Cola. She had been up since five-thirty that morning in a

frenzy of excitement and last-minute packing and was beginning to feel this could not be the same day. She looked
away, trying to focus her eyes on a cluster of sailboats to
the left of the shoreline beyond. Could she really believe
she was sitting there now, in Palm Beach—a century-old
settlement of the super wealthy, on a narrow strip of sandy
island ten miles long, on Florida's southeast coast? She
remembered the drive in from the airport with the lawyers:
once one crossed the bridge over Lake Worth, which separated the island of Palm Beach from the mainland, one
entered a curiously well-preserved little town with the look
of a village in the south of France. The broad avenues of
towering royal palms, the cramped lanes of the residential
streets with their stucco walls, clipped hedges and topiary
trees looked more European than American. And there were
elegant shopping streets like Worth Avenue, with its St.
Laurent Rive Gauche, Bonwit's, Gucci and Lily Pulitzer,
which extended the feel of the French and Italian Riviera.
Farther along the main drives of County Road and Ocean
Drive, guard gates shut off whole compounds of red-tile-
roofed mansions surrounded by tropical gardens of palm
trees, banyan, hibiscus and oleander. In the hurried tour the
lawyers had given her on the way to *Ca' ad Carlo,* Francesca
had seen copies of giant Renaissance palaces, French country houses, Côte d'Azur villas, and miles and miles of clipped
lawns, shaved hedges, palms and more palms—all silently
simmering under the white Florida sun of midsummer.

In the murmur of voices returning to her, and breaking
into her thoughts, Francesca heard Maurice Newman re-
marking that it was late, and that they should be getting
back to Miami.


THE silver-haired estate lawyer drew Francesca aside as the
others filed out the door and down the small flight of steps
which led to a side path and eventually the front of the
house.

With the air of someone who has saved the most important thing to last, he drew a folded piece of newsprint from an inner pocket of his suit jacket and handed it to her.

"You're going to want to see these things, my dear. They're what we talked about earlier. I'm afraid, like everything else connected with wealth, being the new Bloodworth heiress carries a special price. You'll soon have to begin to decide how you want to handle things like this."

The newspaper clipping was dated the day before, from the Miami *Herald*.

### CHAUFFEUR'S DAUGHTER INHERITS BLOOD-WORTH FORTUNE

*Palm Beach*—The daughter of a former employee of the Bloodworth family has been named sole heir to the famed *Ca'ad Carlo* estate and the multimillion dollar fortune of the late Carla Bloodworth Tramm DeLacy Bergstrom, granddaughter of the founder of the worldwide variety store chain.

According to the will disclosed recently in Palm Beach, Mrs. Bergstrom left her entire estate of an estimated $50 to $60 million to a former chauffeur, an Italian immigrant who was briefly in the employ of the Bloodworth family in the 1950s. The chauffeur, now deceased, had one daughter, Francesca Maria Lucchese, 28, of Boston, Mass., who is sole inheritrix under the terms of Mrs. Bergstrom's will.

*Ca'ad Carlo,* the Bloodworth estate in Palm Beach which was completed in 1926, has long been one of south Florida's showplaces, rivaling the Flagler mansion *Whitehall,* also in Palm Beach, and *Vizcaya,* the Deering estate in Miami. Both are now State of Florida museums.

The main house of *Ca'ad Carlo* features authentic Venetian wood paneling, heraldic devices of the 15th and 16th centuries, priceless plasterwork imported from the Adriatic, a Venetian handblown glass collection valued at over a million dollars, and one of the country's most valuable pipe organs.

Charles D. Bloodworth, Jr., was the first to maintain year-around Palm Beach residence when he remained on the 6-acre estate during World War Two while serving as materiel supply advisor to the War Department, Florida District. His daughter, Carla Bloodworth, established legal residence here four years ago while

Francesca couldn't read anymore. All she could think of was that her name was in the papers. She was the subject of a lengthy news story just like someone famous. It was difficult to believe. *The chauffeur's daughter.* Inwardly, Francesca cringed. It was demeaning not only to her, but to her father.

"It comes as something of a shock," Harry Stillman was saying, "to find that one's life has gone suddenly public, doesn't it? The Bloodworth Foundation has a public relations firm that usually handles the press and electronic media, but I think you'll want to double current efforts and get a private secretary to handle a lot of this. How do you feel about a secretary?"

Francesca felt numb. She could only stare at him.

After a moment he said, "Well, there will be all sorts of events, you know—requests for interviews, photographers who want a shot of you at any price, invitations to do fashion shows, charity balls and to lend your name to a thousand different organizations, ranging from political parties to antinuclear groups. It's difficult even for people who are born into this life to cope with this sort of pressure, believe me, so it's not going to be easy. But my dear, we'd like to offer you a very nice person from our Miami office on a temporary basis. You'll find she's a life saver. When you screen a permanent application, you'll want someone with a good PR background, as well as—"

"Do I have to?" she said suddenly. She already felt surrounded by people. It was a strange sensation. Before she'd come to Palm Beach she'd had some vague idea of living quietly on the big estate, slipping in and out of *Ca'ad Carlo* while she got used to things—the plan outlined by Harry Stillman in her office in Boston weeks ago. She really didn't want things to suddenly speed up, faster than she could become adjusted to them.

"My dear," the lawyer said gently, "I'm also afraid you're going to need some security people. I don't want to frighten you, but newspaper publicity can make life very—complex. In the past few years security at *Ca'ad Carlo* was rather low key. Carla was confined to her bed, and John Turtle filled in for what was required, and only the gate guards were doubled in the busy season. But surely you can see you're going to make a great difference, my dear, as demonstrated by the item in the Miami *Herald*. I think the safest thing for you, now, is to have a security person around the clock."

"A *bodyguard?*" She couldn't keep the astonishment out of her voice. In all the hectic events of the past few weeks Francesca had never considered such an idea.

"I'm well aware many people don't even like the sound of the word, but you'll find security people are not all that uncommon here in Palm Beach. That's why I suggested you try to keep John Turtle around for a while. He and Peavey are tough young men; they know how to keep an eye out for trouble." When Francesca looked at him doubtfully, the lawyer said, "As for instance, they'll get you in and out of shops without interference, restaurants, and doctors' and dentists' offices, so that you won't be bothered by curiosity seekers, people with an ax to grind, or just plain cranks. You know, Carla was stopped once, years ago, in New York on her way into the Waldorf Astoria by a woman who claimed she was Charles Bloodworth, Sr.'s illegitimate daughter and who tried to assault her with a hammer. Carla was such a tiny little thing, if the bodyguard hadn't rescued her, the woman would have done a great deal of damage. You also have disgruntled Bloodworth employees from some store somewhere, stockholders with a grievance, union dissidents, religious types looking for contributions, and finally those who simply hate the rich. There are plenty of those."

"A bodyguard," Francesca repeated, trying to make it real.

"Now that the *Herald*'s got the story of Carla's will, apparently from the courthouse here, you can count on the media's interest. You're a working girl from Boston who's suddenly inherited one of the world's largest fortunes in a very unusual way. It's a good story. You'll be approached for interviews. My advice is, don't respond to any of them if you hope to retain a shred of privacy. Once they're interested in you, the media will try to penetrate your household staff, the local merchants, friends, acquaintances, to try to get what they can out of them. No detail is too small, either—what you had for dinner, what kind of clothes you wear, nothing too insignificant."

"Oh, no," Francesca whispered. It was becoming realizable, now; she was beginning to see the scope of it and it alarmed her. She had a sudden thought that if she had known all this back in Boston, perhaps none of this would have come true. As it was coming true now.

The lawyer took her arm. "A good secretary will keep up the barriers, and a couple of security men will do the rest. Don't look so stricken. It's only learning to adjust to a different regimen, and you have plenty of people around to help you. Remember, Palm Beach looks after its own; otherwise it would cease to exist. The media doesn't get much from the local people. And it's been my experience that if you hold your ground and don't give way, the press and electronic media will back off. Bloodworth offices in New York can pull a few strings, too. Carla used to be very tough about putting pressure on media higher-ups to get their employees to lay off, even threatening to bring a few invasion of privacy suits when necessary. And she generally succeeded. So did her father, Charles, Junior. It was only old Charlie Bloodworth, Sr., who lived high, and loved publicity."

The lawyer held the screen door open for Francesca. The late afternoon heat, bouncing back from the terrace, struck them fiercely. Even the wind from the Gulf Stream was burningly hot. In the distance the sailboats had rounded their buoy and were racing back, brilliantly colored spinnaker sails blossoming like flowers as they ran before the wind.

He took her arm as they descended the steps. "Palm Beach is a lovely place, my dear. You'll hear a lot of stories. It's rather an ingrown little town with a very special population, the very rich who've become accustomed to the power, and isolation, money brings. There's a wild crowd, just as in any community, and there's the Old Guard holed up in their County Road mansions, and some types you would never want to know. And some who are very wholesome and charming. There are simply different ground rules here, that's all. And in some cases—bodyguards."

"I didn't think about all this," Francesca managed. Her heart was beating painfully; she was still struggling with the idea that anyone, someone you didn't even know, would try to harm you. A demented woman with a hammer had tried to attack Carla Bloodworth.

"Fortunately," Harry Stillman continued, "you're going to be here for a few weeks during the summer when it's quiet, nothing much going on, and that will give you time to become accustomed to a lot of things. And we're still hoping to keep you pretty much hidden out here at *Ca'ad Carlo.*"

"It's frightening," Francesca whispered.

The lawyer's grip on her arm tightened. "Now, now. Your young life is ahead of you. You have to concentrate on what's coming with your youth and beauty and now a great fortune. It's going to be a glorious future."

# Chapter Three

The maid had put Francesca's luggage in one of the many spacious bedrooms that lined the second-floor gallery. The room—twice as large as the entire studio apartment Francesca had left in Boston—looked out onto a small balcony. From there the oceanside shoreline of Palm Beach could be seen as a bastion of concrete sea walls above a severely eroded beach, which gave a clifflike, Mediterranean aspect to the flat south Florida coastline. Clusters of sago and queen and royal palms clashed their dry fronds in the ocean breeze. The red-tiled rooftops of the big houses of other estates could be seen through the dense green foliage.

The bedroom suite, Francesca saw with some relief, was neither overwhelmingly masculine nor fussily feminine, but pleasantly furnished in inexpensive rattan furniture in South Seas style. An ancient air conditioner wheezed full blast, pouring out deliciously cool air. Francesca peeled off the sticky pants suit and headed for the bath. The window there was too small for an air conditioner, but a brand new electric fan with deep blue transparent blades had been provided. It sat on a white-painted bath stool. Francesca saw a price sticker on the plastic base which said: *Bloodworth's, $29.95.* There was, she thought, nothing like patronizing the family store.

As she slid into the warm water of the enormous sunken porphyry tub with its gold-plated fixtures, she tried to accustom herself to the idea that all those thousands, perhaps tens of thousands, of Bloodworth variety stores were *hers,* now, but the full realization escaped her. Too much had happened. Her senses were still assaulted by the new and unexpected. And deep inside she was still Francesca Lucchese, single working woman from Boston, with a big Italian family, a not very pretentious person. She sat soaping her arms and shoulders for a long time, thinking about it while the fan sent a cool jet of air on her shoulderblades, wondering when and if she would change.


WHILE she was in her bath Mrs. Schoener had come in and set out a silver tray with an opened split of champagne in a silver bucket. There was also a shallow crystal bowl with two deep red and orange blooms as exotic as orchids floating in it, blooms which Francesca recognized as the estate's hybrid hibiscus blossoms the lawyers had pointed out to her. Next to the champagne bucket was a folded cream-colored slip of notepaper which said:

*I've invited myself to dinner. A drive around Palm Beach comes after if it pleases you.*

It was signed, *Kurt B.*

The maid had laid out Francesca's clothes on the bed. It was a strange feeling to see one's clothing selected and put out, and know that the maid had sorted through one's things, even underwear. Francesca stared down at the two new outfits from Filene's—a voile shirtwaist dress in emerald green, and a striped jersey top and matching white pleated skirt.

Rubbing her body slowly with the big bath towel, Francesca examined her new dresses with dissatisfaction, realizing that her clothes-buying sense needed some upgrading. What was right for Marblehead and Cambridge was obviously not a head-turning event in Palm Beach. The clothes in the boutiques on Worth Avenue, even glimpsed briefly from the car, were exotically different, very *haut monde*.

Carefully, Francesca stretched out on the bed beside her Boston clothes and dialed the area code number for that city and then her aunt and uncle's number. She wiped off a few drops of water from her smooth, satiny belly and heavy breasts with the bath towel.

It was her Uncle Carmine who answered.

"I just wanted to let you know I got here safely," Francesca said, feeling suddenly homesick. She had struggled for so long to get away from her overprotective, loving aunts and uncles and be independent—and now, in a rush, she missed them terribly. She felt tears welling up in her eyes and blinked them back. "The lawyers and an accountant met me at the Palm Beach airport, and they stayed all afternoon and then they showed me the house. Mr. Stillman— you remember him—said I ought to get a private secretary. And I signed something called a certificate of occupancy which means, among other things, that all the estate bank accounts were turned over to me."

Francesca could hear screams and laughter in the background as she talked and she knew it was her cousins, Joanie and little Sal. She swallowed the persistent lump in her throat while her uncle roared into the distance for some quiet around here, Frannie is on the telephone from Palm Beach.

"Those kids are fighting over Frogger video again," her uncle said. Then, "Well, baby, how's it going?" Her uncle's tone was falsely hearty; she knew he missed her, too, and was fighting back typically Sicilian tears. "Jeez, we haven't gotten used to having you gone! Every five minutes Angela is saying to me, 'I wonder how Frannie is getting along, how she likes that big house down in Palm Beach.' The whole family's been on the telephone all day, everybody calling everybody else, asking them what they've heard. They even called me at work. You know how it is."

Francesca did. She longed, at that moment, to be with them, and to share in the excitement of Frannie, who had gone to Palm Beach to claim her fantastic inheritance. She sighed. "The house is just like the pictures, Uncle Carmine," she said. "It really is a sort of Venetian palace. I'm sure you remember a little bit about it from the time you and Dad were here. But it's hard to believe people actually lived in this place. There are nine bedrooms, can you believe it? And *two* dining rooms, do you remember?"

She talked for several minutes, for the first time consciously trying to describe what was now hers without being too sensational. She told them what she had seen of Palm Beach—*Was it still the same day?* she asked herself again—vistas of wide, palm-shaded avenues within a tiny little tropical town. And the shops and the beautiful Addison Mizner arcade on Worth Avenue with some of the world's most expensive and exclusive boutiques. And the Whitney mansion, the Kennedy compound on North Ocean Boulevard, the Pulitzer house, the Palm Beach Country Club and the great old Breakers hotel where the taxi stand holds nothing but black Cadillac limousines for hire.

Her Aunt Angela came on the line, and Francesca repeated most of it for her aunt and her Cousin Caetano, who had just stopped by after work. Then the kids got on the upstairs telephone extension. There was a lot of excited screaming and talking all at once. When Joanie and little Sal got off the extension Francesca talked to her aunt and uncle about the Rolls-Royce and John Turtle and Peter Peavey, the part-time chauffeurs. There was a sudden silence.

"Your father was a good man, Frannie," her uncle Carmine said heavily. "You come from good people, don't you forget it. They didn't make them any better than my brother. And I don't care what the old lady said in her will, you got a right to hold your head up anywhere. You don't need to take no crap from nobody."

It was a refrain Francesca had heard often enough, but she knew it came from love and concern. She merely said, "Yes, Uncle Carmine," obediently.

What she really wanted to say at that moment was how much she missed them, how—deep down within her—she was frightened with the uncertainties of this new life, and wished some one of them could be with her, to help her. All her self-assurance was deserting her: she needed to discuss with someone the strangeness of having a personal maid who drew your bath and knew your clothing as intimately as you did yourself, and the necessity of a private secretary, and a bodyguard.

Francesca set her lips determinedly. She knew if she even hinted to her family that she was less than happy where she was there would be quick, explosive reactions, lots of advice, misunderstandings and declarations that they were, all of them, coming down on the next plane to help. The whole family would be in an uproar.

"All that about Giovanni being the only man she ever loved," her uncle was saying. "That's nobody's business. All that stuff was between the two of them, years ago, and nobody will ever know the truth. You haven't got anything to be ashamed of."

"Carmine," her aunt said on the upstairs extension.

"Remember," her uncle went on, "you're the one paying the bills, now, and what you say goes, Frannie. You make them understand that."

"The lawyer advised me to get a bodyguard, Uncle Carmine." It was out; now she had to explain. "It's all the money, you know. That is, rich people have to be protected from cranks and people who want to bother them. It's really hard to believe, I mean to consider *me* that way. I can't get used to the idea of a bodyguard—there are all these people around me as it is! Five of them, including the maintenance men. And would you believe the place was built for a staff of twenty-five servants originally? It was like living in the middle of a mob scene!"

"Get a bodyguard," her Aunt Angela said. "Frannie, are you listening? You need some sort of protection down there, you don't know what sort of a place that is, Palm Beach. There are a lot of strange people around these days. And not only rich people need bodyguards, believe me."

"Right, honey." This was her uncle. "Get a bodyguard. But get a good one like an ex-cop, who knows what he's doing. Caetano knows some ex-cops from Dedham, Revere, Brookline. You want me to ask Caetano to look around for you?"

"No, not really," Francesca began. But before she could stop him, her uncle had called Caetano to the telephone. It took Francesca several minutes to persuade her cousin Cae not to send down several well-qualified ex-policemen to apply for the job.

She had to remember that her family only wanted to know that she was safe and happy in Palm Beach. The rest was just a dream as far as they were concerned; a glorious dream in which she, Francesca, was going to be happy ever afterward. They wanted to be told everything was wonderful.

"It's great here," Francesca said, dutifully. "It's a lot different, just like we said, but I've had a wonderful time so far. I'm going out to take a look at Palm Beach tonight. Mr. Ber—somebody's going to show me around. And I really miss all of you."

When she hung up, Francesca threw herself across the bed, careless of her clothes, and rubbed her eyes. There was no turning back. The realization swept over her like a tidal wave. It all looked so easy, and so marvelous, but it was going to be much, much harder than any of them had realized. Finally the brimming tears spilled over and she wept a little.

Then she sat up and wiped her eyes with the back of her hand. In the dressing-table mirror she saw a slender, naked young woman with a pretty face and superb figure, black hair drifting untidily, nose and eyes puffed with weeping.

"Oh, good grief," Francesca muttered under her breath. She ran her fingers through her tightly curling hair, uncertain what to do with it. Her gypsy hair. Kurt Bergstrom had invited himself to dinner. Francesca poured herself a glass of champagne from the bottle in the silver bucket and sat back on the bedspread, legs crossed under her, to watch herself in the mirror. She lifted the glass and watched her naked reflection in the mirror do the same.

She, Francesca Lucchese, was drinking champagne in her own twenty-eight-room mansion in Palm Beach.

"Oh, well," Francesca said out loud. It was real, but she still couldn't believe it.

She chose the red-and-white-striped jersey top and the white pleated skirt from Filene's for dinner with Kurt Bergstrom.

It was a dinner to remember, if not for the right reasons. As Francesca looked down the dinner table she was reminded of a scene from *Alice in Wonderland*, vaguely the Mad Hatter's Tea Party. Nothing seemed to be going right.

The massive silver candelabra needed polishing and were, in places, almost black with tarnish. The tableware was not only tarnished, but mixed with ordinary stainless steel pieces. Some of the plates were dark red and gold bone china, some were English flowered earthenware or dark gray modern pieces. They were served by John Turtle, the grounds and maintenance man, impassive in a white kitchen jacket.

The food was good, but Francesca did not have the appetite for an enormous meal of cold consommé, grilled fish, beef Wellington and salad on such a hot night. Kurt Bergstrom, looking unbelievably handsome in a navy linen blazer and a white silk shirt open at the throat, sent back the first bottle of wine. John Turtle returned with two more, which the blond man examined.

Francesca was getting strong signals that more than one thing was wrong. It was obvious by the cold patience with which they dealt with each other that Kurt Bergstrom and John Turtle were not the best of friends.

"Where is the Reisling?" the man in the Viking beard demanded of the other waiting by his side.

John Turtle regarded him with expressionless black eyes for some length. The hard planes of his face held him rigidly aloof. "Delia Mary doesn't have the keys."

"Why not?" The big man's slow voice held an edge.

The cook must have been listening, for now Delia Mary entered the dining room. The very air seemed opposed to anything Kurt Bergstrom might do.

"They's nothing wrong with that bottle of wine for dinner, Mister Kurt," Delia Mary said. She stood with her hands on the hips of her starched cook's uniform. "I chose it myself."

The big man put one arm on the table and half-turned in his chair to speak to her. "You had the keys this afternoon."

Delia Mary's face did not give an inch. "I gave them keys back to Mr. Stillman. I told you that when you came in here wanting to put all this stuff out for dinner that I ain't got time yet to clean. All this dirty silver what we can't use yet without we finish taking inventory."

Francesca watched them, baffled. They didn't seem to know she existed at the moment; there was some strange continuing thread in this which eluded her. She said suddenly, "I have the keys."

The faces turned to her.

"At least I have lots of keys," she explained. "Mr. Stillman turned them over to me. I'll have to look at their tags."

There was a war going on at *Ca'ad Carlo,* even she could see that. And in this war the staff did not exactly ignore her; they simply acted as though she had no part in it. She gathered it was Delia Mary and John Turtle against

Kurt Bergstrom, who held himself with a sort of icy sufferance. Francesca remembered the Miami lawyer's words: *He ran things around here for years.* Now Kurt Bergstrom was out, and the others were letting him know it. He no longer gave orders. Not even over a bottle of wine, their faces said.

She was suddenly very angry. It was unfair to Kurt Bergstrom to be treated this way. And she was infuriated that they should argue in front of her, as if her presence was the last thing anyone would have to worry about!

She knew she had created this awkward moment herself, by not knowing she had the household keys. But she couldn't absorb everything in one day, they should know that. She knew it would take a damned long time before these people would forget she was only a chauffeur's daughter who had inherited a multimillion-dollar fortune through some scandalous backstairs affair in the past! Cutting Kurt Bergstrom off from an estate that might rightfully be his. *If only Carla had left him something,* Francesca thought, looking down at her plate.

"Just a minute," Francesca said in an ordinary voice. No one paid any attention. They were arguing about missing pieces of china. "I'd like to have your attention," Francesca said, aware of how inadequate her words were, but determined to speak.

She saw John Turtle look up, then, his black eyes connecting with hers. She thought he looked surprised. Francesca reached for the center of the table and the bottle of wine. She picked it up, seeing the label was all in French. It looked very expensive.

"What's wrong with this?" she wanted to know.

Now they turned to her.

Kurt Bergstrom said with the same patient note in his voice, "The white wine. That's a beaujolais."

Francesca held the bottle of wine firmly by the neck and looked down the table. Her Uncle Carmine's words, 'You pay the bills, you tell them what's what,' rang in her ears.

But her uncle hadn't told her what to do when the message was that nobody wanted to listen.

"Miss Lucchese," the cook began.

"Lew-kay-zee," Francesca said, not for the first time in her life. "It's an Italian name." She tried to keep her voice low and patient, too, but her fingers were trembling around the neck of the bottle. "Actually, it's Sicilian. I'm used to drinking red wine with everything. Let's drink this now," she said, brightly, "and I'll bring down the keys in the morning and we'll get the whole thing straightened out."

They only stared at her. Even Kurt Bergstrom.

Well, too bad, she thought, staring back at them. What was the matter with these people? It was like a squabble in the history department of Northeastern; nobody wanted to give it up. But even if Kurt Bergstrom was no longer the master at *Ca'ad Carlo,* he still had the right to be treated civilly. As for the wine—Francesca set her chin stubbornly. She had half a mind to put in a stock of good Italian Chianti in the future and serve nothing else.


WHEN Delia Mary and John Turtle had gone to the kitchen, Francesca looked down the Mad Hatter's table with its over-load of food, flowers and tarnished silver and said, "Well, I'm sorry."

The handsome giant shrugged. "On the contrary, I should apologize to you. I only wanted to make the meal nice for you on this, your first night at *Ca'ad Carlo.* From now on, of course, *you* will send back the wine if it is not right." He turned his attention back to his fish. "The lawyers have told you to get a housekeeper, yes?"

Francesca said Harry Stillman had mentioned something of the sort.

"Or a butler." He poured some of the red wine into his glass and sipped it. "This is not bad." He looked around for John Turtle to pour it and found that he had gone. Kurt

Bergstrom unfolded his big frame and got out of his chair. He came around the table to Francesca with the wine bottle, and filled her glass himself. "Somebody should be in charge of the house."

"I guess I should—" she began.

The bronzed face looked down at her, the sea-blue eyes holding a look that, in the light of the candles, seemed to touch the curls of her heavy black hair, drop to her lips for a moment in a speculative way that set Francesca's heart to beating loudly, and then thoroughly examine the satin light on her bare arms and the swell of her truly superb breasts.

"No, you don't need to do any of this." His eyes still moved over her, lingering on her thighs and admirable legs tucked under her chair. "Carla was sick for a long time; she never went out. It will be a big change to have you here, a good change. You will go to parties, enjoy yourself—didn't the lawyers want you to do that?"

Francesca looked up at him, her head swimming. He towered over her. She could not escape his fresh-washed male scent accented with the perfume of after-shave cologne. She was overpoweringly aware of his body, and the brilliant blue eyes aroused a terrible confusion in her soul. She wondered what it would be like to have those strong, curving lips lower to hers and take them in a kiss.

Rattled, all she could think of to say was "Are you comfortable down where you are, in the guest house?" in a choked voice.

"Sure." The blue eyes caressed her, amused. "After we go out to see Palm Beach I will show you. I will show you my things. And you —are you comfortable in my room?"

It was Kurt Bergstrom's bedroom she was staying in.

"Oh, fine," Francesca said quickly. She tried to put thoughts of what his kiss would be like out of her mind. She lifted her glass and drank a large gulp of red wine and tried not to choke on it.

\* \* \*

"I WAS broke," he said candidly as he drove the Porsche down the floodlit walled lanes of Palm Beach. He drove well and economically, both hands on the wheel like a professional race driver. "My boat, the *Freya,* was in Curaçao. You know I'm *Svensk*—Swede, don't you?" His face was lit by the lights of the dashboard, lips set firmly together in the cropped Viking beard. "I was with some Norwegian friends in Curaçao with the *Freya* up for charter. Business was bad, none of us had any money. My friends left to go to St. Thomas to find work. I owed on *Freya*'s docking, petrol, everything. I was afraid I would lose her for debts. Then Carla and some people came down from Miami on a plane, they were staying at the Royal Christiana and wanted to go to Caracas and gamble. It was Carla's idea; one day she saw me on the dock cleaning the *Freya.* Carla chartered my boat, she paid for everything. She was very good that way. I had no crew, they had gone to St. Thomas, so I was going to singlehand the *Freya.* Except some of these people who were with Carla were nervous for me to sail a big boat like the *Freya* alone. So Carla herself wanted to help, and I picked up a kid to come along. Carla was not much use, but she liked it. We sat up at night and talked while I sailed, and when we got to Caracas we got married. That was five years ago. Five and a half," he corrected himself.

So Carla was a flesh-and-blood person after all! Francesca could imagine how he had looked when the Bloodworth heiress had first seen him—tanned and lean and powerful, a blond sea god down on his luck, money owing on his boat, stuck in some Caribbean port. She was *fifty,* Francesca reminded herself, a rich woman who'd already had two husbands. And who could resist this man?

She was sure she knew what had happened.

"You fell in love with each other," she murmured innocently.

He shot her a quick look. "Love? I took care of Carla. She was a woman who needed someone to take care of her. I carried her in my arms—she was little, you know. Also, she couldn't sleep. It was a habit of a lifetime, the insomnia. I sat up and talked with her, many nights. But Carla was a princess. Everybody had to do what Carla said."

The Porsche turned down County Road, going north of Palm Beach village. He turned to her briefly and in the dim dashboard light she saw the corners of his mouth turned up, amused.

"You want to know why Carla didn't leave me her money, and the house? She was mad at me, maybe. So she left me as she found me, with the *Freya* and not much more. A sailor. And a bum."

They were passing the great estates that lined the wide road in this, the middle part of the island. There were thick stands of giant oaks and trimmed hedges that reached as high as the first story of the houses. Through iron gates Francesca glimpsed a Doric portico and red-tiled roof down an avenue of palms, all bathed in glaring moonlight.

"Oh, don't say that," she protested. "You're not a—" She didn't finish. Distracted, she craned to look at great houses with the shapes of French villas and Medici palazzi.

"Oh, I'm a bum," he said agreeably. "That's the Sproeckels' place," he pointed out, indicating a pink Spanish villa. "A bum is someone who goes everywhere and does everything and has no money, right? I have fought in Africa, in Katanga and Angola. You have heard of Mike Hoare, no? And in Cambodia. I am a very good soldier, my specialty is paratroops. I command. For money."

"A soldier of fortune," Francesca whispered.

"A *mercenary*," he corrected her. "And yes, I suppose you know I have the title of nobility—count. But in Sweden that is nothing. It does not keep one from being a bum. All Swedish titles come from old Vikings who were robbers and grabbed from each other at the point of a sword. There is no aristocracy in Sweden like in England, with dukes and duchesses and viscounts and earls, like that. Do you understand?" He looked through the rearview mirror as he made a sharp lefthand turn. "There are only counts, what

is left of the old Viking robbers, and the king. My house
and land belong to an automobile manufacturer, now. You
have heard of Saab?"

The Porsche drew up to a guard and a uniformed security
man leaned out of them, murmured, "Good evening, Mr.
Bergstrom," and then stepped back.

The man at the wheel put the sports car in gear and it
moved slowly down a driveway arched over with a tall
hibiscus and masking banyan trees.

Francesca floundered in a sea of confusion. A mercenary? He had insisted on the word. He looked tough. And
she could imagine his big, powerful body in a paratrooper's
mottled battle clothes, helmet with chin brace, jumping out
of airplanes into the jungle, leading other mercenaries. It
seemed easier to picture him that way than as he was now,
his big hands casually turning the Porsche up a white shell
drive in the moonlight, impeccably handsome in his linen
blazer and silk shirt.

A bum, he had insisted. Broke and down and out when
Carla found him. Was that why the others at *Ca'ad Carlo*
treated him the way they did? Francesca already knew the
answer.

"Also," he said in the same even voice, "I did some gun
running after Cambodia, when I got the *Freya*. She's a
French boat. I bought her in Bangkok." He stopped the car
before a great sprawling white stone edifice lit by one dim
light bulb over the vast marble steps. He turned off the
ignition and sat back to look at her. "And yes," he said
softly, "I was a husband to Carla, I had sex with her." There
was a pause, while his blue eyes searched her face. "Now,
these are all the answers to the questions you were *not* going
to ask me, right?"

He was laughing at her. Francesca felt a slow, painful
blush rising to her face. Of course he was right. Those were
all the things she'd been dying to find out! And he had
known it!

But then, as he looked at her, she saw his eyes change,

as if urgent, darker currents were beginning to run in the blue-green seas. He suddenly moved toward her, sliding his big arm along the back of the Porsche's passenger seat. And Francesca, her body gone rigid with a strange expectancy, felt his closeness and his male strength.

The blue eyes appraised her. When she trembled, involuntarily, his hand lifted to touch her hair.

"Sweet," he murmured.

As unable to move as though she had suddenly been transformed into stone, Francesca felt his big gentle hand move to the back of her neck, pulling her head forward in order to turn her face up to his. Under his touch she was mesmerized, curiously helpless, yet something deep within her flesh, in the core of her belly, fluttered willingly. The brilliant blue eyes so close to hers seemed to fill up the night, and her breath came with difficulty. There was danger there and the unknown, Francesca knew. But this man's gentle, powerful beauty assailed her senses and drugged her; his clean, musky scent mixed with the spicy perfume of his after-shave lotion filled her nostrils. She thought of his huge, sun-gilded body aroused and wanting her. Closing in on her. And she shuddered.

The powerful fingers stroked her shoulders, threaded through her thick black curls and moved to the crown of her head with hypnotic sureness, pulling her face close while the other hand cupped her chin. Their lips almost touched.

"Francesca," he murmured. She could feel his warm breath on her mouth. "Don't pull away. I want to kiss you."

Numbly, she knew she didn't have the strength to protest, aware that he wanted her. What was happening was happening too fast; she didn't know this man, but he was controlling her body, not she. To her horror a small, quaking sound rose in her throat—a whimper of surrender. Whether she wanted to or not, her whole body was melting in his arms.

In answer, she saw his eyes darken. Kurt Bergstrom's mouth touched hers very lightly, and her own lips were stiff and trembling in response; she was as awkward as though she had never been kissed before. Then his mouth opened against hers and, very softly, he parted her lips with his tongue as if teaching her how to respond to him. Francesca clung to him with both hands, but a slow fire spread from his probing, confident mouth into hers. His tongue penetrated the sweetness of her own, tasting, exploring, kissing her in an almost leisurely way, but deeply and thoroughly. Francesca's body jerked against his in tense, puppetlike response, stirred by an uncontrollable heat in her flesh. Her head was swimming. What was he doing to her? What was his magic? She had kissed men before—now she felt like a child in the arms of this handsome, terrifying man.

She dimly realized that his hands stroked her back, caressed the fabric over her shoulderblades, and then inserted themselves under the jersey top and against her damp, silky skin. His big hands stroked her to the waist, pressing her body against him, then pushed down through the waistband of the pleated skirt to explore the top of her panties, then through them to cup the ample soft curves of her hips, finally grasping the cushioned roundness of her bottom in strong fingers.

"Beautiful Francesca," he murmured into her lips.

At his words, Francesca shuddered with a sudden release of sensual tension. Both his powerful hands grasped the luxurious softness of her bottom and pressed her body against him so that she could distinctly feel the big, hard presence of his arousal through their clothing.

The feel of his wanting her dragged Francesca back to reality. In spite of her body's sensuous throbbing, she was suddenly aware that her clothes were twisted, that she lay back uncomfortably against the front seat of the Porsche and that Kurt Bergstrom's arms held her immobile. She was fully, painfully ready for him and her soft flesh clamored for release. Her body wanted him wildly and savagely. She felt the blood pounding in her face, fully aware that he could make love to her right there, in the front seat of the Porsche, in the driveway of some strange house in Palm Beach, and she doubted that she would have any strength to deny him. She had never felt like that before in her life.

Quite abruptly, he smiled. He pulled his hands away, grasped her shoulders and pulled her upright. His mouth found hers for a deep kiss, and then he said, with a slight edge to his voice, "I think you could make me drunk with you, Francesca."

Her senses reeling, she swayed toward him and then pulled back. "What?" she whispered.

His hand cupped her chin to look down into her eyes. The blue look seemed to be amused, again.

"Do you want to go inside and meet some Palm Beach people? Some of them are crazy, but you will see what I mean. And they want to meet you."

For a moment Francesca couldn't answer. She wasn't quite sure her body was going to obey her. It still leaned toward him, wanting the feel of his kisses. She managed to pull herself upright in the seat and raised her hand to her turbulent hair, to smooth the black curls. The huge white house loomed over them in the moonlight. From somewhere inside came the amplified sound of loud, hard rock music.

She straightened the white pleated skirt from Filene's, feeling suddenly and unbearably dissatisfied with the way she looked. Her new clothes were so ugly she couldn't bear to think about them.

"Of course," she murmured.

# CHAPTER FOUR

A WOMAN came to them across an entrance hall that was
all colonnaded marble pillars and electric *torcheres* in mam-
moth bronze Corinthian-style floor stands. Her high heels
clicked across a vast green marble floor. The light was poor,
but the woman glittered elegantly in a vivid red silk djellaba
shot with gold threads that billowed about her sensuous
body. Masses of artfully puffed and tangled dark red hair
framed a deeply tanned, bony face with large luminous dark
eyes heavily accented with layers of mascara. She walked,
and looked, like a high fashion model. She was indescrib-
ably beautiful.

"Well, at last, here you are!" she cried in a throaty voice.
"I thought you were going to come for supper!"

Francesca opened her mouth to reply but the redheaded
woman floated past her and threw herself on Kurt Bergstrom, mouth opened wide to kiss him. She twined her arms
around him tightly.

A few moments passed and the kiss continued. Francesca looked around the great marble hall, feeling quite unnecessary, and more embarrassed than irritated. At last it was Kurt Bergstrom who pulled away. He held the redhaired woman's hands so that she couldn't wind her arms around his neck again, and said, "Dorrit, why don't you say hello to Francesca Lucchese? You wanted to meet the new owner of *Ca'ad Carlo,* right?

*"Precious!"* the redheaded woman said with entrancing huskiness. She turned and threw her arms around Francesca's neck.

Francesca found herself enveloped in a cloud of Patou's *Joy* and a woman's arms, a woman's body sheathed in silk. An open mouth met her own lips and caressed them boldly with its tongue, like a lover. Francesca jerked back. No one seemed to notice.

The beautiful woman held her at arms length and the dark, sultry eyes examined her thoroughly. "What a lovely baby, really," her shining red lips murmured. "Just like a schoolgirl with all that long curly hair, but not a schoolgirl, right? Maybe thirty? But just think of *all that money*—only Jinkie has more, now, you know!" Francesca was already turning a scalding red but the woman turned and said, over her shoulder, "You'd better lose ten pounds, sweetheart."

"Dorrit, for God's sake." But Kurt Bergstrom's voice was amiable. "Behave yourself."

The woman's voice floated back through the darkness of the marble hall. "Oh shut up, Kurt! Buffy's going to be her friend, we all decided it. Buffy used to be a stewardess or something. They'll have a lot in common."

The big man reached out and caught Francesca's hand and pulled her after him. Francesca allowed herself to be steered down a hall with marble statuary like a museum, but she was seething. The beautiful woman's words had been like blows, sharp, painful, dismissing her as really no one important. For the second time that evening Francesca felt a surge of humiliated rage. First her own employees at *Ca'ad*

*Carlo,* now this. She was ready to quit. But Kurt Bergstrom continued to drag her forward. They entered a smaller corridor made of glass that looked out on both sides into a floodlit, unearthly green jungle. There were purple and white and small green yellow orchids in the jungle greenery and brightly colored birds, parrots and cockatoos, chained to wooden perches. Beyond the jungle corridor was the blast of loud rock music.

"Stop," Francesca said between her teeth, but the only response was a stronger jerk on her wrist.

They descended into a partially enclosed swimming pool area that was a mixture of living room, restaurant-sized bar, and a pool illuminated by underwater lights. There were full-sized palm trees growing beside low couches, blooming orchids under glass-topped tables, and spotlights bathed flowering hibiscus and flame-colored ixora planted in gravel. The jungle motif in the glass-enclosed corridor had been carried into the pool-living area and expanded, Francesca saw. A heady perfume of some sweet and pungent blooming plant filled the air. All the guests seemed to be graying, terribly fit and handsome men in their fifties and sixties, and gorgeous women young enough to be their daughters.

The beautiful girls, Francesca noticed, followed a set style with their lithe bodies and pronounced high breasts, silky tans and beautifully kept long hair. They all wore designer clothes of the type seen in Palm Beach shops, and they all looked as though they studied the same fashion magazines and had their hair done in the same salons. Looking at them, Francesca felt lumpy and too tall, and too awkward in a red-and-white-striped jersey with white pleated skirt. The redheaded woman had said 'a schoolgirl'—if so, she knew she looked a fool.

"I'm Buffy." A tall, gleaming girl in a gray silk jump suit with long straight hair as pale as silver took Francesca's hand. Buffy's eyes followed Francesca's as Dorrit drifted off with Kurt Bergstrom still in tow. "Don't pay any attention to Dorrit. She can be nice when she wants to. And she will, eventually, when she settles it about Kurt. Come have a drink and tell me about *Ca'ad Carlo*. Have you recovered from the shock yet? Is it as weird as they say? Somebody said it looked like 'Othello and Desdemona Visit Disney World,' but it can't be any worse than *Viscaya*, down in Miami."

Buffy pulled Francesca to a bar which featured a waterfall, live orchids and hundreds of mirror-lighted bottles of liquor. There was no bartender, so Buffy stopped behind the bar and brought out a bottle of tonic water and a bottle of vodka. Buffy poured Francesca a glass of white wine from an ordinary glass jug of California chablis.

The ravishingly beautiful Buffy tossed her long silver-gold hair back with one hand and said, "Okay. I'm married to Jock Amberson. He's fishing at Marathon. We're the crowd that lives in Palm Beach the year round, and we're growing, you know. It used to be that you only lived in Palm Beach in the summertime because you didn't have any money to go anywhere else, but that's not true anymore." She shot Francesca a sharp glance. "Look, I met Jock when I was on two weeks' vacation in Montego Bay from Pan Am. He was divorcing his third wife and went ape when he saw me in a bikini." Buffy handed Francesca her glass of white wine. "This was what you wanted, wasn't it? Dorrit has to buy the wine herself, now, so it's El Cheapo. You know, I'm dying to see *Ca'ad Carlo*. You will let people in, now, won't you? Carla wouldn't."

"Why not?" Francesca asked, curious.

The other woman shrugged. "Who knows? They tell me Carla was weird at the last. Poor Kurt tried to change things, he tried to move things around a bit and get rid of some of the Bloodworth junk, but Carla wouldn't let him do that, either. They say Carla wanted to give the place to the state for a museum, like the Flagler mansion here, but she changed her mind. A lot of things have happened there. Do you know Bunny Quigley drowned off the front of the house there at *Ca'ad Carlo?*"

Buffy's drawling recital was consciously funny, and Francesca had to laugh. She had been on edge when Dorrit has escorted them in, but now the feeling was beginning to drop away. Buffy, at least, was warm and friendly.

"He didn't drown at *Ca'ad Carlo*, my lawyers swear. It was somebody else's house. They say it's just another Palm Beach story," she said.

Buffy shrugged again. "Oh well, I really didn't know who he was, it's just what everybody says, you know." Drink in hand, now, Buffy stepped closer for a long appraisal of Francesca. "You're sort of pretty," she said, not unkindly. "There's a kind of sleeping beauty quality, really." When she saw Francesca's expression she said quickly, "Well, it's great you've got all that money, anyway. So many of these people here don't enjoy what they've got. When they inherit their fortunes they're told it's a sacred trust, so that's all they do—look after their money. They're very dull people, a lot of them. And really defensive."

Francesca said, somewhat apprehensive, "You know, Buffy, I'm not really supposed to be here, officially, that is. The transition is going to be difficult for me, to this sort of life, so the lawyers thought I should get used to things gradually. I had a job at Northeastern College—"

Buffy let out a hoot of laughter. "Oh, honey, I was a stew sharing an apartment in Chicago with three other girls when I snagged Jock! He's not in the Bloodworth league, but his mother's a Radney, that's Oklahoma oil, and he does all right in spite of the alimony and child support he ladles out. And look, Dorrit's from noplace—nobody knows where she's from, but here she is living in Bodner's house, which is old money from Philadelphia through Bodner's mother. But Dorrit's a wacko. Bodner's going to kick her out. She has to get her things out by September first, that's why there aren't any servants around, in case you haven't noticed. But she can use up all the booze, and the light bill's paid. Palm Beach has heard all of this, none of these things are any surprise, believe me. So what if Carla died and left all that dime store money to her chauffeur? The

Bloodworths were only poor Irish immigrants like the Kennedys, only they were working in the Pennsylvania coal mines before old Charlie opened his first ten-cent store."

While the beautiful blonde woman talked, Francesca could feel eyes on her. This curious party—could one call it a party—was full of a suppressed excitement which had nothing to do with who she was or why she was there. At the pool there was a ripple of laughter as some of the beautiful young women went skinny-dipping while the trim middle-aged men watched them, and people were smoking pot, she could smell it, rather ostentatiously in a group at the end of the bar. So was she imagining it, or did heads turn in her direction and did whispers follow?

The lawyers had gone to great pains, she knew, to make this rendezvous in Palm Beach as low-key as possible, in order to give her time to adjust to what was, obviously, becoming a rather involved new life. Francesca wondered rather nervously if there was a pipeline of gossip operating in Palm Beach already which knew all too well who she was, and when and why she had arrived. Certainly Buffy seemed to know all about it.

Kurt. She looked around for Kurt Bergstrom. Why now, of all times, had he gone off with the woman called Dorrit and left her?

A short, gray-haired man with a slight paunch and a boy's face, dressed in Bermuda shorts and a somewhat frayed cotton knit shirt drifted up. "You're a nice-looking girl," he said to Francesca. His pale amber eyes examined her thoroughly. "Listen," he said, moving quite close to drop his voice almost to a whisper, "you don't want to hang around with this crowd of Dorrit's. They're only here in Palm Beach because they won't let them in anyplace else."

"Cripes, Jinkie, don't start that!" Buffy cried. To Francesca she said, "Jinkie's hung up on niceness. He's worried Palm Beach is getting very decadent. But actually Palm Beach is not as decadent as Boca Raton. They've got all kinds of weirdies down in Boca—Argentinians, Brazilians, Arab sheiks—you name it. It's like Malibu! Besides, Jinkie," she accused him, "you go other places. You're just back from Newport, right?"

"Palm Beach is not like it was," the little man maintained stubbornly. "Not here, not there, not anywhere. Grandaddy wouldn't like Palm Beach now at all."

"Oh, *screw* Grandaddy, Jinkie!" Buffy exclaimed. "You're hung up on Grandaddy, too."

Jinkie's grandaddy's name was one Francesca recognized at once. The word was a synonym for wealth. If true, and she supposed it was, Jinkie had more money than anybody! While Francesca was staring at Jinkie a small, thirtyish woman with a strained smile came up to them accompanied by a man in tennis shorts. The man was middle-aged and had ugly, hairy bowed legs. He smiled only with his mouth. "Welcome to Palm Beach, Miss Lucchese," he said. "We've been looking forward to meeting you. You're certainly a celebrity! I'm Bernard Binns, and this is Elsa MacLemore."

Buffy thrust her hand, holding a gin and tonic, between them abruptly. "Hold on, Bernie," she said loudly, "go hustle business somewhere else." To Francesca she said, "Bernie's going to tell you to read his diet book and come to his weight loss clinic, but don't do it! If you're going to get made over, go to the Golden Door in Fort Lauderdale. They give the works—body, hair, skin, diet, wardrobe, everything—and they don't give you weirdy shots!"

The small tense woman said quickly to Jinkie, changing the subject, "Kurt Bergstrom's got your diesel boat up for sale, he tells me. He says he's going to broker it for you."

She and the multimillionaire Jinkie began talking about yachts while the diet doctor began an argument with Buffy about shoat placenta injections. The group's conversation was, seemingly, the latest installment on topics they always discussed when with each other. Francesca's head was beginning to throb, her scalp drawing ever tighter with tiredness and tension, and the blare of rock music didn't help at all. She had worried about being recognized; now she felt very much left out!

Francesca searched the room again, looking for Kurt

Bergstrom's towering height and blond head, or Dorrit's flaming red hair. Neither was to be found. What had she done? she asked herself miserably. Had she been too clumsy, too resistant in the car when Kurt Bergstrom had kissed her? The chemistry between them—or at least that *he* offered, she told herself—was very real. Why hadn't she been able to react to this terrifically attractive, worldly man with a little—*poise?* Francesca caught her underlip with her teeth, and frowned unhappily. She was assailed again with the feeling that she was doing everything all wrong. She had on the wrong clothes, she really wasn't up to mixing with all these wealthy Palm Beach people who seemed to know each other so very well, she had been stiff and stupidly inhibited when Kurt Bergstrom had tried to kiss her, and he had disappeared almost immediately once they were inside Dorrit's mansion.

"Something wrong?" It was Elsa MacLemore, the diet doctor's woman friend. "Are you tired? It must be a terribly long day for you."

*Everything was wrong,* her heart cried out. "Yes, tired." Francesca bit down on the words painfully. "And my head is bothering me."

Dr. Binns turned to her now. "My dear, why didn't you say so?" He seemed delighted to be of help. He fished in his pocket and brought out a small glassine paper packet.

"Bernie," the tense woman said.

Jinkie had come up. He stood watching them.

The diet doctor's hand reached for Francesca's wineglass, tilted it toward him, and emptied the contents of the packet into it. He motioned for her to drink it.

"What is it?" Francesca said, looking into the glass. The powder had instantly disappeared. "Is it aspirin? It's not a sedative, is it?" she said doubtfully. "I really don't need anything to slow me down."

"It's better than aspirin," Jinkie volunteered. "Besides, I don't think Dorrit's got any aspirin in this place. I don't think there's even any toilet paper in the head."

Buffy turned to notice what they were doing. "What are you giving her?" she said, suspicious.

"Count to ten and wait," the doctor said, watching Francesca down what remained of the glass of wine in a gulp.

"Oh, Francesca," Buffy said, shaking her head. "This isn't Boston. I don't think you know what you're into, yet."

Count to ten, the diet doctor had said. It took twenty minutes for an aspirin to take effect. How long, then?

A gray-haired, distinguished-looking man in a white linen suit spoke to Francesca in Italian and it was a moment before she recognized the language. The feeling of terrible awkwardness returned, she answered in her high school Italian that actually she knew only a little Sicilian, and not much of that. While she stumbled through the Italian phrases, the man's eyes twinkled. He switched to unaccented American English and began to talk charmingly of the Greek ruins at Siracusa, which he seemed to know quite well. He wasn't Italian. His name was Herb Ostrow and he was a film writer, among other things. He talked about Anna Magnani and the great days of Italian films.

Listening to him, Francesca felt curious things happening. An inward fizzy feeling was taking over, lifting the tiredness so imperceptibly that it was hard to realize it was gone. The throbbing headache was banished. She began to talk to the film writer, discussing some of the Italian films she'd seen. Herb Ostrow seemed spellbound. In return, Francesca sparkled. She began to flirt with him a little, realizing that even *she* had no idea she was that fascinating.

She had lost track of time. When she paused for breath, he said, openly admiring, "You're really quite beautiful, if you'll allow me to say so." He made an expansive gesture. "Not the usual plastic type of television beauty, but the kind the Italians appreciate. Sort of the unaffected, smoldering quality of an early Sophia Loren."

"Gina Lollobrigida," Jinkie put in, coming up to stand with them. He stared pointedly at the front of Francesca's red-and-white-striped cotton shirt.

"Cripes, not Gina Lollobrigida!" Buffy said witheringly. "Who remembers her? She was sort of short and bulging, wasn't she? And what are we talking about, anyway?"

"If she smolders and she bulges, you'd better get a fire extinguisher," Jinkie cackled. "Sounds like the engine's going to blow up!"

"Jinkie's a creep," Buffy said under her breath. She looked down into Francesca's empty wineglass and frowned. "Where the hell's Kurt? He's supposed to be looking after you." She turned and looked around. "Let's see if I can scare him up."

What Francesca really wanted to do was dance. The middle-aged men and their gorgeous young women were dancing at the edge of the pool, gyrating to the hard rock music. She knew she could do better than that. Dredged out of the depths of her unconscious, she knew she wanted to dance with Kurt Bergstrom and she wondered almost shyly if he would. If she asked him. Buffy, she reminded herself, had gone to look for him. She felt so marvelous she could hardly stand still.

A hard-faced young woman with ink black hair and a superbly thorough tan came padding up from the pool. She was still dripping water and she had taken off her bikini top: her narrow, pointing breasts were flawlessly burnished, down to dark rose copper nipples. She bellied over the bar, reaching with one long arm to get the jug of wine to fill her glass, exposing a strip of near-white on each cheek as her bikini bottom hiked up.

"Mine are better than that," Francesca said loudly. She began to laugh, she felt so wonderful. She was not as gauche as people thought she was. The screen writer had thought she was fascinating. And she knew if she gave Jinkie any encouragement, he would, too. At least she knew when her breasts were bigger and better shaped than some scrawny girl without any clothes on.

"Dammit, Kurt," Buffy was saying, "you've really got to *stay* with her! She's high, high—and it's something that bastard Bernie Binns laid on her."

Francesca was floating now. She had never felt so perfectly happy in her whole life. The room, the very air, seemed to sparkle darkly. The loud music filled every fiber of her being and vibrated in her ears and even through her sensitive eye sockets. Nude men and women were swimming in the brightly lit aquamarine waters of the pool.

Buffy took her chin between two fingers to look into her face. Buffy, her own eyes large and brilliant, said: "Oh, cripes, honey—how much? You're really flying!"

Francesca knew other people might be more polished, more sophisticated, more at ease in these surroundings, but, as her Uncle Carmine said, she was the one who had the money! It was supposed to make all the difference in the world. She looked at Buffy and broke into irrepressible giggles.

"You worry too much." It was Kurt Bergstrom's voice, and his strong hand taking hers. Francesca turned to him gratefully, and he looked down at her, handsome and assured. She knew everything was all right.

"Take her home." It was Buffy's voice again. "Francesca, I'll call you in the morning, okay?"

"I really don't want to go home," Francesca said. "I don't feel sleepy at all." She really wanted to dance with Kurt Bergstrom, but she couldn't bring herself to ask him. She wanted him to know that she really was a very good dancer.

She also wanted to talk to Herb Ostrow, the writer, again, but Kurt took her hand and started toward the door that led to the jungle corridor and the front of the house. Suddenly Dorrit appeared, her mass of red hair quite disheveled, her eyes black rounds of smudged mascara, clutching the partly-open *djellaba* to her sensuous body. Even Francesca could see that Dorrit was naked underneath the transparent silk robe. Dorrit waved her arms and seemed to want to speak, but bodies closed around her, and hands reached out and pulled her back into the crowd.

"Good night, honey," Jinkie said as they mounted the stone steps to the exit. "I'll call you in the morning."

Brilliantly alive and awake, Francesca threw her head
back recklessly to laugh. Everyone was going to call her in
the morning. She had made quite a lot of Palm Beach friends,
all in a few hours.

Which was exactly what the lawyer had told her to do.


But they were not, apparently, going to go back to *Ca'ad
Carlo*. The sweltering night had finally cooled and a damp,
satiny wind blew from the sea, smelling faintly of flowers.
The curving coconut palms that lined Ocean Drive clicked
their fronds in the wind. Francesca rode with the Porsche's
window rolled down, amazingly awake, nerves glittering.
She couldn't remember being so full of energy in her life.
Francesca was finding Palm Beach an intoxicating experience; the soft night was endless, one could stay up forever
and there was no job anymore to get up to in the morning!
One could stay up all night and party and sleep late and go
for a swim and enjoy a late brunch served by one's servants,
and try to think of something marvelous to do.

The man next to her—the most attractive man Francesca
had seen all night by far—swept her with his electric blue
eyes, probing for something responding in her, and inwardly
Francesca trembled. This was not Boston, this was some
exotic, unreal and exciting place. And she was not sure she
was Frannie Lucchese, a twenty-eight-year-old spinster
working in the graduate studies office of Northeastern University. Surely the rules were changed now, and one could
play this new game as one never before in one's life had a
chance to play anything.

"Some of the world's best is here." Kurt Bergstrom was
talking about polo. "You will get an invitation to the club,
that is no problem. And an invitation also, to the Everglades
Club, that is the hardest to get into."

Francesca let her hand trail out of the window of the car,
fingers sifting the breeze. She felt as though laughter bub-
bled just under the surface; she felt so joyous she wanted

to shout. Which was odd, since she had always been told she was too serious.

She murmured, "Is it true Dorrit is going to get kicked out of the house she's living in, back there?"

As though he hadn't heard her he said, "The Old Guard is hard to know. They will let you into their clubs because of the Bloodworth money, but Palm Beach people wait a long time before they are really friendly. Maybe years."

"Do you know any of them?" She was curious.

"A few."

"I thought you said it took a long time."

"They were Carla's friends," he said tersely.

The Porsche turned down a gravel road that led down to the water's edge and a marina. They got out of the car and went down a long, narrow dock to an enormous three-masted sailing yacht at the far end. As they crossed over onto the deck of the boat Francesca could hear lilting calypso music from below. A shadow of a man seemed to appear at a hole at their feet.

"Who the hell are you?" it demanded. "No Cambodia-side An Thoc scum allowed here, I told you last time!"

But the burly shadow put its arm around Kurt Bergstrom's shoulders and hugged him. The face of an enormously fat, enormously powerful man peered at Francesca. "Is this the new heiress? Jesus, Kurt, this kid's not bad! And sixty million, too." He came closer and looked into Francesca's face. When she smiled he said, "Ho, ho," softly, under his breath, "and she flies." He took her arm. "Back down the ladder, sweetheart," he told her. "I don't want you wrecking that beautiful rear end on the rungs coming down."

The ladder turned out to be a small stair down into the boat's interior. Francesca came down cautiously. She'd never been on a sailing boat before and one of this size was intimidating. Below, she found, was beautiful, compact but luxurious. The boat was filled with young people in casual clothes, blue jeans and shorts. The calypso music came from two guitars and a steel drummer jammed into a corner of the main cabin. The air was blue with smoke and the sweet, pungent odor of marijuana. A small friendly woman in jeans, tanned, not young, came up and hugged Kurt Bergstrom.

"I didn't think you'd make it." She looked up at him through spiky lashes fondly. Then she looked over Francesca. "Oh Kurt, she looks *nice*. I'm Cassie," she introduced herself, "and the big slob is Angel. I guess Kurt told you— they were together in Bangkok."

Cassie drew her aside as Angel squeezed between them and went forward. Someone passed a drink for Francesca over Cassie's head. It was cola, she found, sipping it, with a slice of lime and something unidentifiable. She shrugged, and drank it.

Cassie hesitated, then drawing Francesca to her so that the others wouldn't overhear, she murmured, "Be good to Kurt, we all love him. And Carla really worked him over. I *know*, I was there."


IT was after four when the Porsche turned into the gates of *Ca' ad Carlo*. A sleepy-looking uniformed security guard, supplied by a West Palm Beach agency, greeted them at the front gate with "Good morning, Miss Lucchese, Mr. Bergstrom," and waved them through.

Francesca settled back in the Porsche's seats. It was *her* security guard, she thought dreamily, and *her* tree-lined drive leading up to her Palm Beach mansion. She could almost feel she was getting used to all this.

She smoothed the pleated white skirt with her hands. The rowdy party on Angel and Cassie's yacht had taken its toll on her Boston clothes; someone had spilled beer on her, and she had torn her jersey top on something jumping down from her seat on a kitchen cabinet. Not to mention crawling around on the floor—*deck*, she corrected herself—doing the limbo. But it didn't matter; she had already decided she was going to throw away all her Boston clothes and start over again in the boutiques in Worth Avenue.

Dreams do come true, Francesca told herself happily. Nothing could break the sparkling mood of the evening. Even now she wasn't feeling sleepy at all, in fact, she had never felt so wonderful. She was vividly, thrillingly wakeful—her veins pumping fire, aware of her silky skin that enveloped her body, of her tingling, curiously sensitized lips, her heavy breasts straining against her bra, the way her long legs slid together through the sheath of nylon pantyhose. Something—perhaps all-night partying, lack of sleep, the wine she had been drinking—had produced a marvelous high. She knew Kurt Bergstrom was watching her out of the corner of his eye.

Everywhere they'd gone that evening, people had greeted Kurt Bergstrom with pleased surprise, and it was obvious he had many friends in Palm Beach. That made it doubly hard to understand the trouble with the staff at *Ca' ad Carlo*. What were the mysteries surrounding this man, Francesca wondered, even when he was so devastatingly candid about himself? He had told her more than she wanted to know, without asking. She felt a nervous thrill through her body just thinking about him, and looked away through the darkened window glass so he wouldn't see her face. She felt foolish, but, she thought, and not for the first time that evening, how could any woman not want him?

"It's late," he said, as he slid the sports car into a parking slot by a lane of daturas. "It's almost morning." His tone was teasing; in the darkness, the gleam of his fine white teeth showed as he spoke. "You don't want to see my house now, do you?"

"Of course I do!" Francesca declared. "Who needs to sleep?" She opened the door of the Porsche and jumped out. "I'm finding nobody sleeps in Palm Beach, anyway."

The party on Angel and Cassie's yacht had been going full blast when they left, and more people had still been coming aboard.

She heard his soft, amiable laugh. "Yes, that is true of Palm Beach. One can always find a party."

Francesca started down the path. It was suddenly very hot under the trees in the dense darkness, and the perfume of the flowering daturas was cloying. When she stumbled, Kurt took her arm.

"Are you all right?" He had taken off his jacket and in the darkness she could make out his white shirt, pale hair and the shadow of his tanned face. The concern in his voice was obvious.

She drew herself up, and her soft flesh brushed the corded muscles of his forearm. She thought his body tensed with the contact. "I'm perfectly all right," she announced. It was true; the magnificent sparkling feeling was still there. "I haven't had all that much to drink—and I wasn't smoking that stuff they were passing around, either, on Cassie and Angel's boat," she added. Her own body was reacting to his closeness; Francesca tried to pull away slightly, but it didn't work.

The tall blond man looked down at her, his pale eyes lit by the faint moonlight beyond the trees. "I wasn't talking about what you had to drink," he said.

The dark path led to a cottage set in a grove of coconut palms, oleanders, and the great white trumpets of the daturas in bloom. He went ahead and unlocked the door.

Francesca waited in the doorway for Kurt to find a lamp and turn it on. When he did, the light revealed a charming room with whitewashed walls, shuttered windows, and a great fireplace of rough-hewn beams and plaster. Framed photographs lined the walls, of men in camouflage combat uniforms against a jungle background, of sailing yachts, a country estate with a large stone house and rolling fields, figures in ski clothes against a range of ragged mountains, and several men and women in the costume of a royal court. One picture showed a handsome woman wearing a diamond tiara and a broad ribbon with a jeweled decoration diagonally across her breast.

A heavy blackwood table before the fireplace held a
collection of Indonesian ceremonial daggers inlaid with
mother-of-pearl, a reclining brass Buddha and several
leatherbound books. The whole room, Francesca saw, was
filled with things from around the world: African artifacts,
Asian art, idols, masks, and what appeared to be a carved
wooden boat prow, very ancient, in the shape of a dragon
mounted on one wall. Under the boat prow was a large
black and white, framed lithograph of a Viking longship
with wind-filled striped sail, moving out on a dawn sea with
the sun rising just above the horizon. The sun's glitter on
the water in the picture was matched by the flames which
shot from the dragon-prowed ship and climbed around the
figure of a man lying on a platform in full battle gear, horned
helmet on his head and his shield placed over his body.

"What's that?" Francesca exclaimed. There were no other
figures on board the Viking ship except the warrior on the
bier with the flames about to devour him.

"It is a Viking burial." He came to stand behind her. "At
dawn they set the ship afire and put it out to sea. This is a
chief's burial, otherwise one would not destroy a good
longship like that. But for a Viking, it was the last great
honor."

She couldn't take her eyes from the picture. It was full
of a dread fascination that she could not express. "Then
what happened?"

"It sank."

When she turned, she was almost in his arms. This sudden assault of his bigness, his maleness, on her senses took
her breath away. The closeness of his body seemed mag-
nified a hundred times, and she could not bring herself to
look up into his strange sea-blue eyes. He already had too
much power over her, Francesca thought. Inwardly, she
shivered. When he spoke, his voice seemed to whisper and
echo in her mind.

"I thought you would be different," he murmured.

Francesca heard his words, but she was suddenly re-

membering Dorrit close to him earlier in the evening, and
Dorrit's hungry, open mouth devouring his. She steadied
her voice enough to say, "Different, how?"

His slow smile seemed to caress her. The precisely molded
planes of his rugged face, his perfectly carved lips with their
amused, upturned corners, his great size and his easy, masculine assurance made Francesca go weak, assailed a thousand treacherous emotions. She could hardly hear his answer.

Vainly, Francesca tried to stay alert to the real danger
in all this; she knew nothing about him. He was a soldier
of fortune, an adventurer, as well as Carla's disinherited
third husband! A feeling of caution deep in Francesca's
consciousness tried to come alive, fighting unsuccessfully
against the wild, glittering feeling with which her body was
filled.

The big man bent his tawny head to her, the sea-blue
eyes boring into her. "I want you very much, Francesca."
His voice had gone very soft and husky. "I'm going to make
love to you. But I want you to want me, too."

Francesca drew a ragged breath. The warning voice in
her mind told her this shouldn't be happening, and for a
very good reason. But before she could speak, his firm,
demanding mouth found hers. Immediately an invisible spark
leaped from his lips and seared deep into her trembling body.
The glittering feeling ignited and burst into soaring flames.

Ruthlessly, his mouth parted her lips, and his tongue
began an exploration of her quivering response. He drew
her face to him with both hands, cupping it, and his kisses
dragged breathless little moans from her.

"Love me," he said against her mouth.

Francesca was no longer capable of resisting. She was
stunned to find she wanted this man with a violent physical
demand that clamored to have him lose himself in her body.
Conscious thought fled; she was giving herself over to whirl-
ing sensations, heightened colors, a sense of his body and
a growing need. Without wanting it, her hips pressed against
his body hungrily. She clung to him with both hands, nails

biting into his arms, astounded at what her body was doing without her consent.

"Wait," she choked. Everything was going too fast, and she acknowledged she had no control over any of it!

But he only smiled. His hands slid down her arms, grasping them, pulling her even closer against his big body, stroking his thighs and the curve of her hips, and then lingering to grasp her buttocks in both hands as his mouth assaulted hers, pressing her against the great aroused rod of flesh she could feel beneath the layers of their clothing.

He wanted her to know how much he desired her, Francesca knew, but her body quailed before the thought of his aroused physical power. She wanted to scream out in her confusion, but all that escaped was a lustful little moan.

His lips and tongue continued to ravish her, trailing fire across her face, into her hair, nibbling gently at the lobe of her ear, then descending into the quivering hollows of her throat. His kisses goaded her, tracing the damp skin of the line of her cheek into her dark curling hair, into her throat and then the cleft between her breasts. Finally she felt his fingers against the heavy round softness of her breasts straining at the jersey top, and then his thumb and forefinger reached for the unbearably sensitive nipple through the cloth. She gave a soft cry.

At the sound, his arms tightened around her. "My God," his lips whispered against her hair, "I want you now, beautiful Francesca."

He picked her up in his arms. Francesca was not a small woman and only his size and strength made it seem effortless. When he started for the bedroom Francesca could make no sound of protest. She no longer had any will of her own, her body was in complete control, driven by a shattering excitement in her flesh. Her own body wanted him now—it didn't mind what her conscious mind objected to at all!

"Wait," Francesca moaned, knowing that he would not hear her. He dropped her gently on his big bed. She felt as though she were losing her mind; her body was like a greedy, clamoring other being, not her own. Around them the room was spinning. All that was real was her willful flesh and this powerful man controlling it.

He pushed her gently back against the bedcovers, and began stripping away her clothes—the cotton jersey top, the pleated skirt, her bra and then her panties. At each brush of his fingers against her silky skin Francesca shuddered. Her hands grasped his wrists as if to restrain him, but no words came out. He stood for a moment looking down at her beautiful long-legged body with its tiny waist and magnificent breasts, and his eyes darkened to a midnight shade.

"You are truly beautiful," he muttered. He turned her face to him, one hand under her chin. "You knew I wanted you when I first saw you, and you saw me, there this afternoon in the kitchen. I could see it in your eyes, then. Yes?"

Francesca tried to protest, but his mouth covered hers, penetrating her soft cries with long, drowning kisses, his tongue probing and overwhelming her lips.

He reached over to turn on the bedside lamp and a soft glow filled the room. Francesca quickly put her hands to her naked breasts, blinking. Her senses had run riot; even the light seemed to shoot sparks into her consciousness. She could only stare at him.

He leaned over her, his shoulders massive under his white silky shirt. "I am not going to hurt you, Francesca," he soothed her. "What a child you are." He pulled her fingers away from her breasts and then cupped them in his big brown hands, watching her start and shiver under his touch. "I want to look at you," he murmured, his eyes following his words. "I want to see your lovely body enjoy what I am doing."

Abruptly he lowered his head, and his tongue touched her glistening pink nipples, circling and caressing them. But she almost screamed out as his mouth then took them firmly, grazing her soft skin with his teeth, his lips pulling at their ripeness. Her treacherous body, goaded feverishly, writhed under his. The feel of his mouth tore little sobs from her and his own body tightened in response. She heard him gasp. His fingers dug into her soft, yielding flesh as his mouth moved to the other passive globe of satiny smoothness. When he lifted his head, Francesca saw his eyes glittering.

After a few seconds he sat up in the bed and then stood up and undressed himself swiftly, throwing the white shirt on the floor. Then he took off his shoes. At last he stood up and unbuckled his belt, and pulled off his white slacks. Francesca could not turn her head. He wore small bikini briefs, abbreviated and expensive-looking, in a gold color that made his flat belly and slim hips appear even more tapered.

Watching her, too, now, he peeled away the bikini briefs quite deliberately and stepped out of them with his solid, assured, masculine gracefulness. He was a handsome man who knew the beauty of his body; his aroused maleness was overwhelming in its size and power. Francesca, mesmerized, could not drag her eyes away. He saw her, and smiled his slow smile.

With a convulsive movement Francesca sat up in the bed as though to leave. But almost immediately he was kneeling beside her, to put his arms around her. In the soft light his thick golden hair and sun-gilded body was like a god's.

"Don't run away," he said. "I am going to make love to you, beautiful Francesca. It is too late to say no to it."

The soft light from the bedside lamp was a thousand brilliant dancing motes about them, floating in the air like diamond dust. Francesca knew her mind played tricks on her as he pressed her back down against the bed, as she felt the sensation of his lips and tongue on her skin, roving over her shoulders, seizing her breasts and trailing sensuous demands down her shuddering soft belly to the nest of dark curling hair in her groin.

"You want this, don't you?" his voice urged her. "Show me, Francesca!"

Like a puppet her body obeyed him. Her body moved under his kisses, tormented, while his hand gripped both her wrists and dragged them over her head to hold her. She thought of the men he had led, paratroopers, and the violence of war, and his menacingly big and powerful body that now so easily subdued hers. The silky patch between her legs was throbbing wildly. She choked back a cry as she felt his mouth smothering her with kisses there. The electrical field had passed from his body into her own flesh, shooting sparks into her aching center.

She was sobbing excitedly as his big body pressed her into the softness of the bed. At that moment she wondered wildly how this bronzed giant had made love to fragile Carla Bloodworth. But Carla had wanted him—fifty-year-old Carla on the dock in Curaçao, seeing a blond, beautiful sea-faring god, wanting him. *Buying him,* her mind told her.

He pulled his big body over her, one leg thrusting between hers, and Francesca's hand slipped against the silky ripples of his muscular back, unable to resist him. She wanted him. But she didn't want him to conquer her and make love to her. She didn't know what she wanted!

"Francesca," he groaned against her mouth.

His big body, shivering with his desire, thrust against her and she gave a little shriek. She braced herself against the invasion of her flesh and sensuous, hurting, her body gave way. She heard him grunt in surprise with the resistance he had found, but he did not stop.

There was an even greater pain as he crowded into her with his great size, and she dug her fingers and teeth into his shoulder, and heard his quick exclamation. Francesca lost all sense of what she was doing. A raging fire burned in her. And she was pinned against the great tearing force of his desire that was no longer gentle. He drove into her with difficulty, and she clawed at him.

She goaded him to even greater passion; he cried out her name in choking gasps as his body slashed against her.

In return Francesca lunged against him, centering on the

maddening ache that was beginning to burn with tiny flames.
His hands dragged at her shoulders, pulling her onto him,
claiming every inch of her. In response, she threw herself
against his big body with a frenzy that ripped the last shred
of control from him.

"Francesca, you firecat," he ground out. His great body
arched as it thrust into her repeatedly. His hands grasped
her hips and pulled them up to meet his violent lunging.
"Love me," he urged her. "Show me."

At his words Francesca's body mounted to an unbearable
peak of fiery sparks. Then it exploded with a force that tore
a wild sound from her. Instantly, his heavy body exploded,
too, matching her own. He managed to cover her wild cries
with his lips and held her, shuddering, gasping, in his arms.

"Francesca, you firecat," his voice murmured against her
lips. "You demon."

She subsided only slowly, still held by that terrible dark
fire in her veins which had made her helpless before all
this. She was filled with exhausted satisfaction; even the
pain was hardly there. And she was still dizzy with her
desire.

He lifted his blond head and looked down at her, his face
wet with the perspiration of his lovemaking.

"Francesca," he said hoarsely, "why did you do this?
How was I to know you were virgin?"

Francesca stared up at him, wanting only to pull his
mouth down to hers for a long, drowning kiss. She could
not think; all inhibitions were gone. And she still wanted
him. She wanted him to spend days, weeks in bed with her
making love. And she wanted to love him, too, she thought,
smiling, and his great golden body, for hours on end.

"Look at me," he told her. His fingers nudged the side
of her face, to bring her eyes to meet his. He muttered,
"Girls are not— American girls are not virgins this long."

Francesca smiled her secret smile and closed her eyes
for a moment. She wouldn't begin to try to tell him how
many men had wanted her, and how badly, and how stern

her uncles had been, especially since her father was dead.
They followed a strict Sicilian code and she had abided by
it. Until, at twenty-eight, one tried not to grow desperate.
One tried not to realize that, after all, there was not only
this, the traditions of her family, but also the devastating
discovery that there was still no man she had found that she
wanted to love.

Thinking of her family, Francesca quickly brought her
knuckles to her mouth in an expression of sudden pain.

*My God, what was she going to do now?*

He saw her face, and sensing something of what she was
thinking, he tightened his arms around her softly. He had
not withdrawn from her; their bodies still lay joined, and
Francesca clung to him. He felt solid and powerful and
reassuring against her. She shivered again, the amazing fires
deep within her still not satisfied. They were beginning again
in the center of her flesh, making her move her hips lan-
guidly against his hard, warm weight resting on her.

"My God," he muttered under his breath. Then, slowly,
he rolled his big body away from her and sat up and reached
for his clothes where he had dropped them on the floor
beside the bed. He didn't look at her. And he swore. Francesca didn't recognize the language, but she could tell by
the tone of his voice that he was cursing softly.

Francesca sat up, too. She was still vibrating with her
newfound sensuousness, and wanted him to look at her.
She had been told her body was more than nice; now she
wanted him to look at it. She lifted her long hair with both
hands and stretched her body, tentatively, feeling rather
shyly pleased with herself.

"What are you saying?" she asked him. The curious
sexual energy still pounded in her veins.

"I am saying 'goddammit,'" he said.

She moved to him then, putting her hands against his
back as he sat on the edge of the bed, stroking the great
muscles under the smooth skin working as he put on his
shoes.

"Make love to me again," she said softly.

He seemed to sigh. He turned to look at her, brilliant eyes flickering over her now. "Francesca, I am going to make a bath for you. You are a little high, you know. You lie in a bath, a cool bath, and try to calm down."

Now that he had turned to face her Francesca boldly took his big hands and placed them on her damp, silky breasts. "I don't want a bath," she said. She found even his light touch against her sore nipples sent a jolt of electricity through her. "I want you to want me again," she whispered, her eyes shining. She couldn't explain to him what the discovery of her own powerful sexuality was doing to her. Her mind was confused and it raced helplessly. His blond Viking aloofness had been shattered by her wild desire, she had seen it. She wanted him to love her again. All sorts of wonderful, half-realized things were happening to her, but one thing was sure—she had found the man she wanted to love forever.

"Yes, I want you," he said patiently. "But I want you in the bath, trying to be quiet. My God, this is a mess." He took his hands from her breasts and turned away from her. "A virgin! What a mistake. The whole damned thing!"

Francesca got to her knees in the bed and twined her arms determinedly around his body, twisting to face him so that she could see him. She held on to his shoulders with both hands to keep from falling and put her mouth against him teasingly, her tongue exploring his adamant lips.

He looked down at her with a curious expression. She ran her fingers through his gold, shining hair and heard the groan deep in his throat. In spite of his words she knew he wanted her very much, too.

"Innocent," he muttered. "My God."

"Please love me," she whispered against his lips. She was still glittering, the feeling refused to go away. Her breasts were tender and hurting from his mouth and her body still ached with his powerful demands on it, but she wanted to make love again.

He shook his head. "Francesca," he said, "you don't want to make love again so soon, it's only the first time for you." He pointed to a spot on the bedcovers. "Look, you bled a little."

She shook her head, dismissing everything. "I want you to make love to me," she insisted. "I want you to want me like you did before." Her hands stroked his hard, muscled belly, down to his thighs where the hair was a golden down against his brown skin, and her fingers brushed his sex. She felt his flesh flutter and grow under her fingers, and she cried, "You do want me!" in triumph.

"Francesca, stop it," he muttered. But his arms tightened around her, nevertheless.

"You want me!" she crowed.

"Yes, I want you." His voice was reluctant. "Do you think I'm crazy, not to want a beautiful girl like you? But this is my fault—I can only blame myself."

The strange burning, glittering energy was still driving Francesca; she hardly heard him. "Say you want me," she demanded, as her hands struggled to pull him over her.

She saw him shake his head. "My God, yes—too much," he said harshly. "Even this way."

# CHAPTER FIVE

FRANCESCA WOKE at one-thirty in the afternoon. The ormolu
clock on the bedside table reminded her of the half hour
with a dulcet chime. She had slept badly—in fact, it had
taken her a long time to go to sleep at all, fighting a restless,
exhausted wakefulness that was, she knew, the outcome of
an all too eventful evening. She felt as though she had lived
a thousand lifetimes since stepping from the Boston plane
at the Palm Beach International Airport only twenty-four
hours ago.

It was difficult, too, to wake in a strange room, in a
place where the blazing afternoon sunshine streaked through
venetian blinds, touching South Seas–style rattan furniture
and a painted ceiling overhead of the inevitable prancing
cupids and satyrs. An old air conditioner wheezed at the
window. The dressing table, the low table by the bed held
wide vases of hibiscus and roses and springs of flame ixora,

and through the open door to the bath Francesca could see
the sunken porphyry tub, the size of a child's swimming
pool.

A strange place. She was surrounded by the six acres of
manicured lawns of *Ca'ad Carlo*, a nine-hole golf course
regrettably not in usable condition, six tennis courts, two
swimming pools, a yacht basin and a twenty-eight-room
mansion complete with one of the world's largest pipe organs.

And she had a terrible metallic taste in her mouth and
felt exhausted. Her head ached, and her body felt as though
it had taken a beating.

*So it had,* she thought, her eyes flying open. How could
she possibly forget all that violent lovemaking in the night?
Francesca took her lower lip between her teeth, her face a
study in consternation. She remembered acting wildly. Oh
God, she *had* gone to bed with someone, she *had* lost her
virginity! And not on her wedding night, either. As the
memories returned in snowballing clarity she saw once again
the weird party at Dorrit's borrowed mansion, Jinkie and
Buffy and the writer who called himself Herb Ostrow, and
the diet doctor and his strange woman friend and yes, Kurt
Bergstrom, the blond giant behind the wheel of the Porsche.
All the pictures, in one fantastic, unbelievable night. And
the party, which for the life of her she couldn't remember
except as a blur, aboard the fat man's—Angel's—yacht.
Angel and Cassie. And oh God, yes, she thought, agonized,
sitting suddenly up in bed—having Kurt Bergstrom make
love to her in his cottage!

It had really happened! She had gone crazy. She hadn't
been in Palm Beach twenty-four hours and she'd lost her
mind over a man she'd never seen before, Carla Bloodworth's third husband! With a slowly thudding heart she
considered what she'd done.

They had walked back to the main house from Kurt's
cottage long after the sun was up. She carried her shoes in
her hand, her arm laced through his, leaning against him.

At the steps he had kissed her, his deeply tanned face rather drawn in the hot early morning sunlight. As he held her in his arms he had murmured against her hair, softly, "Francesca, you don't know what you've done."

Thinking about it, Francesca took her underlip between white teeth and frowned. She hadn't understood the remark then, and she found she didn't understand it now. But Kurt Bergstrom had wanted her, she knew it; his lovemaking had been savage with his desire. It was also unrealistic to expect him, a man of the world, to declare anything more, she told herself.

If only it hadn't happened so fast, there should have been more time. She was an impulsive person—who with a Mediterranean temperament wasn't? But nothing, before, to compare with this! If it hadn't been Kurt—if it had been some fool she'd thrown herself away on—

Francesca pulled herself to her elbows and looked at herself in the dressing-table mirror, wincing at the soreness of her flesh as she did so. A rather haunted young woman looked back, long ringletted black hair hanging over naked shoulders in a gypsyish cascade, eyes like holes with smudged mascara and not all that clear. Francesca sat all the way up in bed suddenly and lifted her arms. There were faint purple spots on her upper arms where Kurt had held her, not realizing the strength of his grip. But she'd been acting like a madwoman, making love. A new rush of blood flooded to her face painfully, and she made a sound that was caught between a moan and laughter. All that legendary Sicilian passion was true, after all!

The bruises would be all right, she supposed, as soon as she got a little suntan.

No, she wasn't sorry, Francesca told the naked-breasted gypsy girl in the dressing-table mirror. What was done was done. She willed the cloud of depressing guilt to go away. She was twenty eight years old and still unmarried; by now she certainly had the right to choose. And she had more or less made her choice, she supposed; if it hadn't exactly been clear-cut at the moment, swept on by reckless passion, he was still the most dazzlingly handsome, most fascinating man she had ever met, and she had wanted him. Yes, as he had said, probably from the moment she had seen him standing on the ladder in the *Ca' ad Carlo* kitchen storeroom. And remembering his body and the way he had desired her, uncontrollably, a familiar warmth flooded all the sore places. She wanted to make love with him again. It sounded terrible, but it was true.

In the mirror she saw the telephone light winking. She turned and picked up the white and gold receiver.

"Miss Lucchese, good afternoon." It was the voice of Delia Mary, the cook. "Your breakfast is ready any time you want it, you just tell me what you'd like to have."

Breakfast at one-thirty in the afternoon.

"I don't know," Francesca murmured. She flung herself back against a wall of pillows. Breakfast as she remembered it was coffee and orange juice standing up in her tiny Boston efficiency apartment kitchen, rushing so as not to be late for work. Out of the corner of her eye she saw herself in the mirror and remembered the beautiful redhaired woman's words. Did she really need to lose ten pounds? Her beautiful breasts, lush and tapering to pronounced points, *were* a little large. So was her bottom. She wondered if all the people at Dorrit's place last night who had said they would call, had called. And how one found out, anyway, at *Ca' ad Carlo,* if there were any telephone messages.

"Miss Lucchese," the cook's voice continued, "we got some nice mangoes, ripe and sweet, Johnny brought them in this morning. And we got some good hot biscuits with orange blossom honey, and you can get any kind of eggs. You want me to just fix you up a nice tray and send it up?"

The cook was making every effort to please her. She said, gratefully, "That sounds good. You do that, thank you."

She put the receiver back in its cradle and fell back against the pillows. A sense of excitement filled her. Whatever had happened, he had kissed her, he had made love to her, he had wanted her! Would her family, all her aunts and uncles and cousins, like Kurt Bergstrom? The answer came all too quickly. *Probably not.* "The other woman's third husband?" She could hear their voices in her ears. "Why didn't she leave all her money to him?" Francesca closed her eyes.

Once her aunts and uncles knew him, they would probably accept him. But *like* him? Francesca thought of Kurt Bergstrom explaining to her Uncle Carmine or her tough little cousin Caetano the story of how he had come to meet and marry Carla Bloodworth when he was down and out in the Caribbean. Or how he had fought as a mercenary around the world. Or anything. She shuddered.

There was a soft knock at the door. Francesca expected it was the maid, Mrs. Schoener, with her breakfast. But it was John Turtle, the maintenance and grounds man, in a white kitchen jacket. Francesca dragged the slippery silk sheets up to her chin and slid down in the bed quickly.

"Good afternoon, Miss Lucchese," he murmured in his expressionless voice. After the first glance, guessing that she was naked, he kept his eyes averted. Under the jacket he wore jeans and heavy brown field boots. He brought the breakfast tray to the bed, snapping open the legs and placing it across Francesca's lap. He adjusted the tray, shoving it up against her stomach. As he did so, Francesca stared down at his arm and his brown hand with small black hairs across the back and wrist, and the heavy gold circle of his wristwatch. Hostile, she told herself. Her head had begun to ache again unpleasantly. There was something very unservantlike about John Turtle. She remembered the scene in the dining room the night before and the way he and the cook had acted toward Kurt Bergstrom.

"Where's Mrs. Schoener?" she wanted to know.

He fixed his dark eyes on the windows. "You sent her to the bank, Miss Lucchese."

Until that moment the morning had been a blank. Now

she remembered. They had been looking for the keys. Delia Mary couldn't unlock half the things in the kitchen without them. That was early morning. The maid had gone to West Palm Beach with the inventories and the occupancy release to be put in the safe deposit box.

Francesca looked up. In the mirror she could see John Turtle standing by her bed. Francesca was sure John Turtle didn't like her. It suddenly occurred to her that the maintenance man may have been more than a little attached to Carla. It was possible. Carla had demonstrated she liked good-looking young men, and this one was certainly attractive in a smoldering way. At that moment Francesca realized that John Turtle was watching *her*, not knowing she could see him in the dressing-table mirror.

The faint bruises on her arms! That was what he was looking at.

John Turtle leaned over her to pour her coffee, and Francesca watched him in the mirror wide-eyed and with the growing certainty that the staff of *Ca'ad Carlo* knew where she had spent her first night in Palm Beach. She had been a fool not to think of it. The lights had been on in Kurt Bergstrom's cottage until dawn, and the Porsche was parked outside. She hadn't returned to the main house until after the sun was well up, and Kurt had been with her—he had even kissed her goodnight on the front steps.

With mounting horror, Francesca knew what the staff was saying. That she certainly hadn't wasted any time. That she hadn't even spent the first night at *Ca'ad Carlo* in her own bed.

These people didn't know her, they could only judge her by her actions. How could they know she had never made love before last night? Who would believe a twenty-eight-year-old Catholic virgin, even though she was sure there were thousands of them existing somewhere? She had been with *Kurt Bergstrom*. That was the real trouble.

John Turtle was saying something to her. Francesca looked up, trying not to meet his eyes, and her hand trembled, sloshing coffee into the saucer.

"You have some mail," he said in his even voice.

Not, Francesca noted, "Miss Lucchese." She was suddenly sensitive to everything. She looked down at the breakfast tray and saw a small pile of letters next to the silver vase with a single yellow rose in it.

With her head ducked, hands still shaking, Francesca said, "From now on I'd like Mrs. Schoener to bring my breakfast. And when the maid isn't here," she continued, "I'd like Delia Mary to bring it up."

He said only, "Very well, if that's what you want."

She knew there was someone else available to bring up breakfast; it didn't have to be John Turtle. And she thought, Was he just satisfying his curiosity about her, now that she had gone to bed with Kurt Bergstrom in record time? She wanted to dislike John Turtle as much as he, obviously, disliked her.

The headache and queasy feeling attacked Francesca again. She put down the coffee cup and swallowed experimentally.

"Just telephone the kitchen if you want anything," he was saying. But his voice was a roaring in Francesca's ears.

She hastily covered her mouth with a napkin, trying to gauge the signals her stomach was relaying. She hadn't drunk all that much wine, but she'd had something on Angel and Cassie's yacht. She had no idea what it was. But if this was a hangover, it was a weird one.

John Turtle looked at her quickly, then stepped closer to the bed. "Are you all right?" he said.

"I'm fine," she choked. If she were going to throw up, she didn't want John Turtle around. "I'm fine," she insisted. "You can go, I don't need anything else."

He waited the barest second, still staring, then turned and went out, closing the door behind him soundlessly.

*Crazy,* Francesca thought, not sure whether to laugh or cry. *Ca'ad Carlo* had a crazy, hostile Indian maintenance man. While she fought down another surge of nausea she knew no one would believe the things that had happened to her since she had arrived in Palm Beach. She had to stop thinking about Kurt Bergstrom and what had happened in his arms last night. There was a fresh new day ahead—or part of one—and she would be seeing the big blond man, talking to him; the thought lifted her spirits tremendously. She tried to smile. Things were going to turn out all right. In all that had happened to her, the good thing was Kurt.

Francesca picked up the small glass of orange juice and sipped it, finding that juice was better than the metallic-tasting coffee. The fluttering in her stomach stopped. With her free hand, Francesca picked up one of the letters that John Turtle had brought up.

There were several pieces of mail addressed to Occupant. So even wealthy people got junk mail, she discovered. A magazine subscription company offered the opportunity of a lifetime to acquire a million dollars if she won their lottery. With a wry smile, she pushed it aside. She didn't need another million—she had enough of her own. There were several envelopes without stamps that were obviously hand-delivered. Francesca paused for a moment, breathing deeply, to let her stomach settle, then picked up the heavy silver letter opener on the breakfast tray and cut the first envelope.

*Come to dinner Thursday, 8 p.m.,* the first letter said. It was signed *Jinkie.* The beautifully engraved letterhead carried Jinkie's famous name. Francesca wondered what sort of people one would find at Jinkie's house for dinner. Or even what sort of place Jinkie lived in. Palatial—one could be sure of that.

The second note on thick blue paper was scrawled in a bold handwriting.

*Where did Kurt take you after you left? I forgot to warn you, boat people are a definite No-No. Also, Dorrit is livid. I hope that explains everything. And welcome to Palm Beach!* It was signed, *Buffy Amberson.* And, *P.S. Call me. I tried to call you but all your telephone numbers are unlisted.*

Another note on typed beige paper said, *I hope you're available for lunch next week. I've thought it over and you're not a young Sophia Loren or a Gina Lollobrigida,*

*but the reincarnation of La Belle Otero. I'll explain who
she was over lobster crepes. But no man could resist her.
Herb Ostrow.*

There was a professional announcement from the diet
doctor, embossed on white paper, giving office hours, telephone numbers and the address of his exclusive clinic in
West Palm Beach. On the bottom of the card in cramped
handwriting was, *Elsa sends best regards*. Francesca turned
the card over in her hands, puzzled. Elsa was Bernard Binns's
strange little woman friend.

The last envelope was cheap paper of the sort one would
buy in drugstores, or even in Bloodworth's variety stores.
It contained a single sheet of white typing paper with cut-
out pieces from newspapers, pasted together to form a message.

It said:

YOU *ARE* going TO DIE *just* LIKE     c A RLa     DID

# CHAPTER SIX

FRANCESCA GRABBED up the gold and white telephone, realizing that she had no idea of the extension numbers on the estate. She jerked open the drawer of the bedside table, finding nothing. There was no telephone list, no directory, no way of dialing anyone. She had to do something. With a shaking hand she dialed 0 for operator and heard it ring. There was the click of a receiver lifted at the other end.

"Shop," a voice said. She could hear an engine running in the background.

"Who is this?" she cried. Her hand holding the telephone was trembling violently. The terrible piece of paper telling her she was going to die was on the breakfast table before her, as menacing as a coiled cobra.

"Miss Lucchese?" A pause, then, "This is John, you've got the maintenance shop."

"Give me the number to Mr. Bergstrom's cottage." She

tried to keep her voice down. "I need to talk to him!"

The sound of the motor stopped. "Miss Lucchese—" the voice began.

"Did you hear me?" Suddenly she was almost screaming. "Get somebody to bring me a list of telephone numbers! I don't know how to call on this thing!"

"Fifty-seven," his voice said.

Francesca slammed down the telephone. Frantic, she picked up the receiver and dialed again. She heard it ring.

"Hello," another voice said. Not Kurt Bergstrom's, she realized.

"I want to speak to Mr. Bergstrom." Her voice trembled on the verge of panic. Had the maintenance man given her the wrong number?

"This is Pete Peavey," the voice said. "I'm down here cleaning. Who is this?"

"This is Francesca. Francesca Lucchese." She tried to make herself sound calmer. "Would you put Mr. Bergstrom on the line, please? This is his number, isn't it?"

Peter Peavey considered this for a long moment. "This is his number, Miss Lucchese, but Mr. Kurt's gone to Bimini. Miss Lucchese, are you calling from the main house?"

"Just tell me when he'll be back, please. Just tell me quick!"

Another pause.

"He didn't say. He took his boat out this morning, Miss Lucchese, that's all I know. If anybody can tell you, it's John. Can you call John Turtle at the maintenance shop? The number is—"

"I know the number," she cried, and hung up. She dialed 0 again with difficulty.

"Shop," John Turtle's voice said.

In a shaking voice, Francesca said, "I want you to tell me where Kurt Bergstrom's gone."

"Miss Lucchese?" When Francesca did not answer he said, "I tried to tell you a minute ago. Mr. Bergstrom's gone to Bimini. He took his boat out this morning."

"Where," Francesca said with desperate calm, "is Bimini?"

"It's down off the coast," his quiet voice told her. "Toward the Bahamas."

Toward where? None of this made any sense. "How do I find out if he's left a message for me?"

"He didn't leave any messages. I brought everything with the mail."

*"Telephone messages!"* She screamed it out, not caring. "Isn't there a switchboard or something here?"

"Not any more. There are four direct lines and the house line, the one you're on now." Guardedly, he said, "Is there anything the matter?"

Francesca clung to the wobbling telephone with both hands. *He was gone.* The world was crashing down. "How long," she said with an effort, "does it take to get to Bimini and back?"

But he said, "Miss Lucchese, do you need anything? What's wrong? Do you want me to send Delia Mary up?"

"How long?" she whispered.

"Maybe a couple of days, depending on whether or not you use power or sails. Maybe three or four."

*Three or four days?* Francesca fell back among the bed pillows. And he had left no messages! She couldn't believe the man who had loved her last night would go away without any sort of explanation! It must have been an emergency, it had to be. Kurt Bergstrom certainly hadn't said anything to her about a boat trip that would last three or four days.

It was either that, or—

It was possible, she thought, that she had made a mistake so terrible last night that her mind could only skirt the edges of it, not wanting to deal with it. She had acted like a fool. Something had possessed her. Even now she couldn't account for her wild behavior. Shock was following shock.

Francesca laid the telephone down on the bedspread in a daze and got out of bed. It was some sort of nightmare—a dream about finding herself in a bizarre house with only a skeleton staff to run it, with a handsome man who had made love to her and then disappeared. And then a letter in the mail telling her she was going to die. She didn't like this dream at all!

Without exactly knowing what she was doing, Francesca picked up her filmy robe from the back of a chair and walked across the room with it in her hands, forgetting to put it on. But if this was a dream, she told herself, looking around, what was she doing here, in Florida? Who was this woman reflecting in the dressing-table mirror who looked just like her, gypsy black hair, staring silver-gray eyes and an expression of terror?

What did it mean, *You are goi     die just like Carla did*?

The lawyers said the cause of Ca. Bergstrom's death was a heart attack. And why would anyone want to send to her, Francesca Lucchese, hate mail? She had never done anything to anyone! Just plain cranks, the Miami lawyer had said. And those who hate the rich.

Francesca bit her lips until they hurt. She couldn't call her family for help; she couldn't telephone her uncles every time something happened. She had fought a long battle to be independent and handle her own affairs. She had to handle this herself. *But where was Kurt Bergstrom?* Why had he disappeared?

Someone was banging loudly on something somewhere nearby; the noise was unbearable. Francesca held her hands clutched to her head, trying to think. *Think,* she told herself. She hadn't done anything right since she arrived in Palm Beach. How could everything have gone so terribly wrong?

The door to the bedroom slammed open with a crash. A large, formidable-looking black woman in a tall chef's hat and white jacket stood in the doorway. A rangy, dark-haired man was behind her.

"Miss Lucchese, you want something?" the cook wanted to know. Her face was concerned. "You having trouble with the telephones? Mr. Kurt's gone off on his boat, he didn't leave no messages. He do that lots of times. You don't want to let that bother you."

"What?" Francesca said. She discovered she was holding the transparent negligee clutched in her hands, barely concealing her nakedness. John Turtle was staring.

Delia Mary made a clucking sound between her teeth and stepped into the room. The maintenance man went to the bed and picked up the telephone receiver from the bedspread and put it back in its cradle.

"Honey, don't you feel all right?" the cook asked. "You want me to call the doctor?"

Francesca shook her head. She didn't need a doctor. She needed someone to help her. And the only one who could help her had just gone away on his boat without a word of explanation. Just give me a minute," she said. She sat down on the bed and tried to slip her arms into the filmy robe while still covering herself.

The cook and John Turtle exchanged looks. The maintenance man turned to leave the room, but Francesca looked up suddenly.

"Wait, just a minute!" she said. The tall man turned and looked at her. "I want to talk to you," Francesca said, "about getting me a bodyguard."


THE estate office had been closed in 1970 when, for budgetary reasons, the household and grounds staff of *Ca'ad Carlo* was reduced in response to the elimination of a large percentage of Bloodworth stores in the United States and abroad. Competition from discount houses had finally left its effect on the old retail chain; it wasn't until two years later, when Bloodworth's, Incorporated, opened the Blo-Co division and expanded into discount retailing under new management systems that the company's profit picture began to improve. By that time Carla Bloodworth Tramm DeLacy had separated from her second husband and was living on the Isle of Capri. The stucco cottage of the estate office was never reopened.

Francesca went to look at the office by the main gate of *Ca'ad Carlo* with John Turtle and Peter Peavey, who were in charge of all the estate buildings. There was a switchboard, she found, but it looked as though it had been there since the time of the original Charles Bloodworth. The plug-in lines and old-fashioned telephones had been replaced, at some time in the past, with the direct lines John Turtle had mentioned; now there were pushbutton extensions at the big swimming pool, the maintenance shop, the uniformed guard's post at the front gate, and in most of the rooms in the main house.

After examining the outdated office and telephone equipment, disturbing the dust in the process, Francesca asked the maintenance men to close up the building again.

The matter of the bodyguard was not so simple. A temporary security man, John Turtle informed Francesca, could be had from Pinkerton's in Miami, but in the long run she would want to find someone well-qualified for the permanent position.

"You don't want anyone too hard-nosed," he told her. "Police training sometimes is not all that much of an advantage. Personal bodyguard detail needs a knack many cops don't have. A personal bodyguard has to develop a split-second ability to evaluate a situation, especially to discriminate between the client's friends and security risks. Otherwise big errors can result. But no matter what type of men you hire, they have to pass maximum federal checks. Don't take them otherwise."

Francesca was rather reluctantly impressed with how much John Turtle knew about security. He had done some moonlighting, was all he would tell her. A maximum security check was an in-depth investigation of the applicant's background, including relatives working for the Bloodworth corporation, family status such as divorce, numbers of dependents, demands of current family ties—the list seemed endless. And, he told her, not all private agencies filtered applicants thoroughly, even when you depended on them to do it. Personal habits had to be impeccable. Nonsmokers preferred, nondrinkers mandatory. A bodyguard had to be bondable.

"I think we're looking for someone who doesn't exist," Francesca said.

He shrugged. "It's tough."

Wealthy people, he told her, and important personalities in government, in show business, kept up an almost constant search for the right bodyguards. Howard Hughes in his later years surrounded himself with security people who were Mormons; their strict faith and personal habits recommended them to the millionaire as people he could trust. But families like the Kennedys tended to hire their poorer relations to work for them. Discretion was a major factor: many wealthy people had learned the hard way that the money to be made from magazine stories and published memoirs was a big temptation to employees to tell all to the press and media. And after all this, he told her, the final consideration was compatibility.

"Compatibility?" Francesca smiled. "It sounds like a dating service."

John Turtle did not smile. As far as Francesca knew, John Turtle never smiled.

He said, evenly, "You don't want a full-time bodyguard around who will get on your nerves. A personal security man is like a shadow—there, but doing his job so well you can forget all about him."

*Moving around silently,* Francesca thought. John Turtle was something of a mystery. "How do you know all about security?" she wanted to know.

"I was Mrs. Bergstrom's bodyguard for a few months when she came back. Then she didn't need one."

The news surprised her. "Why not?"

"She was in bed."

After some prodding, he told her he had been away from

*Ca'ad Carlo* for a number of years. "I went to law school.
I didn't finish. It's on my job application," he said tersely.

LATER that afternoon Francesca got the personnel folders
of estate employees from the carefully prepared synopses
the lawyers had turned over to her. She was curious about
John Turtle, but the personnel briefs also told a lot about
the people she now employed, including their salaries. She
was appalled to find none of them was making much money;
Palm Beach wage scales appeared to be very low. Delia
Mary Williamson was a graduate of West Palm Beach High
School and had worked for several restaurants, including
one in Coral Gables before coming to *Ca'ad Carlo* fourteen
years ago. She had four children and a husband who worked
for the health and rehabilitative services of Palm Beach
County. Gerda Schoener had been a chambermaid for Cun-
ard Lines and several New York hotels, and was a citizen
of West Germany until 1976, when she applied for U.S.
citizenship. Peter Peavey had attended high school in Ar-
cadia, Florida, and had worked briefly for a Martin County
foreign car dealer as a mechanic before coming to *Ca'ad
Carlo*. All of them had been hired by someone called Nina
Pachuko, Personnel Director, the Bloodworth Foundation,
Bloodworth Bldg., 590 Third Ave., New York. Her sig-
nature was on every application but one—John Turtle's.

Francesca picked up the maintenance man's personnel
file. John Turtle was born on Brighton Indian Reservation,
Glades County, Florida. He was a graduate of Glades High
School, where he was a member of the varsity football team
and the debating society. *Debating society?* Francesca
thought. John Turtle was anything but a conversationalist.
Eight years in the Marine Corps, military intelligence and
special services. Credit for college courses taken while in
the service. Two years at the University of Florida Law
School in Gainesville. Harry Stillman, senior partner of
Stillman, Newman and Vance of Miami, had hired him and

signed John Turtle's personnel records, not the lady from
New York.

Francesca was beginning to feel that the Miami lawyers
had a special interest in John Turtle. Harry Stillman had
certainly singled him out.

Lifting the telephone receiver at her bedside, Francesca
dialed the number of Stillman, Newman and Vance in Miami
and was told that Mr. Stillman was not in, but that he
certainly would want to reach her right away if Miss Lucchese wanted anything. He would get right back to her.

Francesca was learning that anything she wanted was
high priority; it was nice to know she could get the Miami
lawyers any time she called. In a few minutes the senior
partner of the law firm called her back, and she talked with
Harry Stillman about hiring a bodyguard.

What he told her about John Turtle was very interesting.


AT dinner in the small dining room Francesca was served
by the maid, Gerda Schoener. A cool fresh breeze of a
waning thundershower, breaking the blistering heat of the
day, stirred the candles in the silver candelabra, now nicely
polished since Delia Mary had regained the household keys.

Francesca had asked John Turtle to come to the main
house so that she could talk to him, and she found him
waiting in the great hall by the hooded fireplace. The floor
lamps were lit, tall bronze stands with Tiffany shades that
lent even more color to the garish room. The maintenance
man stood with his arm propped against the overhanging
fireplace hood, his tall body easy in white shirt, jeans and
heavy field boots.

"Good evening, John," Francesca said. She felt very
awkward using a formal tone, but she was determined to
get off on the right foot with her hostile employee. After
what was admittedly a poor start, she had a long way to
go.

"Good evening, Miss Lucchese," he said, just as formally. He took his arm down from the hood and stood easily, gracefully, his hands at his side, his dark eyes scrutinizing her flatly. The pantherish power in his lean body distracted her, and she looked away.

"I talked to Mr. Stillman in Miami this afternoon," she said.

"Yes, I know. He called me."

She was surprised and shot him a quick look. She found the impact of black eyes meeting hers with a distinct jolt. She told herself there was no reason for the lawyer not to talk to John Turtle, anyway. She said, "Well, Mr. Stillman advised me to hire you as a bodyguard on a temporary basis until he can interview some people in the Miami area for a job." Actually, the lawyer had pressed her to consider John Turtle for a permanent position, but Francesca was convinced they would find someone, as John Turtle himself pointed out, more compatible. "That is," Francesca said, rather lamely, dragging her eyes away, "if it's all right with you."

He didn't think much of her, Francesca knew. But then John Turtle didn't seem to have much tolerance for any human error as far as she could see. He was a rigid, humorless person. She wondered if John Turtle had any girlfriends, anyone he made love to. It was an interesting thought. He was certainly good-looking in a lean, taciturn, *macho* sort of way. But she couldn't imagine those hard black eyes looking at any woman passionately, much less longingly, or that face burning with desire. She certainly couldn't imagine those chiseled lips opening to say: *I want you, I'm going to make love to you.*

He only said, "Miss Lucchese, I like what I'm doing."

Francesca stared at him. What did that mean? Was he rejecting her offer? He couldn't do a thing like that! For one thing, the money was a lot more—the lawyer himself had set the salary and she had thought the final figure very impressive. Francesca wondered if she should offer John Turtle a bonus to accept. Then she thought, *I'm damned if*

*I will.* Why anyone would want to turn down a better job was beyond her. With his attitude, she thought, no wonder he had dropped out of law school!

"But you worked as a bodyguard here before," she told him.

His eyes studied her for a long moment, probingly. Then he said, "Has something happened?"

Francesca opened her mouth and then shut it again. The question had taken her off guard. She didn't want to tell John Turtle about the crank letter, if that was what it was; she didn't want to tell him anything if she could help it. And she certainly wanted to stop being challenged by him. He made her feel like she was a weak, brainless idiot! She heard herself saying, "I had a crank letter. In the mail you brought me this morning."

He never took his black eyes from her face. "Tell me about it," he said.

Francesca licked her lips. She was sorry she'd mentioned it, now. "What was wrong with Carla Bergstrom?" she wanted to know.

"What did the letter say?" he demanded.

"Oh, nothing," Francesca said, looking away. She felt suddenly guilty, as though she had done something wrong. It was hard to remember that actually she had been the target of someone's sick mind. "It was out of the newspaper, the words pasted together. Really, all it said was, 'You are going to die just like Carla did.'" The moment the words were out of her mouth, Francesca experienced a vast sense of relief. It was only John Turtle. But just knowing he would have to help comforted her.

He was still watching her closely. He said, "Have you got the letter?"

"No, I burned it." That was true, she didn't want the hateful thing around. "I understand it's not unusual for people like me to get crank mail. Wealthy people."

He gave her an odd look. "I wouldn't exactly say it's normal, but it happens. However, if you get another one,

don't destroy it. They have to be turned over to the FBI."
He paused and said in a different tone. "Mrs. Bergstrom
died of a heart attack, that was the cause of death given in
the coroner's report. And you look pretty healthy to me."
The dark look raked her. "You don't have any health problems, do you?"

Francesca shook her head. She knew what he thought of
her. She knew what all of them thought of her. She supposed
she would never escape the consequences of her first night
at *Ca'ad Carlo*. She found the blood rising to her face. She
was surprised to see John Turtle was watching her closely,
as though reading her thoughts.

"Don't worry about it." His voice actually seemed to
soften. "You have the right idea, it was a crank letter, so
don't lose any sleep over it. But if it happens again, let me
have it right away."

She lifted her wide gray eyes to him. "Does that mean
you'll take the job?"

He said, "Yes, Miss Lucchese, I told Mr. Stillman I
would."

He had known all along he was going to take the bodyguard job! she realized. He had been playing games with
her to find out what had made up her mind so quickly. She
said between her teeth, "I think you're supposed to sleep
in the main house, now." Harry Stillman had assured her
John Turtle would know what to do.

"I'll take care of it," he said quietly.

Twenty-four hours a day with John Turtle. She'd have
no privacy left at all, she realized with a pang.

Francesca said, "The first thing I want to do is to go
down to a place in Fort Lauderdale called the *Golden Door*.
It's, ah—a spa and weight-loss clinic. Do you know it?"

He said, "I've heard of it."

"I'm going tomorrow. I'll be in a private cottage, so I'm
sure there will be some place for you to stay."

"I'll see to it," he told her.

Francesca stared at him, suppressing a sigh. She had a

bodyguard now, John Turtle. She was reluctantly aware that the idea was somehow comforting. But if anything, she disliked him more than ever.

# 2

## Legacies

# Chapter Seven

"ARE YOU sure that's the way you want to wear your hair?" Stephen of Beverly Hills said. He held the comb poised over Francesca's head, looking at her in the bank of fluorescent-lighted mirrors. His eyebrows were raised and his mouth rounded in a parody of doubt.

Francesca smiled. Her silvery gray eyes, now surrounded by a Zulu-liked tangle of freshly shampooed black curls, looked back at Stephen's impishly. They'd had this conversation from the moment she'd arrived at the *Golden Door* five days ago; if the objective was to wear her down with gentle insistence, she had to admit it usually worked. The staff at the *Golden Door* never used anything but the most elaborately courteous approaches, but they usually got what they wanted.

However, in the matter of her hair, she was holding her own. Although she wanted, now, to be smashingly, flauntingly beautiful with that ineffable, ultra-chic patina of the women she'd seen in Palm Beach, she wanted to avoid what Herb Ostrow, the writer, had called the "plastic television syndrome," where all beautiful women looked dismayingly alike. For nearly a week she had withstood Stephen's pleading to cut her hair or at least give it a complicated permanent that would take some of the curl out of the ends while crimping the roots to enhance its already considerable thickness, or mass it with artful backcombing to three times its normal bulk to make her face look even bonier and more startlingly fragile. Francesca was determined to keep her hair the way she had always worn it. The idea reduced Stephen to paroxysms of despair.

"Darling," he protested, "straight hair went out with the Beatles and vinyl knee boots, when girls used to *iron* themselves senseless. It's not even preppy anymore! And nobody wears yecchy curls." He lifted Francesca's hair in both hands and let it shower darkly through his clever fingers. "Look how beautiful Stephen has made it for you, all sparkles and terribly fantastic health and vitality. It was a *ruin* a week ago, full of split ends and niggly little horrors!"

Francesca eyed herself critically in the mirror's banks of fluorescent lights. Her dark hair accented her storm-gray eyes, and although it was not the utter wreck Stephen claimed a few short days ago, it was immeasurably improved. Mysterious clay packs, honey and wheat-germ-oil treatments, and hours spent in lanolin baths had intensified its softness and color and brought out interesting golden glints around her face. Her hair shimmered like charcoal satin as Stephen let it fall. She knew she definitely did not want it puffed and backcombed, standing out in a giant bush like Dorrit's red mane or the high fashion models in *Vogue* and *Bazaar*.

Sensing her thoughts, Stephen bent down so that his face was beside hers in the mirror image and hissed, "You want to be *ravishingly beautiful*, don't you?"

Startled, Francesca nodded.

"Okay," Stephen said.

Stephen of Beverly Hills gave his attention to only the most select of the *Golden Door*'s clientele who came there to lose weight, regain a more healthful lifestyle and—if only temporarily—restore their minds and bodies. They ranged from the perpetually overweight movie star with the violet eyes to wives of Arab oil sheiks, Washington statesmen, television celebrities, and a few extremely wealthy businessmen who patronized the spa. At the *Golden Door*, one entered a world focused almost exclusively on how one looked, and how one *felt* about one's looks. Francesca had found the experience strange, but not unpleasant, like a steady diet of whipped cream. Behind the spa's high, secluded walls on Poinciana Road in Fort Lauderdale, the most earth-shaking crises would develop over an eighth-of-an-inch roll of fat under the armpit to a suitcase showing of resort wear from a Rodeo Drive boutique which the *Golden Door*'s fashion coordinator demolished with a single word—"incoherent."

"Now, I could cut it severely across the forehead," Stephen said. He never used a word like *bangs*. "But we definitely do not have the real authority to revive the Cleopatra look, even if anybody wanted to."

By "we," Francesca had learned, Stephen of Beverly Hills meant Francesca. She saw him scratch his ear thoughtfully and had the feeling that Stephen was going to win, after all.

"I want you to look like a Botticelli," he said suddenly. "Not the *Venus*, that's such a damned cliché and besides, I'm not going to turn you into a redhead, you'd never be able to keep it up, even if your hair is good and strong. But definitely something High Renaissance, like the *Primavera*."

Before Francesca could open her mouth Stephen cried, "Well, why *not* Botticelli? All wops have got this crazy spiritual, sexy quality I'm one myself! And God knows you're bottle-shaped just like all Botticelli's women. Just look at those hips!"

Francesca turned red. Five pounds was still five pounds,

and she had slaved to take them off under the supervision of the *Golden Door*'s exercise evaluator, a young woman who looked as though she had been put together with nylon string and plastic skin. As it turned out, Francesca was not bottle-shaped. But whole conferences had been devoted to the in-and-out curves that shaped her breasts, waist and hips and which, she had been gently advised, were *much too much* for the drop-dead look she wanted. In *Golden Door* language, Francesca found, much-too-much meant maybe two inches in circumference, maybe less.

THE Botticelli look took three and a half hours. Francesca had to eat her lunch of soybean loaf in fresh asparagus sauce and carrot cocktail supreme in the hairstyling booth at the back of her private cottage on the grounds of the *Golden Door*. Stephen of Beverly Hills took two strands of hair at her temples and subjected them to waving chemicals and bleaches which produced, ultimately, dangling curls touched with moonlight shades to frame her face. The rest of her hair, shaped, and the terrible curls scissored under control, fell soft and dark from the crown of her head to just below her shoulders. The Botticelli look, an original creation by Stephen of Beverly Hills and designed only for her, was discreetly billed at $1,500.

"Don't think of your hair at all today," Stephen told her. "Don't even look at it until tomorrow, when I'll be back for the final comb out."

On his way out Stephen regarded John Turtle, sitting in the cottage's living room in his black business suit and white shirt and tie, with a look that spoke volumes. Stephen had already told Francesca that her bodyguard resembled a hit man for the Mafia or a neophyte Congressman, he wasn't sure which.

Joely, the exercise supervisor, was next. They moved to the cottage's workout room where the mirrors confirmed, as they bounced across the floor on their buttocks, that Francesca's curves weren't flattening out at all. Finally they stood side by side for a last checkout before the room's wall of mirrors, slim shapes in their black leotards and tights.

The small blond supervisor said, "Well, you've worked hard, and there's visible improvement, but the problem's ethnic, at least part of it." Quickly she added, "I hope you don't mind my saying that—but ethnic in a marvelous sort of way! I do wish you'd stay another week."

But Francesca had plans for the coming week. She was going back to *Ca'ad Carlo* "ravishingly beautiful," as Stephen of Beverly Hills had put it.

John Turtle had changed to his jogging suit and track shoes by the time the exercise session was over. Francesca didn't change her black tights and leotard; she merely slipped her Adidas on her feet.

The afternoon run under Florida's summer sun was optional, but it sweated off pounds marvelously, Francesca had found, and with maximum discomfort. As she trotted down the gravel path that wound through poincianas and flame-flower vines, Francesca put her head down grimly, determined, as she had been the entire five days, to match her bodyguard's smooth stride.

*He hasn't lost a pound,* she told herself, feeling the first drops of perspiration beginning to travel down the Botticelli curls. She had seen John Turtle eat. His trays, brought to the private cottage with hers, were heaped with fried chicken, buttery dinner rolls, steak, salads dripping with blue cheese dressing and slabs of pie with ice cream. It was disgusting. Francesca made him take most of his meals at the umbrella tables out back on the terrace, and out of her sight.

And he ran like a jungle cat or something equally graceful and effortless, she thought fretfully. And he not only ate, he *smoked!* John Turtle smoked small brown paper cigarillos—fragrant and very telltale when you couldn't see him— which he split, scattering the tobacco, and rolling the paper into fragments, military-style, when he wanted to discard the butts. None of it affected his wind. Francesca could hardly keep up with him.

Only one other person at the *Golden Door* ran with a

bodyguard, and that was a multimillionaire Chinese-
American businessman from Hawaii. His security man looked
like a moving mountain. The two groups maintained a polite
distance over the three-mile stretch through the palm trees
and grassy lawns of the *Golden Door*. And both caused the
same sort of interested comment among the other guests.
Francesca had grown used to the sight of faces appearing
at windows to see the mysterious occupants of the private
cottages go by with their security men.

She was aware that, even at the *Golden Door,* her status
was impressive. "The Bloodworth millions." It was a phrase
she had heard all her life, like AT&T and Wall Street, and
she still couldn't react to it. The excitement of the past few
weeks had dimmed the impact of where she was and what
she was doing, but every once in a while Francesca allowed
herself to wonder if she really was, as one newspaper had
described her, "one of the richest women in the world."

She certainly was a secluded and important presence at
the *Golden Door*. Her cottage was hidden in the section of
the grounds identified only by a sign which said: ENTRANCE
BY PERMISSION ONLY. The *Golden Door* staffers were the
only ones who passed unchallenged. And of course Dorothea Smithson, her new private secretary, on temporary
leave from the Miami offices of Stillman, Newman and
Vance, who drove in to work at the cottage every day.

Professional was the word for the short, sandy-haired
secretary in her early forties who sorted the day's mail,
brought down from Palm Beach by Peter Peavey in a pickup
truck, and laid it out for Francesca's inspection along with
small handwritten notes suggesting the proper answers.
Francesca found there were already several letters from Palm
Beach area churches and other local institutions, asking for
money. Begging letters, as they were called, were always
forwarded to the Bloodworth Foundation in New York,
which kept a list of approved recipients. Quarterly lists of
approved donations were sent to Francesca for her approval
and updating.

The secretary also handled the press clippings. Dorothea didn't have to look at these if she didn't want to, but there was already quite a collection of newspaper stories and items from the wire services describing the will and the new heiress—"the chauffeur's daughter"—to the Bloodworth millions. A story in the Hearst paper in San Francisco featured several photographs of *Ca'ad Carlo* taken through the South Ocean Boulevard gates, a view of the Bloodworth Building on Third Avenue in New York, and a photograph of Charles D. Bloodworth, the founder of the variety store chain.

Although Francesca was keeping a low profile in Palm Beach according to the lawyers' plan, Dorothea Smithson assured Francesca the press was eager to have pictures and interviews anytime she could grant them. A freelance woman writer for the big women's magazines wanted to interview Francesca and would donate the sale price of the article to Francesca's favorite charity. Both *60 Minutes* and *20/20* television shows had made inquiries through the Bloodworth Foundation office in New York and had been turned down. *Queen* magazine of England had sent an inquiry by cable, as had the German *Stern* and *Paris-Match*.

The new secretary turned thumbs down on any press interviews. "Mr. Stillman's done a great job keeping you under wraps so far, keeping the pressure off so you'd have time to adjust," she said. "You don't know what it can be like once the media singles you out for attention—an ongoing news story they won't let up on. It gets rugged. I think we'd better take a few precautions and have the PR people contact your family in Boston and give them a briefing on what to say and do if the press calls them."

Francesca knew very well her Sicilian family wouldn't talk to the press; she wasn't so sure about the neighbors or the people she had known at work.

"We'll take care of the neighbors," Dorothea Smithson assured her. "Most times just simple requests not to give out interviews will do it. If not, money works. But you have to give them more than what the media is currently

offering. Sometimes that's a bundle. Your news price may
go sky high because you're very good-looking, a good photo
subject, and millions of women can identify not only with
your being super rich, but with your working-class past."

Francesca and John Turtle pounded down the path toward
the *Golden Door*'s tennis courts. This was where they usually attracted the most attention; the tennis games stopped
completely as they went by. This afternoon was no exception: Francesca saw someone throw down his tennis racket
at a missed volley in disgust.

They rounded the curve by the sauna building and started
for the gravel path which led to the gyms, the sports shops
and the north end of the golf course. Francesca gasped for
air. She couldn't master her breathing as John Turtle did,
but she was determined not to quit.

During the first days of Dorothea's employment Francesca had started the long-distance redecorating of her
bedroom suite at *Ca'ad Carlo*. The secretary held lengthy
discussions with the decorator on the telephone while
Francesca had her morning skin treatment and makeup
sessions. The decorator in Palm Beach could do anything
for a price—even the walls of the suite could be painted
overnight. Francesca chose something called Bermuda
Jonquil while the decorator, on the telephone, worried
that Francesca might not like the final color. The furniture
and lighting were to be done by a firm called Palm Beach
Coordinates. Francesca got the impression the sales director was having a terribly polite nervous breakdown.

"Big estates like the Bloodworths' don't buy much lo-
cally," the secretary told her. "Palm Beach is terribly strat-
ified, you know. There's *some* money, or what makes one
eligible to be called 'rich' in Dothan, Alabama. These people just want a Palm Beach address if they can afford it.
Then there's *money*, which means a lot, probably inherited.
And then there's the very top level, which means so much
money nobody really knows how much because it's all
invested and tied up in trusts and foundations. I don't have
to tell you what level you're on. Palm Beach Coordinates

is flattered out of its mind to have your trade."

Francesca stumbled up the two steps to the *Golden Door* guest cottage and John Turtle, right behind her, caught her arm to keep her from falling. She threw herself into a deck chair.

"It's killing me," she cried. She had really wanted to keep up with him this last run and even pull ahead a little, but all she had accomplished was a terrible stitch in her side. She drew long, shuddering breaths.

By tomorrow, she knew, she would reach the final stage of the *Golden Door*'s transformation of Francesca Lucchese. Sicilian pizza with its thick crust and hot peppers was just a fading dream. Her bust was two inches smaller and her hips would barely support the bottom part of her once-new bikini from Filene's. She was going to be stunningly beautiful. Guaranteed. She already knew she had a very good figure, perhaps better than that. Now she would resemble, among other things, a trendy version of one of Botticelli's nymphs in the *Primavera*. In Stephen of Beverly Hills' own words. She could hardly wait.

"Just take it easy," John Turtle was telling her as she struggled to breathe. "You overdid it again." He knelt before her to slip off her jogging shoes and release her steaming feet. "Relax the diaphragm muscles, try not to gulp for air," he said in his quiet voice.

Francesca looked at the back of her bodyguard's shaggy dark head and was reminded that everything, now, was temporary. John Turtle was only a temporary bodyguard. She had a temporary secretary. Even Peter Peavey was doubling as temporary chauffeur for the Rolls. The redecorating of her bedroom suite at *Ca'ad Carlo* was, in spite of the enormous expense, only temporary. These things waited until she could finally get around to deciding what she wanted permanently. She was finding that if one had the money, temporary *anything* was always affordable. One could take all the time one wanted to make up one's mind when one paid the bills.

John Turtle looked up at her suddenly. He was still on

one knee, with her running shoe in his hand, but the hard planes of his tanned face and straight black brows gave him an expression as smoothly impenetrable as flint.

*He knows,* Francesca thought. Wide-eyed, she met that intent black look. John Turtle knew how temporary everything was. He knew she was only waiting for Kurt Bergstrom to return.

"Thank you for my shoes," Francesca said, as she had said every day for almost a week.

This time he said nothing.


THE final day at the *Golden Door* was unreconstructed chaos.

The maid, Mrs. Schoener, came down with Peter Peavey to pack the wardrobe selected under the supervision of the fashion consultant at the *Golden Door*. Boxes and dresses on hangers were everywhere. The fashion consultant, a tall and beautiful former Halston model, disputed, in a genteel voice, with Stephen of Beverly Hills about scheduling prerogatives while the makeup specialist loaded his equipment into the hairstyling booth where Stephen's tools were still about. Peter Peavey and John Turtle carried out the luggage. A large pile of suitcases and boxes filled up the Rolls and spilled over into the estate's pickup truck. The director of the *Golden Door* arrived with waiters, a bouquet of red roses and two bottles of Dom Perignon in silver ice buckets. Francesca sipped champagne in the hairstyling booth with a plastic sheet around her neck while Stephen of Beverly Hills, Miss Jordan, the fashion coordinator, and the small makeup man fought over her. The telephone rang constantly, mostly calls for the *Golden Door*'s director who, with a glass of Dom Perignon in hand, declared he couldn't leave without seeing the final creation.

Gradually, stage by stage and layer by layer, the finished processes were uncovered. Stephen's Botticelli creation was even better on the second day than the first, as he had predicted. Under the makeup man's skillful hands Francesca's normally olive skin was now Beige de Tunis, her brown eyeshadow Umber, her cheekbones Pomegranate and her lips Special Gloss Number Four, which came in a little ceramic pot. Gold Brilliance, more muted than its name, gave highlights under each carefully shaped eyebrow. The outfit chosen for the final day at the *Golden Door* was a gossamer India cotton in tangerine and yellow. When she was dressed, Francesca went out into the workout room with its mirrored walls to see herself from every angle. The others followed.

She was not, Francesca saw, a duplicate of one of the dancing wood nymphs from Botticelli's *Primavera*. And she was rather glad. But she was ravishingly beautiful, just as Stephen of Beverly Hills had said.

How could one look at oneself and know that? she thought. But she knew she *was;* she thought of all the beautiful women of films and stage and television and somehow she had achieved that, while still being herself. She had metamorphosed from Frannie Lucchese, a tall pretty girl with gray eyes and a spectacular figure usually deliberately hidden in unrevealing academic clothes, to Francesca Lucchese, a genuinely beautiful woman with an electrifyingly lovely, expressive oval face, magnificent eyes that flashed silvery fire, and a mane of gorgeously arranged charcoal curls. A child-woman with a touch of steel. A woman who had had only one lover and one night of lovemaking but whose passionate nature had been set gloriously free at last.

"Enormous statement," the fashion coordinator said in her syrupy voice, "strikingly done."

"Too much lip gloss," the makeup man muttered.

"Exquisite," the director of the *Golden Door* said, impressed.

Even Mrs. Schoener nodded ponderously.

"A real masterpiece," Stephen of Beverly Hills declared.

Even Dorothea Smithson, coming to the door of the workout room with the message that Francesca was wanted on the telephone, stopped and took off her glasses for a better look. "Oh, that's so lovely," she murmured.

The waiter with her lunch tray, John Turtle and Peter Peavey, crowded into the doorway. The bodyguard fixed Francesca with an unwavering stare, but the younger man blurted, "Wow!" loudly, and then flushed.

The waiter opened another bottle of champagne. Francesca went to take the telephone call on the extension in the kitchen.

"I want to see what you look like," the voice of Buffy Amberson said. "I know you're leaving—I called reception to find out. Everybody's talking about you. I just wanted to take a look at you before you go."

"Buffy?" Francesca cried. "Why didn't you tell me you were here? Why didn't you tell me you were coming to the *Golden Door?*"

"I'm staying in a private cottage I can't afford," Buffy's voice went on. "But you'll see when you get here. Phoenix Cottage, Oleander Lane, it's just around the corner."

The line clicked.

Francesca threaded her way through the crowd and walked out the side entrance. The others wouldn't miss her, she knew. The clamor of getting packed had started all over again.


BUFFY opened the door of the guest cottage. The place was strangely quiet in contrast to the havoc taking place in Francesca's quarters. Buffy wore a dressing gown of silver to match her hair. In her hand was a carrot cocktail supreme which smelled of something added. Only her eyes were recognizable. The rest of her face looked like a badly damaged basketball.

"The nose is broken," Buffy said through puffed lips. "They just told me a while ago. I bypassed the hospital in West Palm Beach, not wanting to get on police records and maybe in the newspapers, and came down here. I drove myself. It was hellish. I could hardly see, and I had taken painkillers, so I was tripping like crazy. But I wanted the plastic surgery guy here to see me right away. He's fabulous, he's about the best in the country. He says they can work on the nose from the inside."

Francesca sat down abruptly. Her knees had suddenly turned to rubber. She tried not to stare at Buffy's face. "Oh, God," was all she could find to say.

Buffy turned and strolled away with her practiced, undulating glide. She was barefoot. The back of her hair, Francesca saw, was matted and streaked with dried blood.

"It's going to cost a bundle," Buffy said tonelessly. "A year ago I had a fractured jaw. That cost a bundle, too, and I had wires in my mouth for six weeks. I ate everything out of a blender, through a straw. Last night was Jock's alimony and child support reaction when he saw his quarterly statement. He takes a couple of bottles of José Cuervo and gets it out of his system, but it always costs him money. The big slob can't seem to understand that."

"Why? Why?" Francesca cried. She couldn't imagine anyone wanting to destroy Buffy's beautiful face. No matter how drunk. "Buffy, why do you let him?"

"Let him?" Buffy said, not turning. She finished off the rest of the carrot cocktail supreme. "I don't *let* him, Francesca. I usually run like hell. This time he caught me in the driveway just as I was trying to get in the car. I thought he was going to run me over in the damned thing and get it over with, but he settled for bashing my face against the hood. You should see the Ferrari—that's bodywork, too, and just as expensive!" She turned to face Francesca. "Don't look at my face, please. I'm going to get a new nose, which is all well and good—the old one had a hump in it. Now, I want to look at you and see what the little elves of *Golden Door* have done. Even the chambermaids are talking about what a fantastic project you turned out to be. Stand up, will you? And turn around."

"Buffy," Francesca said, "please tell me—is there anything I can do?"

The blue eyes, sunk in swollen flesh, regarded her calmly. "Yes, sign my line of credit, Francesca. Jock will pay eventually, but I can't wait for him to sober up and get his bank account straightened out. They have to work on my nose in the morning or they say it will fall off or something. Blood clots."

Francesca said hastily, "Oh, yes, of course. I'll do it before I go. Just don't worry about it. Please."

"Cripes, I can hardly see." Buffy peered at her. "Is that you, Francesca? Where's all the pasta curves gone? And the sweet college girl look? Stephen's a maniac with hair, I didn't know he had that much taste. Turn around again."

Francesca turned, the tangerine and yellow skirt billowing out around her knees.

Buffy only said, "Did Kurt tell you he was going off on that damned boat of his, the *Freya?* Never mind, I can see that he didn't. He's back, you know. He got back last night. I telephoned to see if you were home yet, and he answered. Little Frank is very good with makeup, isn't he? He's one of the best makeup men in the country. I think they pay him zillions to stay here at the *Golden Door*." Then she said in an entirely different tone of voice: "Francesca, you were a pretty girl before, but now you're positively beautiful. Maybe too beautiful. Anyhow, you'll find out when you see Kurt. Just watch his eyes."

# Chapter Eight

Francesca knew she was going to have to become accustomed to the varying degrees of uproar her appearance caused when she went out. As she followed the headwaiter across the main dining room of *La Ronde* in West Palm Beach to the table where Herb Ostrow was rising quickly to greet her, there was a growing buzz of voices, of heads turning, which she was coming to know meant that she was being recognized. It was surprising how many people had heard of her in a comparatively short time. Of course, the way she arrived at places was like a blast of trumpets—the Rolls, as impervious to No Parking signs as a battleship pulling up, Peter Peavey in matching gray livery at the wheel, John Turtle jumping out as soon as the Silver Ghost stopped, to clear the way. By the time she got past the front door, sales managers, waiters, attendants, clerks, were already rushing to meet her. The headwaiter of *La Ronde* had been no exception.

127

As Francesca put out her hand to Herb Ostrow she was pleased to see his reaction. She wore a gold-colored silk summer suit with a red silk von Furstenberg scarf tied cowboy-fashion at her throat, which counterpointed her dark hair and vivid makeup. She saw startled, open admiration in his eyes. The writer quickly lifted her hand to his lips. The buzz of comment around them rose several decibels.

It was nice having one's hand kissed, too, even though she couldn't keep from smiling. And to know that this attractive man with his urbane manner and graying hair seemed, at the moment, at a loss for words.

As the headwaiter held her chair for her Herb Ostrow said in a low voice, "My God, you're absolutely beautiful! I can't think of anything right now that doesn't sound stupid, because I'm overwhelmed. But I think you've changed your hair."

She murmured, "I've been enjoying all my money," and saw him throw back his head and laugh.

"Was it fun?"

She sighed. "There's fun, and there's fun." The headwaiter still hovered over them in an excess of attention. "You said lobster crepes in your note, but what I actually have to have for lunch is soybean loaf with fresh asparagus sauce and a big glass of carrot juice."

"We can do better than that," he said, opening the menu.

Francesca had been quite serious. If she ate too much, none of the gorgeous clothes she had brought back from the *Golden Door* would fit. The alterations followed the loss of five and a half pounds so closely that, she was sure, even lobster crepes would show.

And if fun was being transported from one place to another in the Rolls, Francesca thought, opening her menu, it was only because she was finally mastering the routine it took to get her anywhere. First, the limousine stopped. Then John Turtle got out of his seat in front, usually brushing aside any doormen who might be waiting for her, to open the car door himself. She nearly always got out as best she could, remembering to let him get ahead of her if she had to, giving him room if he stayed by her side. They were developing a sort of rhythm; she had only run into him twice in the past few days. Now, Francesca saw, putting down the menu, John Turtle was sitting in the waiting area of the restaurant where she could see him. In his neat black summerweight suit and white shirt and striped tie the head-waiter, at first, had taken him for her husband.

Lunch with Herb Ostrow was fun. Francesca enjoyed herself tremendously, feeling, among other things, a sense of relief to be away from the *Golden Door*.

When the dessert cart came with its cream puffs and napoleons and great slabs of key lime pie, Francesca shook her head, no. It was becoming easier to do. The life she was living was becoming easier, too. Although she was discovering that one could be, as the newspapers were call-ing her, the richest woman in the world and still feel one was starving to death.

Francesca told Herb Ostrow she had received an invi-tation to Seahampton, the Palm Beach home of Mrs. Carlton Hampton, now in her eighties and known as the Queen of Palm Beach.

"There are people who live out their lives and die still waiting for an invitation from Queenie Hampton," Herb Ostrow observed. "Certainly you'll go. Don't miss it."

"I don't know," Francesca murmured. "I'm not going to be very social, you know. I can't. No one's going to let me forget I'm just the chauffeur's daughter, a working girl from Boston. It's pretty obvious, to be invited to tea to be looked over."

"What's wrong with it? Palm Beach has its own version of Boston's 'cliffies,' you know—dowagers who set the social scene. Here, the old girls of Palm Beach keep things in line simply by not inviting anyone into the Palm Beach institutions they're dying to get into—like the Everglades Club, the Racquet Club, and so forth. And they're pretty good at it. The Palm Beach dowagers have set a social tone that's lasted for decades, almost a century now. The trouble is, divorce has ruined the old girls. Men don't keep mistresses anymore, they get married to their young chicks. So older women have begun to pile up in the corners. Remarriage doesn't come all that easily, even when you're rich. Women still outnumber men here about four to one. Need I say the old girls hate the young third and fourth wives with a mortal passion?"

Francesca stirred her coffee. "I've seen some of them," she murmured. "The younger women with older men."

"I'll bet you have." His eyes twinkled. "It's really sort of sad. There are the older women with their divorce settlements and their mansions, including those with the considerable fortunes that were theirs to begin with, and then there are all the aging ex-husbands with their young birds, and sometimes even second families of young kiddies to embarrass the grown-up offspring of the first connection who have young kiddies the age of their step-brothers and sisters. And Palm Beach weddings are a nightmare. You go up to offer felicitations to the teen-age bride and find out she's not the bride—she's the old man's fourth wife! In fact, the bride looks older than her mother-in-law. And of course you have to get past the hurdle of which wife you're talking to. Sometimes they all show up for the same wedding in an excess of goodwill."

When Francesca laughed, the writer went on, "Queenie Hampton is the only dowager left with any power now that Maude DePew is too old and sick to leave Philadelphia. Queenie's one of the few who still keeps up the old mansion, and hasn't settled for a condominium at Lake Worth Shores with around-the-clock nursing and other medical services. Of course, Queenie's so old she doesn't go anywhere, that's why she stays in Palm Beach the year around. But the theory is that she stays alive by meddling in everybody's business. From a distance, of course. She has a phenomenal memory. She can probably recite year-by-year accounts of everything that's happened at *Ca'ad Carlo* since it was built."

Francesca said, thoughtfully, "I'm not sure I know how to go to tea at a Palm Beach mansion. Her note says only, 'Come to tea, four p.m.,' and gives the address, Seahampton, which is that big place out County Line Road with the big stone walls. My maid says an invitation to tea in the old days meant a long afternoon dress with a hat and white gloves."

It was Herb Ostrow's turn to laugh. "I don't think Queenie Hampton expects you to turn up looking like something out of *My Fair Lady,* but you might consider the hat. It would be a nice touch. However, tea with some of the old girls can mean cheese and crackers and manhattans. They're big on manhattans. But when Mrs. Carlton says Hampton tea, she means it. You'll get, I am told, eighteenth-century silver tea service, Spode, watercress sandwiches and a wobbling old family retainer. His name's MacElroy and they tell me he looks just like the late Field Marshal Montgomery."

Francesca said suddenly, "This is awfully nice of you, you know, to offer advice. I'm sure there are not many people who know as much as you do about Palm Beach. Or who would want to help me." She hesitated. "I'm still not sure why Mrs. Hampton invited me."

Herb Ostrow lit a cigarette and blew smoke into the air. "Well, if you'd inherited a little less money, Queenie might not be so curious. But the Bloodworth millions are a little hard to overlook, even you've got to admit that. Queenie knew them all. In fact, Queenie helped organize Palm Beach. She helped Flagler, who was a hustler first in oil with Rockefeller, and then in Florida railroads, to bring important people down here. She brought the Duke of Windsor in the Twenties to play polo, and he held parties for the Whitneys and Mellons and snubbed the Vanderbilts so that they fell all over themselves getting in. She kept out movie people, but she invited the Roosevelts. And of course she helped old Chuckie Bloodworth get his toe in the door socially. The first Bloodworth wife wasn't much, just a hardworking

girl who started out behind the counter and helped old
Bloodworth build his dime store empire. I think it was
Queenie who advised Chuckie to get rid of Wife Number
One and move on to that little spun-sugar doll, Edna Myers,
whose daddy made his money in the San Francisco China
trade, and whose Mamma was Texas oil. Edna didn't have
much substance, but Charlie loved the way she could open
doors for him. And she gave him a son, which the first wife
didn't, to carry on the Bloodworth fortune and family line.
And the son, of course, gave us Carla who, rumor has it,
was a dead ringer for grandmother Edna. I'm sorry—I didn't
know Carla myself, so I can't fill you in much there."

Francesca said, very carefully, "Carla was quite sick for
a long time, wasn't she?"

Herb Ostrow signalled for the waiter to bring him the
check. "I don't really know. Palm Beach is notoriously closemouthed, at least on semi-public levels. Apparently she had
something wrong with her for a long time, yes. In the last
few years she was virtually a recluse, didn't see any of her
friends here, stayed shut up in the house, and took to her
bed at that last. She had Kurt, and he seems to have run
the place after a fashion, looking after her, sticking pretty
close to home until after her death. Even, I understand, not
going out on his boat much, which is the main passion of
his life. Have you seen the *Freya?*"

She shook her head.

"It's quite an item. Boats are boats, especially in Palm
Beach where some of the world's greatest yachts tie up.
But Kurt's got a yawl some Frenchman built in Indochina
and it's apparently the genuine article. As is Kurt, of course—
you see how he looks. They say he can sail this big boat
alone, singlehanding, which takes some doing. I think you
tie down the wheel and run around setting sail. You don't
sleep, apparently, or if you do, you nail yourself to the
mast, or immolate yourself in the bilge, or whatever it is
these boat people talk about. All the salt-water sailors around
here worship him. They think he's the reincarnation of Eric
the Red."

Francesca smiled. "You don't sound very approving. You're not trying to tell me to stay away from him, are you, Herb? I thought everybody loved Kurt Bergstrom."

Herb Ostrow signed the check and sat back. "Oh, I'm not telling you to stay away from him. After all, you seem to have him as Viking-in-residence at the moment, don't you? It's only that, as a writer, I've always found Scandinavian types a bit hard to know, especially the seafaring variety. Even Carla didn't get Kurt until she bought his boat. He seemed to come with it, like the anchor."

"What?" Francesca said.

"Haven't you heard that Carla kept Kurt's boat in escrow, as a way of making sure he stayed? She may have given the *Freya* back to him before she died, but who knows? If the deed's still held by the estate, you own it!"

Francesca stared at him. She couldn't say a word, and was glad when the writer kept talking.

He went on, "You know I'm writing a book about Palm Beach. It's a definitive study of past social structures. I've approached the Bloodworth Foundation several times for permission to have access to the family records and open up the archives, but they don't answer my letters." He hesitated, a little self-consciously. "The legal firm in Miami is about as cooperative as a nest of alligators. Francesca, I know it sounds too damned self-serving, but it would help me a lot if I could get into the Bloodworth family records. Particularly ol' Charlie's days here, when he was building *Ca'ad Carlo*."

There was a moment's silence. Francesca had only been half listening. There had been no mention of Kurt Bergstrom's boat in the will. She had a copy of Carla's will somewhere; she had to remember to find it and read it again. But who had told her the boat and the Porsche were Kurt's? She couldn't remember.

Francesca said, choosing her words slowly, "Carla's second husband was a writer they tell me. He wrote a booklet about the house. They tell me it has an inventory, if that's of any interest to you. I can get it for you, all I have to do is call the lawyers in Miami."

The writer's request was simple enough, but Francesca was developing a great caution about the boundaries of her privacy, and with good reason. She was not exactly enchanted with the idea of showing up in an article or a book sometime, somewhere. And she never wanted to see another crank letter as long as she lived.

"Francesca, please." Impulsively the writer put his hand out to cover hers. "Have lunch with me again. I didn't invite you to *La Ronde* today to get permission from you to look over the Bloodworth family histories, I hope you'll believe that. I asked you to lunch because you're the living spirit of *La Belle Otero*."

She pulled her hand away from his. "How very clever of you, to leave that to last. I think I'm supposed to say, 'Oh, well, you'll have to tell me about *La Belle Otero* the next time we have lunch.'"

"Well?" he asked.

"Oh, sure." Now she shrugged. "'You'll have to tell me about *La Belle Otero* the next time we have lunch.' How's that? Just give me a ring."


THE nerve-wracking whine of an electrical saw greeted Francesca as she came through the upstairs gallery on her way to her bedroom. She hadn't realized it was going to be so noisy arranging for her rooms to be enlarged to make a study and office with a desk for her secretary, from the bedroom of the suite adjoining. In her original burst of enthusiasm for more space in the main house she had supposed the magical effects of Bloodworth money could get the job done as quickly as the bedroom redecorating, but this wasn't the case. Paint-spattered drop cloths were laid all along the hall. The carpenters were working on the other side of the wall but she could hear their voices plainly. The racket of all the drilling and cutting made her ears ring.

Her bedroom, now pale shades of yellow, vivid lime green and white, still entranced her, as did all the wood,

glass and chrome furniture. Her suite had become an oasis
in the midst of *Ca'ad Carlo*'s gaudy murk.

Mrs. Schoener had laid out Francesca's clothes for tea
at Seahampton and, Francesca saw, the hat and white gloves
were there.

Her wardrobe was getting to be a problem, she realized,
throwing her handbag down on the bed. She had gone on
several shopping sprees. She found she just couldn't help
exploring the Worth Avenue shops now that she was the
new Francesca fresh from the *Golden Door*. As a result the
old-fashioned dressing room closets were jammed. She
needed another room with more modern storage space. Even
Mrs. Schoener had agreed.

The secretary had left a pile of messages on the low
chrome and glass bedside table for her. Francesca ran through
them quickly. There were several notes in Dorothea's neat
script. The *Golden Door* had called twice. The spa was still
making inquiries about the credit line she had underwritten
for Buffy Amberson's nose operation. Francesca had the
distinct feeling the *Golden Door* management wanted her
to pay Buffy's bill herself, rather than just backing up
Buffy's credit line. Francesca stared at the note, wondering
who could take care of the problem for her. She could call
the lawyers in Miami, but that would just expose Buffy's
terrible problems, and she couldn't do that. Should she write
the *Golden Door* a check, pay the bill, just to shut them
up? Francesca sighed. Dorothea had left early to meet the
movers bringing things up from Miami to her new apartment
in Palm Beach. The secretary's son was out of school for
the summer and coming up to live with her. The saw on
the other side of the wall shrieked and there was a loud
crash. Francesca wondered if she should send Peter Peavey
over to help Dorothea get moved. If she were still a Boston
working girl, she'd go over and help Dorothea herself.

*Damn, damn,* Francesca thought, feeling harried. A pink
message slip told her Jinkie had called with another dinner
invitation. She put it aside.

There was a small pile of mail that had been opened and

screened by Dorothea, mostly invitations from people in Palm Beach she didn't know. The secretary's note of explanation accompanied each one in case Francesca should want to accept one of them. But the message she was looking for wasn't there.

Francesca sat down on the bed, carefully moving aside the clothes the maid had laid out for her. *How long should she wait for a call?* She had wept over this, lost sleep over it, suffered agonies of guilt and humiliation. Why hadn't he tried to see her? His guest cottage was less than three minutes from the main house. Why hadn't he tried to explain why he left so abruptly? Why had he been gone so long?

Francesca supposed she already knew the brutal truth. She'd made a royal fool of herself, that was all. From the day she arrived at *Ca' ad Carlo* she'd been a ludicrous figure, an overdue twenty-eight-year-old virgin who hadn't found the right man to marry and give her love to. She'd thrown herself at this magnificently worldly, handsome man in a release of wild sexuality that even she had not been able to explain to herself. It was an experience she couldn't think about, even now, without blushing.

She'd been an idiot. She'd rushed at Kurt Bergstrom without giving him any clue as to her total inexperience. And of course, considering what had happened, he'd beaten a hasty retreat. What man wouldn't?

*But he had desired her totally, passionately.* That much was true.

Well, perhaps. She knew she was no judge of how much men wanted women, how they behaved making love, what they said. Or what they promised. He could be just as overwhelming with other women, for all she knew.

Francesca rested her elbows on her knees and pressed her knuckles to her temples, hard, against the nagging misery of her thoughts. She was going to have to ask Kurt Bergstrom to leave. Perhaps when he was gone, her unbearable humiliation would finally disappear. God knows it was too painful to have to deal with as it was!

Yes, she was going to have to write off Kurt Bergstrom as the biggest mistake she had ever made in her whole life. And she didn't even know whether she had the strength to act on it or not.

Francesca reached over to lift the telephone from its cradle, but the shriek of the saw on the other side of the wall shook the air. It was impossible to talk with all the remodeling noise going on. She put the receiver back down again. Face to face was the only way to do it. She knew if she was ever going to end it, she would have to do it at that moment.

Francesca made her way out of the main house quickly, conscious of passing time and her tea date. The air conditioners in the main hall were broken down again; John Turtle and Peter Peavey were working on them outside on the great terrace. The house was merely stuffy, but the full heat of Florida hit her as soon as she stepped outdoors. Francesca hurried down the crushed shell walk carefully in her high heels, then turned into the side path which led to Kurt Bergstrom's guest cottage. Francesca could hear voices, the woman's loud and strident, Kurt's low rumble answering, before the place came in sight. She broke into a jog. What on earth was going on? Whoever was in there with Kurt Bergstrom was having a screaming battle royal, that was clear. She couldn't imagine who it was. But it was the last thing she'd expected to find.

She pushed the door to the cottage open without knocking and stood there in the doorway.

They turned to her at once. Gerda Schoener was holding an armful of bedsheets, her stolid Teutonic face angry and flushed. Francesca didn't know what language they'd been speaking, but it wasn't English. Kurt Bergstrom's face, not so flushed but just as angry, stared at her. His blue eyes were splinters of ice.

"What's going on here?" Francesca said uncertainly. She was jarred to find no reaction in Kurt Bergstrom's eyes, the familiar response of excitement and admiration she'd grown accustomed to since returning from the *Golden Door*. He seemed to look right through her. Francesca said, "What's all this about, Mrs. Schoener?"

Neither of them moved. Whatever Francesca had interrupted, it had been full of fury, one could still feel it in the air. Francesca remembered that she had yet to find anyone at *Ca'ad Carlo* who didn't, apparently, delight in challenging Kurt Bergstrom's right to be there. What they thought of him showed all too plainly.

And what they thought of *her,* she knew, was probably very well concealed. She might only be the former Italian chauffeur's daughter from Carla's past, but she had all the Bloodworth money. Whereas Kurt Bergstrom was only Carla's disinherited lover.

"You can change the bed later," she told the maid. The words fell into the angry silence.

Mrs. Schoener put the sheets down on the arm of a chair and stalked out. As the door closed, the man turned away, putting his back to her. He leaned one arm against the fireplace hood and bent his head to rest against his forearm.

"I'm sorry," he said in a low voice.

Francesca hardly heard him. She looked around the room. His eyes dismissed her as if she hadn't changed. As though nothing had happened. All other eyes reacted to the new and beautiful Francesca. He didn't. There could be only one explanation.

"I have only a moment," she said stiffly. She didn't look at him. "I have an appointment for tea. But I understood you were back, that's all."

"Yes," he said in a toneless voice. "I came back while you were gone. I had to go away, Francesca." The sea-blue eyes lifted suddenly and saw her and they widened. For the first time there was recognition of the new Francesca. "Just watch his eyes," Buffy Amberson had said. Now, finally, his look took in her summer silk dress, bare tanned shoulders, her dark hair floating long. He said, abstracted, "You— you should know why I had to go away."

That was no sort of explanation. Francesca bit her lips,

close to angry tears. Was this the way it was going to end?

"It won't work," he said abruptly. "To talk is useless." He bent his forehead to his hand. "Francesca, go away. Go back to this place you came from, Boston. Or go to the house in Hawaii, get the servants to open it up, you would like it there." His voice turned harsh. "But for God's sake, go away. Get out of this damned place!"

She was astonished at his tone, at his despairing attitude. She felt anger rising, as much anger as had been in the room while he and the maid quarreled.

"Don't be ridiculous." There could be only one reason. "I'm not going to let you people push me around! I'll fire all of them, the staff, if I have to!"

He lifted his head. "What?" he said, baffled.

"And you don't have to say you're sorry, either," she shouted. "As far as I'm concerned you have nothing to be sorry about! Mistakes happen here just like anyplace else. I don't need any of you. I've got too many things to keep me busy!"

"Francesca," he said, staring at her.

She drew herself up with dignity, half blinded by tears. "I have an appointment with Mrs. Carlton Hampton here in Palm Beach for tea. And I have a sick friend, Mrs. Amberson, who needs looking after. So you see I can't really waste time on all this." She turned and started for the door, unseeing, and bumped into the chair with the bed linens on it. "Just do the best you can," she said loudly.

"Francesca, come back," he said.

But she yanked the door open and fled.


MRS. Carlton Hampton was quite fat. It was something of a shock to see her.

Francesca had pictured a woman tall, rather bony, of lofty gentility, dressed in severe grays and pale blues and wearing a single strand of pearls, perhaps seated in a small room with fading French furniture.

Instead, the hot afternoon sun struggled into the drawing

room of Seahampton through partly-drawn velvet drapes of a heavy plum shade. The burning light touched the colors of several Persian rugs, some laid on top of others, and picked out a thousand knickknacks, photographs and relics of Mrs. Carlton Hampton's past. It was hard to know what to look at first, the incredible room or the equally fascinating hostess.

A large oil portrait, larger than life, hung over the eighteenth-century marble fireplace. The mantelpiece was covered with the signed photographs of kings, queens, presidents and the late great of the world. Priceless Chinese figurines in jade-crowded snuff boxes, miniature clocks, framed press clippings, a gold Faberge Easter egg from Czarist Russia, a broken marble head of a Greek Aphrodite, and two Bayer's aspirin bottles.

The woman in the portrait over the fireplace wore a daring white *peau de soie* silk ball gown with a plunging neckline that cut almost to the stiffly corseted but astonishingly tiny waist. The considerable areas of bared skin—arms, throat, nearly naked breasts—glowed with an impossible voluptuousness. Francesca had never seen skin like that, but she didn't doubt it existed. The portrait's ripe pink mouth was opened rather boredly, as if anticipating the praise of its beauty that was sure to come. The painting seemed oddly full of motion, even violence, in the woman's stance, the sweep of the white silk dress, and the ripe flesh.

Francesca accepted a fragile cup and saucer with a small amount of tea in it. It was no mistake, she saw, that Mrs. Carlton Hampton sat in a wing-back chair right under the sensuously raging ghost of her former beauty.

"Augustus John did it," Queenie Hampton said, following Francesca's eyes. "We were down in Devon that summer because the Germans were bombarding London and all one could see was barrage balloons and sandbag entrenchments. So we went down into the country. It was quite a lovely summer. I got dressed up in my Worth gowns from Paris and he painted, and then he went off to do the Duchess of

Marlborough. I heard she wasn't quite as good."

Francesca looked over the rim of her teacup. She wasn't sure she had heard that correctly.

Mrs. Carlton Hampton was also dressed in white silk, the gown as loosely draped as a tent over her ample girth. A choker of faintly yellowed pearls clasped her several chins tightly, and three long gold chains held a bird's-egg-sized diamond surrounded by rubies, a gold-framed miniature of a woman's head painted on ivory, and a Byzantine cross done in flat cut emeralds. Jingling faintly as she moved, Queenie Hampton allowed the gargantuan silver tea pot to swing back upright on its base.

"It was a terrible time, actually," the old lady went on in her still-satiny voice. "The war was going badly, but the Americans had just come in, so hopes were up. Vernon and Irene Castle were entertaining the doughboys." She paused, fixing her black eyes on Francesca's face. "That was World War One. You did know it was that war, didn't you, and not the last one?"

"Oh yes," Francesca murmured. She gathered "the last one" was World War Two. She tucked her feet even farther back under the red velvet sofa she was sitting on and tried to sit up straighter. The tea tasted of flowers.

Francesca had dreaded the tea date with the queen of Palm Beach's dowagers, and had dressed with a sort of frenzied carefulness, not forgetting the white gloves. Now, she saw, it didn't really matter. She doubted Mrs. Carlton Hampton even noticed what she was wearing. The first fifteen minutes' conversation had been mostly a monologue by the old lady about people in Palm Beach Francesca didn't know.

"No, you didn't," Mrs. Carlton Hampton said testily. "No one knows what I'm talking about anymore, but I'm used to it. No one's ever heard of Vernon and Irene Castle or poor Gussie John these days. And we all thought Gussie was going to be immortal! None of us had ever heard of Picasso or Modigliani or any of that crowd. That's a Corot behind you," she said, darting her eyes.

Francesca turned, careful of the eggshell cup and saucer in her hands. The wall behind her was jammed with pictures, the frames almost edge-to-edge. There were views of castles and palaces and villas perched on Mediterranean cliffs, and a large watercolor of a man in ballet tights playing a Pan Pipe with the scrawled word *Nijinski* at the bottom.

Francesca put the teacup and saucer down on one of the small velvet-draped tables that cluttered the room. The house was unbearably hot; if there was any air conditioning one certainly couldn't tell it. Somewhere a clock chimed and was immediately followed by half a dozen others hidden deep in the huge house. It was four-thirty. Francesca wondered how long tea was supposed to last.

Mrs. Carlton Hampton took several tiny sandwiches from a silver plate on the tea table and leaned back in her chair. Her gnarled fat hands were covered with rings.

"Now, you must tell me how you're getting on," she began. Before Francesca had a chance to respond she went on, "You're very young to be handling all this—the Bloodworth lawyers are helping you, aren't they? Tell me, is the pipe organ still there? It was Chuckie Bloodworth's baby, you know—Flagler had one at *Whitehall,* Deering had a monster of a pipe organ at *Viscaya* in Miami, and John Ringling had one built for his place in Sarasota. But Chuckie wanted the biggest and best pipe organ of them all. Which he got. He hired the best men to come down from New York and Boston to play it. He couldn't play a note himself, and he had to wait months for someone to play the thing for him. And when he finally got an organist he'd sit up for hours, far into the night, drunk as a coot, listening to his private concerts. He loved Verdi. Verdi wrote operas, he didn't write anything for the pipe organ as far as I know, but Chuckie would get all these expensive musicians with big reputations to come down and play florid arias from *Aida* and *Rigoletto* until they were half out of their minds." She said abruptly, "How did you feel when you learned you'd inherited all the Bloodworth money?"

"Surprised." Francesca lowered her eyes, trying to look properly modest. She wasn't sure exactly what Mrs. Carlton Hampton wanted.

The old woman eyed her with some skepticism. "I can imagine. You didn't have any money at all, did you?"

Francesca was sure that Mrs. Carlton Hampton knew all about her. She read the papers, she was sure. But it was obvious Queenie Hampton wanted to see for herself.

"No money at all," Francesca admitted. "I worked as a clerk in the history department of a college. I made a little bit more than a secretary, but not much. I hadn't even paid off the notes on my car."

"Well, well, well," the other woman said. The sharp black eyes probed her. "And what do you think of the will, hmmm? It said your father was Carla's lover, you know."

Francesca stiffened. "I don't think the will said that at all," she said carefully. "It said he was the only man she had ever loved. That could mean a lot of things."

"I remember him," Mrs. Carlton Hampton said. "MacElroy asked if I knew specifically who he was and I said, why yes, of course, I remember Vanni very well. Carlo brought him back from Europe in 1960, the middle of November, just before Chuckie's birthday. Of course, Chuckie was dead by then, but his birthday was November 17th. He used to have the most impossible birthday parties, even after Edna died. One drank raw egg with Worcestershire sauce in those days for hangovers, it was all the thing. And they had to bring in eggs by the carload from Jacksonville after one of Chuckie's birthday parties—Palm Beach was laid low for a week. I remember the chauffeur was remarkably good-looking. We remembered Valentino, but Carla's Vanni was really even more attractive. They said Rudy really liked boys, anyway, and one could believe it when one saw that wife, Natasha. A perfect lesbian."

Francesca hadn't understood a word Queenie Hampton had said, but she looked politely interested.

"Well, you want to keep the place up," the old lady continued. "MacElroy tells me one of the Turtles is back keeping it up again, old Sebastian's grandson. Our houses look sound, you know, but they actually deteriorate quickly in this climate. It was madness to build them in a swamp to begin with. Really, so many of them are marginal. Our Palm Beach Association keeps busy with appeals to the owners to keep up their property. There are all these foreigners about—Arabs and South Americans and the Germans, and developers—oh, my dear, I mustn't begin to tell you about the developers! They're the worst of the lot. Once your back is turned these horrible people begin ripping down everything in sight to put up condominiums. They've just about destroyed Lake Worth, and the south part of the island! *El Mirasol* and Mrs. Horace Dodge's beautiful *Playa Riente,* and just recently the Phipps's *Casa Bendita*—all demolished for subdivisions! Now, the Palm Beach Association will get in touch with you, and talk to you about keeping up *Ca'ad Carlo,* and holding the line on these developers."

"I'll be ver—" Francesca began.

But the old lady plunged on, "You've got Vanni's eyes, my dear. Oh, I saw him many a time, he was a charming boy, always so wonderfully good-natured. Light eyes are not all that unusual in Italy, you know; you've only got to travel there, even down in the boot, to know that. Yes, I remember Vanni's smile. And he had perfect manners. One can't surpass the Europeans for manners, even the peasants. I understand the maids were mad for him, but Carla put a stop to that. What a tizzy Carla caused with her chauffeur— one heard it everywhere on the Beach! *Not Carla,* everyone said."

Francesca stared at Mrs. Hampton, unable to speak. She was realizing the subject was her father, and Carla Bloodworth. *Vanni,* the old lady called him.

The ancient butler in his black suit and old-fashioned wing collar came in. Mrs. Hampton turned to him impatiently and said, "No, she's going to stay. I like her. And bring us some sandwiches." She swiveled back to Francesca. "What *was* remarkable was that Carla brought the whole tribe back with her. They camped out like gypsies, the wife, the mother-in-law, the brothers—it gave a certain air to *Ca'ad Carlo*, you know, all those Italians. I don't think Carla had much control over it. Someone had talked her into bringing all of them back with her. They all went off, eventually. All they wanted to do was immigrate, anyway. Carla loved Italy, she had that villa in Capri all the time she was married to Tramm. You must have been the baby," Mrs. Carlton Hampton said. "They all went to Boston, didn't they?"

"Yes," Francesca said softly. "My uncles are located in east Boston. It's still a big family. We—they, own a construction company there."

"Hmmm," Mrs. Carlton Hampton said again. Her fingers searched through the tiny sandwiches on the plate. "You're a very pretty girl. When I was young no one tried to look skinny, flesh was all the thing. White as snow and thick as cream, that was the saying. I see someone's tried to make you look like a Caravallo *ducchesa*. Don't squirm, it's rather clever. Vanni was quite beautiful, you know. They were such good-looking boys then, one wonders where they've gone. All old men now, probably They don't call men beautiful anymore, but Carla's young chauffeur was."

"My father's dead," Francesca said flatly. She was getting tired of listening to her father and her family being discussed as though they were objects, or commodities. "He was a very good person."

Mrs. Carlton Hampton ate another small sandwich. "Oh, he was, you know, Carla's lover. There was never any doubt about that, even though Carla was always very quiet about what went on over there at *Ca'ad Curlo*, like her grandmother Edna. I think they both liked sweet, amiable men. I'm not talking about husbands, now—Chuckie Bloodworth was a juggernaut, you couldn't mix him a drink without arguing over it. And Tramm was just like him. I remember Carla's wedding, the first one. We all knew who had picked Harold Tramm for her, poor dear. But by fifty-nine or sixty Tramm was dead, and so was grandaddy, and the second husband had gone off to Hollywood to get the divorce, and Carla could do as she pleased. And there was Vanni. Carla was mad for him, and they say she made no bones about it. She installed him in one of the guest cottages on the grounds so she could slip down at night to be with him."

Francesca put the cup down in the saucer with a small crash. "We're talking about my father," she said rather loudly. "My father came from very proud people. He wasn't an illiterate peasant, he went to the seminary in Taormina until he had to go to work to support his family. And we're *Sicilians,* not Italians, there's a difference." She looked around. The room was hot and she was trying to control her temper. "Yes, I'm sure they all wanted to immigrate, Mrs. Hampton. America was the land of opportunity for them. My uncles are very hard-working, successful businessmen, and wonderful family men. And, I'd like to say— they're faithful to their wives!"

"Have some tea," Mrs. Carlton Hampton said. "I never said Vanni wasn't an honorable man, my dear. We all knew he never wanted Carla's money or he wouldn't have left her."

Francesca's lips had gone stiff. "That's the very least you can say of him, isn't it—that he didn't want her money? My God," she suddenly burst out, "don't you people think of anything else? He had all his family depending on him! Frankly, I don't think you people understand the way life works. Outside the walls of Palm Beach, that is!"

"Hoity-toity." The old eyes scrutinized Francesca not unkindly. "No need to fly off the handle. Here, have another cup of tea." The fat fingers reached for the giant tea pot and tipped it to pour another cup. "I wasn't born into all this, you know. I was on the stage, it wasn't a very reputable profession then, when I married my first husband, Giannini.

I think it's very difficult to keep from being used—rich women learn all too soon that all anyone wants from them is their money. I sit here many afternoons and think of the men I've loved, and who claimed they loved me, and I tell you, I still haven't made up my mind what it's all about. Don't be too quick to judge." Her hand offered the teacup over the table. "I knew Vanni, I don't think he would have been Carla's lover just to keep his job. On the contrary, I think he had a good heart. She was quite a beautiful little thing, you know, and spoiled rotten. If he loved her, then she was lucky, more than most women here."

"He was my *father*," Francesca gritted. Her head was beginning to ache. She had already been through one scene that afternoon with Kurt at *Ca'ad Carlo*, and didn't need another, but the words just came tumbling out. "My father wasn't a *boy*, a chauffeur—he was a wonderful person. He can't be talked about as though he was just a something! Do you know how he died?" A burst of emotion welled up in her. "He was driving a concrete mixer, the only one the brothers had, and it was night and the road was covered with ice just outside Holbrook and the truck skidded going down a long hill. It skidded for over a mile, Mrs. Hampton, and my father could have jumped free, but they needed the truck and he tried to save it. He lost his life because he tried to save a concrete truck! My uncles never got over it. I thought my Uncle Carmine was going to kill himself. I was fourteen when it happened, old enough to know my father was the handsomest, most wonderful man in the world. And yes, he had a good heart—that's why the concrete truck rolled on him and smashed him. He was so good-hearted he didn't want his brothers to lose it!"

As Francesca dabbed away angry tears the older woman said, very calmly, "I just told you and you weren't listening. I said if the boy loved Carla she was very lucky. One could take just so much of Carla, you know. You didn't know the Bloodworths, but it was quite true. She was always Chuckie's granddaughter. I can't say any of them were really lovable. Old Chuckie was a monster."

"I must go," Francesca muttered. She lifted the teacup distractedly and drank the last of the tea. It was plain, she told herself angrily, that Queenie Hampton didn't know what she was saying.

The other woman went on, "But I don't say it was easy for Carla, either, you know. Old Chuckie was dead so he couldn't lay down the law to her, but fraternizing with the servants was quite beyond the pale! Besides, there'd just been that scandal over at the Rockefellers about the Norwegian maid. The boy insisted on marrying her, although it didn't last long. So tongues certainly wagged over Carla and her beautiful Italian chauffeur. She would keep letting him drive for her, and all Palm Beach fell all over itself to get a look at him. Not everyone was carried away, of course. Old Sebastian Turtle hated the Italians from the moment they arrived. He was still the gardener then. They called them gardeners and not grounds technicians in those days."

"Mrs. Hampton," Francesca said determinedly, "I've enjoyed it, and it was good of you to invite me to tea, but I have to go."

The old lady did not appear to hear her. She cocked her head to one side as though listening to her own voice. "And old Sebastian claimed, or so he told my gardeners, that the woman with Vanni couldn't be his wife. 'What makes old Turtle think that?' I asked MacElroy when he told me. And MacElroy said they hardly saw each other, much less lived with each other, and he had come to the conclusion that she was somebody else's wife. Because, of course, if she'd been his wife Carla wouldn't have tolerated her for a minute."

Francesca stood up. "I think you'll have to call someone to show me the way out," she said firmly.

"Yes, you do that, dear," Queenie Hampton said. She lifted a little silver bell from the tea table and rang it to summon the ancient butler. "I do get tired in the afternoons, drinking tea makes me quite sleepy after a while. You've seen my pictures, haven't you? I have a lovely one of Isadora

Duncan quite naked. She was in London in 1912 when that was taken, living with the sewing machine tycoon. It was Isadora's *forte,* actually, thundering about nearly nude on the stage with those terrible feet and calling it classical Greek dance. The head of Aphrodite up there on the mantel is one she gave me. My dear, she had a dreadful accident, too, only it was against the wheel of an automobile. *'J' vais a gloire,'* she said, and threw this long scarf over her shoulder and it wrapped right around the axle. Killed her outright, I believe."

"Mrs. Hampton," Francesca said.

The black eyes came back to her suddenly. "My dear," the soft old voice whispered, "they're going to call you beautiful, and now you have far too much money. I'm eighty-nine years old, and I've been called beautiful, and I can't think what to tell you." Then, more loudly as she looked around, "Look after Chuckie's lovely house, dear, and don't let it fall to pieces. You're one of us now, you know." She lifted the little bell again. "Tell MacElroy I said you're to come back. I don't see many people these days, but you can come back, tell him I said so."

"Thank you," Francesca murmured. She felt as though she had passed years, not two hours, in the vast stuffy drawing room with its hundreds of relics of the past.

"And remember to see the Palm Beach Association," the old woman called. "They'll tell you what to do."

# Chapter Nine

"Will July never end?" Buffy Amberson moaned.

Francesca, surveying the sea with a pair of high-powered binoculars, didn't answer. The other woman lay beside her in a matching redwood recliner under the oleanders, her still-bruised face shaded by the leaves, but her legs in the sun to tan. Buffy lifted her hand to adjust her sunglasses to a less painful spot on her nose.

"Nobody stays in Palm Beach in the summer," Buffy went on. "If I weren't so much in the hole for face surgery, I'd pack up and go to my mother's. At least Milwaukee isn't Palm Beach. But I haven't even got the price of a bus ticket. Damn Jock for going off and leaving me here! You know where he's gone, don't you? Back to second wife Barbara and the kiddies. He won't stay long, he never does, just long enough to cry all over her and get lots of sympathy. Then when the kids get on his nerves and start driving him up the wall, he takes a plane back to Buffy, the singin' and dancin' sensation of Palm Beach. The bastard."

Below them on the greensward *Ca' ad Carlo*'s main fountain sent an arching spray into the air in a flickering of rainbows. The riding lawnmower from the West Palm Beach custom grounds service turned the corner by the large swimming pool and started back again.

"*I, Carla Bloodworth Bergstrom, being of sound mind and body, do hereby bequeath—*"

Francesca adjusted the binoculars and started again, sweeping the horizon for the spot where the *Freya* was sailing before the wind, her mainsails billowing. Francesca, who was ignorant about such things, still knew it was an exceptionally beautiful boat, large and expensively enough built to be called a yacht. She caught it again in the binoculars and saw the long, low-slung hull as it cut the water, a lip of white foam curling at the bow.

Francesca had reread Carla's will, dated two years after her marriage to Kurt Bergstrom, and witnessed by local bank people and a Palm Beach lawyer. It said nothing about the *Freya*. The last will had not appeared until after Carla's death, when it had been found in a safe deposit box with some jewelry and papers in the bank in Palm Beach. How had it gotten there? And when had it been drawn up and witnessed, if Carla had been such a recluse, confined to her bed?

Francesca watched the *Freya* come about at the entrance to Lake Worth pass, sails flapping as they lost the wind.

Buffy sat up. "Oh, damn, Francesca," she said in a low voice. "I keep forgetting your bodyguard's near enough to hear every word I say. He is, isn't he?"

"I suppose," Francesca murmured, indifferently. The lean, rangy figure of John Turtle in blue jeans and work boots, the smoke from a brown cigarillo curling in the air, was right below them.

"Do you have to have a bodyguard around even at home?" Buffy whispered. "I mean, we're suntanning. I've got everything untied, you can see all of me. Cripes, Francesca, don't you have any privacy?"

"Not much," Francesca admitted. "Besides, it's only John Turtle. I've gotten used to it." She twisted the focusing wheel on the binoculars to find Kurt Bergstrom aboard the *Freya*. She looked for the blond glint of his hair.

"Don't tell me he doesn't look," Buffy persisted. "That's a hunk of man, Francesca. He'd have to be half-dead if he didn't look. Hey, he's got his eyes on you! It's *you* he watches all the time!" She twisted her long, elegant body to roll over on her stomach. "He's really cute. Come on, Francesca, haven't you noticed?"

Francesca shrugged. "He has to watch me, Buffy, that's what he's there for. I got another kidnap threat in the mail this week. It always happens when there's another news story. Would you believe some photographer shot me with a telephoto lens at the little swimming pool? He must have been up a palm tree somewhere. I didn't see the pictures, but my lawyers tell me they're pretty sexy you know, I was wearing a bikini. And that brought out all the cranks. It gives you the creeps when you think about it."

"Creeps? It makes my blood run cold! Oh, Francesca, what in the hell do you do about these threats?"

"Get more people to take care of them," Francesca said calmly. "John Turtle is my personal bodyguard now, and the new security man covers the grounds. He goes up and down the paths looking for trespassers. The police in West Palm Beach and the FBI, they get the kidnap threats. And the Bloodworth Foundation in New York and the Miami lawyers decide who to prosecute and sue. And the public relations people keep it out of the newspapers. I really don't even ask about it anymore. Buffy," she said suddenly, "did you know the Bloodworth Building in New York gets about two bomb threats every year? There are all these terrorist groups which say Bloodworth money has been invested in companies which support military dictatorships. And the lawyers even say the Bloodworth Building gets bomb threats because all the Bloodworth stores are non-union." Francesca frowned. "Do you think I should try to do something about that?"

Buffy was watching John Turtle standing on the terrace below them. She propped her chin on her arms. "What are you going to do, organize the workers?"

Francesca lowered the binoculars. The *Freya* was out of sight. "I don't think unions are a bad thing. All the people I knew, growing up, were construction workers and they all belonged to a union."

"Good grief," Buffy murmured, not moving her eyes from the figure of the bodyguard, "don't say that, Francesca! This is Palm Beach, the Conservative Capital of the World outside of Dallas. All right, tell me—where's Kurt now?"

"Turning the buoy," Francesca said, "the last time I looked."

The beautiful woman lying on her stomach, the untied bikini top under her bare breasts, lifted her silver-gold head and murmured into the distance, "Hey, hunk of man, look at *me*—I haven't got as much money as she has, and my face is out of service right now, but the rest of me is still operating!"

"Buffy, don't do that." Francesca sat down on the lounger. "I don't think John Turtle has much of a sense of humor. Anyway, he's getting paid for what he does. Just leave him alone."

Buffy grunted. "He's not my employee. And I think he's gorgeous. Just look at those shoulders, look at those legs, that mouth—yummy, I love that sort of grim, sexy look around the lips! He reminds me of a panther. Cougar? No, panther, all dark and kind of dangerous and strong. Besides, I'm getting tired of waiting for my nose to heal up into what they tell me is going to be sheer perfection this time." She rolled over on her back, holding the scrap of bikini top carelessly to her small, thrusting breasts. "Well, tell me—how is the *Freya* today? Was Dorrit with him? Is that why you're keeping watch?" When Francesca looked up quickly,

Buffy said, "Forget that I mentioned that," under her breath. "Dorrit's not with Kurt. Dorrit gets seasick, everybody knows that. Buffy should know when to keep her mouth shut."

"Why should Dorrit be with Kurt Bergstrom on the *Freya?*" Francesca said, frowning. When the other woman did not answer she said, "Buffy, why should Dorrit be with Kurt? Has she been with him on the *Freya* before?"

Buffy covered her eyes against the sun. "Francesca dear," she said in a small voice, "you're footing the bill for my face repair until I can shake down my rotten husband to pay you back. You're not going to make me say anything that's going to bust up our friendship, are you?"

"Don't kid around, Buffy," Francesca said sharply. "I mean it. Tell me."

Buffy took her hand away. "Okay, Dorrit's nothing to worry about, Francesca. It's just that Dorrit's broke and she has to leave. Bodner's written her another poison-pen letter telling her she has to be out at the end of August. Which puts Dorrit in the same spot with about a thousand other beautiful Palm Beach whizzers, male and female, who have no place to go after enjoying this summer's forbidden pleasures. It's a shame beauty and talent don't pay off, isn't it? So what does poor Dorrit do? Go back to New York to see if she can get any modeling jobs? Not this year, honey— all the rag business wants is twelve-year-olds. And Dorrit must be pushing *twenty-seven!* Doesn't it make you ill just to think of it? So does Dorrit take up with the local motorcycle gang for new career horizons? It's a thought, but all that wear and tear is pretty hard on the body. No, Dorrit goes looking for friends who can help her replace Larry Bodner. But poor Kurt's not going to replace Bodner, darling Kurt hasn't got any money, either. But he can help Dorrit find a Bodner substitute."

Francesca was remembering that passionate, devouring kiss Dorrit had given Kurt the first night she'd met him. "She wants him, Buffy," Francesca said softly. "She'd take Kurt if she could get him. Money or no money."

Buffy sat up, her lithe, beautiful body glistening with suntan oil. "Half the women in Palm Beach would take Kurt Bergstrom if they could get him, don't you know that? Nobody ever understood why he stayed shut up here with Carla, when he could have gone out on the town, really. So everybody said he was waiting for Carla to die so he could get her money. Then she died, and didn't leave him any money. How do you figure it? From what I'd heard, she would have given him anything he wanted."

Francesca thought of Kurt Bergstrom's words: "She left me as she found me, with the *Freya* and not much more."

"What is it?" Buffy said, watching her. "Has the silent Swede been telling you his life's secrets?"

Francesca lifted her shoulders in a shrug. "Nothing, really. He just said that Carla left him as she found him, with the boat and not much else. It didn't seem to bother him." Except that, Francesca knew, Herb Ostrow had said the *Freya* belonged to Carla after all.

"That sounds like our Kurt, doesn't it? I can never figure him out." Buffy laughed her silvery peal, her head thrown back. "All these boat people, the sailing crowd with the big yachts are really crazy, crazy, crazy. I don't know much about Kurt, actually." Her expression changed abruptly, grew thoughtful. "Except that everybody assumed he was going to get Carla's money when she died. She was so much older than he was. And after all, what do good-looking men want, anyway, except some rich woman's money?"

Francesca stared at her. The blithe words seemed to hang in the air with unconscious import. Beyond Buffy's head she could see John Turtle leaning against the stone balustrade, and in the distance the sparkling jets of the fountain. Of course, that was it! The shadow of the fortune hunter that lay over them all, as it had dogged Giovanni Lucchese. There seemed no way of getting away from it.

Buffy said softly, "Francesca, can I ask—what's with it between you and Kurt? I mean, if you let him stay in Carla's guest cottage—"

"My guest cottage," Francesca reminded her.

"Oh, sorry." Buffy pulled a face. "But you are sleeping with him, aren't you? I mean—"

"I suppose if we paid any attention to each other," Francesca said loudly, "it would look to everybody as though Kurt Bergstrom was setting me up, wouldn't it? The way he set up Carla? That's what you said, you know: 'What do good-looking men in Palm Beach want from women except their money?' And when you look at it like that, it makes anything between Kurt Bergstrom and me impossible, doesn't it, except on a cash-and-carry basis. Because whatever Kurt does, it's going to be because he's after my money!"

"Oh, Francesca," Buffy protested, "you can't mean that!"

But Francesca was remembering how Kurt Bergstrom had taken his boat to Bimini to put as much distance between them as possible. Whatever he said, whatever he did, it was going to appear that he had been after her money from the very first night at *Ca'ad Carlo*. To make it worse, she told herself, chagrined, she had never been to bed with a man before; if he had been counting on a little casual sex, Palm Beach-style, she had really fixed that up. "You know why I had to go away, don't you?" he had asked her.

She did now.

"Francesca darling," Buffy was saying, "will you listen to me a moment? Now look, don't jump to conclusions about Kurt, will you? Not everybody loves Kurt, I ought to tell you that. You've only been seeing his friends. There was a lot of talk after Carla died that—"

"Buffy," Francesca interrupted, "let's go have some lunch. Delia Mary's fixing broiled shrimp and she's taken an oath not to feed me anything fattening."

But her heart was pounding.


THE carpenters had finished the renovation of the adjoining guest room in record time, but it still had taken much longer than Francesca had expected. The newly created room still

smelled faintly of paint and sawn wood and lacked a new
carpet, but it was now fully an office-study. Rosewood desks
were equipped with typewriter wells for both Francesca and
her secretary, and file cabinets were hidden in teakwood
panels. In spite of having been hastily designed, it was the
perfect work area for Francesca's growing correspondence
and the business as head-in-name-only of the Bloodworth
empire.

"Isn't it nice I know how to type," Francesca observed
as she settled into her new work area. "I came equipped
with all the working-girl skills."

Dorothea Smithson handled correspondence and the rapidly growing file on the Bloodworth corporation as well as
the social calendar. Booklets, brochures and beautifully
bound annual reports from the various divisions of the company were accumulating by leaps and bounds, and Francesca
was beginning to get some idea of the Bloodworth empire.
It was obvious that neither Carla Bloodworth nor her father,
Charles, Junior, had been much interested in the company.
Since the early 1950s its operation had largely been in the
hands of the Bloodworth Foundation.

Francesca rather enjoyed reading her way through all the
material sent down from New York. She had a degree in
business administration and analyzing the structure of the
Bloodworth corporation was familiar territory. But she
couldn't help but be curious as to why the Bloodworth
Foundation could not come up with an annual report that
accurately reported the corporation's worth. She'd never
heard of a structure as big as Bloodworth's that really didn't
know how much it would bring on the auction block. Could
it possibly be horribly mismanaged?

The Bloodworth offices in New York had been politely
attentive at first to her requests for information on the comparatively new Blo-Co chain. But after her examination of
the profit and loss sheets and the firing off of several letters
asking for explanations, there was no reply. Instead, the
Foundation Executive Director called the law offices of
Stillman, Newman and Vance in Miami to ask what was

the matter with the new heiress to the Bloodworth millions.

"Why do they think anything's the matter?" Francesca asked Harry Stillman.

"I think you're upsetting them, my dear," was the lawyer's answer. "Nobody's paid so much attention to the company since the days of old Charlie Bloodworth. You might—this is just a suggestion—consider going a little more slowly."

The construction company was another matter.

Blo-Co, Francesca found, had set up its own contractors to build Blo-Co stores in Bloodworth-owned shopping malls. The operation was staggeringly unprofitable. Francesca, who knew more than a little about construction costs, couldn't believe the figures the Foundation forwarded to her. When she called her Uncle Carmine at Lucchese Brothers' Construction and Concrete Company in Boston, though, to suggest her uncle take a temporary job with the Blo-Co construction division to get it straightened out, he refused to take her seriously.

"First of all," Carmine Lucchese rasped, "what you got here is a publicly-held company with stockholders, in spite of the fact that the Bloodworth family owns over fifty percent of the stock. This corporation is not going to let you come in and start pulling out their upper management types to replace with your own relatives, right? If you start to push as hard as that, they're going to fight you. And another thing, Frannie, a big shake-up at Bloodworth's is going to shake up the stock market. Bloodworth's is one of the biggest retail chains in the world, it's got money invested in everything from the space industry to Brazilian government bonds from what you tell me. Okay, so their construction division is screwed up. So what else is new? They could be taking a big tax write-off. Who are Bloodworth's tax lawyers? Can you get in contact with them?"

Francesca didn't know the Bloodworth's corporation tax accountants, but she set Dorothea Smithson to telephoning again to find out.

Her Uncle Carmine had turned down her offer to take

over the reins of the construction division of Blo-Co with a flat no. "Frannie, we're just a bunch of concrete men up here, not management experts. Listen, you keep on doing what you're doing, don't step on any toes. It's going to take you about a year to study a corporation that size, so don't worry about it."

But Francesca was determined that an investigation of Bloodworth's, Inc., wasn't going to take a year if she could help it. And she certainly didn't care whether or not she made New York or Miami extremely nervous in the process.

While Francesca worked, the maid, Mrs. Schoener, usually supplied her with coffee and kept busy with Francesca's clothes. Francesca had never been quite sure what the duties of a ladies' maid were, but she saw that Gerda Schoener worked long hours very diligently assembling, sorting, repairing, pressing and generally maintaining her ever-expanding wardrobe. Each dress and sportswear coordinate went into its own nylon mesh bag and each section of these in the closets was organized so that within minutes a complete outfit could be laid out for any occasion, with accessories. When Miss Lucchese bought furs, the maid told her, they would be hung in a refrigerated storeroom off the kitchen.

Although it was Dorothea Smithson who now oversaw the daily menus and supervised personnel on the estate, including making up the payroll forms, Mrs. Schoener did liaison duty with the staff to make sure that, for instance, John Turtle and the other security man knew within minutes of Francesca's decision to leave the estate, what sort of transportation she would use, where she was going, and address and telephone numbers of her destination in case she had to be reached.

At night the maid turned down Francesca's bed, laid out her nightgown and put out the usual drink, juice, hot tea, or the inevitable carrot cocktail supreme.

"I'll never get through drinking this stuff," Francesca always moaned at the sight of the latter. But she had lost another three pounds. And no matter what the *Golden Door* exercise supervisor had said about the irreducibility of ethnic hips, she had lost an inch and a half there, which kept Mrs. Schoener busy taking in the silken seams of all her Sciavone slacks.

AT four in the afternoon Mrs. Schoener came to take away the coffee cups. Francesca leaned back in her chair and stretched. It was still hot in the afternoons in the upstairs bedrooms. She could appreciate what Buffy had meant about Florida in July—when one of the upstairs air conditioners went out, as they frequently did, she grabbed up her swimsuit and fled the house until John Turtle or Peter Peavey could get it fixed.

In late July John Turtle had called in several engineers for estimates on installing a central air-conditioning system. The figures had been appalling. But a tour of the house with the engineers had shown why. During the time Carla had lived in Europe not much attention had been paid to the slow deterioration of the main house. Nearly everything looked sound enough, but close up an inspection showed the painted wood, the upholstery, even the heraldic banners hanging from the ceiling of the formal dining room, were slowly decaying. Not only did much of *Ca'ad Carlo*'s interiors need restoring, but only air conditioning on a grand scale could prevent the rot from going any further. The high summer temperatures, the invidious Florida humidity and the failure to use what air conditioning there was with any consistency had kept *Ca'ad Carlo*'s treasures in a pressure cooker. One of the engineers took a small file and scraped away some of the gilt on the gallery wood to show it had all but turned to powder. He then plunged the metal file into the wood. It penetrated it like cheese. Francesca was beginning to understand a little of Mrs. Carlton Hampton's obsession with maintaining old Palm Beach property.

Gerda Schoener crossed to the windows that looked out

on the little balcony overlooking the drive. "Mr. Bergstrom is bringing in his boat," the maid observed.

Francesca laid aside the last of the morning's pile of mail and got up. From that angle one could see the northern corner of the green lawns, the stand of oleanders where she and Buffy had been sunning before lunch, and beyond that the concrete sea walls of the old boat basin.

"I didn't think you could use that dock," Francesca murmured.

"*He* can," the maid said. "Mr. Kurt is a fine sailor. He knows what he is doing."

Francesca turned to stare at her. She had thought they didn't like each other. Then what was the tremendous row, she thought, all about in the guest cottage a week ago?

The *Freya* was standing out from the crumbling pier while its master gauged the difficulty of inching it into a docking in a glassy but treacherously rolling sea. The yawl's beautiful gleaming white hull seemed as fragile as eggshell against the slab of seawall. Blue canvas-covered styrofoam bumpers were out and lashed to the *Freya*'s sides to protect them, but a surge of the sea suddenly caught the yacht and lifted it as though to slam it down on the pier's broken edges. The blond man at the wheel calmly held the boat until the swell subsided.

Francesca let out her breath. "What is he bringing his boat in here for?" she wondered. "I thought he kept it in a marina."

Mrs. Schoener did not turn her head. She seemed fascinated, her eyes fixed on the lovely boat and the big man who handled it so effortlessly. "He is getting his things out, Miss Lucchese. This morning, Mr. Kurt cleans out his cottage."

Francesca froze. "That can't be." She watched the yawl closing on the pier. The man at the wheel tossed a line ashore and Peter Peavey caught it and carried it to tie up the *Freya*.

The maid muttered, "Oh, he is a fool, that one. Now he goes away."

Francesca could hardly believe her ears. *Going away?* "But I didn't tell him to leave!" she cried. "Is that what you all think, that I'm making him move out? Why didn't he say something to me?"

Gerda Schoener's stolid blue gaze regarded her impassively.

"You got to ask him that, Miss Lucchese. Not me."

# CHAPTER TEN

FRANCESCA hurried across the lawn, the heels of her French sandals digging into the grass. She broke into a run for the last few feet, glad she was wearing slacks and a soft silk shirt to give her enough freedom of movement to sprint. She leaped down the three steps to the boat basin and virtually skidded to a halt at its edge. Peter Peavey was making fast the boat's lines. Kurt Bergstrom looked up at her from the deck of the *Freya*, smiling, his handsome Viking-bearded face at last showing recognition of the change in her as she stopped breathless, and a little flushed, on the pier.

"What are you doing?" Francesca cried. She gasped for air. "You're not moving out, are you?"

He seemed not to hear her, his eyes busy with all that was new in Francesca—her black hair drifting in the sultry wind, her coloring, the subtle makeup emphasizing her firmly modeled features and her large, cloud-gray eyes, the knowing flattery of the tailored orange silk shirt and skin-smooth slacks. The big man's look acknowledged that she was beautiful. He gave a silent whistle of appreciation, his eyes crinkling at the corners. He motioned with his free hand. "Come aboard."

Francesca looked down doubtfully. The low sea swells took the *Freya*, lifted her, then let her drop. The deck was a half a foot or so beneath Francesca's feet. An expanse of green water widened and then contracted with every rise and fall. She didn't think she could jump that terrible gulf from dock to deck. If she leaped and missed, she could fall into the water between the *Freya* and the old concrete dock and be chewed to hamburger, she was sure, before they could get her out. Kurt Bergstrom was watching her, holding out his hand to her. There was a question in his eyes. Not *can* you do it, but *will* you do it, they said.

Francesca jumped. The deck of the *Freya* rose to meet her feet with a horrific smack that nearly sent her to her knees. She grabbed at the front of his striped jersey, her other hand snatching at the air. The French heels of her sandals nearly pitched her over. But she had made it! She heard him laugh.

"Come on, I'll take you out," he told her. He called to Peter Peavey to cast off the line he had just secured, and reached over Francesca to throw the other line back to free the stern. The *Freya* began to slip, bow in, at right angles to the pier. "Cast off, I told you," he shouted.

Reluctantly, Peter Peavey obeyed. The *Freya*'s stern was loose and the bow line would not hold her, anyway. As he did so, the engines purred up a notch and the yawl moved out into the Gulf Stream.

Francesca still held on to Kurt Bergstrom with both hands. She felt him half stoop in a graceful bending of his body to turn the wheel, the great muscles in his back and shoulders working under her fingertips. Aware at last that she was clutching at him, Francesca looked around for something to hold to and grabbed a small rail at the stern gratefully.

The *Freya*'s bow pitched slowly up and then down into a sea swell and Francesca wondered, briefly, if she were going to be sick. A fresh hot breeze wafted over them as the yacht moved away from land. Francesca gulped the air and felt better. She saw, out of the corner of her eye, a man running over the green grass of *Ca'ad Carlo*'s lawns to the boat basin, a tall, rangy man with a suntanned face wearing a black summerweight business suit, the jacket open, striped tie flapping.

*John Turtle*.

Francesca, remembered, in a wave of dismay, that she had an appointment for drinks with Herb Ostrow at the Palm Beach Country Club at six o'clock. The man running down to the boat basin was her bodyguard, dressed to go with her. It was too late to do anything now, she knew. She turned to say something to the man beside her, but he was busy taking the boat around a point of seawall which separated *Ca'ad Carlo* from the estate of the Whitney family next door.

Francesca saw John Turtle come to a halt at the edge of the grass. He stared at the *Freya* moving out to sea, Peter Peavey beside him. Francesca didn't want to look at their faces. Peter Peavey merely looked astonished. She didn't want to think about John Turtle's expression.

"Turn back," Francesca said, belatedly. "I—we have to get—" She looked at the man beside her, his blond hair stirring in the wind, his face now showing unconcealed amusement. She pointed. "I'm not supposed to leave without him, really," she protested.

Kurt Bergstrom threw back his head and laughed, showing fine white teeth. "To hell with him," was his response.

They kept going.


FRANCESCA sat in the stairwell leading belowdecks and took off her shoes. The heels, Kurt had pointed out, made marks on the deck. Under her bare feet, when she stood up, the polished deck felt warm and strangely buoyant. She felt free, more sure of her balance, barefooted. She tried a few steps, feeling his eyes on her.

What she saw in his eyes now thrilled and excited her and made her even more uncertain. Did he remember what it was like, making love to her? Was this in his mind as he saw her now, more beautiful, more desirable by far than she had been before? Francesca tried to concentrate on getting across the deck without falling.

The sun was hot, but the wind softened its steady burning. Brilliant blue water and clear summer sky and the shoreline moving past in a fringe of white beach and great houses made Palm Beach look very different from this, the ocean side. From this perspective the island had a Disney-like aspect: multimillion-dollar fantasies in stone and glass that merchant princes and empire builders who had flocked to this sandy stretch of Florida coast almost a century ago had lavished with money, out-building each other, out-buying each other, and out-entertaining each other. It was staggering to remember that these palaces were designed only as *winter* homes.

The *Freya* moved out into the Gulf Stream slipping along under diesel power. Kurt Bergstrom braced his big body against the taffrail in the stern, legs lazily extended, bare feet crossed, one hand on the wheel, watching Francesca.

She walked, swaying, across the deck to him. The touch of his eyes warmed her body and made her slightly self-conscious. "It's beautiful," she shouted over the wind. "Everything!"

"Yes, and so are you." His voice was low, almost inaudible, but his look spoke for him. "You are changed."

His free hand reached out and took her by the arm to pull her to him. They were still in sight of those on the shore, Francesca knew. For a moment, electrified, she thought he was going to kiss her. The wind moved her hair across her face and she caught it back with her hand. But he only said, over the noise of the engines and the wind, "Do you want to put up sail?"

She could only nod, her body close to his, the excitement flowing into her, held by that powerful tanned arm.

"Okay," he said, letting go of her. "But you must help."


THE yawl turned its nose into the open sea and Francesca, paralyzed with terror, held the wheel with both hands in a frozen grip. *Keep it steady,* he had told her. The bow of the boat was to be kept pointing straight ahead at an orange triangle called a day marker. A powerboat built for fishing with a Bimini top roared past. Francesca's heart was in her mouth as the *Freya* dipped down steeply into the powerboat's wake and then up again. Someone in the fishing boat's stern waved at her, but she did not dare lift her hands from the wheel. She was very aware of the responsibility Kurt had placed upon her, guiding the beautiful yacht through green-blue ocean waters. Kurt Bergstrom's lovely boat. His passion. Had he let any other woman do this? she wondered.

In bare brown feet, hair whipped by the wind, he moved about setting the yawl's sails. The canvas went up and hung limply, flapping and muttering. He moved as gracefully as a dancer about the deck. He looked at her once or twice to see how she was doing, and grinned.

When the sails were set he came back to her side and put his hands over her hands on the wheel. Gently he pried her fingers away. She saw the boat still kept a straight and steady course. It sailed itself, she saw, astonished.

He was laughing at her. "No," he told her, "you did right. Only it will hold its course for a while if you stay easy."

He cut the engines. In the sudden silence an eeriness settled in the air. It was as though time had stopped.

"Now," he said, taking her hand in his. His fingers were warm as they covered hers and pressed them again on the wheel of the *Freya*. The bow swung to the right. The sails began to fill with wind, cracking and popping, and then rounded out like white clouds. The deck tipped abruptly and hung, the side rail skimming the suddenly racing sea.

Paralyzed with fright, Francesca felt her body slide against his as the yawl did its best to fall sidewise into the green water.

The man beside her laughed again. As long as he laughed, Francesca supposed, the boat was not going to roll completely over and disappear under the waves. But she was not all that sure.

"Go get us some drinks," he told her. "There is Coca-Cola in the galley, and beer. Bring me a Schlitz."

He gave her a push

Francesca started across the slanted deck, resisting the urge to get down on her hands and knees and crawl.

Below, the *Freya*'s hull was narrow; everything formed a sleek, compact line forward. There was a sitting-living area paneled in beautiful wood with a television and costly stereo set. All was more spartan than Angel and Cassie's yacht, although Francesca suspected the *Freya* was larger. The upholstery was handwoven blue and white, which blended with the warm wood tones. The passageway was narrow and the doors opened into neat, tiny staterooms with blue bedspreads on the bunks, washbasin and mirror, and portholes with blue curtains. She could see the sea rushing past.

The area beyond the staterooms widened into a gallery with tables on either side of the passageway and built-in seats and modern kitchen equipment. There was a sense of perfect orderliness, of everything-in-its-place. A man's world. But a special man's world for those who sailed ships.

Francesca found the Coca-Cola in the refrigerator and opened one for herself, and got Kurt Bergstrom a can of beer. Holding the icy containers against her side, she started back up the ladder again.


THEY sailed north, past Palm Beach Shores and then the town of North Palm Beach. The wind was easterly, onshore, and the *Freya* heeled with the wind across her canvas, and dug her bow into rolling swells with a smooth gliding motion. Francesca discovered that she was not going to be seasick. If anything, the air made her hungry. She went back down into the galley and found a box of pretzels and ate most of them, and a banana.

He only laughed at her again. "This is a seasick swell," he told her. "How can you eat in this? What are you eating?" He took part of the banana. "So you are going to make a good sailor, heh?" His eyes teased her.

Francesca had found a piece of string in the galley to tie back her hair. She felt very pleased with herself. And she didn't see how they could have taken John Turtle along, anyway.

The *Freya* beat northward to Juno Beach. There was not much to do except watch the sun descend toward the landward horizon and see the pleasure boats roaring past. People on other sailing craft came to the rails to watch the *Freya* and lift their hands in salute. Kurt Bergstrom's boat was something special, Francesca gathered. And the blond man at the wheel, his body lounging easily against the taffrail, was special, too, from what she saw.

He told her that he had crewed in one of the America's-class ocean racers out of Newport, Rhode Island.

"That is hard work, sailing in those ocean boats out of Newport. They are stripped for speed. You eat cold food as there is nothing to cook on, they don't want the weight of a stove. The hull inside is bare and cold as hell, nobody wants any heating equipment, either. You sleep in hammocks slung from the bulkheads. When you get time to sleep. Over the side is the toilet. Everything is for sail, and for speed. You are always wet and cold like crazy all the time, sleeping or waking, except if you are in the sun. If it is an Atlantic race there is no sun, probably. You get only fog and rain and wind "

"It sounds horrible," Francesca said.

He looked at her thoughtfully. "No, it is very exciting. You are the most alive, then, eating and sleeping and sailing all the time and being damned cold and wet. If we could always be like that, everybody, there would be nothing wrong with us."

They were strange words, Francesca thought, looking at his bronzed face with its brilliant pale eyes. He was talking about being happy. She knew she would be miserable under those conditions. She loved being warm and well-fed and she didn't know that she would ever like the sea that much. When she thought of large bodies of water, she thought of swimming pools. What he was talking about sounded very free and uncomplicated, and very lonely. She knew, without asking, that loneliness didn't bother this man. He turned to look down at her, and she was shaken by that sea-blue gaze.

"I prefer the *Freya*," she said quickly.

"Ah, yes, the *Freya*," he murmured. "She is a beautiful woman." But his eyes were on her.

If he was waiting for her to say they ought to turn back, he gave no sign of it. And Francesca did not ask where they were going. It seemed they just sailed on, blissfully released from the world. The sun set in the rim of the shoreline and he set the running lights and turned the *Freya*'s bow into Jupiter inlet. In the darkness, with the diamond lights of the shore, the boat with its sails set like white ghosts passed silently. But the summer air turned sticky and hot away from the open sea. Kurt took down the sails finally and eased the *Freya* along under engine power, finally dropping anchor in a dark cove with only the lights of a single house a few miles away.

"Come on, let's eat," he told her cheerfully, and went down below.

An awning could be rigged over the stern, making a delightful lounge area. Under it they set out Indonesian print cushions and pillows and a low teakwood table. By the light of candles they ate salad and hamburgers. Francesca carried a bottle of red wine up on deck. That was all he would let her do.

"In the old days out here," he said when they had settled themselves on the cushions, "they drank champagne." He leaned back and pulled a pipe out of his jersey and began to tamp tobacco into it with his forefinger. "There were lots of lights, pretty women, all sorts of wild things going on. A Vietnamese had this boat, one of the royal princes, very rich, very corrupt. They will tell you a Frenchman owned her, but a Frenchman *built* her. Everything the rich Vietnamese wanted was French-made, French-built. In that way I agree with the Buddhists that it is corrupt and decadent not to want and admire one's own culture. But this guy wanted first-class everything, even his mistresses. All blonde women—I think one was Belgian. The boat was made to run fast, with big engines for getting away fast in case the army or the French or the king's police were after him. There was plenty to come after him about, believe me. The inside of this boat was full of junk like a whorehouse, including a screen for dirty films. I took out the junk, all of it. It was a nice clean boat underneath. But don't let them tell you the French don't make good boats, they do. This Frenchman was a genius. When I got her," he said, holding a match to his pipe and sucking on it, "she was in Bangkok where the prince had gone after the police and the army had chased him out, but not the French—this was after Dien Bien Phu. A consortium owned her: two Germans, an Australian and two Hong Kong Chinese, and they had been using her to run raw opium from Burma down into Malay States and over to the Americans in the Philippines. The British had caught them and the Germans were in jail, the Australian had disappeared, and the Chinese paid big bribes to stay out of it. The inside of this boat was a mess. I got the Thais to build all the wood, they're very good at that. The wood came from back in the hills where the elephants bring down the big logs of teak and mahogany. It's beautiful country, there."

The moon came up and Francesca watched silver creep across the waters of the inky bay. The love of his boat was in his voice. She put her chin in her hand and rested it there, thinking. She felt very relaxed. Wherever the deed to the *Freya* was, Francesca knew the yacht belonged to Kurt Bergstrom. It was impossible to think of anyone taking his boat away from him.

"You're getting drunk," he teased her. "Open your eyes."

They had had only a half a bottle of wine, and he knew it. Francesca opened her eyes wide. She might have looked drowsy, but she was drunk only with the moonlight and the water, and the tongues of the candles which flickered in the breeze under the little awning.

"Here, take my glass," he told her. "This will wake you up."

But his glass of wine only burned her throat going down. There was a sudden, unexpected rush of heat to her stomach and she coughed.

When she could get her voice again, she said, "They're expecting me back at *Ca'ad Carlo.*" The thought nagged at her. She had jumped onboard Kurt Bergstrom's boat that afternoon and had disappeared without a word. The sight of John Turtle's face came back to her. And she had not left with just anyone—she had left with Kurt Bergstrom, who was moving out of his guest cottage on the grounds. "They may even be looking for me," she murmured. "Everything's very security-conscious now, since the kidnap threat."

"They know you are with me." The bowl of the pipe glowed in the dark, lighting his face. "They're not going to make any trouble. I take care of you better, anyway, than these servants and bodyguards." He held the glass of wine for her again. "Here, finish it for me."

Francesca sipped it, then made a face. She gave the glass back to him. "What's in that, anyway?" She had grown vaguely restless, wanting to move about. "Perhaps I ought to telephone. Or use the radio. You have a radio or something on the *Freya,* don't you?"

When she stood up there was an alarming surge of burning to her groin. Francesca gasped. She gave him a startled look.

"Don't worry about it," he said. He took her by the hand to pull her back down against the cushions, close beside him. "I told you, I take better care of you than this bodyguard." He paused. In a different tone he said, "He doesn't try to make love to you, does he?"

Francesca was hardly listening, she was so preoccupied with what she was feeling. Her body had gone restless and glittering, full of pinpricks of sensation that seemed to demand some strange relief. She could hardly keep her hips from moving. Her thighs pressed together in response to the throbbing pulse in the heated folds of flesh between her legs. It was all she could do to keep from putting her hands there to try to still the unbearable feeling of need. "Who?" she said distracted.

"The gardener. The bodyguard. You know the one."

"John Turtle?" Francesca put her hand casually in her lap and held it there. She was amazed that anyone could think of John Turtle wanting to make love to her. She choked back a nervous laugh.

"I see the way he looks at you."

That again. Francesca pressed her fingers against her crotch, absorbed by the growing flames there. She had no idea what was the matter. Her body seemed to have suddenly gone crazy. "He's my bodyguard, he's supposed to watch me for as long as he's on duty. I have to get used to it—having security men around."

She couldn't go on. The crazy clamor in her blood could not be ignored. She lay back against the cushions in the stern of the *Freya* almost in Kurt Bergstrom's arms, so close to him she could feel the rise and fall of his big body as he breathed, the hardness of his muscled legs pressed against hers, a powerful arm across the pillows just above her head. She suddenly felt terribly vulnerable. Worse, she knew her body wanted his lovemaking with an urgent longing that was going to force her to do something embarrassing. Waves of nervous turmoil swept through her. She watched his carved, easy lips as they moved, his face so close to hers that she could see the pores in his tanned skin, the straight

brush of light brown lashes framing his blue eyes. She tried
to focus on that strong, incredibly handsome face.

*Try to think of something else,* she told herself dizzily.

With an effort, she said, "I don't want you to move out
of the guest cottage. Please—it's yours for as long as you
want it." In the rising insistence of her body she could hardly
concentrate on what she was saying. "I didn't want you to
move your things out without telling me."

He held the wineglass in his hand, twisting it, looking
down at it. "Not everything," he said in a low voice. "I left
my clothes there, anyway."

The tension that hung in the air was real. Francesca
wanted to reach out and touch his calm, handsome face, to
press her hands against his magnificent body. Was he, she
wondered, remembering how he had made love to her before? Was that what his silence was about? Or did he regret
it? She had seen a curious reluctance in him; it had surfaced
the first time he had made love to her and the same reluctance
had returned, no mistaking it, when he had begged her to
leave *Ca'ad Carlo*. Now they were aboard the *Freya* in
their own isolated world. They had fixed dinner and had
eaten it on deck under the stars. And through it all he had
been perfectly friendly and correct.

She was not going to make some terrible mistake again
if she could help it.

Francesca got to her feet quickly. She had some dim idea
of going down below until her body's heated madness could
subside. With a clumsy gesture she picked up some of the
paper plates and the wineglasses.

She said haltingly, "You don't have to leave the guest
cottage. I want you to know that." She could feel his blue
eyes on her and the knowledge made a riot in her flesh. If
he wasn't thinking of how she had lain in his arms at that
moment, *she* was. She couldn't think of anything else. She
blurted, "You don't have to move your things out—as though
I'm going to throw you out without time to get ready! I
don't treat people that way. If I've done anything to make

it more difficult for you at *Ca'ad Carlo*, I'm sorry. They tell me my big fault is that I do things and then think about them later." A terrible ache had centered deep within her, swelling and throbbing in the silky core of her sex. And he was watching her, watching her, knowing something was happening. "I think you know what I'm talking about," she said desperately. "But I promise you, if you can forget it, so can I." She tried to smile. With a toss of her head she said, "Can we sail back at night? Can we use the sails at night, or do you have to use the engines?"

He stood up, then, bending his head slightly under the awning. His hand reached out and took her wrist and held her, while he took the paper plates and wineglasses and flung them into the dark. There were small distant sounds as they hit the water.

"We're not going back," he said softly. His eyes were pale lights in his bronzed face. "You know we are not going back, don't you, Francesca?"

His big arms went around her. Francesca moaned at the touch of his hard body, she couldn't help it. His hands moved down her back caressingly, seized the heavy roundness of her bottom, and pressed her hips close against him. She felt the big rod of his aroused flesh against her and heard the quickening of his breath. Her own throbbing ache, the hungry pulsing in her breasts and lips, was unbearable.

"Beautiful Francesca," he breathed against her hair. "How was I to know that you would be so beautiful? God, how I want you! I can't help myself."

In one extended motion his arms pressed her back and then his demanding lips were against her face, her throat and moving down to where his free hand pulled away the front of the silken shirt. His fingers hooked into her bra, pulling it down and, released from its confines, her firm rose tipped breasts spilled out boldly.

"My God," he murmured again. His fingers closed over the silky flesh and she shivered uncontrollably as his thumb and forefinger aroused the nipples, making them contract in electric shocks of pleasure. He pressed her back even farther, his mouth sliding down her throat into the soft damp cleft in her bosom. With a rush, his mouth took her breast, his tongue circling the bursting fullness of it, his hands cupping and stroking the other urgently. She cried out. Francesca put her fingers against his hair, small wordless sounds of ecstatic pleasure ripped from her as his mouth grew more savage. With exquisite thoroughness his tongue and his teeth pulled and caressed her smooth creamy flesh, nuzzling, forcing, taking their satisfaction, driving her relentlessly into small animal sounds. His hands pulled her down to the cushions under them.

"Love me, Francesca," he muttered. "Show me how much you want me."

Under partly closed lids his brilliant eyes watched her, his hands stroking her, pulling away her clothes. He left her breasts thrusting out from the constriction of the bra and did not bother to unfasten it; his hands positioned her legs apart, ready for him, stroking their tanned satiny length with his hands. As his hand moved down her tense belly to the silkiness of her crotch, Francesca writhed uncontrollably. At the touch of his hand in the soft patch of her sex, Francesca drew a long sobbing breath and heard the swift intake of his breath in answer. She was completely given over to a passionate uncaring; nothing was important, only the lustful clamoring of her body for the big man who held her in his arms and surveyed her so intently. She let her hips arch wildly against his probing fingers and her body lashed out, almost convulsively, at their invasion. She clung to him, completely at the mercy of what her body was doing, at what this man was doing as he goaded her response. Abruptly he covered her mouth with his and his tongue invaded her. The rhythmic thrusting of his fingers grew faster. She went wild. Francesca seized the great muscular shoulders and half pulled herself up, crying out loudly.

"My darling!" His mouth devoured her, his hand probing her body lashed her into a frenzy. "Show me how you love me," he gasped. She abandoned herself to sheer sexual wildness at his command, lost in his control over her body. At last there came a shock, so intensely pleasurable that she almost screamed with it.

Slowly, very slowly, shaking with aftershocks, Francesca subsided, and Kurt pulled her body under him. The pressure of his weight on her brought a small moan from her lips. He softly withdrew his fingers.

"Francesca." She looked up at him with dazed eyes. He lightly kissed her on the lips. "I wanted you to have your pleasure. It was good, yes?"

She didn't comprehend, still trembling with retreating waves of intensity.

The strange blue eyes searched hers. "Francesca, say that you will come to me if I remain at *Ca'ud Carlo*. That you will come to me and let me make love to you."

She frowned, distracted. The swelling ache of her body responded to his beautiful bronzed length pressing on hers, and she wanted him again.

"I will make life good for you, Francesca." His mouth was against her hair. "Better than you have ever known it. But you have to love me, and trust me. I want you to say that you will."

"Yes," Francesca murmured. She knew she wanted this man shamelessly. She would promise him anything.

He lowered his mouth on hers. His hands moved down her damp, slippery body into the soft hollows of her spine and the curve of her hips, gathering her under him. His fingers stroked the shivering flesh of her soft inner thighs, tracing a fiery trail to the dampness of the cleft where they joined. Then his hands retreated, leaving Francesca moaning, a little breathless. But he took her wrist and guided her hand to his own enormous, bursting flesh, moving them to stroke and caress him. The softest sound, like a groan, fell from his lips at her touch.

"You do love me." The words were husky; he buried his mouth in her hair.

With a growing, fiery need, Francesca pulled at his head to bring his mouth down to hers. He answered quickly, his kiss conquering her lips, his body pressing her down as if to impress his desire, his ownership, on her. His knee moved her legs aside and he moved over with shuddering eagerness. His great bronzed body bent and then thrust heavily into her, taking her powerfully so that she cried out, filling her up with one stroke and then repeating it quickly. His gasping breaths showed his need to have her completely, almost ruthlessly, and Francesca groaned with the onslaught of his bigness and his weight. The breath was jolted out of her with his thrusts and she grew frantic with her own desire. Her fingernails raked his shoulders and back as she lifted her body to him and took his battering wildness. They drove against each other, reaching a desperation that carried them to a volcanic release.

For a moment, at the peak of ecstasy, they clung to each other in a final climactic kiss. The world shattered around them. There had never been anything like it. Then, slowly, Kurt lowered himself, his big body easing to one side against the pillows, hand cupping Francesca's head, his eyes closed. He seemed devastated by the intensity of their lovemaking. Francesca's head drooped against his sun-gilded shoulder, tasting the salt on his skin with languorous lips.

His eyes still closed, he stroked her hair, very peacefully, satiated. He murmured, "Francesca, come to me and be with me always at *Ca'ad Carlo*. I promise you, no one will ever love you like this."

# Chapter Eleven

On the first of August, Buffy Amberson developed nose-bleeds which turned into serious hemorrhages, and beautiful Buffy was panic-stricken. John Turtle drove Francesca over in the rented red Mustang to the Amberson condominium in the exclusive compound of Chantilly on the south part of the island. They found Buffy pacing up and down in the living room, wild-eyed, clutching bloodstained bath towels.

"My God, Buffy," Francesca cried. "For a nosebleed you're supposed to lie down and be quiet. Look at all this mess!"

Buffy looked as though she hadn't heard. "Francesca, I can't pay for any more doctors' bills," she wailed. "I haven't got the money for my damned face! The nose guy at the *Golden Door* says to come on down there and they'll cauterize it and stop the bleeding, but I'm completely out of money!" She grabbed Francesca's arm with bloody fingers. "Oh God, what'll I do if Jock doesn't come back? I'll be out on my ass, like Dorrit! I haven't even got the money to pay the housekeeper this month! Francesca, tell me that he won't stay in Philadelphia with her. Tell me that he won't! Barabara's got all those damned kids, after a while Jock usually wants out so bad he'll buy her anything, a new car, more orthodontics for the brats, anything, just as long as he can come back to Buffy, you know? He will, won't he?" she cried desperately.

Francesca sent John Turtle into the kitchen for some ice cubes while she got Buffy into bed. Then she rolled up the bloodstained towels and took them to the laundry room in back. When she returned, John Turtle had found a rubber ice pack and had filled it with crushed ice. Buffy was holding it to her nose, looking up at the bodyguard with grateful eyes.

When John Turtle went out, Buffy said, "Oh, why couldn't I have met someone like him? Nice teeth, lots of muscles, calm, masterful, sexy—perfect?"

"Because John Turtle hasn't got any money, that's why," Francesca told her. "You wouldn't give him a second look, and you know it."

Buffy said, staring at her, "Francesca, did Kurt really take you out on the *Freya?* He never does, you know. That's the unbroken rule. No women on board. No hanky panky on the sacred boat."

Francesca wiped Buffy's bloody mouth with a clean wet washcloth. "Buffy, how did you know I'd been on the *Freya?* I didn't tell you that."

Buffy stared back at her. "Francesca, for God's sake, half of Palm Beach saw you Thursday afternoon sailing north into Jupiter inlet. Everybody knows the *Freya.* You were standing in the stern holding on to our Viking god with both hands, and everything was very romantic and public and touching. Oh honey," Buffy cried in an anxious voice, "is it really going to be Kurt? Isn't this going awfully fast? Are you really truly sleeping with Carla's third husband that she didn't leave any money to? Oh, wow—that's really going to be very complicated!"

Francesca pressed Buffy back onto the bed. John Turtle had come to stand in the doorway. She knew he had heard every word.

"Tell me, is Kurt all that great?" Buffy cried, holding on to the ice pack with both hands. "Is he going to be worth it, Francesca? Because, you know, they're going to *crucify* you—not for any particular reason, just because it's so—bizarre! After all, how you inherited the money, and now taking over the old husband!"

Francesca met John Turtle's eyes. She saw the most extraordinary expression in them, she couldn't make it out. Then the customary impassivity settled in them, and it was gone.

"Yes, he's great," she said in a steady voice. "Kurt is wonderful. But I haven't made up my mind about anything. I can't." She wanted to avoid using the word *marriage*, it was too soon. "Look, first we have to get you back down to Fort Lauderdale, and let them fix you up. What did they say this morning? Did you talk to the doctor?"

Buffy's voice was nasal, muffled under the ice pack. "Just for me to get the hell down there. But I have to pay for it in advance. Oh, Francesca—"

Francesca patted her arm. "Listen, Buffy, we'll settle when it's all over, right? The only trouble is that you're still having problems with your nose. I'll get my secretary to call and approve another credit line."

"Francesca, they're so damned *tough* about money—"

"I'll fix it," Francesca promised. "We have to have somebody to drive you down. Or do you want to go in an ambulance?"

Buffy shuddered. "Oh God, no. Jock would kill me if he knew I had to be carried out of Chantilly on a stretcher, for any reason! They're so damned particular here, you don't know the background checks we had to go through to be allowed to buy this condo, even for the fortune they wanted for it!" She said, in a low voice, "I'll get Dorrit to drive me down to the *Golden Door*."

Startled, Francesca pulled back from her. "Dorrit? I thought she was in a lot of trouble!"

Buffy said, still muffled, "We're *all* in a lot of trouble, Francesca. What difference does it make?"


THE credit line could not be cleared to allow the doctor in Fort Lauderdale to go ahead with Buffy's treatment. Dorothea Smithson made two lengthy telephone calls to the *Golden Door,* but found them adamant.

"They want you to underwrite the whole thing, obviously," the secretary reported to Francesca. "Instead of just guaranteeing Mrs. Amberson's credit."

"I can't understand what all the fuss is about." Francesca was irritable. "All I hear is how much money is tied up in the Bloodworth fortune, but I can't get the *Golden Door* to give an inch. What's going on?"

Her sandy-haired secretary suppressed a small smile. "I think they know what they're doing. Actually, the worst people in the world to collect from are people with money. They let their unpaid bills drag on for months, they're notorious in that respect. Also, some of the very rich take advantage of their trade. They know it's good advertising and some of them want their bills discounted if they give their business to a certain place. So although it's good publicity to have people like you and all the fat movie actresses in the world patronize the *Golden Door,* customers like Mrs. Amberson don't really count all that much. Am I being delicate enough?"

Francesca said, slowly, "You mean the *Golden Door* knows Buffy hasn't got the money."

"Oh, it's much more than that. I mean the *Golden Door* knows this probably isn't the first time Mrs. Amberson has used a friend to back up her credit when she can't pay off."

"But Buffy says her husband has plenty of money!" Francesca cried. "I don't understand what the problem is."

Francesca called the *Golden Door*'s credit department herself in Fort Lauderdale, but found it difficult to get past the accounts receivable clerk, even when she told them who she was. Everyone was very courteous, but something definitely was wrong. Finally she got the director of the *Golden Door* who told her how wonderful it was to hear from her again, but who was singularly elusive on the subject of Buffy Amberson's medical troubles.

"She's absolutely an adorable person, and we love Mrs. A. dearly, and of course we appreciate she's your friend, Miss Lucchese," he told her. "We've known the Ambersons since Mr. Jock's sister, Mrs. Royce, started coming to us in '72. It's too bad we have this little difficulty now. Frankly, I want you to know why we have to proceed a little cautiously. Let me let you speak to Dr. Von Rauschenberg, he's right here in my office. Dr. Von Rauschenberg was supervising surgeon for Mrs. A's rhinoplasty and reconstruction."

Francesca listened as the doctor's voice droned on with a highly technical account of what he had done to restore Buffy's nose and face three weeks ago.

*"Well?"* her secretary whispered.

Francesca shook her head. They were giving her the runaround, that was plain. She had already decided to pay off all of Buffy's bills and charge it off to friendship: the sight of Buffy struggling all along in her apartment with terrible nosebleeds and no one to help her, had made Francesca very angry—both with the *Golden Door* and their doctors, and with the rotten husband who had smashed up Buffy's beautiful face and then gone off and left her.

The doctor in Fort Lauderdale was saying: "The septum was already partly destroyed, which made the area very vulnerable to the husband's battering. When Dr. Harrison and I went into the nasal passages we saw at once that this latest trauma had put the whole area in a high critical situation and something extensive was indicated, more so than the reconstruction of last year, simply because of the continuing destruction of tissue caused by uninterrupted use of foreign substances. The unfortunate thing about this whole situation is that we warned Mrs. Amberson very specifically what could happen when she had her other operation. We pointed out to her that we were limited as to the number of times we could rebuild the nose and sinuses and still hold the symmetry of the area, or even retain a good color. What you get after too many rhinoplastic constructions is a discoloration called 'cherry ripe' that is very unattractive. The result is one that makes attractive women like Mrs. Amberson very unhappy, and that's what concerns us now, frankly."

"The first time?" Francesca said, puzzled. "You mean Mrs. Amberson's had all this done before?"

There was a pause. The doctor's voice, quite cautious, said, "Miss Lucchese, I discussed all this with your secretary a few days ago when I believe we brought up the subject of liability. There's a large question now as to whether Mrs. Amberson is going to be happy with the outcome of her present reconstruction. This hemorrhaging doesn't make for a very good prognosis. The possibility of litigation—"

"I'll take care of it," Francesca said hastily. "She's not going to sue! Oh, poor Buffy! How bad—" She could hardly bring herself to say the words. "How bad could it get?"

There was another long pause. "I suppose, Miss Lucchese, one could say 'worst case' example would be collapse of the porous bones in the sinus area. They're greatly eroded with cocaine abuse in this subject's case, bringing about a concave condition usually described as 'dish-faced.' At this point, there isn't—"

Francesca held the telephone receiver away from her ear and stared at her secretary. *I don't believe it,* she told herself.

"I see he told you," Dorothea Smithson said. She took the telephone from Francesca's hand, thanked the doctor for his time and assured him a check would be in the mail for the first bill within a few days, and then hung up. "I thought you knew," she said in a low voice. "It was stupid of me not to ask, but I assumed you knew Mrs. Amberson's—ah—problem. She was with you down at the *Golden Door* and I thought you knew why."

Francesca shook her head, disbelieving. "Her husband hit her," was all she could manage.

"I'm sure he did," the secretary said gently. "But that was after. It's called 'the Operation' around here. But they tell me the plastic surgeons are getting pretty unhappy about the numbers of nose reconstruction jobs going right back to their habit within a few weeks, and getting burned-out all over again. The mucous membranes are really very delicate; sniffing cocaine up inside them is just like using a blowtorch after a while."

Francesca sat in a state of shock. *Buffy a cocaine user?* Then how many people that she knew—

It all fell into place. Palm Beach. Drugs. The sensational divorce trials of past years. How could she have been so stupid? She had been so involved with herself, and the transition from the Frannie that was, to the Francesca of now, that she hadn't paid enough attention to what was going on around her.

"How widespread is it?" Francesca said. She shook her head, dazed. "I mean—"

"How many people that we know use cocaine?" the secretary said. She stood with her hands on her hips, looking at Francesca quizzically. "Who knows? It's just like your kids and drugs—it's hard to find out. But you'd be surprised how many smart and sensible people are into cocaine. Sometimes I think this country's gone a little crazy. At some Palm Beach parties they put it out in a bowl like candy, with a sniffer spoon to help yourself. Of course, it's fantastically expensive—that's what makes it so fashionable, and it's easy enough to get in Florida where the boats bring it right in from South America. If you want coke you can get it at the service station when you gas up the car, at the hairdresser, or the boy who cuts the lawn will sell it to you. All you've got to know is the right way to ask for it. The young crowd here are the big users, they do it now with, or instead of, marijuana, but the middle-aged crowd is coming up fast, the jet set that was into hashish just a few years ago."

Francesca rubbed her hands through her hair helplessly. It was all so bizarre. Boston seemed very safe and far away. "Why? *Why?*" she wanted to know. "What's so good about it if it costs so much, and it's so bad for you?"

The secretary studied Francesca for a moment. "You're sure you don't know?" she said softly. When Francesca shook her head, she said, "It makes life more interesting. Of course here, in Palm Beach, life is terribly insular and isolated and dull in spite of all the money. You can play tennis and bridge just so long, and then that's it. Then there's sex. Cocaine makes sex an incredible trip, and everybody does it good for a change when they're on coke. Do you follow me? You can be absolutely tremendous in the sack with a little coke, and couple of pops of cantharides or an ampule of amyl nitrate to send you right through the roof. Some people take a couple of days off and never get out of bed, four or five of them to a coke session."

In spite of herself, Francesca started to laugh. "You're making it up," she said, disbelieving.

"Okay, I'm making it up," the secretary said. "I felt that way, too, when they told me about it." She turned back to her desk. "It's really a shame about Mrs. Amberson's face. She's so very beautiful."

Francesca leaned her head on her hand, elbow propped on her desk, and stared down at the blotter. She knew she really believed the things Dorothea Smithson had told her, believed them without fully comprehending them. Cocaine and sex? It sounded incredible, and yet sensuous love was a mystery, as she was finding out; one that could drag you into its vortex and oblivion with a few seconds' drugging kisses. The incredible feelings that lovemaking with Kurt

aroused in her were feelings that she had never imagined
herself having. And now, she found, she was shameless in
pursuit of desire. The things she had done still sent a hot
wave of blood to her face, thinking about them. Could she
really condemn anyone, then?

But the depression hung on. Poor Buffy. She couldn't
imagine Buffy with her lovely face a collapsed ruin. "Dish-
faced," the doctor had called it. The rotten husband would
never have anything to do with her if that were the case.

Francesca shuffled through the pile of mail in front of
her without paying much attention to what she was doing.
The top sheet of the stack was partly unfolded. Even before
she opened it, Francesca knew that something was wrong.
What ordinarily she would have been prevented from seeing
was printed in cut-out words from newspapers:

ASK YOUR *boy*friend HOw *CARla* DIED

"Oh my God!" Dorothea Smithson cried. She pulled the
small pile of envelopes out from under Francesca's hand,
spilling all of them in the process. They both bent to pick
them up from the floor.

"You're not supposed to see this stuff! How did it get
on your desk? Oh, my dear—" She stared into Francesca's
eyes in genuine dismay. "You never want too see crank
mail, take my word for it! Thank God these are not too bad.
They're not obscene, I mean."

Francesca was still reacting to the initial shock. She held
the letter she had picked up from the mail pile. "How many
of these have you seen?" she said slowly, holding it out.

"I don't know, honey," Dorothea cried. "Actually I try
not to look at these things if I can help it, I turn them over
to John." She pulled the letter from Francesca's fingers.
"Ugh," she said, glancing at it. "I don't think I've seen one
like that before, with newspaper words. Don't take any of
this stuff seriously, will you? It will give you nightmares,
I've seen people crack up under the pressure. It's very

worrisome to see how sick some people can be. But believe me, most of it comes to nothing."

Francesca stared down at the pale green blotter on her new desk with unseeing eyes. It occurred to her that, weeks ago, having all the Bloodworth money was a fantastic dream come true. Or so she had thought.

"I don't think this one is sick," she murmured. "I think I have somebody who really hates me."

Francesca was still upset when she called Herb Ostrow to offer her apologies for not keeping her date with him at the Palm Beach Country Club Thursday evening.

"I went for a sail," Francesca said, knowing how inadequate it sounded. She was aware that by this time Herb Ostrow knew with whom she had gone sailing. "I forgot our date until the last moment. I'm sorry, that's the truth, it sounds pretty stupid, I know. Please forgive me." She could tell she wasn't making it any better. "I hope you didn't wait for me too long."

"As a matter of fact, I waited three hours." The writer's voice was cool. "I was sure something had happened to you. An automobile accident, among other things. I called the main house number several times and finally I got your bodyguard on the line and he told me you'd gone sailing and apparently had forgotten our date. It didn't matter by then, I assure you. I was bombed out of my mind by eight o'clock sitting at the bar in the country club. When I heard it was Kurt Bergstrom you were with, naturally I knew it was all worthwhile," he ended sarcastically.

"I'd like to explain," Francesca said, aware no explanation was acceptable.

He interrupted her. "May I say something to you, Francesca? I don't think you're aware of the impact you've made on all of us. On me. The Bloodworth money has nothing to do with it. You're beautiful, and you're desirable. You see, I'm laboring under the disadvantage of having to adore you from afar. And believe me, it's a hell of a disadvantage when I don't know the back end of a sailing boat from the front. Which is going to be a handicap after Thursday night's events—and after you've gone straight into someone else's arms. Do you follow what I'm saying?"

Francesca's face was suddenly burning. Of course people knew she had been with Kurt Bergstrom. And that probably they had made love. That conclusion was inevitable. And now here was Herb Ostrow blurting it out.

"How do I woo you, lady?" his voice went on angrily. "That is, how do I eliminate what I'm told is unbeatable competition? How do I tell you that you're the most impossibly beautiful and fascinating woman I've ever met?" He paused, then he continued desperately, "Apparently from your silence, I don't. So just forget I said all this."

"Herb," Francesca began. She didn't know what she was going to say. His words had appalled her. This distinguished middle-aged man was in love with her? She couldn't deal with it.

But he went on, "Look, I do want to say one thing, Francesca, and a lot of fairly disinterested parties join me in this request—that is, people you don't know, but who have a good idea what's going on. Who remember a lot of things that have happened at *Ca'ad Carlo.* Which is, Don't trust the people around you. Will you take that advice seriously?"

The writer's voice was full of pain. Francesca wanted to reassure him although she wasn't quite sure how. God knows, she thought, she wasn't interested in Herb Ostrow. There was room for only one man in her life.

"Herb, you asked me about the Bloodworth family records." She plunged ahead with the abrupt change of subject. "About looking into the Bloodworth family correspondence, whatever's in the files in the old office. The Foundation says you can have access to anything you want, just so long as I give you written permission, which I'm glad to do. Do you want to come by and have a drink, or do you want me to mail a letter of permission to you? If you come by we can go down to the office bungalow, they're finishing the painting now, and we can look at the file cabinets together."

There was a prolonged silence. Finally the writer said, "Do you really want to do this, Francesca? You're not just throwing me a few crumbs, are you? Forgive me, but I guess I want you to say that it's not the Bloodworth papers you find interesting for an hour or so, but me."

Francesca, feeling torn, said, "Oh please, Herb, of course I want to do this." She gave a self-conscious laugh. "Since there aren't any Bloodworth survivors, I suppose we're free to take a look. We'll sit down and read everybody's juicy scandals, and secrets."

"This week." He was insistent. "Don't back out on me, Francesca, will you? Let's make it as soon as possible."

"Well, give me a day or two," she said. "I have to ask my secretary to get all the file cabinet keys and everything else we might need. Such as where all these things are stored. I'll get back to you, or I'll have Dorothea call you." She knew this sounded high-handed and tried to modify it. "That's all right, isn't it? To have her give you a message?"

She thought he sighed. "You let me know," he said.


FRANCESCA told herself that it was nobody's business if she had taken a cruise with Kurt Bergstrom, Carla's widower, and they had made love. It did not dispel her uneasiness. She wasn't behaving discreetly, that was obvious. But there was only one layer of Palm Beach that knew, or cared, she told herself. There were other stratas out there—the boy who bagged Delia Mary's groceries in the Publix supermarket on the island, the chauffeurs who stood by their Rolls-Royces in front of the Palm Beach Hotel while waiting for lunch to end, the pipeline among the servants—who probably didn't know her or care one way or the other.

In the beginning she had told herself that Palm Beach would never accept Giovanni Lucchese's daughter no matter how hard she tried, and she wasn't going to let it bother her. Now, she knew, she wanted to be in the right, although she wasn't sure why. She had gone into Kurt Bergstrom's arms eagerly, blissfully, in the kind of happiness she had never known existed. It was not wrong. Not ugly. Whatever gossip swirled about Carla's former husband, or about her, it was not true.

As she lay in Kurt's arms in his cottage, Francesca said, "Have you ever been to dinner at Jinkie's? What's it like?"

He smiled his slow smile, looking down at her naked body curled against his side. "Very big house. Lots of good food. Lots of people who don't know each other."

Francesca laughed. His terse descriptions were always accurate, often funny. She was restless, and he sensed it. She wanted to go somewhere with him. She wanted people to see them together and know how happy they were. She persuaded him to go with her to Jinkie's.

Oak Haven was the largest estate on the north end of the island. No official information on the house had ever been made public, but educated guesses placed Jinkie's Mediterranean villa at eighty rooms, not including two swimming pools and the extensive squash facilities. The grounds were as extensive and well-kept as a municipal park, and terraces and walkways in the back of the main house led down to a large private boat basin on the bay side where Jinkie's current yacht, an impressive 92-foot motor launch named the Ne'er Do Well, was moored. Guests for dinner could stroll, drinks in hand, from the terrace of the main house down to the boat basin where a small bar had been set up in the yacht's stern. There they could get another drink and explore the luxury craft before returning to the house.

Francesca had dressed rather carefully for dinner at Jinkie's, knowing the sort of attention she and Kurt would receive. She wore a green floor-length silk dress shot with gold, exotic and summery, with heavy gold earrings which set off her brunette beauty. Kurt Bergstrom wore a white dinner jacket, tuxedo shirt and navy trousers. They were among the few guests properly attired for a summer dinner party at eight. There were at least two women in slacks, and most of the men wore business suits. One man, introduced as Jinkie's investment broker from New York, had misjudged Palm Beach summer custom by a mile—he appeared in Bermuda shorts, a plaid jacket and a tieless blue shirt. Jinkie himself wore a very correct dinner jacket with a dark red cummerbund and navy trousers—a small man with an ageless boy's face and with an air of one who does not really know what he's wearing, as someone has put him into his clothes in the first place, and sent him on his way.

A battalion of young servants moved smoothly through the guests. Dinner for over forty people at Jinkie's was a buffet served on a vast, glassed-in porch frigid with air conditioning that overlooked the floodlit boat basin and the lights of Lake Worth. But the atmosphere was impersonal; it might have been dinner hour at the Palm Beach Country Club or a local restaurant. And, Francesca saw, Kurt had been right: none of the guests seemed to know each other very well. Two tall men in gray business suits were members of Jinkie's law firm in San Francisco who had flown in that afternoon with details of a land purchase. They were interested only in talking to three young men who were developing miniscule parcels of land still left on the island, which went for fabulous sums. A deeply tanned couple from Australia were people Jinkie had met on a Qantas flight into Singapore several years ago. Francesca recognized the diet doctor, Bernard Binns, and his companion, Elsa MacLemore. Francesca slid away through the crowd before they could find her. Buffy kept Francesa too well supplied with news of the internationally famous Binns-MacLemore Clinic in West Palm Beach. In addition to his diet book, Dr. Binns specialized in vitamin shots that most Palm Beach clients swore by. In fact, presidents of the United States and members of Congress had been Dr. Binns's customers at one time, earning him the name of "Dr. Feelgood" before he abruptly left Washington.

"What a strange group of friends," Francesca murmured to Kurt as they stood having their drinks on the stern of the *Ne'er Do Well*.

He was leaning his arms on the rail, his big shoulders in the white dinner jacket hunched, looking off toward the lights of West Palm Beach across the water. He turned his blond head and gave her a slow smile. "Very rich people don't have friends," he said softly. "Only people they know."

Francesca put her elbows on the rail beside him, shoulders almost touching. "I'm a very rich people," she murmured. "I have friends."

His look was direct. "You're only beginning," he said.

After dinner Francesca talked to a rather nervous young redhaired man who had just sold Jinkie a Bentley sports car. He had a roguish grin. "Tell me," he said to her, "if you sell a car to this guy Jinkie, does he always invite you to dinner?"

Francesca couldn't say. She was watching Kurt Bergstrom standing in the middle of Oak Haven's back lawn, his big blond head bent attentively to the swarm of women around him. She put her arm through that of the young sports car salesman and strolled along the boat basin with him. Old-fashioned light globes on concrete pillars illuminated the walkway. Kurt Bergstrom was the most handsome man in Palm Beach, Francesca was sure. And this was where she wanted to be. Satisfied and happy. In love. Dinner at Jinkie's, the huge white yacht tied up at its berth in the boat basin, uniformed servants serving after-dinner drinks, the dark sea, the murmur of voices and laughter.

"I don't know, I've never sold a car to Jinkie," Francesca said.

The young salesman laced his fingers through hers intimately and gave them a squeeze. His other hand held a joint between thumb and forefinger; between deep inhales he kept his hand cupped around it. His eyes had begun to go a little murky. "This blond guy isn't your husband, is he?" Without waiting for Francesca's answer he said, "Listen, you're absolutely knocking me out, I could make tonight very interesting for you. The most. Anything you want, you beautiful thing. Leave the blond guy here and let me show you, okay?"

Francesca couldn't help smiling. "No," she said, shaking her head.

"Okay." He shrugged. "So bring him along. We can do it that way, the three of us. I go with combinations. I'm broadminded."

Francesca threw back her head and laughed. He stopped, and looked at her as though she were crazy. *Ah, Palm Beach*, she thought.

Nothing could mar her happiness.

# 3

## THE HOUSE OF FRANCESCA

# CHAPTER TWELVE

AT 2 A.M. the telephone rang in the bedroom of the guest bungalow. Jarred from sleep, Francesca stirred against the warm, big body of the man who held her and felt the immediate, wakeful tightening of his arms.

"What?" Kurt murmured against her lips.

The insistent drilling of the telephone bell could only mean some sort of emergency. Whoever was on duty at that hour had to know where Francesca was, to find her. As it kept ringing the only thing she could think of was Buffy Amberson in Fort Lauderdale and that something terrible had happened at the *Golden Door*. She reached out an arm to lift the receiver but Kurt had already taken it.

"*Ja?*" he said softly.

He sat up and swung his legs over the edge of the bed. Francesca watched the satiny ripples of the muscles in his back as he moved to throw the covers away from him. It wasn't about Buffy; the call was for him. Naked, his golden body glistening in the half-light, he sat with a frown on his face and listened. Finally he responded in a Chinese-sounding tongue and hung up.

Still turned away from her, he said, "She has shot and killed him," in a flat voice. "That damned woman."

Francesca sat up quickly. "Shot who?"

He reached for his underwear briefs. "This woman who lives with Bernie Binns. She found him in bed with some girl and shot him until she emptied the clip of the gun into him. It was no accident, she wanted to kill him. She is at the jail, now."

"Elsa MacLemore shot the diet doctor?" Francesca said incredulously.

He was on his feet, stepping into his slacks. "About three or four hours ago." He zipped up his fly, his face preoccupied. "Francesca, quick, put on your clothes. I have to see some friends at once."

"At this hour?" It was the middle of the night. Then she remembered in the middle of the night in Palm Beach meant nothing. "You're going to see Angel, aren't you?"

She had found that Kurt made mysterious trips to see Angel; once or twice Angel, but not Cassie, had been at Kurt's cottage, always leaving after a few minutes, never spending much time to visit.

He found his sailing jersey and pulled it over his head. "Come, I want you to get your clothes on and go up to the house and call Dorothea to come to *Ca'ad Carlo*. Don't do it here," he said as she reached for the bedside phone. "Do it at the big house. But wake her up, she will know this is important. Tell her that you know Binns and the woman, but that you have not been to the clinic. Be sure you tell her you haven't been to the clinic. And that he has prescribed nothing for you, but maybe you are on their mailing lists." He looked up at her quickly, blue eyes darting cold brilliance. "The clinic sent you some mail, right?"

Francesca scrambled out of bed. She was naked, she

looked like a tawny gypsy with her magnificent breasts and tiny waist and sumptuous bottom. She didn't know what was going on, but she caught his great urgency. "I got a notice from the Binns Clinic about office hours, that was all."

He smoothed back his longish gold hair hurriedly with both hands. "Yes, then he has your name in his files. So tell Dorothea that you want to take a flight out this morning, and that she is to book you in a hotel someplace for a week, maybe more. Is your passport current? Can you go to London?"

Francesca stared at him. He didn't look at her, he was rummaging through dresser drawers.

"Why do I have to go anyplace?" she wanted to know. "I haven't done anything! I don't know these people, I've never been to this man's clinic. I haven't even read his diet book!"

"Ah, yes, the diet book," he said, looking about the room. "So many people have read the diet book. This will make a big scandal."

Francesca found her bra and pulled it on, and then her panties. It was hard to realize it was only a little after two in the morning. And that she was in Kurt's bungalow, that they had been sleeping peacefully in each other's arms until the fateful shrilling of the telephone.

"What are we doing all this for?" she cried. "Why have I got to call Dorothea at this hour of the night? And I can't go to London! I don't even have a passport!"

He was swiftly packing a sea bag of blue nylon. He threw some bath articles on top of his clothes and pulled the drawstring. He stood back and looked around the room once more.

He said, almost casually, "Francesca, if anything happens to me, I wish you to have the picture of the Viking longship burial. It is on the wall in the other room."

"What?" Aghast, she stopped what she was doing, her arms half into her silk shirt.

But when he turned to her, she saw his handsome face was quite serious. "And the prow of the longship. Would you like that?"

"What's the matter?" she cried. "What is all this about? It's more than Bernie Binns, isn't it? More than Elsa shooting him?"

But he had turned away again to the closet, pulling out his yellow southwester rain slicker. He tossed it on top of the sea bag.

"I am going away," he said. "I am taking the *Freya*. It will be a week, maybe more, before I get back." He looked at her and saw that she was only half dressed. His eyes widened. "What are you waiting for?"

Francesca couldn't find her silk slacks, the ones she had worn for dinner. She felt only half awake and filled with a curious, indefinable alarm. What was so important about the diet doctor's death that someone had to call *Ca'ad Carlo*, Kurt Bergstrom's bungalow, in the middle of the night? Someone who knew the unlisted telephone numbers. Someone who could converse in something sounding like Chinese.

"I want you to tell me what this is all about," she demanded. "Why do I have to leave town? What's the panic all about? Is there something I should know?"

Now he stopped and turned to her, impatiently. But he said in a voice so low Francesca could hardly make it out, "The less you know the better it is, Francesca. For all of us."

She cried, "Why are you going away, too? You didn't know these people, did you?"

He made a click of irritation with his teeth. "Look," he said, "nobody stays around when there is a murder, right? Even a stupid woman shooting her lover. The police will investigate. They will want to know who her friends are, and his, and her lawyer will want witnesses. They will go after everybody." He waited while she sat down on the bed and pulled on her high-heeled sandals. "Nobody needs to be here in Palm Beach while this is going on, Francesca.

Not you, not me, not anybody who ever knew Bernie and little Elsa, talked to them, went to their clinic. Anybody. Do you understand?"

She shook her head. She knew he wasn't telling her everything, she could feel it. She said, "Why can't I go with you? I can help sail, can't I? Where are you taking the *Freya?*"

"No," was all he said, to all of it. But he pulled her to her feet and kissed her.


THE secretary, Dorothea Smithson, arrived at *Ca'ad Carlo* a little after four a.m. It was still dark in the night sky, but the main house was ablaze with lights. Kurt Bergstrom was gone, having taken the Porsche to the marina where the *Freya* was docked. John Turtle, alerted by Larry, the night security guard, had materialized with amazing speed when Francesca returned to her room. Delia Mary was up and fixing breakfast. And Mrs. Schoener, in a crisp pink maid's uniform but in bedroom slippers she had forgotten, rushed in to draw Francesca's bath.

They were packing. To go somewhere. The airlines telephone lines were jammed, even at that hour, with Palm Beach residents making the same arrangements. Dorothea Smithson was setting up a schedule for a visit to New York and the Bloodworth Foundation offices. She had taken the news of the diet doctor's murder calmly. But when Francesca told her of Kurt's suggestion they take a short trip away, the sandy-haired woman shot her a sharp look, then pursed her lips in a silent whistle.

"What is it?" Francesca cried in exasperation. "What does everybody else around here know but me?"

"Not know," the secretary said. "*Guesses.* Nobody knows what went on at Doctor Binns's clinic, do they? So what you have is not all that bad a rule to follow: when anything happens you want to be able to say that you were out of town."

"But I hardly knew these people! I haven't done anything!"

"You may not have known them, but apparently they knew you. That makes a difference," the secretary said calmly. She began emptying out the drawers in Francesca's desk and putting the contents in several attaché cases. "Don't forget, you're the Bloodworth fortune, now. Every time your name is in the papers the stockholders are going to see it and want to know why. Ever hear of the saying, 'Discretion is the better part of valor'? Well, Harry Stillman brought you down here to learn it, among other things. It means get out of town when anything happens."

"I don't believe it," Francesca said, looking around the bedroom. It was a shambles. Anyone would think she was the criminal fleeing from justice. No one paid any attention to her. Mrs. Schoener was busy in the wardrobe closets, selecting outfits suitable for July in New York. The night security man had already carried down several packed suitcases. Francesca had the distinct impression she knew less about what was going on than even the staff at *Ca' ad Carlo*.

Francesca sat down to her tray of breakfast brought by Delia Mary. It was almost dawn. The telephone started ringing. She took the receiver handed to her by the cook and tucked it under her chin so that she could butter her toast.

The urbane voice of Herb Ostrow said in her ear, "I see you've heard. About Elsa, I mean. I had a hell of a time getting through to you. You've got some kind of Gestapo officer who answers the telephone over there. But I figured you'd be up."

"What's it all about, Herb?" she cried. The words just came tumbling out. "Do you know what we're doing over here? I'm getting ready to leave town! I can't believe it!"

"Where is Kurt?" the writer's voice said very quickly.

"Gone off on the *Freya*. I can't believe that, either! Has everybody gone crazy? I'm going to New York for a special meeting of the board of directors of the Bloodworth Foundation, but they won't know about it until I get there! I've got an eight a.m. flight into Jacksonville, it was all we could get. Would you believe all the charter jets at the Palm Beach airport were taken by two a.m. this morning? What happened? Does anybody know?" Francesca cried.

"She shot him. Elsa shot him," he said. "That for starters. Apparently she and Bernie had been fighting for days, it was quite a mess. Actually, Elsa just seems to have had a series of crises with Bernie that went on until she reached the end of her rope. He was going for younger women and she'd been putting up money for him for years, helping him get his diet book published, footing the bills for the lecture tours, financing the clinic in West Palm." The writer sighed. "You know Bernie was under a cloud. I guess you know that by now, since the federal investigations a year ago about his megavitamin shots that allegedly were boosted with a load of amphetamines. You could lose a lot of weight that way, they tell me. As well as lose your mind."

"Oh," Francesca said. Things were coming together now. Buffy Amberson's remark about going to the *Golden Door* in Fort Lauderdale rather than Dr. Binns's Palm Beach clinic. That it was hard to stop going to Bernard Binns's clinic even after you'd lost weight. Francesca dropped her voice to say, "Herb, what are you going to do? You knew them, didn't you?"

She heard him laugh. "I'm a working writer, lady. I can't leave town when something like this pops. I've already been down to the West Palm Beach slammer tonight while they were booking Elsa, in hopes of getting a word with her. She looked like hell, incidentally. I'd like to do a magazine interview because this is going to be a big story. A lot of people have read Bernie's book, a lot remember him from his Washington days as 'Dr. Feelgood.' Besides, I don't need to leave town. I don't belong to that part of Palm Beach that's rich or important enough to matter. Which brings us back to you. You're not going to stay out of town long, are you? We have a date to go over the Bloodworth archives."

The secretary had come in, signalling that she had another

call waiting. Francesca said, "Oh, Herb, it won't be long, I promise," and then the connection was broken.

Buffy Amberson's voice suddenly said, "Damn, Francesca—your line's been busy as hell! Everybody in Palm Beach is on the telephone and it isn't even dawn, yet, isn't that hysterical? Nobody answers at Jinkie's. He was probably one of the first ones out. He's got his own damned Lear jet."

"Buffy," Francesca cried. "Where are you? Are you in Fort Lauderdale? Dr. Rauschenberg—"

"Francesca, *listen!*" Buffy yelled. "Cripes, I've been running with all my luggage—would you believe?—to catch this plane! They're boarding now, I haven't got time to talk! But I wanted you to know that I called Jock and we both think we ought to take a little time away from Palm Beach with all this going on, you know? Jock thinks Elsa's trial is going to be a big media event since Bernie's book was a bestseller and all that. Although my God—" Buffy's voice screamed into the telephone lines, "Who would have thought of creepy little Elsa *shooting Bernie dead!* And now she gets the whole nine yards, nationwide publicity, time on the witness stand to tell how she did it, what Bernie was doing besides his clinic, which I think was just a cover for—"

"You can't leave the *Golden Door!*" Francesca was yelling now, too. "What about—"

She wanted to say what about Buffy's face, but the other woman apparently didn't want to hear her, for through loud background noise Buffy went on, "Francesca, why do you suppose she did it? They say she emptied the whole gun into him, they say he didn't have a chance! But Jock says he always thought Elsa was the type, you know, putting up with all that screwing actually going on in the office, and people calling him for those fake vitamin shots. Precious, I've got to run," Buffy cried abruptly. "You should see the line of people getting on this damned Eastern flight, and at this time in the morning! It looks like half the Beach is going." There was only the slightest pause. "I'll have to get back to you about the bill for my face fix and nose job later. Rauschenberg did a great job, it's too bad you can't see it. That's all right, isn't it? Bye-bye, I've got to go!"

There was a click as the connection was broken. While Francesca still stared at it, a thoughtful expression on her face, Dorothea Smithson bent over her to say, "I can get nonstop into New York out of Jacksonville, but there are only two first-class seats, so I'll sit in coach." She met Francesca's uncomprehending look with a shrug. "Your bodyguard, remember?"

Francesca sighed.

THE story of the murder was in the New York newspapers when they arrived at Kennedy Airport a little before noon. The New York *Times* featured the story discreetly on page five, but ran a recent picture of Bernie Binns holding a copy of his book, *The Binns Wonder Weight Loss Plan*. The New York *Daily News* ran a front-page banner headline which proclaimed *Mistress Kills Diet Doctor*. The New York *Post* had reached the newsstands by the time Francesca, her secretary and bodyguard had threaded their way through the corridors of Kennedy air terminal. The *Post* showed a front-page photograph of Elsa MacLemore, looking disheveled and wild-eyed, being led down a corridor of the Palm Beach County jail to be booked on a murder charge. The *Post* hinted that it was Elsa who had done most of the writing on *The Binns Wonder Weight Loss Plan*, while allowing the diet doctor to take all the credit.

"But he was such an ugly little man," Francesca marveled. "Now they might give her the chair—right?"

The New York *Times* also reprinted excerpts from the transcript of the Federal Food and Drug Administration hearing on Dr. Binns's megavitamin shots that had taken place several years ago in Washington, D.C. The *Times* also noted an announced investigation of Dr. Binns's Palm Beach clinic by Florida State Drug Control investigators.

Dorothea passed the newspaper, open to that item, back to Francesca.

"New York is going to look awfully good for a while," the secretary said cryptically.

# CHAPTER THIRTEEN

THE FIVE-room suite at New York's elegant Plaza Hotel was serviced by its own elevator, assuring maximum privacy for the heiress to the Bloodworth fortune and her party. An assistant manager of the Plaza, a good-looking blond young man with an upper-class British accent, greeted Francesca briefly, welcoming her to the Prince Otto Suite and the hospitality of a waiting bottle of Moët champagne in its silver ice bucket, a tin of Beluga caviar in a bed of crushed ice and enormous bouquets of roses and chrysanthemums throughout the rooms.

Outside, the city burned in the hot August sun. Inside, all was elegance and a haven of cool comfort, although the telephones began ringing immediately. Francesca's visit to New York, while unannounced, nevertheless deserved the greatest priority treatment possible in the structures of Bloodworth's, Inc. The chairman of the board of directors of the Bloodworth Foundation was out of town but he was flying to New York at once and would be there when Miss Lucchese visited Foundation offices. The chairman's office called Dorothea Smithson repeatedly, setting up and revising Francesca's schedules for the coming week. The entire Bloodworth corporation wished to go on record as being delighted to have Miss Lucchese in New York to visit headquarters.

"Hysterical is more like it," the secretary said to Francesca. "It's roaring chaos today over at 531 Third Avenue, you can bet on it."

"They must think we're crazy," Francesca said, "to be descending on them like this without any advance notice."

"Not the way the MacLemore case is breaking in Palm Beach. I think we're going to get points for getting out of there fast."

For once Dorothea Smithson was wrong. If their sudden appearance in New York to escape the sudden glare of publicity now focused unpleasantly on Palm Beach had created confusion in the Bloodworth corporate structures, it was carefully concealed. Instead, within an amazingly short time an agenda—obviously culled from the regular ones for visiting VIPs—appeared. Bloodworth's, Incorporated opened itself up for Francesca's inspection as if for visiting royalty. But the schedule was staggering. *If you want to look at us,* the company seemed to say, *you're going to have to do it all.*

Francesca, accompanied by Dorothea Smithson and John Turtle, began an arduous two-day briefing and tour of Bloodworth's, from the glass-enclosed four-story lobby with its live plants and trees extending fifty to a hundred feet in the air, to the walnut-paneled sanctuary of the board room of the Foundation. Francesca toured every office. As she was guided through the stock control section of the Blo-Co discount stores division at New York headquarters, some of the data processing clerks, most of them young women her age, climbed on the desks and chairs at the back of the room to get a better look at Francesca.

"They think you're really going to assume control of the company," Dorothea murmured to her. "Look at their faces."

Self-consciously, Francesca looked, and then inwardly cringed. She hadn't planned to promise more than she had any intention of delivering. But a thought nagged away in a small corner of her mind. Women never had any hopes of this kind, and she wouldn't allow herself to think in those terms. Still, she had an MBA, her master's in business administration. Francesca turned and looked back before going out the exit doors and to the freight elevators in the back of the building. Dorothea had been right—women were standing on the desks to get a better look at her.

On the rest of the tour of Bloodworth's, Francesca was well aware of her isolation. It was easier for management levels to deal with her in this way, she was sure; no one expected her to have any real interest in the company. When she asked questions she was given booklets to read. Once in a while an eager young middle-management-level person, always a man, responded to her, but he was nearly always whisked away to be replaced with an older person in authority, who saw that she moved on to her next scheduled appointment.

"How do you break through this?" Francesca asked Dorothea Smithson in exasperation.

There was sympathy in the other woman's eyes. "I don't think you do. You're not supposed to have any real interest in this, and besides, you're a woman. I think you're just supposed to pay attention when the chairman of the board tells you how stunning you are, and the vice-chairman can't take his eyes off your boobies. Don't you want all that?"

"Are you kidding?" Francesca shot her a lightning look from stormy gray eyes. "You know, I'm beginning to feel I might make something of this—the reason I went to night school to get my master's, but it doesn't look as though it will open up to anybody now, does it? This trip really brings back all sorts of familiar feelings. It's as though I'm coming back to the same grind, where I used to work overtime without getting paid for it, and there still isn't any way to open the door, to find out how to get inside of the system. And yet here I am—I've inherited this, I'm sitting on top of the whole structure, watching it work as though I'd never been a part of this very same kind of machine! It's very frustrating."

The secretary was watching her keenly. "You like it, don't you? What do you want to do about it?"

Francesca took her full lower lip between white, even teeth and thought for a long moment.

"The question is whether I *can* do anything about Bloodworth's, even if I wanted to."


DOROTHEA Smithson was not invited to lunch in the Bloodworth Foundation's corporate dining room. Secretaries never were; to have Dorothea with her, the chairman explained to Francesca, was to establish a precedent. Or, as one board member put it, if one secretary were allowed in, then all the Foundation secretaries would want to accompany their bosses inside, too.

When they retired to the executive restroom to freshen up, Dorothea explained to Francesca that the real reason women had never been present in the executive dining room was revealed in the history of Bloodworth's, Inc. There had been no movement to exclude women as such, it was simply that company executives and majority stockholders had always been male. The lone exception, Carla Bloodworth, had never been interested enough in the company to challenge it. Carla had never visited the New York offices, preferring to draw her share of profits from abroad or when she was in residence in Palm Beach.

The secretary assured Francesca she was going to be adequately taken care of. "I'm going to lunch with the administrative assistant to the chairman of the board. They used to be called 'executive secretaries' in the old days—

now note 'administrative assistant.' And some of the lower-management-level women are coming, too. Mostly office supervisors."

The executive restroom was furnished in fruitwood cabinet work with Morocco leather trim; the tile and plumbing fixtures matched the color scheme. The doors to the toilet booths were decorated with hunting scenes. A large triple urinal in beige ceramic stood next to the washbasins.

"You mean all the girls are going to get lunch on the house?" Francesca said, studying the urinal's gleaming surfaces.

Dorothea laughed. "The company's making the grand gesture, so we can't complain, can we? We're going to one of the best and most expensive restaurants in New York, the *Four Seasons*. We'll probably eat better than you do."

Francesca said, her eyes still on the urinal, "Do you have the feeling that we're not exactly at home in these surroundings?" She looked in the mirror over the washbasin at her secretary. Francesca was wearing a severely-tailored gray silk summerweight suit with man-tailored white shirt, but she wasn't projecting the right image, still. The board members were overwhelming her with compliments and small talk of the type reserved for gorgeous young women, and not really listening to what she had to say. "Nobody ever gave old Chuckie Bloodworth the *women's restroom* to use, I'll bet you!" she burst out.

Francesca was holding her purse flacon of Halston in her hand. Dorothea Smithson reached over deliberately and pulled her hand down, tilting the bottle.

"Let's give them something to remember us by," the secretary murmured wickedly.

The Halston poured down the side of the urinal in a golden stream, toward the drain. The reek of the expensive perfume rose up powerfully, filling the room with a choking scent.

"Is that what you call the 'woman's touch'?" Francesca said.

They both burst into gales of muffled laughter.

"We're acting like idiots," the secretary said.

"Let's get out of here," Francesca told her. "I can't breathe."


John Turtle handled the matter of his presence in the executive dining room by simply going ahead of Francesca as he always did. A place was made for him hurriedly, two settings down on her left.

Francesca knew her bodyguard's move had been deliberate. There was no real reason for her to have a bodyguard in the executive dining room, except that John Turtle's presence helped to underline the pecking order of corporate structures: he was a part of *her* group and, as an employee of the majority stockholder, attached to her power. Also, John Turtle was a man, and tough. People at the Bloodworth Foundation treated him with unusual deference, she noted, even though he was only a hired security guard.

John Turtle had a certain something, Francesca thought, leaning forward to see him at his place at the table on her left. People didn't fool around with him. She saw he was making a very hearty lunch of veal *Normande,* Chateau Rothschilde-Salky 1974, potatoes *escalope,* salad, peas in butter sauce, and assorted hot rolls. Francesca sighed. Not many people could eat the way John Turtle did, either, and still be whipcord lean, slim-hipped and move like a jungle cat.

She saw, surprised, that dressed as he was, neat in his black three-piece business suit, his good-looking face set in his usual rigid, impassive expression, that he could, in present company, pass for another top-level executive—an unusually tough-looking one.

Luncheon was served by four waiters, middle-aged men in morning clothes who looked as though they had been serving Bloodworth's executive dining-room lunches for decades. The food was exceptional. Francesca had been told the Foundation employed quite a famous French chef and paid him a small fortune for the menu produced solely for the corporate dining room. The tower room, where meals were served, was furnished in walnut paneling and featured a beautiful Hamadan Persian rug. An almost priceless Tintoretto from the Bloodworth Collection hung on the wall, as well as yet another copy of the familiar full-length portrait of Charles D. Bloodworth, Sr. Francesca couldn't help but be curious about the cost of maintaining the corporate dining room for the eleven members of the board of directors of the Bloodworth Foundation, and the eight or so heads of Bloodworth divisions. Especially since she had learned that the salaries paid Bloodworth retail sales clerks, ninety percent of whom were women, were only a few cents above minimum-wage scale.

The chairman of the board leaned to Francesca and said, "With a little more advance notice, Miss Lucchese, we could have shown you a very nice film on employee services here at Bloodworth's. It gives a very comprehensive idea of our lounges, employee cafeterias, handball courts, and squash facilities on the 9th floor, as well as the glee club—"

"Oh, we can watch it after lunch, can't we?" Francesca said very calmly. She declined a helping of Cherries Jubilee the waiter was serving. "Don't you have a screen here in the dining room where you can show film?"

Her guess was right. After a moment's consternation, someone went off to order the film sent up to the executive dining room. Several board members, visibly irritated, rose to use the telephones in the anteroom to shift their afternoon appointments. Francesca became aware that John Turtle was watching her. The black eyes showed more than their usual interest, and she bit her lip and looked away. *Was it approval?* she wondered. The idea that John Turtle might approve of anything she did made her nervous.

Not that it mattered, though, what anyone thought; now that she was in New York at Bloodworth headquarters, she intended to see everything, especially how the company worked. She knew her uncles would have advised her to do just that.


THE film, entitled *A Great Company to Work For,* had been produced by the Bloodworth Foundation's public relations firm for the annual stockholders' meeting a few years ago when the company's unionization problems were at a peak. It showed the Bloodworth employees at New York headquarters eating in the company cafeteria, which was large and modern, reading magazines in the lounges, and playing squash and handball in the 9th-floor gym.

Francesca said, looking up and meeting the eyes of the chairman of the board, "All the squash and handball players are middle-management-level men, but the majority of your employees here are women clerical workers. Aren't you going to have anything for them?"

Several of the board members smiled.

"I believe we're working on it," the chairman of the board said soothingly.

Francesca remembered all too well how long it had taken to get anything for women clerical workers from the personnel department of Northeastern College.

"I'd like to know," she said, smiling just as sweetly, "how much the film that we've just seen cost. Total figures, if that's not too much trouble."

As the board members made clear, it was a lot of trouble. After several calls from the executive dining room to the public relations firm and the company controller's office to check the figures, the chairman of the board of the Bloodworth Foundation told Francesca, with only a remnant of his former graciousness, that *A Great Company to Work For* had been produced for $215,000, round figures.

The eyes that Francesca met in that moment were John Turtle's, standing by the window of the dining room, smoking one of his little brown cigarillos. And their look seemed to join in agreement—that was almost a quarter of a million dollars!

Francesca knew she was not like Carla Bloodworth, able to pass over the operation of Bloodworth's, Inc., with detached indifference; on the contrary, she remembered all too vividly the 9-to-5 job she had just come from.

A quarter of a million dollars? For a film just to tell employees how great the company was?

The expression on her face, she saw with some shock, was causing the corners of John Turtle's usually grim, straightline lips to curve. He was smiling.

The Bloodworth Foundation executive offices, together with the public relations account executives, arranged a thorough theater and sightseeing program for Francesca and her party, as well as a heavy schedule of informational meetings at the Third Avenue headquarters. In the late afternoons, when Francesca finally took a rented limousine back to the Plaza Hotel with John Turtle and Dorothea Smithson, she felt as though she was investigating every nook and cranny of Bloodworth's, Inc. Overkill was setting in. Brochures and special departmental reports were piling up in the sitting room awaiting her and Dorothea's attention.

Evenings were tightly scheduled, too, with theater tickets arranged for nearly every hit show on Broadway. The evening dates, they found out, were hard to cancel even when they were tired, as they often involved a Bloodworth corporation executive and his wife as hosts for dinner as well as the theater.

Even with their hectic schedule they tried to catch television news, usually while dressing, and reports on the Binns-MacLemore murder case. Elsa MacLemore had retained a famous California lawyer. His press conferences, usually held on the steps of the Palm Beach County Courthouse, focused on the many years Elsa had given to the diet doctor's career, and how little he had rewarded her devotion.

Francesca watched the television screen when it featured an interview with Doctor Binns's grown children, who had come to Palm Beach to testify in behalf of their father's personal reputation. Rumors of drug dealings were still circulating in the national media.

"How could he?" she murmured to the secretary, who was buttoning up the back of Francesca's crimson crepe de chine Dior for dinner at Lutece. "Was it the money, do you suppose?"

"Who, Bernie?" Dorothea said. "Don't ask me why doctors get into drug dealing, but they do. It's the prescription stuff, usually, like Quaaludes, Percodan, and then the rest comes all too easy, I guess." She finished buttoning the dress and Francesca turned around.

"Dorothea," Francesca said quietly, "and who else?"

It was something she had been thinking about for several days. The frantic exodus from Palm Beach not only of the trendy people from Dorrit's circle but, others as well. Bernard Binns's murder had thrown Palm Beach into an uproar. There was no other word to describe it.

But her secretary's gaze slid away. "Who knows who's into drugs?" she said evasively. "A lot of people can do them, your best friends, and you never know, do you?"

The remark reminded Francesca of Buffy Amberson. She hadn't known about that, either, she realized.


THE next day Francesca came to the end of her energy. She'd been winding down steadily for some strange reason; now she had to cancel out her appointments and go to bed with a paralyzing headache. She was exhausted.

"I just don't feel as good in New York as I did in Florida," she moaned as Dorothea helped her between silky sheets. "I just don't know what's the matter."

She slept most of the afternoon and evening away, waking briefly to eat a salad, listlessly, at about 9 p.m., watch a television news roundup and then return to sleep.

A little after 2 a.m., though, the headache returned and dragged Francesca awake. She came out of bed with a knifelike throbbing that seemed to want to saw her head in two pieces. With one hand clutching her forehead, and not wanting to wake Dorothea Smithson, who was almost as tired as she, Francesca groped her way through the silent, flower-fragrant rooms of the Plaza suite to the butler's pantry with the vague idea of finding a tea bag to make some hot tea.

Not only was her head killing her, but odd spasms of cold ran down her arms, across her shoulderblades and into the muscles of her chest. She felt rotten; the hours of rest had only served to make her worse as far as she could tell.

Francesca was poking about helplessly in the cabinets in the dark when the switch was suddenly snapped on. The glare of the light made Francesca blink. Then she saw the figure of John Turtle, barefoot and in red-and-white-striped pajama bottoms, checking out who was roaming around the hotel suite at that hour.

She fixed her eyes on the rigid planes of his face, the almost-shaggy black hair and the obsidian eyes now wary and alert. Then her gaze dropped to John Turtle's body— the pantherish breadth of his naked chest and shoulders and then the muscled sections of his belly, taut and powerfully developed, with the pajama bottoms' drawstringed top sliding precariously on the imperceptible jut of his narrow hips. Lean as he was, his tall body seemed to fill up and crowd the little room. Francesca closed her eyes for a moment, swaying. It would have to be John Turtle. If anybody had to wake, she would have hoped for Dorothea.

"It's these damned headaches," Francesca moaned. She was in a black nightgown that was nearly transparent, but she couldn't be bothered with John Turtle's reaction to her all-too-visible nudity; her head was about to split.

"What's the problem?" he said in his cold, cautious voice.

Francesca saw a tangle of wiry black hairs in the hollow of his breastbone. His rangy body was curiously formidable half-naked, even with the broad red-and-white-striped pajama bottoms. She pressed her hands hard against her pounding temples.

"Do you suppose it could be eyestrain?" she said plaintively. "All these Broadway plays I've been seeing. I feel like I'm going blind sitting in the dark night after night, staring my eyes out." She leaned her elbow against the butler's pantry refrigerator and propped her head in her hand, wincing. "I don't think I'm sick. No brain tumor. Just exhausted."

He put his lean, powerful body against the doorjamb, studying her from that distance. She saw from the flicker of his eyes that he could see through the nightgown. It only vaguely irritated her. "Why don't you take something?" he asked her, his voice softly insinuating. "Don't you have a lot of pills you take? For something like this?"

"Pills?" It was Francesca's turn to stare. "What pills? I don't even have an aspirin. If I had an aspirin," she told him, "I wouldn't be here at two-thirty in the morning looking for a cup of tea, would I?"

She started when he suddenly reached out and grabbed her wrist. His eyes had gone storm-black. She had never seen him look like that. She stared down at the brown hand on her forearm, disbelieving. His glare bored right through her.

"When did you start having headaches?" His voice snapped like a whip.

Bewildered, Francesca said, "A couple of days ago. Why—am I sick? I thought it was just too much New York City."

Harshly, John Turtle said, "You don't mind if I take a look, do you?"

Without waiting for an answer, he pulled her by the wrist through the sitting room and toward her bedroom. The lights were out and Francesca stumbled against furniture, but he did not slow his stride. She had no idea what was wrong with John Turtle. He seemed to have suddenly gone crazy. He switched on the overhead light in her bedroom and rapidly steered her through the dressing room and into the bathroom.

"What are we doing here?" Francesca winced at the sudden impact of fluorescent bathroom lights on her eyes. Her head felt as though ax blows were falling on it.

"Getting what you take to fix yourself up," he said grimly.

Francesca stared at him through a haze of pain. Now she knew he was out of his mind. She wondered if John Turtle was really crazy and, if so, what she was going to do about it at that hour of the morning. She sat down on the edge of the tub with great weariness, feeling the cold slick edge of its surface through the nylon gown.

Except for a bottle of nail polish remover and a box of Band-Aids, the medicine chest was empty, as she could have told him. She heard him make an impatient sound against his teeth. Still gripping her by the wrist, he pulled her up and led her into the dressing room and the dressing table there and searched through the bottles of her cosmetics.

"Where's the rest?" The black eyes blazed into her.

"What rest?" She still clutched the side of her head with one hand, her long black hair falling untidily into her eyes.

His look probed her for a second longer, then he turned back to the dressing table and searched through the bottles and jars again.

He had forgotten he held her hand in a cruel grip. Francesca pulled against him. Her fingers had gone numb, but he didn't seem to notice. She was terribly tired; all she had wanted was an aspirin for her head, and she hadn't wanted to disturb Dorothea.

He wouldn't let her go. Instead, he turned and black eyes raked her. "Tell me what you've been feeling," he said in that deadly soft voice. "Lassitude? Nausea? Loss of appetite?"

"Well, appetite not so good," she admitted. She lifted the mass of black curls away from her face to see him better. "And if lassitude means you could go to sleep standing up, that was me today. I don't know what happened. I thought the Bloodworth Foundation was getting me down." She tried to smile. "I'm still not used to all this," she said apologetically. She was horribly tired. She felt herself winding down

even as they stood there, and his voice seemed to fade into
the distance.

From the way John Turtle looked at her it was obvious
something was wrong. She was jarred, even so, when his
hands seized her and shook her so that her head snapped
back and forth violently.

"Francesca?" He was so close it was as though his very
presence invaded her. "Damn, you're on the nod already,
do you know that? Honey, are you listening? I want you to
tell me again what you just said to me. That you don't take
pills, not even aspirin. Tell me—it's important."

He pulled her to him. Francesca felt the pressure of his
forearm against her soft breast as he gripped her wrist and
held her tightly. The sensitive tip of her nipple touched his
chest through the tissue thinness of the nightgown. She
swayed. Was he angry with her? Why was his voice so
loud? What was so terribly important now, in the middle
of the night? She felt an overpowering desire to sleep. Her
eyelids began to slide down over her eyes.

"Wake up." His voice was close, vibrating through her
body. "Francesca, is this the first time you've had this sort
of reaction?"

She lifted her hands with a great effort and put them
against the warm skin of his chest. She felt springy ringlets
against her palms. She just wanted to lay her head down
somewhere. The overpowering maleness of John Turtle's
body was comforting and familiar, a place where she needed
to be. She thought of curling up close against him. Lying
down. In bed. To have strong arms holding her, a body
enveloping and possessing hers, lips pressed against her
mouth. She sighed. At the first touch of her hands he had
started slightly, a small shudder running through him. But
then his arms closed around her quickly. And she was surrounded by that wildly powerful sensation that seemed always to follow him. Francesca slumped against his body.

Her flesh strained against the film of transparent black
nightgown and where her breasts touched his hard body, it

was sensuous and disturbing. The muscles of his stomach and thighs pressed against her as she clung to him, and she felt the pressure of his hands, fingers spread, against the soft skin of her shoulderblades. She thought dimly that it was impossible to forget how nicely bodies fitted together, male and female, once one had learned how.

"For God's sake," his voice said against her hair. "What are you doing to me? Francesca, listen." But she felt the soft touch of his mouth against her cheek while his hands stroked her back in circles, smoothing it under the nylon. Under his breath he said raggedly, "Man, no one figured this one right."

Francesca clung to the powerful body holding hers. All sensation was melting into a cloud of safe, blissful darkness. Everything was right again. *Kurt,* her mind said.

"Kurt," she breathed.

She felt the arms holding her suddenly stiffen, the lean body go rigid against her own. When she tried to curl herself against it, to go back to that wonderfully blissful feeling, hands like steel held her away. She opened her eyes and saw his dark angry face like a blow. But as she watched, the chiseled features dimmed over and went smooth again.

The voice said, "Wrong number, lady, but I get the idea." While she tried to hold on to him he turned and said, "There are some tea bags in the butler's pantry somewhere. I can fix you a cup of tea, if that's what you want."

But Francesca gave a quiet little sigh and slid to the floor. She heard his quick exclamation, then his body bent over hers. His arms went around her and he lifted her; there was a moment's staggering sensation and then he held her easily in his arms.

Francesca's head lolled against his smooth chest and the bunched muscles of his shoulders. She felt herself being carried to the bed and then put down gently on it, his body leaning over her. With her eyes closed, floating in safe darkness, Francesca rubbed her lips softly against the smooth skin, the tense muscles in John Turtle's throat. Now it was

*her* hands which would not let him get away. The sudden
feeling that she could live like this, in the comfort of this
man's strength, was overpowering. It was a feeling that
willed Francesca from the hectic surroundings of New York,
away from the crowded confusion of the strange life she
was leading with its servants and lawyers and corporation
executives, and carried her back months in time, held in
his arms. Held close. To some distant dream of real happiness.

"I want to go home," she murmured against his warm,
masculine-smelling bare shoulder. Her arms crept around
his neck and clung tightly, and sudden tears sprang against
her eyelids. She was so very tired, so very sleepy. "Home,"
she said softly.

She knew his head bent to hers and his lips touched hers,
lips softer than Kurt's. But then she felt him pull back.

She had meant Boston. Home was Boston, not Palm
Beach. But John Turtle's voice, as if from a great distance,
said, "You can go back to him any time you want to. All
you have to do is get the plane tickets."

But Francesca had drifted off to sleep.


"Do you want an assessment of what we've accomplished
so far?" Dorothea Smithson said.

It was Saturday. They were just finishing breakfast in
the sitting room of the Plaza suite, newspapers scattered all
around them, enjoying the first morning free of schedules
and appointments. A profusion of flowers filled the room
and the elaborate breakfast buffet table had been pushed to
one side, awaiting the waiter to remove it.

Francesca made a face. "We're supposed to have accomplished a place to stay out of the way of Dr. Binns's murder
investigation, I thought." She yawned. "Anything else was
supposed to be secondary."

John Turtle had come out of his room to listen, and the
secretary shot him a quick look over Francesca's head.

"It wasn't such a bad idea," Dorothea observed. "Look at all the things we've done."

"We've seen a thousand Broadway shows and I've gained five pounds eating at expensive restaurants," Francesca groaned.

"We know what it's like to take a Bloodworth's VIP tour," Dorothea offered helpfully. "And we got at least one copy of every piece of literature—every pamphlet and booklet—they've ever published, including the one that mentions President Roosevelt and the National Recovery Act."

"They are a bit out of touch in some ways," Francesca admitted. She was feeling much better at nine a m on Saturday. The brilliant morning sun beating down on Central Park made her want to get out and sightsee New York without the help of the Bloodworth Foundation and their guides.

She noticed John Turtle watched her, for some reason, with a veiled, expectant look that seemed to ask her not if she were feeling better, but if she perhaps remembered something. She shrugged it off; she couldn't begin to guess what was on John Turtle's mind, much less the expressions in those enigmatic dark eyes.

"What bothers me," Francesca said, buttering another piece of toast on her tray, "is that there's a lot going on and you can't find out about it. It doesn't seem to be a secret that they're losing money on the Blo-Co stores, but they shut you out every time you ask about it. It just doesn't make sense."

John Turtle said from the doorway, quite unexpectedly, "You should be trying to get your proxies back so you can vote your majority stockholder's shares."

Both women jumped. It was seldom John Turtle ventured an opinion.

"My lord, he's right," Dorothea said. "You found out the chairmain of the board has the proxies, and has voted those shares since the days of Charles Bloodworth, Jr."

Francesca stared at her secretary. "I can't do all that, can I?"

From the doorway John Turtle said, "There isn't much that can be done in a big corporation without an all-out fight." He moved into the sitting room and stood in front of Francesca, dark-browed and frowning. "But if you're interested, you have to write a letter to the chairman of the board telling him that you rescind his right to vote your proxies. And that you're going to vote your shares yourself. And that you expect to attend all corporate board meetings from now on."

Francesca regarded his tall figure for a long thoughtful moment. Everything John Turtle said was true. "As simple as that?" she whispered.

He nodded. "Yes, for starters. Then they'll think of something to counter, you can bet on it." He paused for the briefest second and his eyes seemed to hold a question in their black depths. Reluctantly, he said, "You know what they think of you, don't you?"

"No." Francesca was impressed with his air of authority, the same toughness she had marked at lunch that day in the Bloodworth Foundation dining room. "What?"

"You're just an upstart, Miss Lucchese," he said in a cold voice. "A young woman of no particular training or background for this sort of thing, and they know you can be eliminated fairly easily. They intend for you to go back to being the company figurehead the last two Bloodworths were. So the corporation will put up a fight. They can do a bunch of things. Like 'lose' information you need. Like organizing the minority stockholders against you—and some of these are topflight Wall Street investment firms, by the way. And oppose you any way they can. They'll put on a fairly discreet campaign to discredit you, which means they'll dig up any scandal. In effect, they'll neutralize you as soon as they can find a good way to do it."

Francesca's eyes were on his face, mesmerized, his quiet words sinking into her consciousness. John Turtle was right. She couldn't understand why he hadn't said something, advised them, before. "What happens if I get my majority shareholder votes back?" she murmured.

His stony, handsome face was darkly expressionless. His eyes bored into her. "You'll control the company," he said softly.

Dorothea Smithson sucked in her breath. It was a moment before she could say, "Johnny!" in a choked voice. Then "Oh, it's so complicated—it takes a lot of people, lawyers, expertise, really!"

Francesca said nothing.

John Turtle said, just as quietly, "Do you want to do it?"

Francesca waited a moment before she answered. She felt excited, uncertain; as Dorothea had pointed out it was a daring move, full of unexplored possibilities. Taking the initiative as no one had done since old Chuckie Bloodworth, the founder.

"I guess the answer is, Why not?" Francesca said softly. "The present Bloodworth management isn't doing all that great. Nobody seems to be working very hard. The week we've just spent there shows that. The board of directors doesn't seem to want to discuss discount stores. They seem to have the attitude that just because the Bloodworth Foundation has gone into discount retailing with Blo-Co they've got it made, when quite the opposite is true. Discount chains are having a lot of problems, all you have to do is read the *Wall Street Journal* to find that out. And not only do they give the impression they're not doing much to earn their salaries, the board has just voted themselves some salary increases that will make your eyes bug out. A quarter of a million top salary, according to the latest copy of the annual report, isn't unusual! Just about what they paid for that awful promotion film. I really can't figure out what they're doing. The president of the Blo-Co division gets almost a million a year with extras, and that's the Bloodworth company that's losing all the money!" Francesca bit her lip. Then she said, "Can we write a letter asking for the proxies or whatever, so that it's all nice and legal?"

John Turtle's eyes had never left her face. "I'll get on

the phone to Miami and get it roughed up, if Mrs. Smithson will final-type it for me. I'm not much of a typist."

Francesca smiled. She'd hardly expected John Turtle to have typing skills, but nothing about him was what she expected, she thought, studying the rangy figure in his black business suit and neat white shirt and dark tie. No trace of the powerful, tough presence in blue jeans and work boots was detectable, but she knew it was there. As she studied him, something about John Turtle, something that had happened or that she had to tell him, nagged at her, but she couldn't remember it clearly. But it was nice to have him friendly for a change; she had thought he detested her.

"Why did you leave law school?" she asked, curious.

The closed look returned to his face. "I found I didn't like lawyers." He said nothing more.

ON Monday Francesca was checking over some outgoing letters Dorothea had prepared, before leaving to see a performance of the New York City Ballet, when a call came through from *Ca'ad Carlo*.

Dorothea Smithson was beside her in the sitting room, fixing stamps to envelopes. Francesca took the call there. John Turtle was in the butler's pantry, mixing drinks.

"I am back," the familiar voice said in her ear, "and you were not here. This is a terrible place without you."

*"Kurt,"* she breathed, knowing the others could hear, but ecstatic and not caring. "It's terrible here without you, too! You don't know how good your voice sounds." Her own voice nearly broke on a sob. When she had control of it again she said, "I miss you so much! Can we come back to Palm Beach now?"

"Who knows?" His amiable laughter rippled in the receiver. "Things are still crazy here. The state attorney's office has called twice to ask you if you are available to come down and make a statement about what you know about Bernard Binns and Elsa. I told them you were out of town indefinitely. They are getting used to that, I think. Half of Palm Beach is out of town indefinitely this summer. But yes, come back if you still love me. Do you still love me?" the voice asked huskily.

Francesca held the telephone to her ear with both hands. She knew Dorothea Smithson was trying not to listen. John Turtle had come to the door of the butler's pantry, his face gone more than usually rigid.

"I love you, I love you," Francesca cried. "I want to come back. I even miss *Ca'ad Carlo!*"

"Good," Kurt's voice said promptly. "Then when you come back I will ask you to marry me. Francesca, will you marry me? Did you hear what I said?"

"Yes," Francesca said, closing her eyes.

# CHAPTER FOURTEEN

BELOW, on the front terrace, John Turtle's two-way radio blared something, breaking the morning's hot, sunny stillness. Dorothea, running down the gallery and then down the stairs to the outside of the house, returned with the message that there was a security problem at the front gate of *Ca'ad Carlo*.

The small woman looked somewhat hesitant. "It's your friend, Mrs. Amberson," she told Francesca.

Francesca jumped up from her desk, spilling wedding invitation lists and printer's samples of wedding announcements onto the floor. *Buffy?* The last she had heard of Buffy she was with her husband somewhere. And a breezy telephone message, Francesca remembered, the night of the Bernard Binns shooting, had left their friendship dangling by the string of several thousand dollars' worth of medical bills from the *Golden Door,* which were still owing.

Still, who could resist Buffy? was Francesca's second thought. She had missed Buffy's sharp tongue and hilarious comments as well as the sensitivity which served to point up the beautiful woman's tenuous hold on happiness—and Jock Amberson.

"I'll be right back," Francesca told her secretary. She rushed out into the gallery and down the steps that led to *Ca'ad Carlo*'s great hall. She couldn't imagine what could involve Buffy in a security problem. Why hadn't Buffy just driven all the way through to the main house the way she always did?

"Wait," Francesca cried futilely to the retreating back of John Turtle halfway down the drive. She knew he heard her, but she also knew he wouldn't stop. She started running after him. At the last curve of the driveway the front gate and the guard's post suddenly came into view. Francesca saw Buffy Amberson, gorgeous in a yellow silk suit, her silvery-gold hair brilliant in the glaring sunshine, pressed to John Turtle with one arm twined tightly around his neck. Buffy's white Lincoln convertible was drawn at a crazy angle through the gates, almost blocking the drive. And Buffy's free hand wobbled in the direction of a low-slung Italian sports car parked under the trees across South Ocean Drive.

"Francesca!" Buffy screamed.

She quickly disentangled herself from John Turtle's rangy body and started toward Francesca. "They wouldn't let me in, I didn't know what in the hell to do," Buffy sobbed. "It's Jock—the son of a bitch chased me through Palm Beach! I kept going south on the island in the convertible and then I thought of *Ca'ad Carlo!* I pulled in here thinking I was saved, and then your guard told me I wasn't cleared to drive on through." Buffy grabbed Francesca's arms with both hands and clung to her, fingernails biting into Francesca's skin. "Oh, I'm so damned glad you were here!"

Francesca drew back a little. Her first impulse had been

to hurry Buffy away from the gate, up to the main house. Now she wasn't so sure.

"Please calm down, will you?" she said to her. The hot sun beat down on the driveway. John Turtle was standing with the gate guard who was on the telephone in his booth. "Is that Jock over there?"

She could see a very handsome, very youthful man with a tanned face and gray hair sitting behind the wheel of the Ferrari. But there was no doubt about it, he was watching the group at the entrance gate to *Ca'ad Carlo*.

"What's going on?" Francesca wanted to know. Then, with a surge of raw anger that turned her gray eyes to cold silver, "He's not trying to hurt you, is he, Buffy?"

Buffy's face contorted with fear. "Dear God, Francesca—he says he's going to wreck my face if I don't give him a divorce! You know he can, don't you? I mean, the doctors at the *Golden Door* told you all about it, I guess." Her eyes slid away guiltily. "My face can't take much more. I guess everybody in Palm Beach knows what a wreck I am. He said—" Buffy's voice rose hysterically. "He said, he said *all he had to do was smash it against the wall a couple of times*, and they'd never be able to put it back together again! And it's true, oh God, it's true! But Jock was the one who turned me on to coke in the first place, Francesca. It was supposed to be such a great high, then great in bed—but it was those damned shots of Bernie's that started Jock with it—all those uppers, amphetamines, in Washington! Now he acts as though I did it all by myself! I was just a dumb stew from Chicago, Francesca—you've got to believe me! I didn't know how to handle drugs. Then I hit this rotten place!"

"Good grief," Francesca cried. She was sickened at what she was hearing, helpless with a sobbing Buffy clutching her. And there was the ominous presence of the man across the roadway in the Ferrari, boldly waiting out his next move. "Is he really chasing you to beat you up again?" Francesca demanded. "Is that what he's waiting for?"

John Turtle had come up. "Mrs. Amberson," he said to Buffy, "if you could move your car so that—"

Francesca interrupted him. "Do you know what he's doing over there?" she asked him indignantly. "He's waiting for her to come out! He's chasing her, trying to beat her up!"

His lips tightened. "If Mrs. Amberson will give me the keys I'll move the car myself. She's blocking the driveway."

The bright sunshine was pounding in Francesca's eyes. She had slept poorly, another in a succession of restless nights since they had returned from New York, and her nerves were on edge. Buffy's screaming and the mess Buffy had dragged right to the gates of *Ca'ad Carlo* didn't help.

"I want him out of here," Francesca cried. What Buffy's husband planned to do to her if she didn't give him a divorce enraged her. "He has no right to sit in front of the gates like this and threaten people!"

John Turtle turned to her, eyes narrowed. "He's not threatening anybody, he's in a public road. But I'd like to get Mrs. Amberson's car clear of the driveway, Miss Lucchese, just in case we need—"

"Don't let him in!" Buffy wailed loudly. "Oh, God, Francesca, don't let him near me! Jock isn't kidding. He'd do anything to get this divorce! He wants me to sign away any right to alimony, community property, everything, so he can get married. Oh yes, he's going to get married again! She's *nineteen!*"

It was hot in the unshaded driveway. The sun bounced back from the white shell surface into Francesca's face. Buffy Amberson's panic, the presence of the man in the sports car watching them and John Turtle's refusal to do anything about it rubbed her already shaky nerves raw.

She turned her fury on the tall man. "Why haven't you told him to get out of here?" she blazed. At the same time she tried to pry Buffy's frantic fingernails from her arm. "You tell Jock Amberson to get out of here, or I'll all the police!"

She saw a spark of anger flare in John Turtle's black

eyes, then it died. "He's not on the property, Miss Lucchese," he said in an even voice. "Actually he has every right to be where he is. I'd like to get Mrs. Amberson's car out of—"

Something in Francesca ripped apart, crazily. She suddenly knew who had given orders not to let Buffy Amberson past *Ca'ad Carlo*'s gates.

"Did you *hear me?*" she screamed. Beside her, Buffy was crying hysterically. She had to raise her voice to be heard over the racket. "I'm not going to be threatened on my own property! Go over there and tell him to get out of here! I don't want him around here. I don't even want him looking at us!"

The planes of John Turtle's face hardened stubbornly. "The man's not trespassing, Miss Lucchese, he's in a public roadway. He hasn't done anything threatening so far. But—"

Francesca pushed Buffy away from her. "I want him out of here!" she raged. She realized her Italian temper was up, but nobody appeared to be paying any attention to what she was saying. She turned a furious face to John Turtle, her fists clenched. Damn him! He was always sneering at her. She had an overwhelming desire to satisfy her frustration by punching him right in the stomach. "If you're afraid to tell this—*wifebeater*, to get out of here, then I'll have to do it myself!"

She slammed both hands into the middle of his chest, pushed hard and brushed past him. He only went back a half step and then, lightning quick, he reached out and seized her wrist and yanked her to him. It was so unexpected and so quick, that iron grip on her arm literally snatching her backward, that Francesca almost lost her balance. She gasped with shock.

When she got her breath she yelled, "What do you think you're doing?" She tried to drag her wrist out of his grasp and couldn't. There was a ludicrous moment as she struggled wildly. All she could think of was that on the other side of

South Ocean Drive the man behind the wheel of the Ferrari sat and watched the melee.

"Just a minute," he told her. "Calm down, you're not going anywhere."

"Of all the stupid—" Francesca cried, and could not finish.

She was suddenly weak in the knees and her heart was pounding; the sun was too hot. John Turtle saw it, too, and relaxed his hold on her a fraction. Francesca closed her eyes, waiting for the dizzy spell to go away. She didn't know it, but she had gone quite ashen.

She heard John Turtle say, "Mrs. Amberson is hysterical, and she's trying to throw everybody else off, too. Your friend uses drugs, Miss Lucchese—she's six miles high right now and flying, but you never seem to notice. Her husband is a user, too, as everybody but you seems to know. Now, I'm not going across the road to tell him anything and neither are you. We don't know if he's carrying a concealed weapon or not, but frankly I'm not interested in finding out the hard way."

Francesca wrenched at her arm angrily, and he let it go. Buffy was clawing at her.

"Don't, Francesca," she was crying. "Listen, stay away from Jock! Please—he'll do anything this time, I know! He even says he'll take me to court on grounds I had, you know, experiences with other women."

John Turtle said quickly, "What?"

"He has pictures," Buffy moaned. She made a distracted gesture. "Oh, Francesca, it was Bodner's idea, and it really turned Jock on. I mean, Jock was there, what could I do? And Dorrit—"

John Turtle cut in. "More than once?" he wanted to know.

Buffy's hysterical sobs had dwindled away. "Yes," she said in a barely audible voice.

"Oh God." Francesca turned and walked a few steps away. What Buffy had just said had stunned and sickened her. She heard John Turtle following her; the sound of his work boots was loud on the crushed shell of the driveway.

"Are you all right?" he wanted to know.

John Turtle's cold caution revolted her, too. She knew he would prefer to close the gates of *Ca'ad Carlo* and let Buffy and Jock Amberson fight it out elsewhere. She knew he condemned her for having made friends with Buffy to begin with. John Turtle had given orders to keep Buffy out, she was sure, then he had refused to warn off Jock Amberson as she had ordered. And he had manhandled her in front of the others. She was sick of trying to deal with John Turtle!

The man in the car, she saw, was still sitting there, watching them, boldly daring them to do anything about it. It was useless, now, to call the police.

Buffy was watching her with an anxious face. Francesca turned away. Buffy was hopeless, she thought bitterly. "Give her some money and get rid of her," Francesca said to John Turtle. She felt as though she hated everyone at that moment. "Dorothea Smithson can come down to the gate with some money for her. We ought to be able to find some money without having to go to the bank, I don't know. But I'm tired of wasting money on her—I want her to get out of here! Her mother lives in Milwaukee, she can go back there."

"Francesca." Buffy took a few steps toward her. "Look, I'm not going to involve you in any of this, I swear." She looked around furtively. "It was a mistake trying to come here this morning, I realize that now. But he was *chasing me*—"

"Please," Francesca said. She wanted Buffy out of her sight forever. "Just don't bother me again, will you? He," she said, indicating John Turtle, "will see that you get some money and get out of town before your husband ruins you for life and leaves you without a face. That's about it, isn't it?"

Buffy's eyes filled with tears. "Oh damn, Francesca, I *swear* Jock won't use anything in court! I mean, it's just a bluff. Jock doesn't want to split with any more of his money

again for an ex-wife, so he's trying everything! But
you—"

"Will you shut up!" Francesca screamed. She saw John
Turtle move toward her, as if to stop her, but she was beyond
caring. "I haven't had group sex with you, or your husband,
or Dorrit—or anybody! How did I get myself into this! I
don't know what's the matter with you people! Are you so
bored out of your minds that you can't turn down any cheap
thrill? I don't take drugs, I haven't made a mess of myself
and bothered *you*, have I? I want you to get out of here!"
Anger with Buffy Amberson, with herself, with the whole
world, burst out of Francesca. Buffy backed away.

The other woman regarded her, wide-eyed. Buffy drew
herself up with exaggerated dignity.

"Boy, have you changed, Francesca," she said in a low
voice. "All that money really makes a difference. It never
fails. Even with a nice Italian working-class girl like you.
And I used to like you so much!"

"I don't want to listen to this," Francesca cried. She
turned on her heel and started back to the house.

Buffy's voice followed her. "No, you don't want to listen
to it. And I don't blame you. But don't get too self-righteous,
Francesca, about other people's mistakes. Just consider the
ones you're making!"

Francesca walked on. She was sick to her stomach, which
was literally jumping and contracting painfully. There was
no escape, apparently, from the relentless Florida sun beating down on her.

She saw the path to the estate office bungalow and turned
into it. She had to sit down for a moment. John Turtle could
take care of Buffy. They deserved each other.

"I'll take your money, Francesca," Buffy shouted after
her. "Just don't fall off your pedestal too hard, will you?"


HERB Ostrow had been at work for over a week in the old
estate office, but Francesca hadn't had time to come by and

see how he was doing since her return from New York. The office was not much cooler than the outside. Francesca held her throbbing head with one hand and looked around for a place to sit.

The ancient file cabinets that held all the estate records and some of the papers of the Bloodworth family had been opened and emptied of their contents. Herb Ostrow obviously had some system of organization, but it was hard to tell what it was. The place was covered with files and loose papers. The gray-haired writer was shirtless, wearing only a pair of tennis shorts and sandals. His torso glistened with sweat.

"Who would think office work would generate this much dirt?" He grinned at her and then ran the back of his hand over his nose, leaving a black smear. When Francesca tried to sit down, he grabbed her arm. "No, not there! That's a fascinating era, nineteen forty-three. Charles Junior was a dollar-a-year man for the War Department in Florida." He flashed her a boyish smile. "Well, fascinating to me, anyway. You don't mind sitting on the edge of the desk, do you?"

He was, Francesca saw, full of enthusiasm for what he was doing. She couldn't help but remember how strained their last conversation had been; now he seemed to have forgotten about it completely. She perched on the edge of the desk, still trembling with odd exhaustion, trying to collect her thoughts after the scene at the guard gate. The office still smelled of fresh paint. The air conditioners had not yet been installed, but a large electric fan turned at one of the open windows.

"I walked down to the front gate," Francesca said. She found she didn't want to tell Herb Ostrow what had been going on. Apparently he hadn't heard any of the commotion, even though the guard post was only a couple of hundred feet away. He was totally absorbed in what he was doing. She took a deep breath.

She said, "Did you ever get your interview with Elsa

MacLemore?" The Bernard Binns affair had rapidly receded from the front pages and the television evening news; everyone now awaited the setting of the trial date.

"Nope," he said cheerfully. "And she's not answering any of my letters or telephone calls. Frankly, I'd give next year's royalties for an interview, but the L.A. lawyer she's got is keeping her under wraps. Which is smart. I hear some of Bernie Binns's former customers have gone all the way to Colombia and Nicaragua until the trial is over. And you know the Feds are still all over the island watching everybody. The only safe place these days is your swimming pool." The writer looked around the littered office. "Under the circumstances, I'm happy right here. If I work hard enough, I may be able to spin off some of this historical material on how Palm Beach got this way to some of the European and Japanese news services. They go for that sort of stuff."

"Yes," Francesca murmured. She wasn't really listening. Her head was still buzzing with the implications of the scene that had taken place at the front gate. Scandal on scandal! She really *had* been Buffy's friend—Buffy had spent most of the summer swimming and lunching at *Ca' ad Carlo*. And as for the *Golden Door*, she had not only paid the bills for Buffy's medical care, but had learned that Buffy was a cocaine user. Francesca supposed people would make of that what they would, especially if Jock Amberson decided to turn his divorce into a lurid courtroom trial to avoid a property settlement and alimony.

But inwardly she cringed. She hated the thought of publicity in this mess. And she knew her family in Boston would never come to terms with this sort of thing; they simply had no frame of reference except the scandals of the wealthy they read in the papers. As for the board of directors of the Bloodworth Foundation, she would certainly become a liability in corporate eyes. She remembered that Dorothea Smithson had just mailed off the letter to the board of directors asking for her shareholder votes to be turned over to her so that she, as majority stockholder, could have a determining part in running the Bloodworth empire.

"Penny for your thoughts," Herb Ostrow said in the sudden silence. His mouth drew up ironically. "Or is this just the traditional daydreaming we have to expect from the lovely bride-to-be?"

Francesca snapped back to reality. She looked around the office, not sure what she should say. "Dorothea feels we should bring someone in, a bridal consultant, and get rid of all the work. But I wanted to keep it quiet and small. We can't use the Catholic church in the village because Kurt isn't Catholic. But then I'm not in very good standing, either. I haven't gone to Mass since I've been here." She tried to smile. "But they did send a priest to talk to me about making a big contribution."

The writer smiled, too. "You can't blame them. They wouldn't have gotten much out of old Charlie Bloodworth."

Francesca got up and restlessly moved to the window that looked out on the junglelike foliage that separated the bungalow from the front drive. Madagascar palms, hibiscus heavy with crimson blossoms, the thick boles of banyan trees filled up the view; one couldn't even hear the traffic on South Ocean Drive.

She supposed John Turtle had gotten Buffy some money now and had arranged for her to leave the gate area. It was too much to hope that Buffy had gone straight to the airport. She probably had to pack her things and come to terms with Jock Amberson's demands, somehow. Francesca shivered.

She put up her hand to touch the window glass, hesitantly. Marrying Kurt Bergstrom was still not a reality, only a dream. She supposed it would come true, but it seemed she moved toward her wedding day with excruciating slowness. She was determined to close her eyes to all the unpleasant things—all that would be said when she married Carla's third husband, all that would be said about Kurt—and concentrate on how happy she would be when they were finally together. He was really everything Francesca had

ever wanted—handsome, magnetic, worldly, brave—the
most desirable man she had ever met. And she loved him
wildly; they were going to be deliriously happy. They had
already talked of moving to Hawaii and opening up and
refurbishing the old Bloodworth estate on Maui. She had
no idea why she felt so vaguely *un*happy.

Francesca watched a mockingbird flitting in the small
green palm trees. She heard the writer clear his throat behind
her.

"Francesca?" She heard the rustle of papers. "Are you
in the mood for a small present?" When she turned he held
out a package of envelopes tied with faded satin ribbon.
"How's your Italian? Can you read it at all?"

Francesca grimaced. The bundle of letters, like all paper
in the soft Florida climate, felt damp and crumbling to the
touch. But the dates were only those of the 1950s. She
selected a letter from the top and opened it up. It began,
*Mi amor*.

Francesca lifted her eyes to Herb Ostrow. "Love letters?"

He nodded. "From Giovanni to Carla. There are no post-
marks. They used a drop someplace on the grounds, there's
a mention of it several times but nothing to tell where or
what it was. Obviously it was better than using the telephone. They must have thought they were safe enough,
writing in Italian. Carla was fluent in it, you know, from
so many years on Capri."

Francesca read a few words, uncertain of her knowledge
of the language. It was plain the writer was an impassioned
young lover expressing his desire for his mistress in very
ardent terms. She felt her face growing red. Watching her,
Herb Ostrow laughed softly.

"Okay, he was an Italian and in love," he said quickly.
"These letters weren't intended for our eyes."

"You can say that again." The question of whether or
not her father loved the Bloodworth heiress was certainly
answered by these love letters. In one of them, in an idiom
she could hardly understand, he raged jealously about some-

thing or other. She couldn't make it out.

"Dinner," the writer said. "She was going out to dinner here with friends. But you know it must have galled him to know she socialized in Palm Beach, and he couldn't go with her. Not as the chauffeur."

Francesca put the letter back with the others. She murmured, "I can't believe this is my father. He was the most beautiful, handsome man, but always so quiet. Sort of aloof. My uncles called him 'the priest.' He'd been a student at the seminary in Sicily, you know." Francesca tied the ribbon back in place. "But here he's so *young*, and so jealous, and so in love. It's like someone I don't know, and never knew. The question is, Did she love him, too? Or was she just fooling around? Are there any of her letters?"

The writer shook his head. "Not that I've found. Women save love letters, not men. But in the letters he says she loves him, and there's no reason not to take his word for it. One letter says he waited all night for her and she never showed. Apparently they rendezvoused in the guest cottage he used, and she came down from the main house through a lane of daturas he mentions. He waited for her in the lane sometimes. He says, very poetically, 'In the shadows I wait for you, in the way I must love you, in this life.' He tells her that if she doesn't come to him in his cottage he will come to the main house, to her bedroom, and make love to her there and 'end this farce.' I don't know at what point in their relationship these letters were written, but one gets the feeling a dead end was approaching. He seems to know it. Perhaps Carla did, too." He paused. "Another penny for your thoughts, Francesca."

She roused herself from her reverie with an effort. She was trying not to think of the lane of daturas, knowing whose cottage this was now. It seemed too fateful. She pressed her lips together.

"Yes, but while this was going on, remember, my mother was there, too. She's like a shadow nobody mentions, but it's always been this way. I never knew anything about her.

I was told that she went to Chicago, but I think Chicago was only a name they decided on. Later they told me she had died. I don't think I believed that, either. So it's okay to talk about how madly in love my father and Carla were, but what about my mother? While they were making love in one of the guest cottages, my mother was living in the servants' quarters with her baby. That doesn't sound too great, does it?"

He looked at his feet stretched out before him. "Does it bother you, Francesca?"

She gave an elaborate shrug. "I can't say that it's driving me crazy, but it's there. Especially since I'm about to get married myself. I've been thinking a lot about what men and women promise each other. And how well they live up to it."

"What about Kurt Bergstrom?"

"Leave Kurt out of it, please." Francesca knew how Herb Ostrow felt about Kurt.

He said, "Your father was only a man, Francesca. Sooner or later you'll have to stop seeing him with a little girl's eyes."

Francesca turned the packet of letters over and over restlessly in her hands.

"Sordid," she said flatly. "That's the right word, isn't it? I got my money through a sordid affair. Almost as sordid as Elsa MacLemore shooting Bernie Binns because he used her money to deal in drugs and make love to his patients when she wasn't looking. Almost as sordid as Buffy Amb—" She caught herself in time. "Almost as sordid as Buffy Amberson hanging on to her husband in spite of his beating her up."

"What's the matter, Francesca?" He watched her, arms folded across his chest, leaning against the desk. "You know how you got your money. Carla's will spelled it out plain enough. Carla left all her money to her chauffeur. They had an affair. Whether it was sordid or not depends on your viewpoint."

Francesca averted her face. "This isn't turning out very

well, you know. I suppose it's about time a reaction was setting in. 'Poor little rich girl.' Or in my case it should be 'Rich little *poor* girl,' right?" Francesca turned from the window. "I'm finding that nobody can live with all this money without being at least a little crazy. Jinkie is the richest of us all—and he's just a strange little boy who will probably never grow up. Jock Amberson doesn't love his wives and his children, only his money. And money was all Mrs. Carlton Hampton ever wanted, I think. Carla was the same way. The way it looks, all Carla wanted to do was fool around with fantastically good-looking men. What is it—the isolation and the boredom?"

"You're letting it get to you," he warned.

"Of course I am! I was told this morning that I'd really changed, that all the money was changing me. That shook me up, you know? I've only had the Bloodworth money a few months, so I'm new at this. But I'm trying. Still, I'm asking myself, Do I have to be as weird as the rest of them?"

Francesca was in the center of the small office, her hands on her hips, a tall and stunningly beautiful young woman dressed simply in a cotton dress that would have cost her total monthly salary as a working girl a few weeks ago. She was all woman in the high thrust of her magnificent breasts, tiny waist and luscious bottom, part child in the wide, gray-eyed look and her unstudied grace as she moved. But a slight air of exhaustion hung around her, and there were circles under her eyes.

"You're beautiful," the writer said simply. "But you don't look like you get enough sleep. Are you staying out all night, going to engagement parties?"

Francesca shot him a reproachful look, but she colored slightly. Late nights were spent in Kurt Bergstrom's bungalow, as she was sure he guessed. "You weren't even listening." She looked around the office again. "Will you remember that we agreed you aren't to use any of this material about Giovanni and Carla, nothing that relates to me?"

"Francesca, I—" the writer began. But if he was going

to say something about his feeling for her, the look on her face stopped him. "I remember, and I understand," he said quickly. "I'm actually very grateful to have this opportunity to go into the Bloodworth files, you know." He paused, and looked up at her. "Francesca, let me ask you a question. This business of your father and Carla Bloodworth intrigues me, there seem to be so many missing pieces." Without waiting for her response he went on, "You mentioned your mother, before. How much do you know about her? Anything? Any description of what she looked like? Your father was dark, I know. Did he have dark eyes, too?"

She stared at him. "Gray, like mine. Italians can have gray eyes, you know. I have my father's eyes. Why?"

"Nothing," he said quickly. "I told you, I was just curious."


FRANCESCA walked back to the house slowly. The heat still bothered her as she was sure it would continue to bother her for the rest of this seemingly endless Florida summer, but she felt slightly better than she had before. It was nearly noon.

She wanted to be with Kurt. Only Kurt could understand what had happened with Buffy Amberson this morning, understand and not be surprised. Kurt knew Palm Beach. More than anyone else he was the one she could talk to, and depend on. She needed his honesty, his easygoing acceptance, and his arms around her. Certainly that. More than anyone, Kurt understood and came between her and the crazy, uncontrollable world around her.

Francesca quickened her pace. She needed Kurt, and she was going to him, she wasn't going to wait until he returned to *Ca'ad Carlo*. And for once she was going by herself, she decided, slipping away without taking John Turtle or the alternate bodyguard. Kurt was on board the *Freya*. She had never gone to the marina or gone onboard the *Freya* without telling Kurt first, but this time she was going to go straight ahead. She felt she had to.

The estate pickup truck, the new station wagon and the rented red Mustang were in the small parking spaces in front of the main door. The ignition keys were in all of them. Francesca was due in the informal dining room in a few minutes for lunch with Dorothea Smithson and the morning's wrap-up of mail, but she put thoughts of that out of her mind. She quickly slipped behind the wheel of the Mustang and started the engine, and then moved it out into the drive. She held her breath. No one had heard the car being started, apparently, for there were no voices calling for her. She stepped on the gas pedal as she approached the guard gate, and roared through before the astonished guard could even see who was leaving.

The inside of the Mustang was blisteringly hot from the sun, and the air conditioning labored to cool it, but Francesca felt better than she had all morning. The irony of having to escape from one's own house made her smile very slightly. She kicked off her high-heeled sandals.

She turned the Mustang into the village of Palm Beach and took Royal Palm Way to the bridge and the mainland. Traffic was heavy in spite of the heat. From Route 41 she cut back to the shoreline of Lake Worth and then into a side street which led down between nondescript concrete warehouses and a bait store and then the marina itself, a seemingly endless maze of wooden walkways with boats of all sizes in their slips, a testimony to the wealth concentrated in Palm Beach and the surrounding areas. It was past noon. The marina baked in the hottest part of the day. Gulls wheeled overhead. A few of the bigger sailing boats hummed with air conditioners. The tinny voices of television rose from a handsome, black-hulled sloop out of Wilmington, Delaware; someone was watching daytime soap operas. And on the hot breeze there was the odor of lunch cooking.

The *Freya* was at the very end of the last slip. The wooden boards of the *Freya*'s gangplank were hot to Francesca's bare feet, as were the metal parts of the railing. Here, too, there was the thrum of air conditioning from below. She supposed Kurt was fixing lunch, or perhaps stretched out on one of the built-in lounges in the saloon, with the stereo on loud. She could hear the recorded sound of the Modern Jazz Quartet.

Francesca pushed open the hatch doors and descended the few steps into the *Freya*. She felt a little dizzy again; coming down the ladder one steeply and quickly found oneself in the middle of the lounge area of the yawl with its recessed lighting, the low, carved table from Thailand and the enveloping loud music on the sound system. It was like dropping straight down into a living room. The Modern Jazz Quartet rippled through "Night in Tunis," but not loudly enough to cover an insistent sound of moaning.

Francesca whirled to face the stern. In the curved area against the bulkhead, the built-in settee in blue handwoven tweed was large enough to accommodate two people; it could be used as a bed if the small staterooms were full. She recognized Kurt's naked body at once. It was impossible not to know the size of him, his massive sun-bronzed muscles rippling under silky skin that became a band of white across his small, hard buttocks, the mark of shorts and swim trunks. His head was bent, a shock of gold hair falling forward over his face. A woman's hands, fingers spread like starfish against his brown back, held him tightly, cradling him between her legs and groaning loudly. His body moved rhythmically to his choking gasps, clenching and then releasing like a driven spring into her.

With a sense of shock that stunned her, Francesca noted how beautiful their bodies were. Naked bodies, totally absorbed in each other. The sounds were the loud, mounting moans of passion. She saw the woman's green eyes look over Kurt's shoulder, staring in growing recognition and horror, a face surrounded by a tangled mass of lovely red hair that could only belong to Dorrit.

# 4

## Ghosts

# Chapter Fifteen

"WHAT THE devil, she had no place to go," Kurt had told her. "I let her stay on the *Freya* a few days, that was all."

Francesca knew that wasn't right. She knew Kurt wouldn't lie to her, he was too forthrightly honest for that. But hadn't Buffy Amberson said that Kurt never allowed women aboard the *Freya* as a rule?

The late afternoon sun streamed in the windows of Francesca's bedroom. The blinds had not yet been drawn against the onslaught of heat and light that the pounding air conditioners would not quite dispel. The bridal consultant, a plump woman visibly damp with perspiration, and the alterations woman fussed over the crisp folds of the beautiful wedding dress.

Francesca had reached the point where she could no longer think. Her brain was strangely muddled these days, and there were times when she felt helplessly adrift in a sea of insoluble problems. What was she going to do about anything? she thought, regarding herself in the mirror. She'd lost more weight. Another woman looked back at her from the glass, a hollow-eyed girl with an increasingly fragile beauty. Her long hair had grown gypsy wild again, she saw, and certainly needed Stephen of Beverly Hills' attention.

"I think this will have to be taken in again," the bridal consultant said. She picked up handfuls of pale pink silk organdy and tugged at it. "Of course high heels make a difference, but we'd better take in about half an inch to be on the safe side." Her plump lips pursed in disapproval. "I don't understand what you've been doing since this last fitting, Miss Lucchese. You look as though you've lost another two or three pounds."

Francesca was growing used to that look. She had lost weight, she supposed, because of the terrible sleeplessness that attacked her healthy body, and the fact that her once ravenous appetite had completely deserted her. Just thinking about it made her confused. She didn't know—she might not even get married, even though everyone expected the wedding to take place. There was a large numb spot in her brain that would not respond to the word "marriage" at all.

Nothing Kurt said to her seemed to make it any better, either.

"Francesca, I made a mistake," he tried to tell her very patiently, very earnestly. "I am not a fool for women, you know me better than that. How can I tell you this? It was damned hard to get away from her, that was all. She was around all the time. The boat is not all that big. Sure, I know—the first mistake was to give her a place to sleep."

Francesca bit her lips. Of course it *would* have to be Dorrit! There had always been unfinished business there, a person had to be blind not to see it. She had never forgotten that devouring kiss in the darkened hall the first night she'd been in Palm Beach, and Dorrit's hungry body twined against Kurt Bergstrom's. In that moment it was plain to see they had been lovers. Were perhaps still lovers.

What a fool she had been, right from the beginning! In all her life she had never imagined that she could be so wrong about everything, so misled by Palm Beach, rattled out of any sense she might have.

She hadn't wanted to listen to Kurt's explanations. She had flung herself away from him, screaming her pain and anger, not caring who heard. She was a woman about to be married who had just found her husband-to-be in bed with another woman! There wasn't much explaining that could be done about that. In a burst of very Italian fury she had thrown herself against him and pounded his body with her fists, hearing him grunt in surprise. It was a few seconds before he could grab her wrists, hold her to him, and calm her a little.

"I apologize, I was a fool." His voice was soft, his bronzed face calm, sea-blue eyes intent on her. When she had left the boat he had quickly run after her, wearing only the old khaki shorts he had thrown on in his hurry. But even like that, and barefoot, he was still the sun-gilded Viking god—powerful, serene, commanding.

Still holding her wrist, his other hand had lifted to stroke her hair as one would to soothe an angry and unreasonable child. "I admit I have just made a damned fool of myself. But Francesca, don't say these things to me, that you hate me. Please."

Francesca had managed to tear herself loose from his hands then, afraid that she would surrender to him in spite of everything. She couldn't get the picture of what she had just seen aboard the *Freya* out of her head. It was as though it was seared into her memory, the sight of Kurt's brown, powerful body raking Dorrit's with such unleashed sensuality, Dorrit reaching for each savage thrust in a flash of silky brown legs and driving naked hips, loudly moaning her pleasure.

Driven by what she remembered, Francesca had screamed at him what Buffy had told her that morning about Dorrit: the four of them—Bodner and Dorrit and Buffy and Jock

Amberson—playing the Palm Beach game of sex and drugs, with one of them taking pictures.

If she had expected to startle him she was doomed to disappointment. He only lifted his eyebrows, then shrugged. "Dorrit wanted to marry Bodner pretty bad. So she did what she could to please him." His voice, too, was calm. "Dorrit is a very beautiful woman. And Francesca, she is not the only tramp in Palm Beach. Give her a break."

"You disgust me!" she had cried. "All of you!"

But even as she said it, she knew she did not mean to include Kurt Bergstrom. She still loved him. She supposed it would always be that way.

"You're going to make a lovely bride," the alterations woman was saying. "You do need to get a little more rest, Miss Lucchese, otherwise it's going to show even more than it does now."

The bridal consultant agreed. "The first year you have to get adjusted to Florida summers; the second year is usually better. But you can't fight it. Your maid tells me she's been trying to get you to take a nap in the middle of the day. That's a very good idea, you know. September isn't a cool month at all. Sometimes I think it's worse than July."

The bridal consultant's voice ran on about the climate of the south Florida coast, and Francesca stared into the mirror. She tried to tell herself that she didn't look all that bad unless one got up close and saw the heavy dark shadows of fatigue under her eyes. The patrician gloss was still there: Gerda Schoener saw to it that she was made up as skillfully every morning as she had been at the *Golden Door*. She sighed. She didn't know what she would do without Mrs. Schoener, now.

Following Dorothea Smithson's abrupt departure after their return from New York, the maid had become a tower of strength, doing a great many things to fill in for the secretary—arranging daily menus, coordinating the household staff, handling the telephones. Everything, Francesca thought, except interviewing Dorothea's would-be replacement. Nobody wanted to do that. It was becoming apparent they would never find anyone to fill her capable shoes.

"Miss Lucchese, you aren't listening," the bridal consultant said.

The understanding had been, as Francesca well remembered, that Dorothea would be only a temporary employee. But she had done her job so well she had become nearly indispensable. The reason given for her leaving was that her son hadn't wanted to leave the Miami high school he attended the year he was due to graduate in order to transfer to the West Palm Beach school. Dorothea had been full of apologies and genuine regret, but the fact was that she had resigned. The first job candidates from local employment services had been so discouraging Francesca hadn't the heart to go any further; she had turned the problem over to the Miami lawyers and they had promised to supply someone within a few weeks.

The bridal consultant and the alterations seamstress were looking at Francesca as though they expected her to respond to some question. In the other room Gerda Schoener was turning down the bedcovers of Francesca's bed for an afternoon nap. The ormolu clock on the bedside table said three o'clock.

The two women exchanged looks.

"The date, Miss Lucchese," the bridal consultant said. "Are we still aiming for a September 18th wedding?"

Francesca tried to smile, embarrassed, for the moment, that she didn't really know. Dorothea Smithson had been handling the details of the wedding, and now all those plans were in chaos. What did the wedding invitations say? she wondered. As far as she knew, they hadn't even completed the list of invited guests.

From the other room Gerda Schoener, who had been listening, said, "Miss Lucchese will have someone call you and give you the date. Perhaps Mr. Kurt will do that. But whatever, you will send the gown right away, when it is ready this time."

When the women looked at Francesca, she nodded. She supposed it was right if Mrs. Schoener said so.

When they were through, and the maid had herded them to the door with their promises to have the pink bridal dress altered and ready as soon as possible, Francesca sank down into her desk chair. She rested her head in her hand, trying to shake off a curious, nagging sense of despair that lurked deep within her. She probably was not going to get married, she told herself. To marry a man she had surprised in bed with a tramp like Dorrit was to invite lifelong disaster. It had all been a terrible mistake, Kurt had explained. But a small voice within her fretted that he shouldn't have invited Dorrit to stay aboard in the first place. The small voice found it hard to accept any explanations, reasonable or not. They were *lovers* before, it told her. And all along—and *after?*

"Miss Lucchese," the maid reminded her. The bed was ready for her nap.

She needed it, Francesca told herself wearily. She wasn't becoming adjusted to the Florida heat at all. The only way to escape was to crawl between cool, satiny sheets, sink into the bed's softness, and sleep away the doldrums.

Francesca looked down at the top of her desk with the past few days' mail scattered carelessly over it. With Dorothea Smithson gone there was just no one to attend to it. But Francesca hated to see things in a mess; her years of office training revolted at the thought of work piling up. She picked up an envelope listlessly and ran her fingernail across the top to open it. It was a bill. She flipped it to the back of the green desk blotter. Another envelope, opened, contained a report from the Bloodworth public relations firm in New York. A passage jumped out at her at once.

. . . a Deborah Walton interview on NBC-TV network news which might be a wonderful opportunity to present the Bloodworth corporation with a glamorous new image as represented by you, and that would tend

to reassure the public about any adjustments taking
place in the Blo-Co stores division...

Francesca tossed the television interview proposal after
the bill. In the same envelope there were several clippings
from newspapers that the public relations firm always forwarded.

The top clipping in the pack was from the August 17th
issue of *Barron's* business weekly, announcing Bloodworth's majority stockholder, Francesca Lucchese, had requested the voting power of her corporation shares be
transferred back to her. The *Barron's* article made a passing
reference to "Bloodworth's troubled Blo-Co division."

*Troubled.* So they were having problems, Francesca
thought. It was the first time the admission had been made
publicly, as far as she knew.

There was a tear sheet from what appeared to be an
advance issue of the *National Enquirer* with a note from
the Bloodworth's public relations account executive which
said: "We put pressure on them to hand over the copy from
the first press run which we enclose, but it was too late for
an injunction according to our legal department."

The ink on the sheet was so fresh it was sticky to the
touch. But there were photographs of *Ca'ad Carlo* taken
from the air which showed its vast stretch across Palm Beach
island from oceanfront almost to the Lake Worth side,
showing plainly the abandoned greensward of the nine-hole
golf course, the main house and the cluster of tile-roofed
guest bungalows, stands of coconut palms and thick vege-
tation, the terrace, the boat basin, and the two sparkling
lakes of the swimming pools. There was also a shot of a
beautiful girl with long gypsy black hair walking across a
pool area in a bikini so brief that at first glance it looked
as though she was naked.

Francesca looked at herself indifferently. Another time
she would have been horrified. Now she recognized the
picture as the infamous telephoto lens shot taken a few

weeks ago that had already appeared in West Coast newspapers.

Another photograph at the bottom of the *Enquirer* page
showed a handsome blond giant of a man in a white dinner
jacket and the same darkhaired girl leaving a Palm Beach
restaurant. Kurt Bergstrom had his arm around her waist
protectingly, and Francesca held her head down, preparing
to slide into the front seat of the Porsche. The headline said:

### CINDERELLA HEIRESS IN PALM BEACH HIDEAWAY
### WITH DISINHERITED THIRD HUSBAND

In a bizarre turn of events which has left even
the ultra-sophisticated resort colony of Palm
Beach gasping, the daughter of a former chauffeur who inherited a dime store fortune estimated at $60 million is now involved with the
late Bloodworth heiress's disinherited third husband, who just happens to live in a guest cottage
on her estate.

"They are really fascinated with each other," a
Palm Beach resident and close friend admitted.
"He was living on the grounds when she arrived,
and she let him stay on because he was broke.
Naturally, they saw a great deal of each other,
and now they're inseparable. I wouldn't be surprised if they got married."

In her will the late Carla Bloodworth Tramm
DeLacy Bergstrom passed over her current husband, Count Kurt Bendt Bergstrom, to leave her
entire fortune to a former chauffeur who was
briefly in her employ some twenty-five years
ago. The chauffeur, Giovanni Lucchese, described by the Bloodworth heiress in her will as
"the only man I truly ever loved," is succeeded
by his daughter, Francesca Maria, 28, a resident

of Boston, Mass. A striking willowy brunette,
Miss Lucchese is reported to have spent $25,000
recently at Florida's famous *Golden Door* health
and beauty spa. The results, Palm Beach ob-
servers say, have been spectacular. "She's really
stunning," says one. "She could have any guy
she wants. But this Bergstrom is a real lady
killer."

Bergstrom, a Swedish citizen and internationally famed yachtsman, continues to live on the
Bloodworth Palm Beach estate, which is surrounded by high walls and patrolled by security
guards. But intimates say his quarters are only
a short walk from the main house. There has
been no explanation as to why the late Carla
Bloodworth did not include him in her will.

Francesca closed her eyes wearily. She wasn't even curious as to who the "Palm Beach resident and close friend"
was. She not only needed Dorothea Smithson at times like
this, but she missed her, too. She got up and went into her
bedroom with dragging feet.

Francesca waited patiently while the maid slipped her
silk shirtwaist dress over her head, and then unsnapped her
brassiere. The blinds in the bedroom had been drawn and
it was dim and cool. The steady pumping of the old window
air conditioner was as reassuring as a heartbeat. Francesca
sat down on the edge of her bed and Mrs. Schoener knelt
to take off her high-heeled pumps.

Mrs. Schoener said, not looking up, "Miss Lucchese,
that Johnny Turtle asked to see you. He says he wants to
make an appointment to talk to you. He didn't like it when
I didn't let him in a while ago. But I told him I would tell
you."

"No," Francesca murmured. She could hardly keep her
eyes open. John Turtle was the last person she wanted to

see. "He wants to know when I'm going out, or something, so he can get the car and things ready." She yawned. "I'm not going out. Just don't tell him anything."

Francesca took a tall, delicious-looking glass of iced tea the maid handed her, a slice of lemon floating against the ice cubes, and sank back against the satin bed pillows gratefully. After a few sips she could hardly hold up the glass.

"And Mr. Kurt called, too." The maid's stolid face seemed to show a slight apprehension. "He wants to talk to you, Miss Lucchese."

She supposed he did. Francesca closed her eyes, feeling a cloud of uncertainty intrude on the drowsy feeling of being comfortably in bed. Sometime, somewhere, she was going to have to make up her mind not to get married.

"I don't know," Francesca murmured. She didn't want anything settled right now; she didn't want to talk to anyone."

The maid's voice, insistent, said: "You think about it, Miss Lucchese. Mr. Kurt is a fine person, I've known him a long time. You ought to talk to him."

It was odd for Gerda Schoener, usually so closemouthed, to go on and on about anything like that. A lovely blue glow behind Francesca's eyelids was wiping away all care, smoothing out knotted muscles, making way for a remarkable psychedelic display of purple, lavender and pink—a marvelous light show drowning her senses in luminous color. Francesca drifted happily, ready for a long sleep. The maid took the glass of iced tea from her unresisting hands and waves of darkness crept over the colors in Francesca's eyes. Over everything.

A few seconds later Francesca dreamed that a door opened and closed and someone with heavy footsteps approached. There were voices, a man's and a woman's—it took a moment to realize they were not speaking English. The first voice was Mrs. Schoener's. The second voice, a man's, Francesca recognized only after some time as Kurt Bergstrom's. They were arguing again, as they had been arguing the day she surprised them in Kurt's cottage. This time not so loudly, but just as fiercely.

Francesca knew she was dreaming. All of this had happened before.


SHE awoke with Mrs. Schoener bending over her with a cup of coffee in her hands. The windows showed darkness and the hot velvet night. The clock on the night table said ten-fifteen. Francesca sat up, dizzily, aghast that it was so late. She had only intended to take a nap. Now half the evening was gone! She was vaguely and unpleasantly aware that her head was still filled with wonderful colors and shimmering lights that showed themselves when she moved too quickly. It was a curious sensation but she felt better and, if not more rested, at least more relaxed than when she had gone to bed.

She sat naked on the edge of the bed and sipped the coffee, black and strong and with a metallic taste that lately had come to flavor everything. But when she had finished and Mrs. Schoener had brought her a second cup, Francesca began to feel energy and a welcome sense of well-being pumping through her veins. She was not quite steady on her feet when she went to take a shower. When she came back Mrs. Schoener was waiting for her at the dressing table and motioned for her to sit down.

"Where am I going?" Francesca wanted to know as she slid into the seat. If she was going somewhere at that hour she had forgotten all about it.

The maid's strong hands seized the back of her neck and began to massage the tight muscles there. "You need to go down to see Mr. Kurt," she said firmly. "You have to talk with him. You can't judge him like these others. For him, life is different. The blood of the old kings, the Ynglinga, is in his veins. He is not like this—" She stopped, searching for a word. "Trash," she finished, with a sour look.

Francesca was not really listening. Mrs. Schoener's hands

deftly worked the skin of her shoulders and back and then down the arms to her elbows. Under the expert pounding her body turned rosy pink, and began to glow. The color came back to her face.

Kurt Bergstrom had a defender in Gerda Schoener, obviously. But if they were friends, why had they had such screaming rows? she wondered.

Francesca wanted to say something about Kurt but the other woman took her by the hand and lifted her from the dressing table seat and pushed her toward the bed. Francesca protested weakly as she was shoved against the bedspread.

"Now," the other woman grunted, "we make you ready."

The maid started with the left leg at the ankle and began long, punishing strokes of her hands and knuckles that loosened the muscles all the way to the knees. Then she began on the thighs. It was a strenuous massage; Francesca began to gasp between the pummeling.

"He makes mistakes, that is true," the maid was muttering. Her broad plain face was screwed up into a troubled expression. "He is human—it is human to make mistakes. But he is all man, you should know that. He has made good love to you in bed." The woman's hands began to pursue the muscles of Francesca's thighs into intimate places and Francesca tried to pull up on her elbows. She was shoved back. "I make your body nice, be still. It is a very good body, good for sex. I make it even more so."

The knuckles worked painfully across Francesca's abdomen, tearing out the stiffness there and replacing it with a warm, erotic sensation. Francesca put her hands over her breasts but the maid pulled them away. Her fingers began to shape the superb golden flesh, pinching the nipples into contracted points. Francesca squirmed, unable to breathe or speak.

"You should go to him, hear what he has to say," the woman went on relentlessly. "You are not getting any younger, you will be thirty in a few years, and with so much money you will not attract good men. Mr. Kurt is worth

ten of these who want to be around you. You know the ones
I mean, like this writer." The voice dropped to a feral hiss.
"They all want your money. That is what they want, even
when you are beautiful, only the money."

Francesca moaned, not able to stop the pounding hands
on her body. She writhed in curious response to those hammering, probing blows. But at the same time she knew the
result would be wonderful. That she would emerge marvelously, sensuously alive.

Suddenly the massage ceased and the maid hauled her
to her feet, pushing her once more to her seat before the
dressing table. She lifted Francesca's mane of rusty-black
curls and ran a brush under it briskly.

"Nothing better will come to you." The hands reached
over Francesca's shoulders to pick up the brushes and bottles
of makeup. "And he can give you children. You should
think of that. Beautiful children." The voice turned a little
hoarse. "You will be a lucky woman. Mr. Kurt is not just
anyone—he is a king, a god. He should have a young
princess for a wife. This time it is good, I am sure of it."

Mrs. Schoener's hands skillfully applied rouge and eye
makeup. An impossibly beautiful glowing creature began
to emerge in the dressing table mirror—a woman with dark
massed curls surrounding a perfect oval face with eyes of
luminous silver-gray light. An enchanting beauty. The proud
lift of her chin made her a princess, indeed.

The maid slipped a glittering silver threaded caftan over
Francesca's head and then sprayed her hair lavishly with an
atomizer of *Joy* perfume.

"Where am I going?" Francesca said again. She was
naked under the glittering robe, but her body was bursting
with ripe feeling. The gown was not quite opaque: she could
see the pink shadows of her nipples thrusting forward under
the silk. She thought she looked like a great sparkling bird
in the loose caftan, a dream bird enveloped in silver sparkles
with matching silvery eyes and a mane of midnight hair that
flowed untamed over her shoulders and arms.

Francesca now felt so much better, energized, that the thought of going somewhere at that hour was intriguing. She was having trouble remembering from one moment to the next. The pink and purple clouds were still in her head.

The maid lifted her from her seat and gave her a shove toward the door.

"Go down to Mr. Kurt's cottage," she told her. "He is waiting for you."

FRANCESCA made her way uncertainly down from the main house. The full moon shed a bright white light on the shell path as she wavered along it, at times taking wrong turnings and careening into bushes. She was barefoot, and stepped on the edge of the caftan when she was not careful. Several times she almost tripped and fell. The night was smotheringly warm. Her bare skin under the faintly scratchy, nearly-transparent silver caftan would not let her forget her nakedness; her flesh still trembled a little from the erotic pounding she had received at Mrs. Schoener's hands.

In spite of her dizziness Francesca became aware after a while that someone was following her. Deliberately she stepped off a path and under the tangled trunks of a banyan, smacking her forehead against a limb in the process. Her eyes were still watering with unshed tears when she smelled the smoke of a small brown cigarillo in the air. She stood very still, hoping he would not see her. She gave a small sigh as John Turtle stopped, turned in her direction and then came in under the limbs to drag her out.

"What are you doing down here?" he demanded. Francesca felt his look raking her: the bare feet, her naked body visible under the glittering gown, and she heard the swift intake of his breath as he looked into her glowing, artfully made-up face. "Damn, *damn,*" she heard him mutter. His hands tightened around her upper arms as he held her.

"It doesn't matter what I'm doing," she told him, drawing herself up with great dignity. "It's none of your business, John Turtle. Go back to bed."

"I wasn't in bed." His voice was harsh. The mist of *Joy* hung in the air around them, perfuming the night. He held on to her as though he could not take his eyes from her. He said in a strange voice, "Dammit, Francesca, don't do this. Go back up to the house." He seemed to hesitate. "Listen—you're pretty well out of it and I don't think you realize it. You don't need to—you don't need to go running around like this in the dark."

She pushed him away. Under her hands his chest was as hard as a stone. She said, very precisely, *"Miss Lucchese* to you, John Turtle. Have you forgotten that? And I want you to stop following me!"

His hands tried to turn her in the direction of *Ca'ad Carlo's* main house. "Francesca, I've been trying to see you. But I can't talk to you like this, now. When you're like this. How long are you going to stay shut up in your room? I can't—"

She didn't want to hear any of this. "I want you to keep your hands off me!" she cried. "How many times do I have to tell you that? I am going somewhere and you can't do anything about it! That is, follow me, or anything!"

Francesca sidestepped, tripping on the caftan. Before he could take her arm to steady her she bolted, lifting the sparkling silver gown in her hands to run.

No footsteps followed her. She ran down the lane of daturas toward Kurt Bergstrom's cottage, conscious of the white flowers in bloom over her head and their narcotic perfume. The moonlight was brilliant. Daturas could make one dizzy. By the time she reached the front terrace of Kurt Bergstrom's cottage her head was spinning.

Francesca half stumbled through the front door. She was almost through the living room when she heard the sound of the shower. The door slammed behind her and at the sound, the water stopped. Kurt Bergstrom appeared quickly at the door with a bath towel around his waist. He was tall and brown and gleaming, and even as Francesca moved toward him she felt her own flesh quiver in response.

His brilliant blue eyes caught her and examined her with

growing intentness as she came toward him, taking in the diaphanous silver gown, her mop of long curls and her glowing face with surprise and appreciation.

"I forget how beautiful you are from one time to the next," he murmured, "like silver fire. Thank God you have come to me."

In a few steps he was close enough to wrap his big arms around her. The bath towel dropped away and he enveloped her in his wet and aroused body, his flesh faintly cool, surging with the strength coiled in him. What Francesca meant to say, the questions and the half-apologies, fled from her mind. With a soft moan on her lips she let her body cling to him. She felt his hard sex press against her loins, hungry for her.

"My darling, my darling," she heard him whisper. His hands laced behind her head, tangling in her hair. He pulled her head back to look down into her face. The strange clear eyes seemed to bore into her soul. "This is crazy," he muttered, "to love like this. Francesca, I tell you the truth, now—I want you as I have wanted no other woman in my life."

Very slowly, he lowered his mouth to her lips. At the electric touch of it Francesca's lips trembled apart and she took his tongue, circling and tasting, boldly probing into hers, confidently possessing her. Her body melted willingly against his. Then his mouth pulled away quickly and brushed her cheek, then the soft convolutions of her ear, exploring it, making hidden nerve endings tingle unbearably. His lips dropped to smooth her throat with gentle, insistent kisses. Francesca threw back her head to receive them, her long hair swinging over his bare arm. His hands stroked down her back to the curve of her waist, settling against her gorgeous bottom and pressing her hips to him tightly.

Francesca was afire, her body responding to his with an aching, pulsing rhythm; all she knew was that she needed this man's easygoing strength, his masculine assurance, the sure rapture of their lovemaking. His hands were unbuttoning the shimmering caftan. In the silver sparkle of the opened fabric her breasts thrust out full and heavy, with tapering glistening pink nipples, magnificent and a little savage. His hands cupped and stroked them sinuously. When he bent his head his eyes filled up her vision, intoxicating her senses. When he kissed her it was provocatively, his lips touching hers over and over again lightly as he murmured love words to her.

"My beautiful Francesca with the most beautiful breasts, the most beautiful body—how could I forget that you were virgin for me?" He took her hand and guided it to his naked loins, closing her fingers around his hard, aroused flesh. "Love me, caress me, my darling," he breathed.

Francesca's touch stroked and explored him, wanting to know his body as intimately as he knew hers; she learned the movement that pleased him and set him to gasping. She couldn't help but know that to this man she had first revealed her passionate nature and that this innocence stimulated him greatly. He was the first and only man she had ever known. His breaths grew heavy and loud in her ear as she continued to caress him with her hand. Then, abruptly, he groaned, and his mouth descended on hers, his teeth nibbling her lips hungrily, his tongue goading her.

Francesca clung to him dizzily. She lifted her mouth eagerly to his at the same time she felt his fingers slip into the soft cleft between her thighs and enter its tight moistness. She cried out with a suddenly accelerated need for him, wanting him to take her. Her mouth strained for his kisses, feeling under her hands the great muscles of his back and shoulders contracting as his hands stroked and held her.

"Show me how you love me, Francesca," he murmured. His blue eyes were like cold flames of desire. "I need you to love me, my darling."

With her head flung back over his arm, dark hair tangling in his fingers, Francesca rose to meet his mounting tension. His big body quivered, and he drowned her mouth in kisses.

"You are going to marry me, Francesca," he promised. "Say you love me."

She could only moan, her hips circling his, full of a raw

ache that begged to be released. She was only half aware
that he picked her up in his arms and carried her to the
bedroom and put her down on the bed. His hands pulled at
the silvery gown, stripping it out of his way. In the dim
light Francesca raised on her elbows to see his beautiful
bronzed body with its powerful arousal, the stalk of his flesh
swollen with desire for her, his skin still glistening faintly
with the sheen of his shower.

He knelt beside her on the bed. "You will marry me,
Francesca," he insisted. "You have forgiven me. Say it, my
darling."

She was barely aware that he moved over her. Her eyes
and senses were full of wildly reeling colors and his potent
nearness. But he held himself from her.

"I want you," he said softly. "I want you to marry me,
Francesca. I wish to love you like this, as your husband,
in our bed in the house of *Ca' ad Carlo*. Do you understand?"

His words, his soft voice and his urgency destroyed the
last of her doubts. Francesca put her arms around his neck.
"Yes," she sobbed, surrendering to him.

She took the great thrusting mass of his flesh with a small
sensuous shriek as he entered her. It was as though his body
sealed his complete possession of her; he crowded her,
stretched her, thrusting into her powerfully, jolting gasps
of pleasure from her lips. Holding her hips high against him
as he knelt before her, he drove into her in impassioned
bursts, his blond hair flailing, his bronze face suffused with
desire. Francesca groaned as stormy waves of his lovemaking wracked her body, and as his fingers dug into her
soft, full bottom, lifting it to receive him. When she began
to shudder with the impact of skyrocketing flames he gave
a choking cry and then his body exploded savagely into
hers.

It lasted only a few moments. Almost as soon as his
release had begun he caught himself, holding her, letting
her go wild in his arms as she enjoyed the joyous climax
of her love. When she quieted at last, going limp and ex-

hausted, his hands met in the curve of her waist and gently lowered her to the bed. He rested his big body lightly on hers, his deep breaths moving her rib cage in and out in time with his, small trickles of sweat running down onto her skin.

Francesca drifted back slowly, her flesh still ringing with the receding tides of passion. As confused as she was, she could still give herself over to a languid feeling of complete happiness in his arms, of being safe and loved. And of loving him totally as he lightly touched his lips to her forehead and outlined the edge of her dark curling hair with his kisses. In return Francesca lifted her hands to caress his warm, damp throat and the sensitive area behind his ears where his hair was thick and drenched with perspiration. She felt his body answer her touch with an almost imperceptible quiver.

"Francesca, my love," he whispered against her hair.

In his arms Francesca knew there was no need to answer the questions that whirled around them—who he was, his position as Carla's third husband, his lack of money. She had only to close her eyes and concentrate on the fact that she loved this big, gentle, golden man, and wanted him, and was going to be his wife.

His free hand stroked her wet hair back from her face, "I will make you happy, I swear it," he murmured. "My God, I love you. I can't believe it. I want you to marry me tomorrow."

Francesca didn't respond to the words immediately. She didn't think he was serious, but he was. Then she felt a small rush of panic. *Tomorrow?* The nagging confusion dulled her mind and she couldn't unravel the implications. Tomorrow meant—there would be only the bride and groom. The wonderful wedding plans crumbled into ruins before they had even begun.

"I can't—" she began, but his fingers touched her mouth to silence her.

"Tomorrow, yes," he said firmly. The strange sea-blue

eyes looked down at her. "Francesca, I want you to do this for me. Time is running out." His voice held an odd note of irritation. "I don't want to lose you. I want us to be married right away—tomorrow."

She didn't understand his words at all. They had the marriage license, she supposed it could be done, but it was rushing things, jumbling all their plans into chaos.

"I'll take care of it," he said softly. "I will make it beautiful for you, I promise."

"I want my dress." She was going to be adamant about that. She wanted to wear the pale silk wedding dress with its billowing skirt and the rose-colored veil and be beautiful for him. She wasn't going to give that up. "I have my wedding dress—it's being altered—" she began doubtfully. The wedding gown was her dream. She wanted him to see her in it.

She saw him smile. His tanned face broke into a tender, indulgent expression, a loving smile, as he looked down into her wide, silvery eyes. His arms tightened around her.

"You will have it. We will get it ready, send for it, I will see to that myself." His lips began to stroke her mouth gently. She felt the warm touch of his breath as he said against it, "I will do everything for you from now on, my darling."

# CHAPTER SIXTEEN

FRANCESCA WOKE in her own bed in the main house.

The first thing she saw on opening her eyes was the rose-tinted bridal gown laid over the satin slipper chair by the window, the billowing yards of tissue-thin silk like the opened petals of a giant moonflower. Over the dress was carefully laid the deeper rose-colored bridal veil, yards of tulle spilling from a circlet of white silk tea roses. The sight bored into her consciousness and jolted her fully awake.

Someone—Kurt—had gone for her beautiful bridal dress, fetching it from the West Palm Beach couturiere. She really was going to get married! Today.

Even as she realized it, Francesca clutched her head and moaned. The terrible headache had found her again. She lay back in bed quickly and lifted the telephone to call Gerda Schoener and help.

* * *

AFTER the maid had brought her the breakfast tray and a
pot of coffee and Francesca had drained most of it, Francesca slowly came alive again, lying comfortably in bed in
a mist of growing happiness. The decision had been made
to get married; it was out of her hands. The coffee sent a
familiar fiery warmth flowing through her veins, and a sense
of sanity returned. The day was going to be perfect, she
decided, stretching in the nest of silky sheets—hot clear
September Florida weather. A cloudless sky showed through
the bedroom windows and indicated all was right with the
world. She convinced herself that everything was going to
be wonderful. She had decided she didn't want to know,
or feel, any more than that.

"Whatever's in your coffee," Francesca called to the
maid in the wardrobe room, "Blo-Co division could use
some of it. You ought to try to sell them your recipe."

There was no answer.

Francesca stretched again luxuriously, remembering what
had taken place in Kurt Bergstrom's cottage. *He loved her.*
He wanted to be married right away. How could anyone be
so happy? she marveled.

Without much interest she sorted through the morning's
mail that had begun to appear again on her breakfast tray.
Since Dorothea Smithson's departure she had fallen into the
habit of taking only what appeared to be personal correspondence and discarding the rest. There was always the
possibility, in unidentified correspondence, that another death
or kidnap threat might be lurking among the seemingly
innocent envelopes. Francesca wanted to avoid, at all cost,
the shock of some sick mind's ravings springing out at her
from the mail. As she was opening the top letter the telephone shrilled. Francesca grabbed it up.

"Miss Lucchese," Delia Mary's voice said on the other
end of the line, "are you fixing to get married today? Mister
Kurt came down here and told me we need champagne for

about fifteen people and little sandwiches down in the rose garden because you're going to get married today. And I told him I don't know nothing about no such thing, that Mrs. Smithson, your secretary, wasn't here no more, and you hadn't said a word to anybody about changing your wedding day. And if I was going to fix something for a wedding I was going to have to hear it from you, yourself. And nobody else."

*Oh dear,* Francesca thought, and closed her eyes. The war had started all over again. She didn't think she could cope with any of this; she realized she couldn't answer any of Delia Mary's questions. She really didn't know much about her own wedding. She didn't have any idea who was going to marry her, or even the time of the ceremony.

"Yes, I'm going to be married today," Francesca said a little unsteadily. "You just do what Mr. Kurt says, Delia Mary. He's in charge of things."

Mrs. Schoener, waiting by her side, took the telephone from her hands to finish the conversation with the cook. Francesca got out of bed and went into the bathroom where, she saw, her bath was already drawn. She could hear Mrs. Schoener's voice, loud, giving orders to Delia Mary, even from there.

FRANCESCA carried her mail into the bathroom and read it as she took a slow-motion, leisurely bath. There was a letter from Harry Stillman of the Miami law firm mentioning her upcoming marriage and enclosing a list of jewelry from the Bloodworth estate, just released by the insurance company auditors. The lawyers hoped she would regard the turning over of Carla's jewels to her as something of a wedding gift. Francesca went down the list of jewelry quickly. There were things like a diamond necklace and a choker of black pearls from the collection of Mrs. Charles Bloodworth, Sr., as well as several diamond rings, a ruby and emerald bracelet, a sapphire and diamond tiara— the list seemed endless.

Francesca accidentally dropped the lawyer's letter into the bath water and had to fish it out and lay it on the edge of the tub to dry. She was still mentally blurry, and having a tremendous lot of jewelry didn't seem real. Where did one wear diamond and ruby bracelets anyway—not to mention a tiara!

There was a long letter from Herb Ostrow.

Francesca smiled. He was so earnest, and she knew he didn't like the idea of her getting married to Kurt Bergstrom at all.

She ripped open the envelope raggedly with her fingernail and began to read.

Dear Francesca:

When you get this I will probably be out of town on a short trip to see my agent in New York, who had great hopes for the Palm Beach book with the new Bloodworth material. But the real truth of the matter is, lovely lady, I don't want to be around for the upcoming nuptials. You know the reason why.

However, with that in mind, I'm hastening to get the enclosed letters to you as I think you will find they contain news that will give you a different perspective on your life and, who knows? perhaps change it in some way. It's too much to hope, I suppose, that they would influence you to alter your current decision to marry, but I think I might prevail on you to at least reconsider.

Francesca, I don't know how to approach you with what I've found in the old Bloodworth office records and family correspondence bins. I've been sitting around for a couple of days rereading your father's letters and I've had to choose between coming to you in person with this and having you ask me questions I can't answer, or falling back on that which I know best—writing it all out for you. I've chosen the latter.

* * *

Mrs. Schoener came to the door. "It's getting late, Miss Lucchese," she said. "Mr. Kurt will have the gentleman from West Palm, the justice of the peace, in the rose garden at one o'clock. That is where you are to come to be married."

Francesca dried off the first page of Herb Ostrow's letter with the bath towel and followed the maid into the bedroom. The pink bridal dress hung on a hanger, a luscious candy-colored drift of yards of silk organdy and clouds of rose-pink veil. Francesca sat down at the dressing table, subduing a funny floating feeling that attacked her when she walked across the room. In the mirror her face was unnaturally flushed, giving her more color than she had had in weeks. Her eyes were like stars with deep, widened pupils. She looked, even freshly bathed and without makeup, brilliantly lovely, her face framed in a riot of damp black curls.

Francesca propped the rest of Herb Ostrow's letter against the dressing table mirror as the maid began to brush her hair.

*Something which could change her life?* she thought. She couldn't imagine what he meant.

The letters are undated, perhaps deliberately. The Italian is a little obscure—an academic interest leads me to believe that in spite of your father's Sicilian background he and Carla used the local Capri dialect with which both were familiar, as a sort of screen for their communications. As you will see, there was a real need for secrecy, after all.

Gerda Schoener attacked Francesca's long hair vigorously with the hair brush, jerking her head back. Francesca had to pick the letter up and hold it at eye level in order to read it. Herb Ostrow was so solemn about his project, she thought; he sounded as though he were writing world history.

These two letters turned up in some sealed envelopes, interestingly enough, which someone at some time had put aside, perhaps realizing the future importance of their contents. At any rate, this being neither here nor there—only to explain why these weren't with the other letters from Vanni to Carla that I turned over to you. The additional sheets are where I've copied out a close translation of the letters' Italian, impenetrable dialect and all, for your attention. But to save you time and trouble and perhaps provide some psychological cushion, the jist of the two letters from your father to Carla more than twenty-five years ago can be put this way:

In letter number one (so marked) he tells Carla that he is going away and taking the child with him. And for the first time we find that he tells Carla how sorry he is for the great wrong he says he's done her, and his family as well, in this matter. And that he hopes to make it up through his future loving care and devotion to his daughter. He says that he understands why Carla will let the child go with him and he says—perhaps putting a good light on it—that he knows she will always love her child.

At this point it becomes clear to all who read the first letter that the baby at *Ca'ad Carlo* was Carla's child. The reference to the woman who was supposedly the mother indicates she was a Lucchese cousin or distant relative brought along to foster the idea that your father was married and that the child was the offspring of that marriage.

By now you must be aware of the story that emerges: Carla Bloodworth, at that time Carla DeLacy, had a child by Giovanni Lucchese in Italy somewhere, but probably not Capri where Carla lived most of the time. And brought the baby back from Italy with her accompanied by the father, Giovanni, and a good number of his family who wanted to immigrate. The three of them—Carla, Giovanni, and their baby, spent 1956 and part of 1957 at *Ca'ad Carlo*. Then, for some reason, Carla seemed willing to let Giovanni go away, taking their baby daughter with them.

Francesca made a convulsive movement to stand up, her face gone pale, but Mrs. Schoener put her hands on her shoulders and pushed her back down into the chair in front of the dressing table.

"Be still," she said. "I am making you beautiful for Mr. Kurt. Keep your mind on what you are doing."

Francesca stared at the letter in her hand. She was having trouble absorbing the message completely; for some reason she couldn't seem to gather her wits. But she understood enough.

The rustling folds of the silk wedding dress suddenly descended over her head, shutting out light and air, and Francesca waited obediently while the maid pulled her arms into the armholes and began buttoning it up the back. Francesca caught a glimpse of her face in the mirror and couldn't respond to that awful look.

The letter went on:

All this is pretty baffling, I realize. If Carla was your mother, why didn't she and your father marry? Mere social inequality wouldn't have mattered all that much in that day and age in Palm Beach. We can speculate that Carla had Vanni's child to move the issue of marriage to its natural conclusion—in other words, she got pregnant in order to have him marry her. But why did Carla agree to let your father go to Boston and take you with him, presumably never to see you—her own daughter—again?

The second letter seems to answer some of these questions. It appears to have been written in Italy shortly before you were born. The emotion expressed makes it pretty harrowing to read—I'd advise you to

wait a while before you tackle the translation. A man
literally lays bare his soul in this. Your father seems
to have suspected that Carla had his child to force the
issue of marriage, and in the letter he tells her why
he can't marry her. He reveals something that probably at the time only his brothers—your uncles—
knew, and their lips were sealed. I believe the word
in Sicilian for that kind of silence is *omerta*. You,
Francesca, will know what that kind of vow implies.
The secret of the family was that Giovanni, the be-
loved and beautiful younger brother, had taken his
vows as a priest before he left the seminary.

The decision not to break the vows and marry must
have been a difficult one, but this was the Fifties,
remember—runaway priests who acquired wives and
children were not as common as they were to be in
the coming decade, and Giovanni was a religious man.
His and Carla's love affair must have been consid-
erably more tormented than the earlier letters show.
Poor Carla—for once something she wanted was not
attainable!

I find it easier to understand, now, why she would
let you go. Her move had been futile—even the presence of a child would not allow Vanni to marry her.
And she was in an awkward position to raise you on
her own, acknowledging your illegitimacy. And considering that your father had been her chauffeur. So
she let you go. The situation between them was fray-
ing, anyway, according to the last letters—under the
pressures of Carla's money and lifestyle and Vanni's
jealousy and dissatisfaction. The solution was to let
you go to Boston with the brothers and their families,
and let you settle down to a normal life.

Francesca held Herb Ostrow's letter in her hand and
found that she could not think rationally. There was only
one thing she could really absorb—*Carla Bloodworth was
her mother!*

In the back of her head a small voice denied this. Stunned, disbelieving, but clear. She couldn't be Carla's child. She *couldn't*.

Read the letters, Francesca. You will find your mother and father loved each other deeply, in the face of much that was dangerous to them. Carla was a spoiled, beautiful little butterfly who hadn't known much love until your father came into her life. Then I think she was rocked to the core of her being. She wanted Vanni desperately enough to get pregnant or, who knows?, perhaps she wanted his child for the best of reasons—for love. Your father was perhaps just as indulged—he seems to have been the brilliant one of his family, with all their pride and adoration centered on him. No one knows much about the crisis of faith that drove him to abandon the priesthood and then, when he was working as her chauffeur in Capri, fall in love with a beautiful American dime store princess who was trying to survive her unhappy second marriage.

You can fill in the gaps by reading the letters. Vanni says how much he loves her. He writes to Carla that she vows she loves him, too—and he will hold her to that through all eternity.

The bottom line here, as you must realize by now, is that years later when Carla was dying, she called in a local lawyer to rewrite her last will and testament, leaving everything to your father and, ultimately, to you. Even then she was true to their secret: she did not reveal that you were her daughter.

I think they must have taken a vow on it, not to let you know that you were their child, in order to save you from the kind of pain they lived with.

This time Francesca made it to her feet in an agonized frenzy. She looked around the room, not really seeing it, her mind circling in helpless confusion. There was only one person who could help her.

"I have to see Kurt," she cried.

What was in the letters would, as Herb Ostrow had testified, perhaps change her life. She had to talk to Kurt about it. She had to tell him *before* the wedding! She didn't know why, but she did.

"Now," Gerda Schoener was saying, "you look nice. I think it is good you wear this dress and veil after all. You are not virgin, but you were for him when he made love to you. So it is all right."

Francesca stared into the mirror as the maid's hands turned her about.

The woman in the glass was tall, with a superb body that set the wedding gown off to perfection. The skirt billowed about her body like the petals of a pink rose. The black-brown hair, piled high and cascading down to ringlets across her bare shoulders, drew attention to the pale gold sleekness of her fine skin. The pink of the silk gown was echoed subtly in her flushed face, giving her naturally olive complexion a hectic light that was reflected in her silvery eyes. The wedding dress was modestly cut across the bosom, featuring small puffed sleeves as a gesture to the hot Florida summer, cinched tightly at the waist, then drifting out to yards of tissue silk in the skirt. Distractedly, Francesca knew that she had never been so beautiful. Even Gerda Schoener's face showed it.

Francesca started for the door.

"Where are you going?" the other woman cried. When Francesca struggled to get past her she said grimly, "You don't go anywhere now, your wedding is at one o'clock. You will wait here."

"No," Francesca said stubbornly. But when Gerda Schoener seized her arm she stopped, assailed by a returning bout of confusion and not quite sure what she was doing. Then she remembered Kurt.

He was the only one in the world who loved her and could help her.

The maid blocked her way, scowling. "Go back and sit down, I told you. You don't go anyplace like that, in your wedding gown. If you go to see Mr. Kurt he will tell you same thing. It's bad luck to see the bride before the wedding."

Francesca only knew that Gerda Schoener had placed herself so that she was an obstruction on the path to Kurt Bergstrom. And she intended to get around one way or another. She stepped toward her, feinted, then stepped to the other side quickly and darted past the broad-shouldered woman, who let out a bark of dismay.

Francesca skipped through the bedroom in a second, holding the silken skirt up in a great wad with one hand.

Francesca was down the gallery stairs and through the great hall of *Ca' ad Carlo* in seconds, and burst out into the searing sunshine of the front circular drive. She had dropped Herb Ostrow's letter somewhere in her flight, but she told herself it didn't matter. She could explain the contents when she got to Kurt's cottage.

The shell drive crunched under her feet as she ran, holding the heavy skirts of the bridal dress up in both hands, her hair streaming like a dark flag behind her. She ran unsteadily. The trees wavered in the brilliant hot light—at times she felt as if she were a figure in a dream, floating in time and air. Her feet didn't seem to touch the ground.

The sunlight dazzled the eyes at noon. The vivid jungle-like growth of green Palm Beach island was unreal. The shell path was full of wavering ghosts in the white, flaming brightness. The ground tilted, and Francesca closed her eyes and stumbled and almost fell. She had to keep going.

There was Carla's ghost, coming down the lane of dream-poisoned daturas in the night to meet her lover. Carla in Vanni's arms. She, Francesca, had moved down that same lane in the night to her lover, too.

The dark jungle trees, the burning light, the white path before her melted and ran together. For a moment she forgot why she was running. What was driving her so relentlessly. Or why, now, she was dressed as a bride.

Francesca flung open the door of the cottage and stumbled headlong into it, her heart pounding with the terrible exertion of running as hard as she had ever run in her life. She lost her grip on the layers of the big silk skirt and stepped on it and nearly pitched headfirst. She knew she didn't have enough breath to speak, to call out. She saw the open door to the bathroom. She lurched against the wall, hit her shoulder on the side of the narrow hallway, and put out her hand to the doorjamb of the bathroom to keep from falling. She could only manage a small sob, calling his name. It would be all right when she was safe in Kurt's arms.

Francesca completely surprised him. Her entrance had been in such a rush that he hadn't heard her approaching until the last few feet, the last few seconds as she staggered to the door of the bungalow's bathroom. Kurt turned.

The surface of the bathroom cabinet near the washbasin was littered with various articles—a teaspoon, a clear plastic sandwich bag which held a quantity of white powder, a length of surgical rubber tubing, several puffs of red-tipped absorbent cotton, and a candle which was still lighted.

When Kurt turned his big body to Francesca the sea-blue eyes in his tanned face were strangely unfocused, but his mouth brimmed with bright red blood. Some of it spilled over in the corners of his mouth and leaked down in red rivulets to his chin. It gave him a monstrous, ghoulish look. He still had the hypodermic syringe in his right hand. The thumb of that hand was covered with blood, too.

For that second it was as though Francesca was suspended in time. She heard her own long, ragged gasping for breath as she clung to the door frame, her free hand still clutching the billowing skirts of her wedding dress.

The blood dripped down out of his mouth, turning him into a monster, and still he stared at her with dead eyes, not able to speak.

Francesca screamed. It came ripping out of her mindlessly, that terrible sound, and would not stop. There was no response in his look.

Francesca kept screaming. And screaming. Everything was coming to an end. A steamroller of darkness leaped up in the back of her eyes and rushed over her. Her head turned and jerked spasmodically. And then she fainted.

# CHAPTER SEVENTEEN

THE SUN was hot in the receiving line in spite of the occasional shade of a royal palm which swung its fronds over them in the intermittent gusts of wind from the ocean. Francesca, stiff and disoriented, felt as though she would break in two if she bent too far, so most of the wedding guests who were not her own height or taller struggled as best they could to reach her cheek and kiss it, before they passed down the line formed by the bride and groom and Cassie and Angel, the groom's best man, and the matron of honor.

But Harry Stillman took a piercing look at Francesca when he approached and then turned to the man next to him to mutter, "My God—it's worse than I'd heard. She's completely out of it."

Francesca smiled again vaguely. A length of the bridal veil's pink tulle drifted against her mouth, moved by the hot breeze in the *Ca'ad Carlo* rose garden. The sound of

bees in the flowers was loud; at times the buzzing filled
Francesca's ears so that she couldn't hear what people were
saying. But she had heard Harry Stillman very clearly. What
she did not understand was the heavy tone of disgust in his
voice.

In fact she couldn't understand why the Miami lawyer
was at her wedding at all. She didn't remember inviting
him. And she had seen the stiff, angry look on Kurt Bergstrom's face when the lawyer had arrived. No one really
wanted him there. The man in the gray business suit with
him was unfriendly, too.

She turned her face to Kurt next to her for reassurance.
He was blond and smiling, and her eyes lingered on the
handsome bearded man who was her husband and the breadth
of his shoulders and his height, and the occasional caress
of his blue eyes when he turned to gaze at her. Now, as
she looked at him, she felt his fingers tighten around hers.
He had held her hand since they had come down from the
main house, never letting it go, not even during the marriage
ceremony.

Something about his hand holding hers—

He never let her go, she remembered. Kurt held her so
that she wouldn't drift away from his side. She was very
prone to drifting. She felt that unless anchored down she
might drift away on the ocean wind to the top of the palm
trees and be wafted out to sea. There were dark, subterra-
nean memories in the back of her head. A strong woman
who held her arm and wound a piece of rubber tubing around
it while she screamed.

She shivered, and told herself they were only dreams.

Francesca kept smiling. The wedding guests seemed to
be enjoying themselves, even though they numbered only
a handful, and certainly the food and champagne seemed
to have been prepared for a much larger crowd. The man
from West Palm Beach, Francesca saw, Mr. Owens, the
justice of the peace, was sipping champagne with Angel
and Cassie. Mrs. Schoener, sturdy as a pine tree in her black

and white maid's uniform, stood with them. In a separate group, nearer to the path to the main house, were Peter Peavey and Larry, the alternate bodyguard and, for a few moments before she went back to the kitchen, Delia Mary. But John Turtle wasn't there.

Dorothea Smithson, her secretary, and John Turtle, her bodyguard, were both gone. It seemed incredible but it was what she had been told. Someone had said that John Turtle was no longer employed at Ca'ad Carlo. It seemed hard to believe.

There were not as many people as Delia Mary had provided food and champagne for, and the rose garden looked rather empty in the glaring sunshine. But everyone said the wedding had been beautiful. And that Francesca was the most beautiful bride anyone had ever seen. Angel's wife Cassie looked beautiful, too, Francesca thought. Cassie wore a long yellow silk *bo dai* that came from southeast Asia. Francesca had been very surprised to see Angel and Cassie after so long a time, but after a few minutes it had seemed very right to have them.

"Darling, lift up your head," Kurt's voice said to her.

Francesca lifted her head obediently and looked around the rose garden. There were a few things she was not supposed to tell anyone under any circumstance. One secret was that she and Kurt were going to sail away on the *Freya* to Hawaii for their honeymoon. The yawl had been moved from the marina and lay tied up in Ca'ad Carlo's crumbling old yacht basin, waiting for them. It was going to be a long journey from Florida through the Panama canal to the Pacific ocean, and it would be a little frightening with anyone but Kurt. They were going to open up the Bloodworth estate on Maui and live there for a while.

The other secret was that something had happened just before the ceremony. The stolid face of the woman who had held her down on Kurt Bergstrom's bed came back to haunt her, and she could feel the twist of rubber tubing biting into her arm again very clearly. Francesca trembled.

It was better to try to put nightmares safely away in the
deep recesses of one's memory, and not let them pop out
like that.

Francesca turned to Kurt with pleading eyes. Beside her,
her husband was a handsome presence in a perfectly tailored
navy blue blazer with the America's Cup insignia on the
left breast pocket, massive shoulders straining against the
blue cloth as he moved. The deep tan of his skin was en-
hanced by his white silk shirt and dove-gray tie. Most of
all, there was the impact of his good-humored self-assurance
that was, to Francesca, as warm and comforting as the hot
Florida sunshine that bathed them. She could see that there
was nothing to mar this man's happiness now; he had what
he wanted. And she sighed with relief.

She had what she wanted, too. It was no exaggeration
to say that she could love Kurt forever. Now, they were
man and wife.

A few moments after the justice of the peace had declared
them wed Kurt had turned to Francesca with love shining
from his clear blue eyes. His hands lifted the pale pink cloud
of bridal veil reverently and she had seen in his face, as
though for the first time, that he found her very beautiful,
indeed. He threw back the veil and then moved his hands
to cup her face very softly, lifting it to his, shutting out the
watching guests. It was a moment only for the two of them.

Something dark and alien stirred in the depths of his sea-
blue eyes at that moment which might have been sadness.

"I love you, Francesca," he had murmured. "I have never
said this to any woman but, God help me, I say it now. I
will try to change for you, so you must love me. And forgive
me, if that time comes."

They were strange words. She had not understood him,
only his eager kiss as his lips met hers, ending the ceremony.
She understood only one thing, that he loved her.

"Are there enough people around to throw rice?" Cassie
said loudly. Angel's wife came up to them carrying a silver
tray with little nylon net bags full of rice, tied with pink

and blue ribbons. Angel, his fat body encased in an already
rumpled white linen suit, looked around.

"Where did all the lawyers go?" Angel wanted to know.
"Do you know who tipped them off, Kurt?"

Francesca wasn't paying attention. She was watching the
long sweep of *Ca'ad Carlo*'s greensward that stretched from
the rose garden and the big fountain on the ocean side, down
to where it was bisected by the paths that led to the large
swimming pool and the guest cottages. At the curve in the
driveway a black sedan raced up, skidded to a stop, raising
a cloud of white shell dust. Three men in black business
suits got out of the automobile and started sprinting toward
the long lawn and the hedges surrounding the rose garden.

At first none of the wedding guests noticed. Francesca
thought it was so unusual to see anyone running at *Ca'ad
Carlo* that there must be a fire somewhere, although these
people certainly weren't dressed like firemen. Another black
sedan skidded up and passed the one stopped in its path by
mounting the low curb and cutting through some ixora bushes
before it, too, screeched to a stop.

Angel, a glass of champagne in his hand, whirled in the
direction of the noise. Kurt dropped Francesca's hand for
the first time that afternoon.

Several men piled out of the second black sedan and ran
after the first group, which had reached the low hedge on
that side of the rose garden. Three men vaulted the hedge
and, not able to stop, careened into the buffet table with its
load of food, silver champagne buckets and massed floral
arrangements. Figures in black business suits went down
with the buffet in a tangle.

Cassie screamed. Angel, moving astonishingly fast for
a fat man, pushed Francesca aside and grabbed Kurt Bergstrom's arm, shouting something.

Instantly the two men moved in concert, never looking
behind at the women they were leaving, and headed for the
thick stand of foliage that separated Ca'ad Carlo from the
Whitney estate next door. The second group of men in black

suits had seen the downed buffet table and skirted it. They headed at an angle for the sprinting figures of Kurt Bergstrom and Angel to intercept them.

Francesca watched with an open mouth as a man ran past her carrying a gun in his hand that glinted metallic blue in the hard sunlight. She turned and found the lawyer Harry Stillman at her side. He put a restraining hand on her arm.

"Stay right here, my dear," he told her. "We don't want to get in the way."

More men ran past, this time in the beige and green uniforms of the Florida State Patrol. More cars screeched to a stop in the main driveway.

A tall man with a hard familiar face, carrying a blaring two-way radio in his hand, jogged up to Harry Stillman and slapped a folded white paper in his hand.

"The damned warrant," he said. John Turtle's black eyes raked Francesca, seeing the beautiful pale pink wedding dress, her tumbling black hair and the vacant expression in her eyes. "My God," he muttered. Then, to Harry Stillman, "They're already married?"

The lawyer nodded.

"Hello, John Turtle," Francesca said. She had to raise her voice over the sound of sirens on South Ocean Drive. She saw John Turtle was wearing a black suit, too, and a white shirt and striped tie. "I'm glad you could come to my wedding."

John Turtle gave her one final look, a quick glance that reluctantly testified to how beautiful she was, mixed with something murderous, before he jogged off. The black-suited men were now crashing through the jungle growth that separated the two Palm Beach estates.

The hollow voices of two-way radios continued to echo in the sultry air. Peter Peavey and the other bodyguard set the buffet table back on its legs. Francesca felt an irresistible desire to laugh.

The wedding was obviously over. The justice of the peace, Mr. Owens, was talking to the lawyer in the gray suit who had come from Miami with Harry Stillman. Everyone seemed excited.

"Francesca," the lawyer said gently, "I'm going to have Mrs. Schoener take you up to your room now. You're better off out of this for a while. Francesca, my dear, you do hear me, don't you?" He lifted his hand and slowly turned her face to him. "That's better. Now go upstairs with Mrs. Schoener and lie down, and she'll take care of you until things clear out a bit down here."

Francesca smiled at him.

"Good lord." He suddenly peered into her face. "We'd better have a doctor look at this girl right away!" He turned to Mrs. Schoener and said, "Put her to bed and keep her quiet. I'll see what I can do about sending someone up in a few minutes to look at her."

"Where's Kurt?" Francesca said pleasantly.

No one paid any attention to her. Even Gerda Schoener seemed preoccupied. The maid steered her rather roughly in the direction of the house, telling her to hurry, hurry, every few feet. There was a great deal of noise going on at the Whitney's next door. Near the main house there were more uniformed state police on the pathways, signalling through their radios to a power launch that was patrolling the waters in front of Ca'nd Carlo's great red-tile terrace that faced the sea. The Freya, rolling gently in a sea swell, was still tied to the crumbling dock. Still waiting for them to begin their honeymoon voyage.

At the massive carved wood front door Francesca stopped, not sure she wanted to go inside. Some vague unpleasant memory nagged at her that would not surface in her consciousness. She didn't want to lie down and rest in the midst of her wedding celebration. She was just beginning to remember who had given her the injection. Kurt Bergstrom had held her hand all through it; he hadn't let go of her hand afterward, even to be married

"Wait," Francesca said. She grabbed at the doorjamb, the wood in the sun hot to her fingers. She couldn't go inside. Something might happen to her in there. She didn't think she could trust Mrs. Schoener. "Where's Kurt?" she cried.

She was married to Kurt, she was his wife. She wanted him with her. Not this grim woman who now had her arm and was trying to pull her over the threshold.

The door swung open.

The great hall of *Ca'ad Carlo* was perfectly silent, dark and cool in contrast to the blazing outdoors. Behind them people were milling through the shrubbery with walkie-talkies and there was a police boat patrolling the sea off the front terrace. But there was no one inside the silent house at all. Mrs. Schoener pried at Francesca's clinging fingers impatiently, loosening them one by one from the door frame. Francesca stared; the maid's hands were like a man's.

"I'm going to stay outside," Francesca pleaded. Light and dark moved in the great room just beyond. She didn't want to go in there. "I'll wait for Kurt," she cried desperately.

A man came up the circular drive before the house, portable radio glued to his mouth, and trotted on. Mrs. Schoener had Francesca's wrist, dragging her.

"Mr. Kurt is coming back for you," she hissed. "He will come back and take you away, stupid girl! You must change your clothes and get ready for him."

Francesca backed away from the other woman, reluctantly retreating into the shadows of the great hall. She didn't trust the maid. She twisted her arm in that hard grip, trying to free it.

"I'll do it myself!" she stammered. "I'll dress myself. You don't have to come!"

Francesca rushed inside. In the silence her high-heeled sandals made clicking noises on the smooth marble floor. The big flowing skirt of the wedding dress hampered her movements. With her free hand she tried to pull off the tulle veil which floated in front of her eyes, but the circlet of wire to which it was attached wouldn't budge. She told herself she didn't want to fight with Mrs. Schoener about anything; she wanted to get away from her. She needed Kurt.

"Where am I going?" Francesca cried, confused.

The maid turned to pull her up the gallery stairs. "You're going to change your dress. To do what Mr. Stillman the lawyer told you to do."

"Yes," Francesca said doubtfully. She was beginning to remember.

He had held her with his big hands easily, pressing her down on his bed in the guest cottage while Mrs. Schoener stood over her. He had kissed her gently, telling her that it was going to be all right. That she had to love and trust him. Mrs. Schoener had knotted the rubber tubing around Francesca's left arm to make the blue-dark vein stand out in the hollow of her elbow.

Kurt's seafarer eyes had been so close they filled up everything. "It's just a little one, my darling. And some morphia."

Francesca wrenched her hand from Mrs. Schoener's grip so hard she staggered back and teetered at the top of the first landing perilously. The nightmare was closing in!

She whirled, and gathered the skirts of the wedding dress up in both hands. The only safe place, now, was her room. The shadows of *Ca' ad Carlo* were closing around her.

She heard Mrs. Schoener's heavy feet thundering behind her on the wooden staircase. As Francesca reached the top of the stairs and the gallery she trod on her skirt again and heard something rip. She went down on her knees. She tried to scream for help. There were people just a few feet from where they were, on the outside. No one seemed to know what was taking place.

The maid's brutal hands grabbed her under the shoulders and began dragging her away from the top of the stairs. Dizzy, feeling as though she were moving in slow motion, Francesca got her feet under her, tangled in yards of rustling fabric, and slid back down again. One sleeve of the wedding dress gave way. Gerda Schoener was behind her, holding her under the arms like a wrestler with a hammerlock, immobilizing her, dragging her backwards down the gallery. Away from her bedroom. The wooden walkway echoed to the sound of their grunts and laboring gasps.

"Not where they can find you," the other woman was saying in a hard monotone. "These doctors and lawyers they want to bring up here."

Francesca managed to reach over her shoulder and claw into the maid's face blindly. Mrs. Schoener grunted in pain but did not let her go. "Not where anyone can find you. Only him."

A door swung open in the murky dimness. Francesca braced her foot against the door frame, sobbing hoarsely, resisting with all her strength. They were somewhere on the gallery, at the door to one of the unused bedrooms, she could not tell which. The maid was trying to drag her inside. Francesca screamed. The sound echoed up into the vaulted reaches above them, high in the great hall's decorated ceiling, and then died away. There was no one to hear.

Although her head was swimming and she could not see very well, Francesca did not have to be taught how to fight for herself. She threw all her youth and strength into defending herself against the onslaughts of this juggernaut woman bent on dragging her into the room. She got one leg between Mrs. Schoener's legs and pitched forward deliberately, dragging her after, and they both fell, the heavy woman on top of her, momentarily knocking the breath out of her. But Francesca had broken her grip. She got to her knees and lashed out. Her fist caught the other woman on the side of the face. She heard an exclamation of pain. But the heavy woman's arms groped out, the iron hands closing on her arms and shoulders, locking her into a terrible bear hug. Francesca could not break that grip. She sank her teeth into the woman's shoulder, grinding down until she tasted blood and bone. No sound came, but the grip was broken again, and she scrambled away on her knees.

The wedding dress coiled around her and clutched at her like an adversary; she could not move fast enough in it. Dazedly, she saw the room out of the corner of her eye. It was the pink and yellowed lace decor of Carla Bloodworth's room. Edna Bloodworth's room, too. The air inside was shut up, stagnant, and steaming. Francesca was already slick and dirty with perspiration.

On her hands and knees Francesca scurried over the dusty Chinese rug in the direction of the bathroom. She would fling herself inside it and lock the door. She saw the door-knob at eye level and dragged herself up just as Mrs. Schoener dropped on her from behind.

At any other time, less encumbered by the sea of silk that was the bridal gown and not slowed by what had been given her before the wedding ceremony, they might have struggled to a draw. Gerda Schoener was oxlike in her powerful movements and seemingly impervious to pain. But Francesca was young and had a superbly strong body, and she fought with the desperation of her Latin temperament, like a tigress. But she could hardly see now--a terrible gray haze had descended over her eyes and mind. The room was so suffocatingly hot she could not breathe. More and more slowly she hammered her fist into Gerda Schoener's face, listening to her animal grunts, then tore at her eyes hopelessly.

A great, unexpected blow on the side of her head broke Francesca's resistance, and she was catapulted into dark space. She sprawled on the floor, face smacking against a leg of the bed.

Stars. Lights.

Then blackness.

SHE dreamed that she was roasting in the hot sunshine. Tied to a chair in the middle of a vast garden that was filled with millions of roses and buzzing hordes of invisible honey bees that one could hear but not see. Her face was so sunburned that it had ballooned to ten times normal size. Her head was a great aching globe that Francesca turned from side to side futilely in search of a cool breeze. Her arms and legs were tied to the chair with huge pink satin bows.

Francesca groaned.

"He will come to you." It was a madwoman's voice, close to her ear, and Francesca tried to draw away. The rose garden faded and there was darkness, instead. The voice went on, "We will wait for him because he is coming for you in a little while. They will not bother him, these others. A king's blood runs in his veins, the blood of the Ynglinga, he cannot be defeated." The voice sank to a low, lunatic despair. "What a god he would have been in the old world, the age of the heroes! My golden one, my beautiful little boy."

"Water," Francesca said hoarsely.

The voice muttered on in its own secret message, its craziness like the low rustling of trees in the wind.

"The bathroom door is locked," Gerda Schoener said. "We are here. Yes, we are here, waiting for him. There is no water. We must endure this and wait for him like the *vig*-wanderers. On the long voyages in the longships."

Francesca sank back down into the darkness again.


FINALLY the madwoman groaned to her feet. Francesca stirred and opened her eyes, stunned with thirst and heat and only half awake.

"I will go pack your clothes," the mad voice said. "Like a queen you will go on the great sea voyage with my brother beside you. You will make him happy, a young and beautiful woman like you."

Heavy footsteps began to pace back and forth around Francesca's head. She tried to focus her eyes, tried to concentrate on the woman's words. The room was dim with drawn blinds, but the splayed shafts of sunlight that crept in between the slats and the dusty yellowed lace at the windows were like beams of fire. One fell across Francesca's eyes, blinding her. She tried to move her head away from it and moaned.

The dead monotone said, "The woman was too old, and plenty crazy, like an old bitch with her clothes and jewels and the drugs. What good was she, anyhow? Now he gets a young tigress." The presence bent over Francesca and she could hear the heavy, ragged sound of her breaths. "A beautiful young tigress, and the money."

There was a long pause then the footsteps receded and came back again. In the heavy gasps there was an intermittent sound, the low animal grunts of something, someone, in torment. The voice wandered off.

There was a silence. Then the door slammed.

After several moments of dazed drifting, Francesca gathered her conscious thoughts enough to concentrate on turning over. She found she was lying on the musty Chinese carpet of Carla Bloodworth's room. The furniture was covered with sheets for summer storage, giving them a ghostly look. But Carla's bed with its pink satin undersheet was uncovered, as though someone still slept in it.

With a violent effort Francesca pulled herself up in a sitting position and tried to lift her head. The windows were closed and the temperature in the room was unbearable. Dimly she remembered the old air conditioners had been removed from the unused parts of the house.

Doggedly she pulled herself to her knees. She was in danger; she had to help herself and be quick about it before the madwoman came back. Her groping hands came in contact with the edge of something warm and smooth, and lacy fabric. She hauled herself up to see that it was Carla Bloodworth's dressing table. There were the silver-backed toilet articles, the crystal perfume atomizers and the photographs in their gold frames: her father in his chauffeur's uniform, and the blonde woman with the flowerlike face. Smiling. Bright pale eyes. *Mother*.

It was a preposterous thought. Francesca turned her head away and the room spun dizzily. Her heat-swollen face was pounding and her long hair was dripping with perspiration.

She tore at the veil with one hand, hearing it rip and the answering sharp stinging pain as the rose circlet tore loose from its anchorings in her hair. Holding on to the dressing table, she clawed at the front of the wedding gown and it fought back, but she knew she had to get out of the layers of the dress or it would kill her. One silk sleeve fell down, exposing a bare breast. She let go of the dressing table and, panting, tore at the front of the gown with both hands.

Francesca ripped away what remained of the front of the bridal dress, the tissue thin silk in her hands parting with a thin squeaking sound. But she succeeded in rendering herself only half nude; the waistband of the voluminous skirt would not give. She couldn't find the zippered opening and could not remember the dress closed up the back. The blood pounded in her face and she knew she would drift back into unconsciousness again. Her eyes were confused by the return of the bright swirling colors that circled about again in her head.

The window. She fixed her thoughts on the window.

She grabbed the sill with both hands and pulled herself up to her feet. It was terribly hot in front of the glass. She parted the blinds and saw through beating sunshine a piece of the red-tile terrace, the long beautiful lines of the *Freya* bobbing in the old boat basin and the aquamarine Gulf Stream sliding in the sea beyond.

The window was shut. Locked. Sealed. Francesca put her hands on it and strained to lift it and her flushed face felt as though it would explode. Her eyes began to be obscured with a dark film. Slowly she sank to her knees and knelt there, clinging to the windowsill with both hands. A marvelous swirling cloud of lavender and pink and blue coiled through her mind and there was a singing in her ears.

She rested her cheek against the windowsill and closed her eyes.

*  *  *

IT was becoming harder to breathe. The heat and dust clogged her nostrils and made a choking film in her throat. She put her face and body down against the Chinese carpet and pushed painfully toward the door on her belly, smelling grit and long-accumulated dust and hearing the sound of her own tearing gasps. The long skirt of the wedding gown strained and tore with each push. At last she dragged herself up by the doorknob and tried to turn it.

It was locked.

"Kurt," she whispered. She had to get out of the locked room if he was coming for her.

Then the blackness returned.

THE next time she was sick. Her body felt as though it was losing its battle against the airless room. She crawled back across the floor to pull herself up at the windowsill again. She kept forgetting what she was trying to do.

Now it was growing dark. The sun sank in the trees of the shoreline behind *Ca'ad Carlo*. Lights had begun to appear in the velvet sky in the north, beyond the pass to Lake Worth.

Francesca fell across the edge of the dressing table and stretched her arm over the littered surface, hearing the crystal perfume flacons scattering, to seize one of the heavy gold-framed photographs there. She dragged the picture to her, then lifted her arm and began to batter the glass of the window with it. The photograph in the frame was that of a beautiful blonde woman.

"Help me, someone," she muttered thickly.

She lifted the heavy gold frame and smashed it against the windowpane and heard the glass shatter and break. She struck again and the gold frame spun out of her hands and through the broken glass to drop below. Immediately a thin stream of cool air from the broken pane brushed Francesca's lips and face. She held the windowsill with both hands, trying not to slump below the vent of delicious cool wind

coming in from the evening sea. Her eyes cleared. She drew
a deep, aching breath.

The tops of the palm trees came into focus, then the clear
deepening blue of the sky. Only gradually did she notice
the position of the boat below. The *Freya* had slipped from
its mooring and, like a ghost or a derelict was softly moving
toward open water. Francesca's vision blurred and for a
second she thought she only imagined it. But when her eyes
cleared she saw that the *Freya,* now caught in the last light
of the sun, had picked up speed. Someone had set the small
jib and it moved slowly and stealthily on the evening breeze.
Although it looked abandoned there was someone aboard.

Francesca grabbed the windowsill with both hands and
clung to it, wanting to cry out. A wave of nausea swept
over her that made her groan and she fought to stay on her
feet. The *Freya* was several hundred yards from the crumbling dock, now. In a few moments it would cut on its
engines and make a break for it. But for a long moment it
slipped toward the east and the open ocean like an unearthly
silent spirit, a dream of something that could not be happening.

*Why was he taking the* Freya *without her? Was she going
to be left there in that abandoned room to die?*

Francesca rested her head against the warm glass of the
windowpane, listlessly turning the questions over in her
mind without realizing the sense of them. She was too tired
to think, and too ill.

Two rakish-looking cruisers slipped into the sea from the
northernmost point of Palm Beach Island. Francesca was
so intent on the *Freya*'s ghostly run in the fading light that
she hardly noticed them until they came into the channel.
Francesca sagged against the window frame. It was like
watching a dream. The setting sun cast strange gold paths
upon the sea, nagging at memory. Where had she last seen
a boat sailing into the night?

The Coast Guard cutters ran a course set to converge on
the *Freya* and intercept it. The yawl's engines were driving

it through the water now at a speed calculated to give it a chance to slip past, running without lights in the increasing darkness, and into the open sea and freedom.

With a growing sense of dread Francesca clenched her fists. The powerful cruisers were closing in on the racing yacht; the *Freya* couldn't outrun them now, positioned as they were between it and the open sea. There was something doomed in the ships playing out their drama against the sundown water and the arching sapphire sky.

Francesca closed her eyes for a moment. She knew Kurt Bergstrom was aboard the *Freya*—no one else could sneak it from its mooring so skillfully, taking advantage of the silence of sail for the first few minutes and the fading light. In the odd stillness of her prison she remembered the strange import of his eyes caressing her, and his words as he lifted the bridal veil to look down into her face. "I will try to change for you, so you must love me. And forgive me, if that time comes."

Without words, with only a dread intuitive leap of understanding, Francesca knew what was about to happen.

"Don't!" The word was only a harsh croak of anguish in her parched throat.

The *Freya* lost headway in the sapphire sea. It began a large, aimless half-circle before the cruisers blocking its way to freedom as though no one manned the wheel.

Francesca rasped a hoarse, painful scream as she threw herself against the window. At the blow, another burst of glass shattered down onto the terrace below, but there was no one to hear. *Don't let it happen!* she prayed.

She had the vision of the Viking boat from the picture in Kurt Bergstrom's cottage clearly in her eyes. Imprisoned in *Ca'ad Carlo*'s walls she could not touch him, call out to him, beg him to stop! But that something that had always lingered fatefully in his amiable sea-blue eyes, that belonged to no one, that owed allegiance to no one, would not respond to her, she knew.

A small red flower burst into flame at the *Freya*'s stern.

A series of red and orange glows followed, running from stern to bow, as with someone lighting them with a can of gasoline. The fire climbed into the *Freya*'s rigging in creeping fingers. Then a sudden billowing ball of yellow and orange enveloped the stern of the yawl as the fuel tanks caught.

"Please, please," Francesca whispered, knowing it was futile to wish that it wouldn't happen. She pressed her mouth and face against the window glass, feeling that her soul would tear itself to pieces. The heat that throbbed in her face and brain was echoed in the terrible inferno of the burning ship. For a moment she thought she saw a figure outlined against the flames. Then it was gone.

*They set the Viking burial ship afire and sent it out to sea.*

Then what happened? she wanted to know.

*It sank.*

How could she have forgotten the picture of the Viking sea burial in Kurt Bergstrom's cottage? Or the look on his face when he explained it to her? Now no one would have the *Freya*, only its master.

Francesca slumped against the window glass. He had made a break for the open sea in the *Freya*, knowing, probably, that it was a long shot, and that he had no chance to make it. Knowing what he would do, then, if he failed. Now the *Freya* would burn, drifting out to sea, and then it would sink. And Kurt was dead.

*Forgive me,* he had said when he lifted the bridal veil to kiss her.

Francesca closed her eyes again, wearily. She would die, too, if no one found her. Perhaps that was the way it was meant to end, after all. She slid to her knees and rested her head on the windowsill.

The darkness returned.

# Chapter Eighteen

The flashlight shone in Francesca's face. It was a moment before the mad voice intoned in the darkness, "He is dead. It is all over. My beautiful golden boy is dead."

The cool air from the open door mingled with the breeze flowing in from the broken window. Francesca turned her face to it, surprised that she was still alive. How long had she been there?

Except for the flashlight beam the darkness was deep. Only a faint sky shine showed at the broken window.

Hands dragged her to a sitting position, her back against the windowsill. Cascades of dusty-smelling lace curtains flowed around Francesca. She tried to lick her swollen lips but her parched tongue wouldn't obey.

"A little water," she said thickly.

But the strange mad voice went on, "My beautiful brother is dead, like a king, like a great *Jarl* of the Viking longships, and his boat is gone with him, in the old way. So it is ended, done." The voice cracked in the darkness, full of its grief. "And there will be no children, now. And there will be none of us left of Hallsturm. And the line is ended. We are lost."

Francesca moaned deep in her throat. Gerda Schoener's strong hands gripped her by the upper arms and she couldn't move. Dimly Francesca was aware that in the house below them there were stirrings, noises, and doors slamming. A car engine raced in the driveway.

The maid's finger probed her forearm hurriedly in the flashlight beam. The dead monotone went on, "He was a Volsung hero, my brother. A god." Her thumb pressed a spot below the elbow. "You do not know how lucky you were, a girl like you, from the sort of people you come from, to have Count Kurt Bergstrom give his love to you."

Francesca couldn't struggle. All her strength was drained away by the terrible heat.

"I will send you to him, now. You will go with him, to be his forever."

There were loud voices and the sound of heavy running feet right outside in the gallery.

Francesca tried to scream for someone to find her, but her tongue was too swollen to allow a sound to come out. She felt a sudden sharp, tearing jab of something digging into the skin of her forearm, and winced. There was a burning sensation under her skin, and then her arm began to ache.

The door to Carla's bedroom banged back with a crash. Great white lights exploded against Francesca's eyelids. There were sounds of things falling, and Gerda Schoener's hoarse screams. Then someone cursing a light switch which would not work.

Strong arms went around Francesca roughly and John Turtle's voice, harsh with relief, said, "My God, she wasn't on that damned boat after all!"

"Is she alive?" a voice wanted to know.

Francesca peered up in the darkness, her mouth too swollen to speak. Her arm was growing numb. She felt someone taking her pulse, holding her wrist, swearing softly.

"She's been shot up with something. Here's the needle. We'd better get her the hell out of here."

The strong arms lifted Francesca, brushed her against other bodies milling about in Carla Bloodworth's room, then hurried her through a crowded doorway. More lights. Her head drooped against the faintly damp fabric of John Turtle's suit jacket, still not able to speak. Her nostrils were full of the strongly comforting odor of masculine sweat and soap and small brown cigarillos.

The sensation of being rushed rapidly along the gallery above the main hall made Francesca's head swim; there were people all around them with portable lights and blaring walkie-talkies. Cooler air bathed her face and burning skin. Someone kept pace with them all the way, fingers on her wrist to monitor her pulse. John Turtle's worried voice ran like a thread through the confusion.

"Francesca," he was saying, "keep your eyes open, baby. You have to fight going to sleep until we can get you to the hospital and run some tests and see what Gerda's pumped into you. Can you hear me?"

She was carried down steps, through lights and noise and into the hot, moist night. Hands helped them into a van, freed the billowing skirt of the wrecked bridal dress when it caught on something.

Someone said in a low voice, "Is she going to make it?"

Francesca lay back against a hard surface while a blanket was pulled over her bare breasts and tucked around her. She wanted to tell them it was too hot for a blanket but no words came out. She could hardly open her eyes.

"What's the holdup?" John Turtle's voice cracked like a whip.

Another voice said, "Take it easy, Johnny."

The door slammed.

Francesca wanted to sleep. The air in the van was stifling.

Through languid half-opened eyes she knew they careened out of *Ca'ad Carlo*'s front gate, tires squealing, and into South Ocean Drive. A police siren began to shriek. John Turtle slipped his arm under Francesca's head and pulled her to him, to cradle her in his arms while they sat on the floor of the speeding van. His hard, tense face was very close and his black eyes bore into hers, compelling her to listen to him, and do what he said.

"Don't go to sleep," his low voice urged her. "Look at me, listen to me, Francesca. You can't do this to me, you've got to help. Francesca, open your eyes."

But she tried to turn her face away from him. Why should she do anything John Turtle said? Kurt Bergstrom was dead. And she knew how much this man had hated him. She wanted to die—to slip away into easeful, drowsy darkness was the only thing left for her.

But his hands shook her roughly. "Francesca, damn you," his voice grated, "wake up! And snap out of it. I'm not going to lose you to some damned drug-dealing junkie who couldn't make love to you unless you were both juiced to your eyeballs!"

The hard, ugly words cut into Francesca's consciousness like knives. And as they did so, as full realization of what they meant sank into her consciousness, she moaned in protest. She didn't want anyone—anything—dragging her back into the world! Her mouth was swollen partly open and her tongue couldn't move enough to speak, but she ached to scream at John Turtle to leave her alone. Why did it have to be John Turtle of all people here—now—to torment her?

Through half-opened eyes she saw that black look intent on her face. He felt her body twitch in anger and he quickly murmured, "That's the girl. I might have known you wouldn't let me put down Count Wonderful."

His face was just inches from hers, hard and impassive as ever, his shaggy black hair rumpled in the sticky heat. But his eyes were alive with burning emotion. She shut her eyes so she wouldn't have to look into them and groaned again. With her cheek pressed against his jacket and shirt she could hear the queer, quick pounding of John Turtle's heart and sense the incredible lean toughness of the body and arms that held her. It was easy to remember how hostile this man had been, always.

He went on softly, "You can't say that God's gift to Palm Beach wasn't a hell of a lot more, can you? Except maybe an accomplished boat bum."

Now her eyes snapped open. She managed a choked, angry sound. John Turtle would never understand how much she had loved Kurt. *Juiced to the eyeballs?* What was he talking about? She didn't want to understand the filthy insinuation. She wanted to die. There was nothing to live for—Kurt would never be there in the cottage down the lane of daturas at *Ca'ad Carlo*. The ghosts were not exorcised—they had won!

But John Turtle kept right on talking.

"If it makes you any happier," he was saying, "this is my damned fault. Francesca, are you listening? I should have known there were two of them—It figures, now that Gerda's out in the open. But who would know Count Wonderful has a sister operating in his plans? I'd been watching him like a hawk since our conversation about aspirin in New York, when you said you didn't pop pills, and getting no place. I couldn't find that he was passing you anything just as we could never prove he was supplying Carla, either. So the question was: if you weren't taking the stuff yourself, who was giving it to you? The answer was Gerda. When we opened her room this afternoon we found a wonderland of drugs which she'd been using, apparently, to dose you up in some pretty strange ways. We won't know exactly what she had in there until we sort it all out."

"No," Francesca groaned. She wanted him to stop. His voice was prodding her, hatefully, and there was no escape. She couldn't even sit up by herself.

But the black eyes continued to hold her and force her

to listen. "I really needed those warrants," he said. He held her close in his arms; she felt his warm breath touch her eyelids and her cheekbones softly. "You don't know how much I wanted to nail him, Francesca. And incidentally, you owe a big vote of thanks to Elsa MacLemore. Do you hear me? Early this morning her attorney agreed to plea bargaining in return for what Elsa knows. And at noon Elsa turned over a list of Dr. Bernie Binns's drug suppliers to the state attorney's office. Francesca, wake up. There they were, Count Wonderful and his pal Angel, at the top of the list. The Palm Beach operation wasn't big stuff for them, not like their great days running drugs and guns in Southeast Asia, but they were beginning to do all right for themselves—and it was a hell of a lot less dangerous. I couldn't get the warrant for Bergstrom's arrest fast enough." His arms tightened around her. "I wanted to be there before he shanghaied you into marrying him. But I missed on that one, too."

Francesca quivered with unfocused anger. A hard pulse was throbbing painfully in her temples, but it was not as strong as her raging desire to get away from this man who held her. She couldn't listen to him any longer. She hated him, hated what he was saying—hated him for trying to drag her back into the world. But she was powerless to do anything when he lifted his hand to softly move the sweat-drenched curls from her forehead and stroke her cheek with his fingers. She saw the gleam of his eyes boring into hers. The van swayed, and his legs and thighs gripped her to hold her.

"Liar," she rasped. The sound was mushy in her throat but she saw he understood the word.

"Liar?" He lifted his voice over the sound of the police siren which followed them. "Francesca, you don't seem to understand what the hell's been going on. Baby, the consensus of opinion up until recently was that you had a large drug habit, even Harry Stillman was convinced—especially since you shacked up with Bergstrom in record time. I hope

I'm putting it delicately enough. It really threw us. You
didn't exactly come across all that convincingly as a real
swinger, but you were trying hard as hell to act like one."
When Francesca made a sudden, jerking movement of anger
he pulled her close and his arms gripped her even more
tightly. "But I could kick myself for not catching on that
Count Wonderful and Gerda were doing the same thing to
you that they did to Carla. I really didn't have a handle on
anything at that point, I was groping. And I probably
shouldn't have pulled Dorothea out when I did, she didn't
want to go, but I had to pressure Bergstrom to make his
move." His voice lowered, suddenly harsh. "Francesca, do
you want me to tell you what it felt like to watch you floating
down to the guest cottage every night for this guy's Late
Late Show?"

Francesca gave a low sound of pain. She was desperate
to tell him how much she hated what he was doing to her.
And what he had done to her in the past. In the swaying,
speeding van her body rocked against his, cradled in the V
of his thighs, his legs stretched out on either side of her.
He held her prisoner.

The van bumped over something, turned into a brightly
lit area. The siren choked off its scream abruptly as the
vehicle came to a jolting stop.

In the sudden silence Francesca watched helplessly as
the dark man lifted her hand, gently straightened the fingers
and then placed it palm up, against his lips. The black eyes
burned at her in that tanned, carved face, but his mouth
was soft and cool.

He said, his voice slightly muffled, "It was sort of hell,
Francesca, this whole thing. The last time, I tried to turn
you around and make you go back to the main house, I
couldn't take any more of it." He allowed her to fold her
fingers back up into a fist, but he still held her hand, covering
it with his, as he looked down at her. "What happened,
Francesca? Did you find out he was still shacked up with
Dorrit? Is that what suddenly made him want to wrap you

up in a hurry? Or did you find out about his nasty little heroin habit he picked up in Saigon?"

Francesca shook her fist, trying to break loose, and could not. John Turtle's voice had begun to fade, replaced by a growing roar that filled her ears.

"I haven't done much to make you like me." His voice was low, ironic. "And I know how grateful you are right now. I can only hope you get over it eventually." He hesitated for only a second. "Francesca, I'm a U.S. Customs Service agent working out of Miami. This was my case. What else can I tell you?" Someone threw open the rear door and there were voices. He said quickly, "I fell in love with you from the moment I saw you sitting on the terrace at *Ca'ad Carlo* with the Miami lawyers, and I knew then you were going to complicate my whole life. Because it was going to be hard to live without you."

Hands were lifting Francesca. But she wanted John Turtle to understand one thing. She swam up through the dark unconsciousness waiting to claim her, intent on it, struggling to form the words. The thick sounds that emerged were hardly understandable.

"You killed him," she croaked.

She was being lowered to a stretcher. No one heard.

# 5

## BOSTON

# Chapter Nineteen

OCTOBER CAME to New England in a classic gold shower of brilliant leaves and bright blue weather, but November edged into dreary grayness and cold rain––which suited her mood better, Francesca thought.

Just after Thanksgiving, when she no longer needed to be with her family at night, she moved her things to the attic third floor of her Uncle Carmine's house, to the room she had had as a child, when all the brothers and their families had lived together in the old brick row house on Framingham Street.

No one was especially happy with the move to an isolated part of the house except Francesca; her family didn't feel she was well enough to be up there at the top of the house by herself. On the other hand, they wanted her to be satisfied. They didn't want to do anything that would bring back the nightmares that had kept them all awake the first few weeks. The one thing that really concerned them was that Francesca had no desire to leave the house.

But she was happy enough. In her young cousins' slang she had found her hole and had crawled into it and that, she had decided, was the way she wanted it to be for a while. She picked up the threads of family life, especially on Sunday when all the Luccheses and Dellafiores gathered for Sunday dinner, and she often watched television for hours with her cousins Joanie and little Sal. No one mentioned Palm Beach. "A few weeks rest" had been the prescription at the hospital, and as the prescribed rest stretched into its second month the families' unspoken feeling was that it would take time. And time was what they could best give Francesca.

The childhood room on the third floor was Francesca's ultimate refuge. She could lie on the narrow bed, surrounded by shelves of her old books from first-grade Easy Readers on through to Nancy Drew and framed photographs from high school and even college days and enjoy a view from the small dormer window of what was still referred to in the east Boston Italian section as "the Neighborhood"—brick row houses and backyards, and the backs of stores, the grade school, and the broad yellow brick sides of St. Anthony of Padua's church. It was good to be home, even if home belonged to a child and not a grown up woman of twenty-eight who was still heiress to a $60 million fortune.

And she had plenty of time to think. She, who hadn't even had time to formulate an idea of how she intended to live and what she intended to do with her money before disaster struck in Palm Beach, now, in Boston, had time to spare to review it all. To think about Carla and Vanni and the things her uncles had not told her. That her father had been a young priest who had regretted his vows for some reason almost as soon as they had been taken, but who had not been able to throw off that commitment, regardless, for the rest of his life. And the truth, that her uncles must have suspected for years, that Carla Bloodworth was her real mother.

Her uncles still had not spoken to her about any of this; the Sicilian vow of silence was real. Francesca supposed she could have children of her own, and they could grow up and have their children, without ever hearing of it. She knew that if anyone broke the *omerta*, it would have to be she.

She tried not to think about the other things that had happened in Palm Beach. They were tied to what she was planning to do with her life in the future and the onslaught of the past had been so devastating she still could not bring herself to think about that. How could one plan what one was going to do when one still couldn't face what one had failed to do before? In the depths of real misery Francesca would only allow her mind to skip from one half-remembered point to another—she had married Kurt Bergstrom, who was even then, during the marriage ceremony, being sought by the police for his implication in a Palm Beach drug smuggling operation of which Dr. Bernard Binns had been a part. And over whom the cloud of Carla Bloodworth's death still hung in spite of the coroner's report of death due to natural causes. This, Francesca thought in an agony, was the man she had loved! Her mind stopped there and would go no further, afraid to remember the rest.


MAIL arrived at the Framingham Street address, forwarded both from the Bloodworth offices in Manhattan and from *Ca'ad Carlo* in Palm Beach. Francesca let it accumulate unopened. But in October the new personal secretary hired out of Miami came to Boston to see Francesca and see what could be done about catching up, including the mail. Francesca stayed in her room in the top part of the house and had her Aunt Angela send the secretary away. But several envelopes were left for her attention, among them one from the Board of Directors of the Bloodworth Foundation dealing with her right to vote the majority stockholder's shares.

By mid-November, though, it was inevitable that Harry Stillman and Maurice Newman, the estate lawyers from Miami, would come to Boston with a backlog of legal documents Francesca could not refuse to see. And some bad news.

The senior partner looked apologetic. "Blo-Co division will shut down as of January one," he said. "This is a blow, of course, psychological as well as actual. There's been little interest in buying the division, unfortunately, as existing assets will be minimal after debts. So it will be a complete phase-out. Of course some plan will have to be worked up for Blo-Co shopping centers. There's going to be quite a loss when construction costs are absorbed. However," he said, looking determinedly cheerful, "the current Blo-Co management is running an analysis of what went wrong, and it will be ready around the first of the year. But I'm afraid there's no hiding the fact that Bloodworth's faces its worst situation since 1933."

They were sitting on the glassed-in sun porch drinking coffee. A cold November rain poured relentlessly beyond the panes.

"What does that mean exactly?" Francesca wanted to know.

The lawyers exchanged cautious looks.

"Bloodworth's will try to survive," Harry Stillman said. "It must. There are too many peripheral effects that would be disastrous in the event of a complete collapse—the stock market, for one, would react severely, and there are a number of banks at risk. Blo-Co discount stores are a big part of the Bloodworth pie. They represent about forty percent of corporate worth."

No one said anything for a long moment.

Francesca remembered this had been coming since last summer, when executives in New York had taken cover behind a wall of secrecy. Blo-Co then had been so mismanaged it was impossible not to suspect big trouble. Now, it seemed to her, the Bloodworth structure was allowing the very same management that had destroyed Blo-Co to submit an account of how they did it!

She got up and went to the windows of the sun porch and looked out at the dreary fall rain. When she had been released after her week's stay in the West Palm Beach hospital in September she had returned to Boston to make up her mind about continuing her life as the heiress to the Bloodworth fortune. It was probably ridiculous—at least in other people's minds—to be in doubt about whether one wanted sixty million dollars, *Ca'ad Carlo* and the majority of stock in the Bloodworth corporation, but Francesca had really needed time to reconsider it. She had been rushed into a life she had been ill-prepared for and, as far as she was concerned, she supposed she had made a mess of it. To look back on anything, she was finding, was to be drowned in a sense of terrible humiliation over mistakes made, and guilt at being so naive.

As she stood at the window Francesca knew she presented a very different picture of herself to the estate lawyers— one tremendously changed from the sleek, expensively turned-out Palm Beach socialite she had tried to be that summer. She had, with the help of her Aunt Angela's pasta, put back on the five pounds she had lost at the *Golden Door* and she had become Frannie Lucchese of east Boston again. She wore her heavy mane of rusty-black curls swept back in nondescript style as she had when she worked in the history department at Northeastern, and she wore old jeans and her Cousin Caetano's poor boy sweater, many sizes too large for her. She was still entrancingly beautiful, and her superb figure triumphed over the baggy clothes, but there was definitely something both stronger and unhappier in her silvery-gray eyes.

She turned back to them, the corners of her mouth quirking up in an ironic half-smile. "Evidently it's impossible to fire bad management at Bloodworth's. It looks like Blo-Co executives are going to hang on for a while because nobody

wants to admit they made a mistake in hiring them in the
first place. I found out last summer nobody at Bloodworth's
ever admits they make mistakes, you know."

The lawyers looked uncomfortable, but neither of them
denied it. Harry Stillman took off his glasses and polished
them at great length, not wanting to meet her eyes.

"They do want to change, actually. It's being forced on
them," he said. "In fact, they'd like to remind you that your
shares of voting stock are now in your possession. Miss
Robinson, the new secretary, left the forms for you several
weeks ago."

Francesca looked at the gray-haired senior lawyer. For
once, she noted, he hadn't called her "my dear," or "young
lady."

"The board of directors," he added, "accepts your voting
strength in the Bloodworth corporation and wishes to co-
operate with you."

Francesca shook her head but couldn't suppress a smile.
*That was darned generous of them,* she thought. "Not as a
media front for the company. I've heard all that before."

Harry Stillman cocked an eyebrow at her. "You can be
a media figure or not, as you want. But you *are* the majority
stockholder. You would be the deciding vote in the running
of the company."

"Of course, it's up to you," the other lawyer put in, "but
if you would graciously accept some high-level orientation
and a bit of training procedure, the Foundation board members would be deeply appreciative."

Francesca looked at both men with real skepticism. It
sounded good. But she was wary, now, of what was being
told her and what was being left out. When he had visited
her that first week in the West Palm Beach hospital Harry
Stillman had divulged how he had been the moving force
in re-interesting state and federal law enforcement officials
in the suspicious circumstances surrounding Carla Bloodworth's death, and how they then had put an undercover
drug investigation agent from the U.S. Customs Service at

*Ca'ad Carlo*. The logical choice had been John Turtle, who had worked at *Ca'ad Carlo* briefly after military intelligence service in Vietnam, and whose family had been employed by the Bloodworth estate in the past.

"I'm sorry," Harry Stillman was saying. "I knew this would be painful for you, but there was no way to avoid necessary business."

From his briefcase Maurice Newman produced copies of the indictments brought against Angelo and Cassandra Nerolo on multiple counts of drug smuggling. *Angel and Cassie*, Francesca thought. A copy of the indictment against Gerda Schoener cited attempted murder, assault and conspiracy. Francesca glanced at it quickly and then handed it back. She still could not face what had happened that sunny September afternoon at *Ca'ad Carlo*.

"Probably a plea of insanity," the other lawyer said hastily, seeing her face. "And I gather she'll get it, too."

Francesca could not bring herself to hate Gerda Schoener, even if she still could not think of the maid as Kurt Bergstrom's sister. She still heard that hoarse, mad voice in her nightmares, crying that Kurt Bergstrom was a god, and a hero like the Vikings of old.

Newman handed her a photocopy of the federal warrant for the arrest of Doris Fleischenheimer on a charge of using the United States mail to send threatening letters.

Harry Stillman said, "John Turtle did a final wrap-up on this young lady before he left, so you have him to thank for it. You do remember a series of threatening notes cut out of newsprint?"

Francesca stared at him for a long moment. "Dorrit?" she whispered.

"Alias Dorrit Fenton, yes."

At that moment Francesca was overwhelmed with the incongruity of it all. Sensuous, witchy, conniving and incomparably beautiful Dorrit was only Doris Fleischenheimer, after all! The vicious author of poison-pen letters telling her she was going to die seemed to collapse under the burden of a name like Fleischenheimer.

Harry Stillman said, "Are you all right, Miss Lucchese?"

"Yes," Francesca gurgled. It was the first time she had laughed in months. And, once started, she didn't know if she could stop. She had been threatened by good old Doris Fleischenheimer, after all was said and done! She wiped away the tears of hilarity with the back of her hand. Both men had been watching her closely.

"Private joke," Francesca murmured, and saw them smile, relieved.

"It wasn't all a tragedy, you know," Harry Stillman said.

Francesca only shook her head, not able to speak.


THE last item was a suit filed by Carla's surviving ex-husband, Grandison DeLacy in the California courts challenging Carla's final will naming her chauffeur as heir.

"It was to be expected, I suppose," Harry Stillman said. "We've had a rash of litigation since you hit the newspapers, all the way to suits in Italian courts by people who claim to be your father's long-lost relatives. DeLacy's always been a clever devil and he may have an arguable point—that he was Carla's legal husband with a more valid claim than someone who happened to be her chauffeur for a time."

"He's angling for an out-of-court settlement," the other lawyer offered.

Francesca stared down at her hands. With a word, now, she could spare them all the expense and trouble of answering Grandison DeLacy's suit and tell them she was Carla Bloodworth's daughter. The letters which Herb Ostrow had given her that her father had written were still at *Ca' ad Carlo* somewhere. There were records of her birth, too, in some place in Italy; she supposed the Bloodworth millions, astute lawyers like the Miami firm and a few private investigators could turn up proof of her birth eventually. The problem was: Did she want to be what she was?

After a moment Francesca stood up and said, "Let me

know about the lawsuit by Mr. DeLacy, won't you?"

The lawyers stood up, also, and assured her they would.

A LETTER came from Buffy. Francesca couldn't resist opening it; she recognized the handwriting immediately.

Francesca, sweetie—

They tell me you've gone away to New York or someplace after what happened, so I'm addressing this to *Ca'ad Carlo,* knowing someone over there will forward it.

Oh, Francesca! I really can't get over all this, first Bernie Binns and then Kurt! There's nothing I can say, really, to tell you how I feel. Kurt was one in a million, the truly perfect man, and the burning of the *Freya* is an image I can't get out of my mind. I'm so glad I wasn't there to see it, I think it would have destroyed me!

You know we all feel deeply for you, Francesca! I've heard so many people mention you and say how sorry they were, since Jock and I returned to Palm Beach. Our loving thoughts are with you at this terrible time of bereavement, but you're such a strong person, I know you'll triumph over this as you did everything else. We will never forget Kurt, will we? Our memories will be a testimonial—but only the good ones, not the bad ones!

Everything is so low profile in Palm Beach you wouldn't believe it! Of course it's pre-season, but the people who are coming back this year are very subdued, really. But Palm Beach will survive—it always does!

Jock and I are back in the condo at Chantilly, but not for long—we have to move before Christmas. The wonderful, super news is that I'm pregnant and the baby will arrive some time in March the doctor says. Isn't this marvelous? I really had to write and

tell you. Jock is very pleased, you know how crazy
he is about his damned kids. Now, as I keep reminding
him, we're growing our own major attraction right
here.

  Francesca, with this new family expansion project
I'm almost too embarrassed to bring this up, but it's
going to be a while before we can repay you any of
the money you laid out for me last summer. The condo
doesn't allow children or pets, so it looks as though
we're going to have to scrape up a really horrendous
down payment on a house somewhere on the island,
and I'm staggered by what doctors are charging just
to catch babies. So please give us some time to take
care of this!

  Jock and I send all our love. Don't forget us!

                                      Buffy.


Francesca sat down at the little student desk in her attic
room and decided to laugh. "Jock and I send all our love."
She remembered the last time she had seen Buffy and how
terrified, there in the driveway of *Ca'ad Carlo,* Buffy had
been of dear Jock sitting across the road in his Ferrari.
Waiting to bash Buffy's face in permanently if she didn't
give him a divorce.

  And Buffy's cocaine habit? Francesca turned the envelope over in her hands. Buffy wasn't evil—just thoroughly
foolish and deluded. Was that a good enough foundation to
start a family—raise a baby? Even in Palm Beach? With a
loving parent like Jock?

  *I must be the one who's crazy,* Francesca told herself. If
you don't look too close, Buffy's the one who's got everything—Jock, money, social position in Palm Beach and now
a baby.

  She supposed she could be thankful that wherever Buffy's life was headed it was not, thank goodness, on a col-
lision course of that of Francesca Lucchese. And she supposed
she could forget about her. And the several thousand dollars

he had paid for Buffy's facial reconstruction.

She supposed she was also going to have to get used to he idea that she wasn't going to have any real friends, now hat she was rich.


THEN came John Turtle.

# CHAPTER TWENTY

As SHE opened the door and saw his set, darkly handsome face, Francesca's reaction was one of total recall: she was back again sitting on the floor of the police van as they sped through the night to the hospital in West Palm Beach, John Turtle holding her cradled against his hard body. John Turtle lifting her hand to his mouth to softly press his lips against it, and kiss it.

"Hello, Francesca," he said in his quiet voice.

She turned away from him at once, her heart thudding painfully. Until this moment John Turtle had been one of the dreams slowly fading from memory. And she had wanted to believe so desperately that none of this had happened. But now he was here, his lean, rangy body filling the door frame, challenging her just by the way he looked at her.

"I don't want you in here," Francesca said, her back to

him. "I don't know who sent you up here, but they didn't ask me about it."

He was silent for a moment, then he said, "You look like a kid." His eyes traveled over her, seeing the tight jeans and the old sweater clinging to her breasts. "A slightly fat kid," he added, his gaze on her hips.

Francesca's face burned with a sudden rush of blood. She wasn't fat, and he knew it! She thought bitterly that it was impossible to imagine that John Turtle had ever held her hand to his grim mouth to kiss it again and again, gently. She'd had some delusion in the van, that was all.

He threw a corduroy stadium coat on the top of the small desk and sat down on the bed. Standing over him, Francesca could see the top of his head, the thick black hair slightly wet with autumn rain, and the long black eyelashes that struck an almost feminine note in that hard, uncompromising face. She looked away quickly.

He said, in his even voice, "I volunteered to come and talk to you and Harry Stillman took me up on it." He looked up at her then, and the force of his tough, masculine presence seemed to suddenly crowd the little room. He said very quietly, "Francesca, I promised Harry I'd answer any questions about what happened the day of the raid at *Ca'ad Carlo*. Because Harry seems to think you're not going to feel any better about Kurt Bergstrom's death unless you get a chance to talk it out. Since I was undercover agent on the operation, I said I'd do it."

Francesca turned toward the window, her body shaking with some reaction she could not explain. John Turtle's being there disturbed her far more than bringing back the events at *Ca'ad Carlo* the day of her wedding. Sudden, brief pictures rose up from her memory of John Turtle running with her on the secluded paths of the *Golden Door*, trying to alter his long stride to fit hers and keep her from collapsing; John Turtle piling out of the front seat of the Rolls-Royce to intercept gawkers on the sidewalk; John Turtle impassive in a dark suit, tough and unapproachable in the executive dining room of the Bloodworth Foundation; John Turtle holding her close in the butler's pantry of the Plaza Hotel. Francesca quickly groped for an image of Kurt Bergstrom in all his golden smiling handsomeness and found nothing.

"I don't know why you're here!" she cried in a thin, trembling voice. "This is my bedroom—and in case you didn't know it, we're all Sicilians here. Nobody's *ever* allowed in a woman's bedroom!"

"Francesca," he said.

She cried, "If my Uncle Carmine were here he'd come up and throw you out!"

"Francesca," he said, less patiently. "I just spent an hour with your uncle. He knows I'm here."

Her mouth dropped open. Before she could think of anything to say he went on, "Why don't you just sit down and listen?" He indicated a place on the bed beside him.

Francesca turned her back on him abruptly. She made herself stare out the little window under the eaves to the bleak November rain falling in the backyards. She was genuinely alarmed at the way both her mind and her senses were reacting to John Turtle. She couldn't seem to get him out of her head. Strange pictures, memories, continued to rise up and confront her.

She remembered how Buffy Amberson had ogled him when he was her bodyguard, when they'd been sunbathing. And John Turtle intercepting her, furiously angry, on her way to Kurt Bergstrom's cottage in the dark. The sight of his face then was that of a man goaded almost beyond endurance.

*Why was she thinking these things?* Francesca held a shaking hand to her forehead. Having him appear at her door like this was like confronting a ghost. Everything from the past rose up to plague her. But it was more than that, she knew. It was John Turtle *himself*.

He was watching her closely. And he said, in his quiet voice, "Francesca, you've got your family scared half to

death, you know that, don't you? You've shut yourself up
here and won't talk to anybody. You won't answer your
mail, you won't talk to anybody about what happened in
Palm Beach last summer. Your aunts and uncles are afraid
to do anything they think might upset your delicate emo-
tional balance and send you over the edge." He paused,
watching her. "You seem to have your family pretty well
conned into treating you like a mental case while you sulk
up here."

The words stung. Francesca whirled on him with several
months' accumulation of anger finally boiling to the surface.
"You *shut up!*" she cried. "I lost my husband because of
you!"

His black eyes narrowed in his taut, handsome face.
"You're not a grieving widow, Francesca, even though you're
trying pretty hard. As you probably know, you were never
legally married." At her gasp he said evenly, "Hell, that's
right—no wedding ceremony is valid when either party is
under the influence of drugs."

She stepped back as though he had struck her, one hand
to her throat. But he went on, "I'm sorry if that shakes you
up, but it ought to clear up that point, anyway. Listen, I
don't know what kind of romantic scenario you've been
hanging on to about Kurt Bergstrom, who made a drug
addict out of Carla and tried to do the same thing to you,
but let me guess. Is it the operatic ending where he roasted
himself alive? Well, spare me your tears. By the time the
Coast Guard trapped Count Wonderful outside Lake Worth
pass he was looking at several consecutive long-term charges
pending here and overseas that even his crazy sister couldn't
get him out of. And a lifetime in the slammer is not a pretty
prospect—not for a modern-day Viking and America's
Cup-type like our hero. As far as I'm concerned he saved
the courts and the U.S. Customs Service a lot of time and
money when he decided to charbroil himself." His voice
dropped softly. "But it's too bad about the fancy boat. I
understand it was a very nice item."

"I'm not going to listen to any of this!" Francesca yelled. His hard, flat words had broken the spell of her shock. She started for the door but he stood up and his tall body blocked the way.

"Of course you wouldn't understand him," she cried contemptuously. "He was a famous international sailor, an aristocrat, a—a paratrooper who fought your wars for you—"

He reached out for her instantly. His hands seized her shoulders, almost lifting her from her feet. She cringed before the raging black fire in his eyes.

"Don't tell me Kurt Bergstrom fought my wars for me, Francesca." His voice was deceptively soft. "I was in Viet Nam for four years. I went in a nineteen-year-old kid and came out somebody even *I* didn't know very well. I had a bellyful of operators like Bergstrom. They brought in drugs that American troops got hooked on. I was in an intelligence unit that went after people like our Count, who thought American fighting men would make a great drug market."

His hands released her and he turned from her abruptly, his face more than usually stony. He said, "Bergstrom and his friend Angel had a milk run from Burma that made them millionaires until they got stupid and tried to doublecross their backers. Then they had to leave Southeast Asia in a hurry. But Francesca, I want you to understand that guys like Bergstrom who called themselves mercenaries didn't fight any wars for me. He operated one or two dirty missions up in the mountains with the *Montagnards* and managed to sacrifice a couple of hundred of them when his operation shut down. He got out in one piece, naturally. The best thing I can say for this megalomaniac junkie is that at least he was a user of his own stuff, and in time it would have killed him." He stopped, and looked down at her darkly "You know why you couldn't find any needle marks on his body, don't you? He used the old trick of shooting up into his mouth, into one of the veins under his tongue. It's risky, but it's neater."

Francesca lunged at him with both hands. Lightning fast, he caught them before they could reach his face and held them. He yanked her against him, powerful arms like steel bands around her, so that she could not move.

"You bastard!" she gasped. "You killed him! You always hated him!"

His face was calm. He said, very softly, "You caught him shooting up, didn't you? It isn't pretty, I know. Francesca, you didn't know all that great godlike charm was the high of a heroin addict, did you? Until you caught him shooting up a little smack?"

"Shut up!" she yelled. But her body began to crumple. Unwillingly, she went slack in his arms.

It was useless to run from it any longer. John Turtle's words painted the picture she had so desperately wanted to forget. That she had buried in the back of her mind for weeks. A picture that was even more terrifying than Gerda Schoener's attempts to kill her in the suffocating, shut-up room at *Ca'ad Carlo*. With a moan Francesca slumped against John Turtle's hard body. She *couldn't* have loved a monster instead of the wonderful man she had thought! It couldn't have all been an ugly, desperate plot to give her drugs so that she and her fortune could be easily manipulated. Was there nothing in all of it that had been good, and real? The answers were ones she couldn't face. The whole world had turned against her.

John Turtle's arms held her, and his free hand stroked her hair for several long minutes.

"I can't face anybody," she said against his hard strong chest. Her voice broke on a sob. "I was so stupid. Such a fool!"

His voice vibrated against her when he spoke. "Francesca, don't take it so hard. Maybe I was wrong. Maybe Kurt Bergstrom was a noble soul and nobody noticed. Does that make you feel better?"

She lifted her eyes to his face. "Do you always have to be so tough?" she said bitterly.

"Yes." But his hands stroked the back of her neck gently, his fingers against the collar of the old sweater. "Frannie, I wanted Bergstrom like hell, from the time he and his sister got Carla hooked on drugs. Carla was good to me when I was a kid. I owed her that much."

His fingers softly threaded through the mass of curls at the back of her head, stroking and comforting, sensuously smoothing the tense muscles there. The moment stretched on and Francesca could not move. Something in the back of her mind marveled that she was there, in John Turtle's arms, and that it felt so natural. She was assailed by a strange feeling she did not want to admit, not even to herself. Had he been a dark, waiting presence always, in the back of her consciousness? One couldn't be —aware—of one man and marry another, that was insane. But the small voice questioned this, too. She groaned aloud. She had made so many mistakes. Certainly she couldn't have made a mistake as great as this one? Trembling, she pressed her face against him. All she could think of was that she wanted him to go away and leave her alone so that she could think. But her fingers dug into the front of his shirt.

She said in a small voice, "Why do you hate me?"

"Hate you?" His arms tightened around her. "What in the hell gave you that idea?" She heard him catch his breath as though reluctant to say what he was compelled to say. "How could I hate you," he said huskily, "when it's so easy to love you?"

"No," she said, turning her face away. Her heart was racing to hear these strange, terrifying words coming from John Turtle.

"When I first saw you," he murmured, "you were like some beautiful innocent kid that had wandered into Palm Beach, where everybody is burned out before they're twenty, from getting everything they want in life. I couldn't believe what I saw the most gorgeous, real, loving woman, and I knew you didn't know what in the hell you were getting into. Even though you acted like you did." When he felt her struggle against him his arms tightened, and he raised his voice slightly. "Francesca, what's the matter with you? Don't you know what effect you have on me by now? You can't be blind to the way you look, the way you are. Even Count Wonderful got caught up in it. You knocked all his plans to hell when you showed up at *Ca'ad Carlo* and he fell in love with you. He'd survived war and gun running and drug smuggling and even the Palm Beach jet set, and then you came here with your quicksilver eyes and your beautiful body and your dazzling kid's smile, and it blew the whole thing. If it hadn't been for his sister I don't think he would have gone ahead with it."

"Don't," she cried, pushing frantically against him.

But he said, "Don't say don't to me, Francesca. I wasn't any different, either. The thought of you in his arms, of his making love to you, didn't just make me hate him. I wanted to kill him. I came right to the brink a couple of times, but I managed to stop when I couldn't bring myself to throw away an undercover operation of almost a year because I had fallen in love with one of the principals in the case."

"Don't tell me these things!" she wailed. She gave up struggling to put her hands over her ears. "I don't want to hear about loving! I'm all through with that."

He wouldn't let her go. "No, you're not," he told her. The carved planes of his dark, handsome face tightened. "How," he murmured, "could a woman who's made for love say she's through with it?"

His hands caught the back of her head to turn her face up to him. Francesca couldn't control a small shudder. Things were so mixed up. She couldn't believe this was John Turtle holding her, speaking to her like this. Or that her own body quivered, yearning for him, as though it had anticipated this moment all along—

His thick dark eyelashes swept down over eyes gone smoky as he bent his head to her. "You're not through with loving, Francesca," he said softly.

His lips were so warm, she thought, startled. There was

an utter gentleness in that lean, tough body. As her lips
parted under the insistent pressure of his mouth she felt an
answering tremor in the muscles of the powerful arms that
held her. *He wanted her!* This hard, taciturn man wanted
her so much that his body actually trembled with his desire.

Francesca's emotions were set instantly in an uproar with
the realization. She clung to him with both hands, fingers
digging into his muscled forearms as his kiss explored her
lips, caressed them with a sort of wonder, trying to ignite
an answering spark. As she tasted the tender, careful caress,
so different from what she had expected from John Turtle,
she opened her eyes wide and gave a breathy sound against
his lips. As she did so, a lightning current seemed to leap
from his mouth into hers.

"You're so damned beautiful," he whispered

The blood was hammering in Francesca's ears, and she
found her own mouth answering just as eagerly. Her whole
body wanted to flow into his lean strength, to fit against
his flat belly, his hip bones, his long thighs in denim jeans.

He murmured against her lips, "Come back with me,
Francesca. You can't run away." When her eyes opened to
stare into his he said, "You might as well come back to
*Ca'ad Carlo* and pick up where you left off."

While she looked up into those blazing black eyes Francesca heard warning bells in her head. She pulled her mouth
away. She leaned back, away from him, in his arms. "What?"
she said.

The question, What was she doing in John Turtle's arms?,
rose up to plague her. What was she doing in John Turtle's
arms, being kissed so thoroughly? The answer was all too
plain.

"Is that what they sent you to Boston to do?" she cried.
"To talk me into coming back so that I can look after all
the Bloodworth money, and keep things going?"

He stared at her from under dark brows. "Damn you,
Francesca," he muttered. "Now what?"

She pulled all the way back from him and he let her go.

She turned to walk quickly down the length of the little room, to put as much distance as possible between them.

"Oh, come on, the lawyers were here," she said, her voice heavy with sarcasm. "And I suppose you don't know I've been requested to take a seat on the board of directors of the Bloodworth Foundation—now that they think they might be able to use my image! And now that the company is in so much trouble." She reached up to push tumbled black hair from her face. "But I've got news for you. I'm not cooperating. I'm sure you all wish I would. Why, I might be able to liquidate some of the Bloodworth real estate like the ranch in Wyoming and all the jewelry, and be persuaded to pump the proceeds into the company, right?" She swung around to face him. "Why do you people bother?" she cried. "I never want to go back to Palm Beach, or New York, or—*anyplace,* as long as I live!"

When John Turtle reached out to pull her to him she slammed her fists against him in a fury, wanting to hurt him. It was like pounding a wall of stone.

"Leave me alone!" she yelled. Large tears cascaded down her cheeks. She was wracked with the release of weeks of pent-up emotions. "That's what I've found in this whole mess," she sobbed. "That people will fight, and connive, and lie, and yes—even try to kill you to get what they want out of you! What are you getting out of it, John Turtle," she accused, "that made them drag you all the way up from Florida with this sales talk about my going back?"

He stared at her, holding her upper arms in a grip that hurt. But his voice was quiet when he said, "I'm not getting paid to do anything. I volunteered to come up here, just as I told you. And I don't want your money, so you can rest easy on that score. But I'm not afraid of it, either, Francesca." He drew a long, determined breath. "I'm not going to back off just because you've got more millions than you know what to do with. There's only half of me that has the white man's hang-ups—the Indian half couldn't care less." His eyes searched her face. "I don't know what you're talking about. If the Bloodworth Foundation wants you to be on the board of directors, then take them up on it. You own the company. And you can't do any worse than the crowd that's in there now. You'd probably do a lot better. I saw you in action in New York, remember."

As she continued to sob angrily his expression softened. "As for coming here to Boston, why, I thought you'd let me persuade you that Count Wonderful was a perfectly normal mistake for any woman to make. He was a professional charm—"

When her hand flew up to hit him he caught it in mid-air. Before she could react his other hand tangled in her heavy hair, pulling her head back, while his mouth lowered, not gently this time, to hers. She struggled against him in vain, her face turned to one side.

"Francesca, for God's sake," he said, with a voice gone suddenly rough and urgent. "What are you trying to do to me, woman? Is it because I can offer you only plain, dumb love, no hyped-up excitement, no pills, no thrills? Just man to woman, me to you? What are you afraid of?"

His mouth took hers with hungry authority, forcing her lips open, transmitting an eager fire. His arms drew her to the tips of her toes, compelling her to lean heavily against him, against his hard body and the leashed desire that shook his rangy frame. Francesca's senses swirled in an onrushing mist of arousal that she had never experienced before. She had never known this sort of bleak, rough need for her, nor the response that she was feeling. Her heart was pounding. She was afraid he would find out how fearful she was. A jolt of warm tingling electricity ran from his lips to hers, connecting with every nerve ending in her body. She arched against him, stunned to discover that she wanted him, too. She was astounded how quickly this had happened, in John Turtle's arms.

"Oh no," she breathed. She knew it was impossible to understand this wild longing, this still-hesitant desire to have him make love to her that warred with the terror of becoming

involved again so soon after disaster. It was all jumbled up
in her mind. She was going crazy. With a rush of panic she
tried to squirm out of his arms. "Wait," she tried to tell
him. "Oh, you don't know as much as you think you do,"
she wailed. "You don't know what a terrible fool I've made
of myself! You don't know, you *can't!*"

She couldn't meet those black, possessive eyes boring
into her. She twisted her head away.

"Francesca," he began.

"I threw myself at him," she cried. "I really made an ass
of myself. You'll never understand." When he scowled,
tears sprang to her eyes. "I hadn't had any experience at
all, I made myself totally ridiculous. I was a—a virgin!"

"What?" The scowl remained. He was beginning to look
puzzled.

She fixed her gaze at a point over his shoulder. She
couldn't bear to look at him. She couldn't even bear to think
of it herself. "It's stupid, isn't it? A twenty-eight-year-old
virgin. I don't expect anybody to really believe it. I didn't
really know what I was doing, I realize that now. I thought
he was the most wonderful man in the world. I was blind
to everything, making such a fool of myself. When all the
time he was actually a sort of professional fortune hunter,
a junkie, a terrible—"

"Okay," he said softly. When she did not resist, his arms
folded her to him. He said nothing for several long moments,
holding her as she choked back her tears, his free hand
stroking her hair. Then he said in a changed voice, "You're
right, I don't know as much as I thought I did. I'm sorry."

John Turtle had just said he was sorry. She heard it
numbly.

"It was a hell of a poor introduction to love, wasn't it?"
he murmured against her hair. "Listen, honey. Are you
listening to me?"

But she clung to him with both hands, eyes unseeing.
She had made her stumbling confession, washing away the
last of the shame and anger that had held her a prisoner in
the childhood room. Now he knew the truth about her. She

was not really grieving for Kurt Bergstrom. She'd been sunk in a desolate terror of not ever having a chance to live, or feel, again.

Against her own body he felt strong, unassailable. She had ruined this, too, she told herself miserably. Now he knew how humiliated she was. She wished suddenly that the whole dreadful summer had never happened, and that she could start over again.

But he only murmured, "Frannie, I'm sorry as hell all this happened to you. Now I understand what your uncle was trying to tell me, about the way you were raised, how protected you've been. You were entitled to something better, the first time." His voice was deep, husky. "I wish it had been me. But I guess you know that. How can I convince you, now, that you didn't make all that much of a mistake? That most of us give our love to the wrong people a couple of times before we get it right?" His hand moved to her throat, tracing a soft line from the throbbing pulse there to the top of her chin with his finger. "When I came here this afternoon," he murmured, "I didn't want to answer any questions about what happened that day at *Ca'ad Carlo* or discuss Kurt Bergstrom with you. That was a lie. What brought me here was that I had to take you in my arms and kiss those beautiful lips and tell you that a couple of months had passed and I couldn't wait any longer for you to feel better about things. I need you. I love you too much." He lowered his dark head to her. "Honey, snap out of it. You've got to walk away from the whole damned thing, that's what we told them in Nam. Pick up your whole self and walk away and forget it. It can be done."

His mouth descended on hers and this time there was no denying him or pulling back. Francesca knew he was certain of the signals her body was sending to him, her mouth opening for his, the trembling of her hands against his shoulders. *He had said he loved her*. While she considered the strangeness of it his kisses moved to possess her eyes, her cheeks, the hollows of her throat, his lips nibbling away her doubts and resistance.

While she still tried to cling to him he gently disengaged her hands and seized the old sweater and stripped it over her head. Her magnificent heavy breasts spilled into his hands and he curved his fingers around them. Francesca shuddered at his touch and swayed toward him with a little gasp. His mouth touched her bare shoulders and then, with tantalizing slowness, moved over her breasts with the sureness of a man who knows how a woman's body would respond to his caresses.

Francesca caught a ragged breath when she felt his lips against her breasts, first one, then the other. A jolt of fire ran from his tongue circling the sensitive tips, and her body arched to his mouth helplessly.

"Francesca, I swore I wouldn't—" he said thickly. "I promised myself I wouldn't rush you." His words ended with a groan as he pressed her back against the bed. "Francesca, unbutton my shirt," he said huskily.

He watched her with a waiting expression, his eyes gleaming under half-opened lids. Her head was swimming. The sense of him, demanding and troubled, filled her with nothing but confusion. She knew she had to follow her heart. He was waiting for a sign from her. Could she trust herself to be right, for once?

Tentatively she reached for the first button on his shirt. It was an insane idea, she thought suddenly, to take their clothes off and make love up in her room, only a few feet away from her strict Sicilian family! But the heat of wanting him, the impact of sudden discovery, made it impossible to think. She bent her head, gone absurdly shy as he shifted to lean his long body over her. Lovemaking with Kurt Bergstrom had been wild, unreal. This was real enough, and a commitment. She trembled when she thought of how terrible it could be if it failed.

"No," she muttered.

She could feel his warm breath touching her face as he said, "Oh yes, honey. Do it. Tell me that you want me."

Under her fingers his shirt opened and his tanned, hard-muscled chest was revealed. There were several wiry black hairs against the coppery skin. She brushed them with her fingers as she pulled away the shirt.

"I need you," he said simply.

Francesca bent her head and placed her cheek and then her mouth against John Turtle's skin, against the slow thudding of his heart. Dreamlike, she felt his arm tighten around her as she lay back against the narrow bed, his free hand stroking her face softly, and then her hair, infinitely tender. She kissed the smooth satiny skin of his chest and slid her hand around the curve of his ribs, palm flattened against his skin, and heard the swift, hoarse intake of his breath.

"My God," he whispered.

She unbuckled his belt with its large brass buckle and pulled it to one side. But when her fingers touched the waistband of his jeans he abruptly pulled her up into his arms. His mouth found hers, drowning her senses with long ardent kisses while his hands caressed her breasts, and undid the fastenings of her slacks. Every part of her body warmed to his touch, wanting to be close to him, to have him take her.

With her eyes closed, she prepared to surrender to their final lovemaking but instead he stopped, holding her for several long minutes, looking down at her. Finally she opened her eyes and looked up at him.

"Before we go any further," he said softly, "I have something to say to you."

When her eyes widened, he let her go and sat up. She sat up too, rather nervously, and licked her lips.

"I intend to love you on a permanent basis, Francesca." His face was quite expressionless, only his black eyes caught and held her. "We come from plain people, both of us, so you know what I'm talking about."

While she stared, he took a moment to bend and pull off his boots and then his socks. He stood up, clad only in his jeans.

"My father's still alive, and he tells me he'd like to have some grandchildren."

He went to the desk and lifted the brown corduroy stadium coat from the desk and took something from the pocket

He held out his hand to her, still impassive, and Francesca, stunned, took a small blue velvet box. When she opened it she found a diamond ring. Not a terribly expensive ring, but expensive enough. She looked up at him with startled, then misty eyes.

"Oh, you're—" she began. Tears were close to the surface, and yet she wanted to laugh. "Why—"

"Francesca," his soft voice said, "I'm going to make love to you. If you don't want me to, now's the time to say it.' When she was silent for a long moment, her head bent, looking down at the ring in the blue velvet box, he said, "I don't think you're going to believe me until I do."

Silently, he unzipped his jeans and stepped out of them. He did it as he did everything else, with assurance and his peculiarly pantherish grace. As he peeled off his underwear Francesca looked, then quickly glanced away, feeling not only confused but foolish. She was startled to see how very male he was, and how very aroused. His coppery body was breathtaking. One couldn't ignore the impact of his broad shoulders, a flat, tightly muscled belly and slim hips, the pale golden color of his skin where he was not deeply tanned.

He sat down beside her and helped her off with her jeans and his black eyes caressed her. When he held her in his arms his warm hands stroked the silky skin of her back and hips, and he whispered, "Do you want me to love you, Francesca? You've got to say something to me."

She looked up into his eyes and for the first time Francesca felt the floodgates of joy opening. She was astonished at the sudden, ridiculous feeling of happiness that swept over her. Nothing like this had ever happened before. The man who held her in his arms was gentle, tough and proud, and he loved her. That was what he was trying to tell her. Dizzily she knew that she loved him, too, and did not stop to question how or when it had begun. Perhaps it had always been there.

When she nodded, her shining eyes drowning in his dark ones, he cupped his hand under her chin and lifted her mouth to his and said softly, "Love me back, sweetheart." He guided her hand down to touch his own throbbing flesh and pulled her close to him.

Perhaps he wanted to show her the difference, the gentleness of his love. But she experienced the strength and intimacy of John Turtle's body as she had never known lovemaking before. Just as clearly, just as sweetly, his hands explored her body, raising her to heights of trembling desire where his passion and hers matched perfectly. When he moved his hard, strong body over her soft one several minutes later Francesca threw her arms around his neck in a welcoming of inexpressible joy. When he entered her, Francesca gasped at his forceful tenderness, filling up every inch of her, possessive and commanding. Her soft cries when he moved goaded him to wildness, her name on his lips bursting against her own. Together they drowned in a whirlpool of loving pleasure. He lifted her hips with his hands and drove her to a last, shattering ecstasy, and the world exploded in lights. Then slowly, his body still contracting with expended desire, he let his weight down on her softly.

The echoing tide of their lovemaking receded slowly. He kissed her lips and her face and her hair again and again, murmuring her name. Through languid half-closed eyes Francesca saw his face, his black hair spiky with perspiration, and felt a rush of love as she lifted her fingers to touch and stroke him. She ran her fingers over his smooth, taut jawline and then his thin, soft lips.

"I must have been blind," she whispered.

"Ummm," he responded. He bent his wet head to kiss her shoulder and rubbed his mouth lingeringly against her skin.

"Don't let's go back," she said suddenly. The moment was shattered. He looked up at her. "I can't go back to *Ca'ad Carlo*," she cried. "I just can't do it, now!"

His expression said that he didn't take her seriously.

"Yeah," he said, his hands settling her more comfortably under him. He rubbed his mouth into the hollows of her throat and made a wordless sound of deep contentment. " want you again, Francesca," he growled softly.

"I'd rather live here, in Boston," she said, frowning.

Now he raised himself on one elbow to look down into her face. "What's this all about?" When she turned pleading eyes to him he said, "Francesca, you're not this afraid What's the matter? Listen, if you don't want *Ca'ad Carlo* turn it over to the State of Florida. That's what Carla wanted to do for years. Half of Palm Beach is going to end up in a museum anyway. That is, the half that doesn't cave in from damp rot."

When she shut her eyes, trying to resist, he said, "Come back with me, Frannie. You can't back away from all this it won't work. You're smart, you've got Sicilian guts and a lot of old Charlie Bloodworth in you, and that's a hell o a combination. Who knows? You might be able to pu Bloodworth's back together again."

Her eyes flew open and she stared up at him for a long moment, not able to speak, not able to cope with the shock of his casual words.

"What did you say?" she whispered.

The dark, ironic look returned to his face but his mouth was smiling. "What—that you're Carla's daughter? Miss Lucchese, you haven't kept up with backstairs gossip in Palm Beach, but it's very reliable. My grandfather could tell you all about it. He was only the gardener at *Ca'ad Carlo*, but the people who work the estates are the last ones you can fool. 'Miss Carla's little girl,' he always called you. He never understood why she let you go."

Francesca stared at him. The dread secret was demolished by his quiet words. Now there was no longer any vow o silence to hold any of them anymore.

"Oh no," she moaned, disbelieving.

She saw his chiseled lips quirk up at the corners. He moved his body softly against hers, still desirous. "Don' take it so hard, sweetheart," he murmured. "I like you better when you've got old Charlie Bloodworth in your eyes, temper up and horsey as hell and ready to stare down the opposition. You were damned tough on bodyguards—did I ever tell you that?" His lips nuzzled her throat and trailed warmth up to the tip of her chin. He made another feline growl of pleasure against her skin. "I can't get enough of you," he muttered.

She shook her head. "You don't understand," she protested. She tried to push his heavy body away with both hands, but he only tightened his grip on her. "Will you listen to me? Harry Stillman says there's a lawsuit by Carla's former husband, DeLacy—"

"Right," he said. His lips and tongue traced the lobe of her ear interestedly.

"Stop," she told him, fighting the electricity that tingled through her at the feel of his mouth. "You're not paying attention! My father was a pr—"

But his lips found hers, ignoring her words. "Francesca," he murmured against her mouth, "I want you again. I want to keep loving you. You belong to me now, I'm going to love you the rest of my life, you adorable, beautiful fascinating damned woman." The hard, good-looking face with its adamant black eyes looked down at her. "Everything else is irrelevant. I want you to remember that when I want to make love to you, everything else runs a poor second. Including Bloodworth's, Inc., and your sixty million dollars. Do you hear me?"

Francesca met his eyes for a long second. John Turtle wasn't joking. He meant every word. And if any man was capable of living up to his words, he was. She sighed, a low, contented sound of acknowledgment that he did not miss. He was a challenge; she was still not used to the driving, assured force of his love. But she knew that with this man everything would be a challenge and that she could grow, that he would allow her to be her own woman. He even insisted on it. All that he wanted back was the ultimate commitment. To love him in return. Completely.

Without hesitation Francesca flung her arms around his neck and lifted her mouth to his eager kiss. "I love you," she cried. "Oh—why couldn't I see it sooner? Everything—"

"Forget that part," he told her, his mouth imprinting soft kisses on her eyes, her nose, her forehead. "We'll make up for it, sweetheart, I promise you."

"And," Francesca vowed, "if all that money gets to be a problem, I'll just give it away."

She knew she would love him forever when she heard him laugh like that.